BEACH

ENJOY THE BOOK!

[signature]

EDITED AND WITH AN INTRODUCTION
BY **LENA LENČEK** AND **GIDEON BOSKER**

PHOTOGRAPHS BY
MITTIE HELLMICH

BEACH

STORIES BY THE SAND AND SEA

MARLOWE & COMPANY
NEW YORK

Published by
Marlowe & Company
841 Broadway, 4th Floor
New York, NY 10003

BEACH: *Stories by the Sand and Sea*
Compilation and introduction copyright © 2000
by Lena Lenček and Gideon Bosker
Photographs copyright © 2000 by Mittie Hellmich
Pages 331–332 represent a continuation of the copyright page.

Library of Congress Cataloging-in-Publication Data

Beach : stories by the sand and sea / edited by
Lena Lenček and Gideon Bosker.
p. cm.
ISBN 1-56924-636-X
1. Sea stories.   2. Beaches—Literary collections.
I. Lenček, Lena   II. Bosker, Gideon.
PN6071.S4 B42 2000
808.83'932146—dc21
00-021650

9 8 7 6 5 4 3 2 1

DESIGNED BY PAULINE NEUWIRTH, NEUWIRTH & ASSOCIATES, INC.

Printed in the United States of America
Distributed by Publishers Group West

to christian f. hubert,
helio-bibliophile par excellence

Fair Vida by the seashore washing,

Her sick child's linens on the shore,

Looked up to see a Blackmoor sailing

And heard the words the sea wind bore:

"Fair Vida, why are you no longer

As fair as once you were before?"

"How should I still be fair and lovely

As fair I was once before,

When my old husband sits at home

When my sick child can't be alone?

All day my old man coughs and moans,

All night my sick child weeps and groans"

The Blackmoor brought his boat to shore,

"Come with me, leave them all behind,

Come with me, be fair forevermore . . ."

—FROM "FAIR VIDA," A TRADITIONAL SLOVENE BALLAD

contents

for a great many of us, there is no sweeter pleasure than a day at the beach. You wake up early in the morning, squint up at the sky to see if the hazy margin that promises a scorcher is smudging the horizon, pack a couple of towels, a hat, and some sunblock, snatch a bottle of water and a snack, and dash out the door. You run back for the book you left on the table, then dive into traffic that bumps and grinds along with blatant disregard for your agenda, or, if you're lucky, jump on a bike for the quick pedal seaward. Meanwhile, your adrenaline is pumping in fierce anticipation, and finally, there it is: that excruciating, hip-hop sprint across hot sand and the spine-tingling, eyeball-rolling leap into the surf. Bingo! All your senses are buzzing with the intoxicating elixir of elements.

It's water time! Half submerged, at one with the great blue-green aqueous mystery below, you bob in the waves, something between fish, fowl, and terrestrial biped. The rest of you, exposed to sun and air from the neck up, swivels now one direction—toward the wide horizon—now the other, back to the shore, checking to see how far the tide has carried you from your day's place on the beach. You're on sensory overload, and you haven't even broken any laws. You feel at one with the world—perhaps because the soothing riff of breakers, the rock and roll of waves, and the yielding warmth subliminally recall our secure uterine life before life.

Or perhaps it is the knowledge that the ocean is the wellspring of all organisms, and that the beach is the stage on which our ancestors first crawled into history. Slowly, you surrender to the rhythm and your mind goes as blank as the sky. You swim a few strokes, turn on to your back and float, letting the energy of the waves pass around and through you. After a while, you find your legs, shuffle out of the water, and flop onto a towel in a coma of ecstasy. Your head settles back into a sand pillow. A doze, perhaps, or, more likely, you adjust your sunglasses, angle the visor on your cap, open your book, and settle into nirvana. Beach bum goes beach brain. "There is rapture on the lonely shore," wrote the British Romantic Lord Byron who, not coincidentally, was one of the greatest swimmers of all time. "There is society where none intrudes/ By the deep Sea, and music in its roar:/ I love not man the less, but Nature more."

Ever since the British invented the beach holiday in the early eighteenth century, bathers have been packing books for a day by the sea. Back then, beachgoers were likely to also be armed with collapsible sun bonnets, watercolors, slippers, gloves, scarves, bizarre flotational devices, and parasols for their therapeutic sojourn—in winter, no less—on the North Sea. Healthy and wealthy young males took off on a Grand Tour to the shores of the Mediterranean, where they consulted leather-bound volumes of Homer and Virgil, and, later, Byron and Swinburne, as they gazed out over the sea and rhapsodized about the power and majesty of nature. In the nineteenth century, under a watery, winter sun, capacious beach chairs on the boardwalk at Deauville or Brighton would fill with readers tucked into novels by Austen, Flaubert, or Dickens.

The contents of the beach bag may have changed dramatically over the last two hundred years, but one item remains constant: the reading material. Books and beaches go together like gin and tonics, fish and chips, sun and tan. Look around a crowded beach—Bondi or Copacabana, Coney Island or St. Tropez, Hatteras or Miami, Laguna or the Hamptons—and you'll see enough books to stock a respectable town library. People who ordinarily limit their reading to the backs of cereal boxes and stock market quotes are nose-deep in bestsellers, romances, and classics. What accounts for such bibliophilia? We like to think it's the fact that on a purely psycho-sensory level, geology makes the beach a perfect site on which to unpack fantasies of pleasure and pain, glory and gain, and to tease out of hiding deep insecurities and secret, megalomaniacal passions. Put briefly, the beach makes us think, dream, and de-repress.

Storytellers since time immemorial have recognized this fact and given us a virtually inexhaustible supply of tales set on the beach. These are stories that explore the marvelous, aberrant things that humans do when they come to the shifting border of earth, water and sky, where all the elements that make up life come together, and where birth and death, creation and destruction are on permanent display. The very sand under our feet takes us far back in time and place. As Walter Benjamin wrote, "Nothing is more epic than the sea."

Coming to grips with the uncertainties of existence, our ancestors concocted myths of beauties and beasts, gods and demons, heavenly rewards and divine retribution—all staged on the beach. Homer, Hesiod, Pindar, Virgil, Ovid, and countless, nameless bards have spun plots of supernatural metamorphoses, erotic transgressions, fateful loves, irresolvable strife, and miraculous homecomings that are lifted directly from the script of nature. In the feelings stirred by the perpetual shifting of land, water, sand, and clouds, the beach has inspired profound and beautiful poetry and prose. As Herman Melville wrote in *Moby Dick*, "There is, one knows not what sweet mystery about this sea, whose gently awful stirrings speak of some hidden soul beneath."

Literary representations of the beach are as nuanced and myriad as its topography. The Biblical account of the Deluge, for example, casts the shore as a scarred, ravaged, and defiled landscape that bears the imprint of a wrathful divinity wreaking catastrophic judgment on a sinful humanity. At the other pole, the Greeks and Romans, and later, the writers of the Enlightenment, picture the beach as a paradise, uncorrupted by civilization, and inhabited by innocent, sensuous, and noble savages. Throughout the Middle Ages, the seashore figured as battleground and treacherous boundary where raiders unleashed rapine and terror, inspiring ballads that told of bold abductions and merciless appropriations.

Sentimental writers—from Addison, Burke, Macpherson, to Zhukovsky and Karamzin—sang the merits of uninhabited, rugged seashores for meditating on mortality, vanity, and the sublime. To Romantic poets, infatuated with the sea as the mirror of a psychologized nature, the beach spoke both of our wrenching solitude and our intimate connection with the universe and its elements. The beach has aroused wonder and curiosity, fear, awe, and exaltation in the minds and hearts of the world's greatest thinkers, artists, and scientists. Modernists, like Joseph Conrad, Virginia Woolf, Thomas Mann, and James Joyce, saw the beach as the place where the scattered flotsam and jetsam of our subconscious washed up into consciousness and where we struggle to compose coherent narratives from the hopelessly scrambled fragments of our lives.

But, above all, the beach is where we have our most intense sexual experiences. After all, the inherent sensuality of the beach stimulates a thundering chromatic scale of sensations—tactile, visual, olfactory, gustatory, and kinetic. Every age and stage of our lives has its own fixed experience of the beach: courtship, honeymoon, parenthood, divorce, retirement. Budding adolescents discover the hidden bonus of the beach as a theater of erotic delights as they train their voyeuristic gaze on vast expanses of naked human flesh. Young men and women display their bodies in joyful mating rituals, while honeymooners embrace in the shade of solitary palapas, in musky oceanside motels, or luxurious beach hideaways. Mature conjugal love comes to renew itself—licitly, or more often, illicitly—by the sea. The divorced and the chronically mis-mated come for sexual renewal, and for one more chance on the erotic merry-go-around. In the end, there is an irreducible simplicity to life at the beach, which T. S. Eliot articulated when, in "The Love Song of J. Alfred Prufrock," he pondered: "Do I dare to eat a peach? / I shall wear white flannel trousers, and walk upon the beach."

This anthology of great beach stories seeks to bring pleasure—
sensual, aesthetic, and intellectual—to the glorious practice of
reading on the beach. If there was a single principle guiding our
selection of pieces, it was the idea that taken together, they should
capture the torments and the ecstasies, the crises and epiphanies
which so often transpire on the beach, the life-transforming
moments, the rituals of family, love and friendship to which the
beach plays host. From dozens and dozens of narratives, we've
selected the most evocative and intelligent, the most revelatory
sketches, and we've then submitted these to the goose-bumps-
on-the-nape test recommended by Vladimir Nabokov as the
most reliable guide to aesthetic perfection.

When it came to the final cut, the selections that raised the
hairs on the backs of our necks, regardless of how often we'd read
them, announced themselves as our "must haves." Such, for
example, are Rachel Carson's incantatory "The Marginal World,"
surely one of the most luminous pieces of writing on natural science, and John Steinbeck's description, from *Cannery Row*, of the
secret life of the tide pool, rendered with the sweeping scope and
measured rhythm of Homeric epic.

Many of the stories evoke the entirely sensual happiness of
Albert Camus' sun-drenched "unconquerable summer" that cul-
minates inevitably in some sort of apocalyptic expulsion from
Eden. Such is T. Coraghessan Boyle's glimpse at the Rabelaisian
indulgences of mass-tourism. His "Mexico" wickedly charts the
peripety of a gringo's quest for R and R—Romance and
Relaxation—in a south-of-the-border resort awash in guacamole, margaritas, and sweat. Jamaica Kincaid's chronicle of a
torrid affair starts with the premise that the lover's "mouth was
like an island in the sea that was his face" and goes on to explore
the sensual intelligence that lurks at the heart of hedonism. In
Cyrus Colter's "The Beach Umbrella," the beach itself is the
provocateur that seduces an upright, henpecked family man into
lying and cheating just so that he too can have a little bit of that
groin-tingling, gin-swilling, hip-swiveling bit of paradise that
sprouts every Sunday on Chicago's Thirty-first Street Beach.

Ever since imperial Rome, when seaside resorts such as Baiae attracted profligates, loose women, gamblers and gourmands to its sparkling shores, the beach has been synonymous with dissipation, hedonism, and vice. Every coastal nation has had its "dirty weekend destination," a place of immorality and indolence, commercial sex and infidelity. The British had their Brighton, the French their Monte Carlo, the Americans, their Coney Island and Jersey shore, and the Russians their Yalta—where Anton Chekhov set, with consummate delicacy, "The Lady with the Pet Dog."

Illicit doings, however, did nothing to diminish the beach's reputation as a site for life-changing transitions, practically miraculous in nature, both religious and therapeutic. The theme of spiritual conversion informs Takeshi Kaiko's "The Duel," in which a young man comes to the sea to learn the unyielding law of life: kill or be killed, eat or be eaten. Diane Johnson's "Great Barrier Reef" gives a sardonic twist to the image of the beach as the threshold of spiritual renewal. Here the beach is a tawdry outpost filled with ugly natives selling ugly souvenirs to ugly tourists, and the sea, seductively beautiful, enticingly warm, is in fact, "riddled with poisonous creatures, deadly toxins, and sharks." For Michel Tournier, the continual cycles of construction and deconstruction, revelation and concealment which transpire on the beach proffer the formula of regeneration to a couple in crisis. In "The Midnight Love Feast," a philosophical dialogue on the nature of marriage, Tournier argues that the ideal condition of matrimony, like that of the beach, lies in its ephemerality. This same suspension of the ordinary underwrites the reconciliation between brothers and the cementing of family in Ethan Mordden's "I Read My Nephew Stories."

Like the proverbial pharmacon—a potent death-or-life dealing medical agent—the beach can both heal and harm. Such is the case in Vladimir Nabokov's "Perfection" in which the Bolshevik Revolution deposits a meek, neurasthenic Russian on a Baltic beach with nothing but the clothes on his back and some mental baggage left over from a first-rate university education. As his adolescent ward soaks in the vital forces of the sun and the sea, the displaced tutor languishes and eventually perishes. More

typical are the stories that render the beach as the symbolic setting for rites of passage, quasi-miraculous encounters with the
self that are staged as near-death experiences. Graham Swift's
"Learning to Swim" shows us this ritual from the perspective of
parents vying for formative control of their child. In Doris
Lessing's "Through the Tunnel," the young boy's epiphanic feat is
a purely private act of self-generation, complete with passage
through a figurative, submarine birth canal.

As Jonathan Raban so aptly put it, "The beach is a marginal
place where marginal people congregate and respectable people
come to do marginal things." In John Cheever's "Goodbye, My
Brother," blood lust and criminality swim to the genteel surface of
sociability and erupt in a fratricidal encounter on the beach. Kay
Boyle, in "Black Boy," shows us the beach as a special place apart,
where barriers of race and age and status are suspended and where
unmediated encounters with other individuals are momentarily
stripped of their social status. In "Turtle Turtle," Monica
Wesolowska describes the yearning and discontent of a coffee-
colored Mayan Mexican, rocked by the sea, day in day out, staring with envy at gringo Mandarins as they debouche from fiber-
glass sailboats, buxom blondes in tow, beer and dope in hand,
throwing money into the sea. Wesolowska has entered the mind
of the disenfranchised, autochtonous noble savage reaching for the
silver stud in the colonizer's nostril, dreaming of becoming one of
the Chucks or Bobs or Bills who seasonally migrate to the warm
Mexican beaches to mate and perform enigmatic cultural rituals.

Whitney Balliett's "A Floor of Flounders" offers one of the
most enchanting portraits we've ever read of the marginal beach
bum, the prototypical old man by the sea, who mediates the
profligacy and simplicity of the beach to all urban comers, known
and unknown. Against his "piscatorial idyll," David Malouf's "A
Change of Scene" resonates as a sinister antithesis. As political
upheaval touches a perfect Mediterranean island, it not only
splinters the delicate harmony between outsider and native, but
fractures the psychic integrity and sense of cultural continuity
which the protagonists sought and fleetingly found in their lit-
toral refuge. One of the sweetest and, for us, most exciting finds

was the selection "Ancestral Houses" from Russ Rymer's non-fictional *American Beach*, which reconstructs the lost world of a unique Black coastal resort, as presented through the haunting presence of master raconteur MaVynee Betsch.

Finally, we think that every anthology needs a bit of a chuckle and self-parody. So, for good measure, we've thrown in J. G. Ballard's sci-fi "The Largest Theme Park in the World," which explodes the fantasy of the endless summer by tracking the implications of a hypothetical "totalitarian system based on leisure" that fills the beaches of the world with professional hedonists. And a book of stories set at the beach would be seriously deficient if it were to omit the subject of the lifeguard, that icon of virile pulchritude who has preside at beaches, fueling female fantasies and, occasionally, descending, Perseus-like, to snatch a drowning swimmer from the jaws of death. John Updike's "Lifeguard" inverts the usual optic according to which the tanned Adonis on the pedestal is the mute object of our gaze, and presents him instead from the inside out, as a delusional Narcissus scrutinizing our bloated, flawed, and dimpled bodies with arch distaste.

Compiling this anthology has given us the greatest pleasure. We hope that it will inspire in you, as it does in us, the depth of feeling and wonder that lies at the very core of the beach experience. If, in turning the pages of this book, you catch the distant perfume of the sea and, like Mary Betsch in Rymer's *American Beach*, glimpse "the shape of sanctuary" in the image of the beach, then we will have succeeded in our goal.

—LENA LENČEK AND GIDEON BOSKER

BEACH

the marginal world

from *The Edge of the Sea*

R ACHEL C ARSON

the edge of the sea is a strange and beautiful place. All through the long history of Earth it has been an area of unrest where waves have broken heavily against the land, where the tides have pressed forward over the continents, receded, and then returned. For no two successive days is the shore line precisely the same. Not only do the tides advance and retreat in their eternal rhythms, but the level of the sea itself is never at rest. It rises or falls as the glaciers melt or grow, as the floor of the deep ocean basins shifts under its increasing load of sediments, or as the earth's crust along the continental margins warps up or down in adjustment to strain and tension. Today a little more land may belong to the sea, tomorrow a little less. Always the edge of the sea remains an elusive and indefinable boundary.

The shore has a dual nature, changing with the swing of the tides, belonging now to the land, now to the sea. On the ebb tide it knows the harsh extremes of the land world, being exposed to heat and cold, to wind, to rain and drying sun. On the flood tide it is a water world, returning briefly to the relative stability of the open sea.

Only the most hardy and adaptable can survive in a region so mutable, yet the area between the tide lines is crowded with plants and animals. In this difficult world of the shore, life displays its enormous toughness and vitality by occupying almost every conceivable niche. Visibly, it carpets the intertidal rocks; or half hidden, it descends into fissures and crevices, or hides under boulders, or lurks in the wet gloom of sea caves. Invisibly, where the casual observer would say there is no life, it lies deep in the sand, in burrows and tubes and passageways. It tunnels into solid rock and bores into peat and clay. It encrusts weeds or drifting spars or the hard, chitinous shell of a lobster. It exists minutely, as the film of bacteria that spreads over a rock surface or a wharf piling; as spheres of protozoa, small as pinpricks, sparkling at the surface of the sea; and as Lilliputian beings swimming through dark pools that lie between the grains of sand.

The shore is an ancient world, for as long as there has been an earth and sea there has been this place of the meeting of land and water. Yet it is a world that keeps alive the sense of continuing creation and of the relentless drive of life. Each time that I enter it, I gain some new awareness of its beauty and its deeper meanings, sensing that intricate fabric of life by which one creature is linked with another, and each with its surroundings.

In my thoughts of the shore, one place stands apart for its revelation of exquisite beauty. It is a pool hidden within a cave that one can visit only rarely and briefly when the lowest of the year's low tides fall below it, and perhaps from that very fact it acquires some of its special beauty. Choosing such a tide, I hoped for a glimpse of the pool. The ebb was to fall early in the morning. I knew that if the wind held from the northwest and no interfering swell ran in from a distant storm the level of the sea should drop below the entrance to the pool. There had been sudden ominous showers in the night, with rain like handfuls of gravel flung on the roof. When I looked out into the early morning the sky was full of a gray dawn light but the sun had not yet risen. Water and air were pallid. Across the bay the moon was a luminous disc in the western sky, suspended above the dim line of distant shore—the full August moon, drawing the tide to the low, low levels of the threshold of the alien sea world. As I watched, a gull flew by, above the spruces. Its breast was rosy with the light of the uprisen sun. The day was, after all, to be fair.

Later, as I stood above the tide near the entrance to the pool, the promise of that rosy light was sustained. From the base of the steep wall of rock on which I stood, a moss-covered ledge jutted seaward into deep water. In the surge at the rim of the ledge the dark fronds of oarweeds swayed, smooth and gleaming as leather. The projecting ledge was the path to the small hidden cave and its pool. Occasionally a swell, stronger than the rest, rolled smoothly over the rim and broke in foam against the cliff. But the intervals between such swells were long enough to admit me to the ledge and long enough for a glimpse of that fairy pool, so seldom and so briefly exposed.

And so I knelt on the wet carpet of sea moss and looked back into the dark cavern that held the pool in a shallow basin. The floor of the cave was only a few inches below the roof, and a mirror had been created in which all that grew on the ceiling was reflected in the still water below.

Under water that was clear as glass the pool was carpeted with green sponge. Gray patches of sea squirts glistened on the ceiling and colonies of soft coral were a pale apricot color. In the moment when I looked into the cave a little elfin starfish hung down, suspended by the merest thread, perhaps by only a single tube foot. It reached down to touch its own reflection, so perfectly delineated that there might have been, not one starfish, but two. The beauty of the reflected images and of the limpid pool itself was the poignant beauty of things that are ephemeral, existing only until the sea should return to fill the little cave.

Whenever I go down into this magical zone of the low water of the spring tides, I look for the most delicately beautiful of all the shore's inhabitants—flowers that are not plant but animal, blooming on the threshold of the deeper sea. In that fairy cave I was not disappointed. Hanging from its roof were the pendent flowers of the hydroid Tubularia, pale pink, fringed and delicate as the wind flower. Here were creatures so exquisitely fashioned that they seemed unreal, their beauty too fragile to exist in a world of crushing force. Yet every detail was functionally useful, every stalk and hydranth and petal-like tentacle fashioned for dealing with the realities of existence. I knew that they were merely waiting, in that moment of the tide's ebbing, for the return of the sea. Then in the rush of water, in the surge of surf and the pressure of the incoming tide, the delicate flower heads would stir with life. They would sway on their slender stalks, and their long tentacles would sweep the returning water, finding in it all that they needed for life.

And so in that enchanted place on the threshold of the sea the realities that possessed my mind were far from those of the land world I had left an hour before. In a different way the same sense of remoteness and of a world apart came to me in a twilight hour on a great beach on the coast of Georgia. I had come down after sunset and walked far out over sands that lay wet and gleaming, to the very edge of the retreating sea. Looking back across that immense flat, crossed by winding, water-filled gullies and here and there holding shallow pools left by the tide, I was filled with awareness that this intertidal area, although abandoned briefly and rhythmically by the sea, is always reclaimed by the rising tide. There at the edge of low water the beach with its reminders of the land seemed far away. The only sounds were those of the wind and the sea and the birds. There was one sound of wind moving over water, and another of water sliding over the sand and tumbling down the faces of its own wave forms. The flats were astir with birds, and the voice of the willet rang insistently. One of them stood at the edge of the water and gave its loud, urgent cry; an answer came from far up the beach and the two birds flew to join each other.

The flats took on a mysterious quality as dusk approached and the last evening light was reflected from the scattered pools and creeks. Then birds became only dark shadows, with no color discernible. Sanderlings scurried across the beach like little ghosts, and here and there the darker forms of the willets stood out. Often I could come very close to them before they would start up in alarm—the sanderlings running, the willets flying up, crying. Black skimmers flew along the ocean's edge silhouetted against the dull, metallic gleam, or they went flitting above the sand like large, dimly seen moths. Sometimes they "skimmed" the winding creeks of tidal water, where little spreading surface ripples marked the presence of small fish.

The shore at night is a different world, in which the very darkness that hides the distractions of daylight brings into sharper focus the elemental realities. Once, exploring the night beach, I surprised a small ghost crab in the searching beam of my torch. He was lying in a pit he had dug just above the surf, as though watching the sea and waiting. The blackness of the night possessed water, air, and beach. It was the darkness of an older world, before Man. There was no sound but the all-enveloping, primeval sounds of wind blowing over water and sand, and of waves crashing on the beach. There was no other visible life—just one small crab near the sea. I have seen hundreds of ghost crabs in other settings, but suddenly I was filled with the odd sensation that for the first time I knew the creature in its own world—that I understood, as never before, the essence of its being. In that moment time was suspended; the world to which I belonged did not exist and I might have been an onlooker from outer space. The little crab alone with the sea became a symbol that stood for life itself—for the delicate, destructible, yet incredibly vital force that somehow holds its place amid the harsh realities of the inorganic world.

The sense of creation comes with memories of a southern coast, where the sea and the mangroves, working together, are building a wilderness of thousands of small islands off the southwestern coast of Florida, separated from each other by a tortuous pattern of bays, lagoons, and narrow waterways. I remember a winter day when the sky was blue and drenched with sunlight; though there was no wind one was conscious of flowing air like cold clear crystal. I had landed on the surf-washed tip of one of those islands, and then worked my way around to the sheltered bay side. There I found the tide far out, exposing the broad mud flat of a cove bordered by the mangroves with their twisted branches, their glossy leaves, and their long prop roots reaching down, grasping and holding the mud, building the land out a little more, then again a little more.

The mud flats were strewn with the shells of that small, exquisitely colored mollusk, the rose tellin, looking like scattered petals of pink roses. There must have been a colony nearby, living buried just under the surface of the mud. At first the only creature visible was a small heron in gray and rusty plumage—a reddish egret that waded across the flat with the stealthy, hesitant movements of its kind. But other land creatures had been there, for a line of fresh tracks wound in and out among the mangrove roots, marking the path of a raccoon feeding on the oysters that gripped the supporting roots with projections from their shells. Soon I found the tracks of a shore bird, probably a sanderling, and followed them a little; then they turned toward the water and were lost, for the tide had erased them and made them as though they had never been.

Looking out over the cove I felt a strong sense of the interchangeability of land and sea in this marginal world of the shore, and of the links between the life of the two. There was also an awareness of the past and of the continuing flow of time, obliterating much that had gone before, as the sea had that morning washed away the tracks of the bird.

The sequence and meaning of the drift of time were quietly summarized in the existence of hundreds of small snails—the mangrove periwinkles—browsing on the branches and roots of the trees. Once their ancestors had been sea dwellers, bound to the salt waters by every tie of their life processes. Little by little over the thousands and millions of years the ties had been broken, the snails had adjusted themselves to life out of water, and now today they were living many feet above the tide to which they only occasionally returned. And perhaps, who could say how many ages hence, there would be in their descendants not even this gesture of remembrance for the sea.

The spiral shells of other snails—these quite minute—left winding tracks on the mud as they moved about in search of food. They were horn shells, and when I saw them I had a nos-

talgic moment when I wished I might see what Audubon saw, a
century and more ago. For such little horn shells were the food
of the flamingo, once so numerous on this coast, and when I half
closed my eyes I could almost imagine a flock of these magnificent flame birds feeding in that cove, filling it with their color. It
was a mere yesterday in the life of the earth that they were there;
in nature, time and space are relative matters, perhaps most truly
perceived subjectively in occasional flashes of insight, sparked by
such a magical hour and place.

There is a common thread that links these scenes and memories the spectacle of life in all its varied manifestations as it has
appeared, evolved, and sometimes died out. Underlying the beauty of the spectacle there is meaning and significance. It is the elu-
siveness of that meaning that haunts us, that sends us again and
again into the natural world where the key to the riddle is hidden. It sends us back to the edge of the sea, where the drama of
life played its first scene on earth and perhaps even its prelude;
where the forces of evolution are at work today, as they have been
since the appearance of what we know as life: and where the
spectacle of living creatures faced by the cosmic realities of their
world is crystal clear.

the largest theme
park in the world

J. G. BALLARD

the creation of a united Europe, so long desired and so
bitterly contested, had certain unexpected consequences. The
fulfilment of this age-old dream was a cause of justified celebration, of countless street festivals, banquets and speeches of self-
congratulation. But the Europe which had given birth to the
Renaissance and the Protestant Reformation, to modern science
and the industrial revolution, had one last surprise up its sleeve.

Needless to say, nothing of this was apparent in 1993. The
demolition of so many fiscal and bureaucratic barriers to trade led
directly to the goal of a Europe at last united in a political and cultural federation. In 1995, the headiest year since 1968, the necessary legislation was swiftly passed by a dozen parliaments, which
dissolved themselves and assigned their powers to the European
Assembly at Strasbourg. So there came into being the new
Europe, a visionary realm that would miraculously fuse the spirits
of Charlemagne and the smart card, Michelangelo and Club Med,
St Augustine and St Laurent.

Happily exhausted by their efforts, the new Europeans took off for the beaches of the Mediterranean, their tribal mating ground. Blessed by a benevolent sun and a greenhouse sky, the summer of 1995 ran from April to October. A hundred million Europeans basked on the sand, leaving behind little more than an army of caretakers to supervise the museums, galleries and cathedrals. Excited by the idea of a federal Europe, a vast influx of tourists arrived from the United States, Japan and the newly liberated nations of the Soviet bloc. Guide-books in hand, they gorged themselves on the culture and history of Europe, which had now achieved its spiritual destiny of becoming the largest theme park in the world.

Sustained by these tourist revenues, the ecu soared above the dollar and yen, even though offices and factories remained deserted from Athens to the Atlantic. Indeed, it was only in the autumn of 1995 that the economists at Brussels resigned themselves to the paradox which no previous government had accepted—contrary to the Protestant ethic, which had failed so lamentably in the past, the less that Europe worked the more prosperous and contented it became. Delighted to prove this point, the millions of vacationing Europeans on the beaches of the Mediterranean scarcely stirred from their sun-mattresses. Autoroutes and motorways were silent, and graphs of industrial production remained as flat as the cerebral functions of the brain-dead.

An even more significant fact soon emerged. Most of the vacationing Europeans had extended their holidays from two to three months, but a substantial minority had decided not to return at all. Along the beaches of the Costa del Sol and Côte d'Azur, thousands of French, British and German tourists failed to catch their return flights from the nearby airport. Instead, they remained in their hotels and apartments, lay beside their swimming pools and dedicated themselves to the worship of their own skins.

At first this decision to stay was largely confined to the young and unmarried, to former students and the traditional lumpen-intelligentsia of the beach. But these latter-day refuseniks soon included lawyers, doctors and accountants. Even families with children chose to remain on perpetual holiday. Ignoring the telegrams and phone calls from their anxious employers in Amsterdam, Paris and Düsseldorf, they made polite excuses, applied sun oil to their shoulders and returned to their sail-boats and pedalos. It became all too clear that in rejecting the old Europe of frontiers and national self-interest they had also rejected the bourgeois values that hid behind them. A demanding occupation, a high disposable income, a future mortgaged to the gods of social and professional status, had all been abandoned.

At any event, a movement confined to a few resorts along the Mediterranean coast had, by November 1995, involved tens of thousands of holidaymakers. Those who returned home did so with mixed feelings. By the spring of 1996 more than a million expatriates had settled in permanent exile among the hotels and apartment complexes of the Mediterranean.

By summer this number vastly increased, and brought with it huge demographic and psychological changes. So far, the effects of the beach exodus on the European economy had been slight. Tourism and the sale of large sections of industry to eager Japanese corporations had kept the ecu afloat. As for the exiles in Minorca, Mykonos and the Costa Brava, the cost of living was low and basic necessities few. The hippies and ex-students turned to petty theft and slept on the beach. The lawyers and accountants were able to borrow from their banks when their own resources ran out, offering their homes and businesses as collateral. Wives sold their jewellery, and elderly relatives were badgered into small loans.

Fortunately, the sun continued to shine through the numerous ozone windows and the hottest summer of the century was widely forecast. The determination of the exiles never to return to their offices and factories was underpinned by a new philosophy of leisure and a sense of what constituted a worthwhile life. The logic of the annual beach holiday, which had sustained Europe since the Second World War, had merely been taken to its conclusion. Crime and delinquency were non-existent and the social and racial tolerance of those reclining in adjacent poolside chairs was virtually infinite.

Was Europe about to lead the world in another breakthrough for the third millennium? A relaxed and unpuritan sexual regime now flourished and there was a new-found pride in physical excellence. A host of sporting activities took place, there were classes in judo and karate, aerobics and tai-chi. The variety of fringe philosophies began to rival those of California. The first solar cults emerged on the beaches of Torremolinos and St Tropez. Where once the Mediterranean coast had been Europe's Florida, a bland parade of marinas and hotels, it was now set to be its Venice Beach, a hot-house of muscle-building and millennial dreams.

In the summer of 1996 the first challenge occurred to this regime of leisure. By now the beach communities comprised some five million exiles, and their financial resources were exhausted. Credit cards had long been cancelled, bank accounts frozen, and governments in Paris, London and Bonn waited for the return of the expatriates to their desks and work-benches.

Surprisingly, the determination of the beach communities never wavered. Far from catching their long-delayed return flights, the exiles decided to hold on to their place in the sun. Soon this brought them into direct conflict with local hoteliers and apartment owners, who found themselves housing a huge population of non-paying guests. The police were called in, and the first open riots occurred on the beaches of Malaga, Menton and Rimini.

The exiles, however, were difficult to dislodge. A year of sun and exercise had turned them into a corps of superb athletes, for whom the local shopkeepers, waiters and hoteliers were no match. Gangs of muscular young women, expert in the martial arts, roamed the supermarkets of Spain and the Côte d'Azur, fearlessly helping themselves from the shelves. Acts of open intimidation quickly subdued the managers of hotels and apartment houses.

Local police chiefs, for their part, were reluctant to intervene, for fear of damaging the imminent summer tourist trade. The lawyers and accountants among the exiles, all far more educated and intelligent than their provincial rivals, were adept at chal-

lenging any eviction orders or charges of theft. The once passive
regime of sun and sand had given way to a more militant mood,
sustained by the exiles' conviction in the moral and spiritual
rightness of their cause. Acting together, they commandeered any
empty villas or apartment houses, whose owners were either too
terrified to protest or fled the scene altogether.

The cult of physical perfection had gripped everyone's imagination. Bodies deformed by years bent over the word-processor
and fast-food counter were now slim and upright, as ideally proportioned as the figures on the Parthenon frieze. The new evan-
gelism concealed behind the exercise and fitness fads of the 1980s
now reappeared. A devotion to physical perfection ruled their
lives more strictly than any industrial taskmaster.

Out of necessity, leisure had moved into a more disciplined
phase. At dawn the resort beaches of the Mediterranean were
filled with companies of martial art enthusiasts, kicking and
grunting in unison. Brigades of handsomely tanned men and
women drilled together as they faced the sun. No longer did they
devote their spare time to lying on the sand, but to competitive
sports and fiercely contested track events.

Already the first community leaders had emerged from the
strongest and most charismatic of the men and women. The casual anarchy of the earliest days had given way to a sensible and
cooperative democracy, where members of informal beach
groups had voted on their best course of action before seizing an
empty hotel or raiding a wine-store. But this democratic phase
had failed to meet the needs and emotions of the hour, and the
beach communities soon evolved into more authoritarian form.

The 1996 holiday season brought a welcome respite and millions of new recruits, whose purses were bulging with ecus.
When they arrived at Marbella, Ibiza, La Grande Motte and
Sestri Levante they found themselves eagerly invited to join the
new beach communities. By August 1996, when almost the
whole of Europe had set off for the coasts of the sun, the governments of its member countries were faced with the real possibility that much of their populations would not return. Not
only would offices and factories be closed forever, but there

would be no one left to man the museums and galleries, to collect the dollars, yen and roubles of the foreign tourists who alone
sustained their economies. The prospect appeared that the Louvre
and Buckingham Palace might be sold to a Japanese hotel cor-
poration, that Chartres and Cologne cathedrals would become
subsidiaries of the Disney company.

Forced to act, the Strasbourg Assembly dispatched a number of
task forces to the south. Posing as holidaymakers, teams of inves-
tigators roamed the cafés and swimming pools. But the pathetic
attempts of these bikini bureaucrats to infiltrate and destabilise
the beach enclaves came to nothing, and many defected to the
ranks of the exiles.

So at last, in October 1996, the Strasbourg Assembly
announced that the beaches of the Mediterranean were closed,
that all forms of exercise outside the workplace or the bedroom
were illegal, and that the suntan was a prohibited skin embellish-
ment. Lastly, the Assembly ordered its 30 million absent citizens
to return home.

Needless to say, these commands were ignored. The beach
people who occupied the linear city of the Mediterranean coast,
some 3,000 miles long and 300 metres wide, were now a very
different breed. The police and gendarmerie who arrived at the
coastal resorts found militant bands of body-worshippers who
had no intention of resuming their previous lives.

Aware that a clash with the authorities would take place, they
had begun to defend their territory, blockading the beach roads
with abandoned cars, fortifying the entrances to hotels and apartment houses. By day their scuba teams hunted the coastal waters
for fish, while at night raiding parties moved inland, stealing
sheep and looting the fields of their vegetable crops. Large sections of Malaga, St Tropez and Corfu were now occupied by
exiles, while many of the smaller resorts such as Rosas and
Formentera were wholly under their control.

The first open conflict, at Golfe-Juan, was typically short-lived
and indecisive. Perhaps unconsciously expecting the Emperor to
come ashore, as he had done after his escape from Elba, the police
were unable to cope with the militant brigade of bronzed and

naked mothers, chanting green and feminist slogans, who advanced towards their water-cannon. Commandos of dentists and architects, releasing their fiercest karate kicks, strutted through the narrow streets in what seemed to be a display of a new folk tradition, attracting unmanageable crowds of American and Japanese tourists from their Cannes hotels. At Port-Vendres, Sitges, Bari and Fréjus the police fell back in confusion, unable to distinguish between the exiles and authentic visiting holiday-makers.

When the police returned in force, supported by units of the army, their arrival only increased the determination of the beach people. The polyglot flavour of the original settlers had given way to a series of national groups recruiting their members from their traditional resorts—the British at Torremolinos, Germans at Rosas, French at Juan les Pins. The resistance within these enclaves reflected their national identity—a rabble of drunken British hooligans roamed the streets of Torremolinos, exposing their fearsome buttocks to the riot police. The Germans devoted themselves to hard work and duty, erecting a Siegfried Line of sand bunkers around the beaches of Rosas, while the massed nipples of Juan were more than enough to hopelessly dazzle the gendarmerie.

In return, each of these national enclaves produced its characteristic leaders. The British resorts were dominated by any number of would-be Thatchers, fierce ladies in one-piece bathing suits who invoked the memory of Churchill and proclaimed their determination to "fight them on the beaches and never, *never* surrender". Gaullist throwbacks spoke loftily of the grandeur of French sun and sand, while the Italians proclaimed their "mare nostrum."

But above all the tone of these beach-führers was uniformly authoritarian. The sometime holiday exiles now enjoyed lives of fierce self-discipline coupled with a mystical belief in the powers of physical strength. Athletic prowess was admired above all, a cult of bodily perfection mediated through group gymnastic displays on the beaches, quasi-fascistic rallies, in which thousands of well-drilled participants slashed the dawn air with their karate chops and chanted in a single voice at the sun. These bronzed and hand-some figures with their thoughtless sexuality looked down on their tourist compatriots with a sense of almost racial superiority.

It was clear that Europe, where so much of Western civilisation had originated, had given birth to yet another significant trend, the first totalitarian system based on leisure. From the sun-lounge and the swimming pool, from the gymnasium and disco, had come a nationalistic and authoritarian creed with its roots in the realm of pleasure rather than that of work.

By the spring of 1997, as Brussels fumbled and Strasbourg debated, the 30 million people of the beach were beginning to look north for the first time. They listened to their leaders talk-ing of national living space, of the hordes of alien tourists with their soulless dollars and yen, of the tired blood of their compa-triots yearning to be invigorated. As they stood on the beaches of Marbella, Juan, Rimini and Naxos they swung their arms in uni-son, chanting their exercise songs as they heard the call to march north, expel the invading tourists and reclaim their historic heartlands.

So, in the summer of 1997 they set off along the deserted autoroutes and motorways in the greatest invasion which Europe has ever known, intent on seizing their former homes, determined to reinstate a forgotten Europe of nations, each jealous of its fron-tiers, happy to guard its history, tariff barriers and insularity.

mexico

T. CORAGHESSAN BOYLE

he didn't know much about Mexico, not really, if you discount the odd Margarita and a determined crawl through the pages of "Under the Volcano" in an alcoholic haze twenty years ago, but here he was, emerging pale and heavy from the sleek envelope of the airliner and into the fecund embrace of Puerto Escondido. All this—the scorching blacktop, the distant arc of the beach, the heat, the scent of the flowers and the jet fuel, and the faint lingering memory of yesterday's fish—was an accident. A happy accident. A charity thing at work—give five bucks to benefit the Battered Women's Shelter and win a free trip for two to the jewel of Oaxaca. Well, he'd won. And to save face and forestall questions he'd told everybody he was bringing his girlfriend along, for two weeks of R. and R.—Romance and Relaxation. He even invented a name for her—Yolanda—and yes, she was Mexican on her mother's side, gray eyes from her father, skin like burnished copper, and was she ever something in bed . . .

There were no formalities at the airport—they'd taken care of all that in Mexico City with a series of impatient gestures and incomprehensible commands—and he went through the heavy glass doors with his carry-on bag and ducked into the first cab he saw. The driver greeted him in English, swivelling round to wipe an imaginary speck of dust from the seat with a faded pink handkerchief. He gave a little speech Lester couldn't follow, tossing each word up in the air as if it were a tight-stitched ball that had to be driven high over the fence, then shrank back into himself and said "Where to?" in a diminished voice. Lester gave the name of his hotel—the best one in town—and sat back to let the ripe breeze wash over his face.

He was sweating. Sweating because he was in some steaming thick tropical place and because he was overweight, grossly overweight, carrying fifty pounds too many and all of it concentrated in his gut. He was going to do something about that when he got back to San Francisco—join a club, start jogging, whatever—but right now he was just a big sweating overweight man with bare pale legs set like stanchions on the floor of the cab and a belly that soaked right through the front of his cotton-rayon, open-necked shirt with the blue and yellow parrots cavorting all over it. And there was the beach, scalloped and white, chasing along beside the car, with palm trees and a hint of maritime cool, and before ten minutes had ticked off his watch he was at the hotel, paying the driver from a wad of worn velvety bills that didn't seem quite real. The driver had no problem with them—the bills, that is—and he accepted a fat velvety tip, too, and seven and a half minutes after that Lester was sitting in the middle of a shady tiled dining room open to the sea on one side and the pool on the other, a room key in his pocket and his first Mexican cocktail clenched in his sweaty fist.

He'd negotiated the cocktail with the faintest glimmer of half-remembered high-school Spanish—jooze *naranja*, soda cloob and vodka, tall, with ice, *hielo, yes, hielo*—and a whole repertoire of mimicry he didn't know he possessed. What he'd really wanted was a Greyhound, but he didn't know the Spanish word for grapefruit, so he'd fallen back on the orange juice and vodka, though there'd been some confusion over the meaning of the venerable Russian term for clear distilled spirits until he hit on the inspiration of naming the brand, Smirnoff. The waitress, grinning and nodding while holding herself perfectly erect in her starched white peasant dress, repeated the brand name in a creaking singsong voice and went off to fetch his drink. Of course, by the time she set it down he'd already drunk the better half of it and he immediately ordered another and then another, until for the first twenty minutes or so he had the waitress and bartender working in perfect synchronization to combat his thirst and any real or imagined pangs he might have suffered on the long trip down.

After the fifth drink he began to feel settled, any anxiety over travelling dissolved in the sweet flow of alcohol and juice. He was pleased with himself. Here he was, in a foreign country, ordering cocktails like a native and contemplating a bite to eat—guacamole and nachos, maybe—and then a stroll on the beach and a nap before dinner. He wasn't sweating anymore. The waitress was his favorite person in the world, and the bartender came next.

He'd just drained his glass and turned to flag down the waitress—one more, he was thinking, and then maybe the nachos—when he noticed that the table at the far end of the veranda was occupied. A woman had slipped in while he was gazing out to sea, and she was seated facing him, bare-legged, in a rust-colored bikini and a loose black robe. She looked to be about thirty, slim, muscular, with a high tight chest and feathered hair that showed off her bloodshot eyes and the puffed bow of her mouth. There was a plate of something steaming at her elbow—fish, it looked like, the specialty of the house, breaded, grilled, stuffed, baked, fried, or sautéed with peppers, onion, and cilantro—and she was drinking a Margarita rocks. He watched in fascination—semi-drunken fascination—for a minute, until she looked up, chewing, and he turned away to stare out over the water as if he were just taking in the sights like any other calm and dignified tourist.

He was momentarily flustered when the waitress appeared to ask if he wanted another drink, but he let the alcohol sing in his veins and said, "Why not?"—*"por qué no?"*—and the waitress giggled and walked off with her increasingly admirable rump moving at the center of that long white gown. When he stole another glance at the woman in the corner, she was still looking his way. He smiled. She smiled back. He turned away again and bided his time, but when his drink came he tossed some money on the table, rose massively from the chair, and tottered across the room.

"Hi," he said, looming over the chewing woman, the drink rigid in his hand, his teeth clenched round a defrosted smile. "I mean, *Buenas tardes. Or noches.*"

He watched her face for a reaction, but she just stared at him. "Uh, *Cómo está Usted? Or tú. Cómo estás tu?*"

"Sit down, why don't you," she said in a voice that was as American as Hillary Clinton's. "Take a load off."

Suddenly he felt dizzy. The drink in his hand had somehow concentrated itself till it was as dense as a meteorite. He pulled out a chair and sat heavily. "I thought . . . I thought you were—?"

"I'm Italian," she said. "From Buffalo, originally. All four of my grandparents came from Tuscany. That's where I get my exotic Latin looks." She let out a short bark of a laugh, forked up a slab of fish, and began chewing vigorously, all the while studying him out of eyes that were like scalpels.

He finished his drink in a gulp and looked over his shoulder for the waitress. "You want another one?" he asked though he saw she hadn't half finished her first.

Still chewing, she smiled up at him. "Sure."

When the transaction was complete and the waitress had presented them with two fresh drinks, he thought to ask her name, but the silence had gone on too long, and when they both began to speak at the same time he deferred to her. "So what do you do for a living?" she asked.

"Biotech. I work for a company in the East Bay—Oakland, that is."

Her eyebrows lifted. "Really? Is that like making potatoes that walk around the kitchen and peel themselves? Cloning sheep? Two-headed dogs?"

Lester laughed. He was feeling good Better than good. "Not exactly."

"My name's Gina," she said, reaching out her hand, "but you might know me as the Puma. Gina (the Puma) Caramella."

He took her hand, which was dry and small and nearly lost in his own. He was drunk, gloriously drunk, and so far he hadn't been ripped off by the Federales or assailed by the screaming shits or leached dry by malarial mosquitoes and vampire bats or any of the other myriad horrors he'd been warned against, and that made him feel pretty near invulnerable. "What do you mean? You're an actress?"

She gave a little laugh. "I wish." Ducking her head, she chased the remnants of the fish around the plate with her fork and the plane of her left index finger. "No," she said. "I'm a boxer."

The alcohol percolated through him. He wanted to laugh, but he fought down the urge. "A boxer? You don't mean like *boxing*, do you? Fisticuffs? Pugilism?"

"Twenty-three, two, and one," she said. She took a sip of her drink. Her eyes were bright. "What I'm doing right now is agonizing over my defeat two weeks ago at the Shrine by one of the queen bitches in the game, DeeDee DeCarlo, and my manager thought it would be nice for me to just get away for a bit, you know what I mean?"

He was electrified. He'd never met a female boxer before— didn't even know there was such a thing. Mud-wrestling he could see—in fact, since his wife had died he'd become a big fan, Tuesday nights and sometimes on Fridays—but boxing? That wasn't a woman's sport. Drunkenly, he scrutinized her face, and it was a good face, a pretty face, but for the bridge of her nose, a telltale depression there, just the faintest misalignment—and sure, sure, how had he missed it? "But doesn't it hurt? I mean, when you get punched in the . . . body punches, I mean?"

"In the tits?"

He just nodded.

"Sure it hurts, what do you think? But I wear a padded bra, wrap 'em up, pull 'em flat across the rib cage so my opponent won't have a clear target, but really, it's the abdominal blows that take it out of you," and she was demonstrating with her hands now, the naked slope of her belly and the slit of her navel, firm, but nothing like those freakish female body-builders they threw at you on ESPN, nice abs, nice navel, nice, nice, nice.

"You doing anything for dinner tonight?" he heard himself say.

She looked down at the denuded plate before her, nothing left but lettuce, don't eat the lettuce, never eat the lettuce, not in Mexico. She shrugged. "I guess I could. I guess in a couple of hours."

He lifted the slab of his arm and consulted his watch with a frown of concentration. "Nine o'clock?"

She shrugged again. "Sure."

"By the way," he said. "I'm Lester."

April had been dead two years now. She'd been struck and killed by a car a block from their apartment, and though the driver was a teen-age kid frozen behind the wheel of his father's Suburban, it wasn't entirely his fault. For one thing, April had stepped out in front of him, twenty feet from the crosswalk, and, as if that wasn't bad enough, she was blindfolded at the time. Blindfolded and feeling her way with one of those flexible fibreglass sticks the blind use to register the world at their feet. It was for a psychology course she was taking in San Francisco State—"Strategies of the Physically Challenged." The professor had asked for two volunteers to remain blindfolded for an entire week, even at night, even in bed, no cheating and April had been the first to raise her hand. She and Lester had been married for two years at the time—his first, her second—and now she was two years dead.

Lester had always been a drinker, drink, but after April's death he seemed to enjoy drinking less and need it more. He knew it, and he fought it. Still, when he got back to his room, sailing on the high of his chance meeting with Gina—Gina the Puma—he couldn't help digging out the bottle of Herradura he'd bought in the duty-free and taking a good long cleansing hit.

There was no TV in the room, but the air-conditioner worked just fine and he stood in front of it awhile before stripping off his sodden shirt and stepping into the shower. The water was tepid, but it did him good. He shaved, brushed his teeth, and repositioned himself in front of the air-conditioner. When he saw the bottle standing there on the night table, he thought he'd have just one more hit—just one—because he didn't want to be utterly wasted when he took Gina the Puma out for dinner. But then he looked at his watch and saw that it was only seven-twenty, and figured what the hell, two drinks, three, he just wanted to have a good time. Too wired to sleep, he flung himself down on the bed like a big wet dripping fish and began poking through the yellowed paperback copy of "Under the Volcano" he'd brought along because he couldn't resist the symmetry of it. What else was he going to read in Mexico—Proust?

"No se puede vivir sin amar," he read, "You can't live without love," and he saw April stepping out into the street with her puny fibreglass stick and the black velvet sleep mask pulled tight over her eyes. But he didn't like that picture not at all, so he took another drink and thought of Gina. He hadn't had a date in six months and he was ready. And who knew? Anything could happen. Especially on vacation. Especially down here. He tipped back the bottle, and then he flipped to the end of the book, where the Consul, cored and gutted and beyond all hope, tumbles dead down the ravine and they throw the bloated corpse of a dog down after him.

The first time Lester had read it, he'd thought it was funny, in a grim sort of way. But now he wasn't so sure.

Gina was waiting for him at the bar when he came down at quarter to nine. The place was lit with paper lanterns strung from the thatched ceiling, there was the hint of a breeze off the ocean, the sound of the surf, a smell of citrus and jasmine. All the tables were full, people leaning into the candlelight over their fish and Margaritas and murmuring to each other in Spanish, French, German. It was good. It was perfect. But as Lester ascended the ten steps from the patio and crossed the room to the bar, his legs felt dead, as if they'd been shot out from under him and then magically reattached, all in the space of an instant. Food. He needed food. Just a bite, that was all. For equilibrium.

"Hey," he said, nudging Gina with his shoulder.

"Hey," she said, flashing a smile. She was wearing shorts and heels and a blue halter top glistening with tiny blue beads.

He was amazed at how small she was—she couldn't have weighed more than a hundred pounds. April's size. April's size exactly.

He ordered a Herradura-and-tonic, his forearms laid out like bricks on the bar. "You weren't kidding before," he said, turning to her, "about boxing, I mean? Don't take offense, but you're so— well, small. I was just wondering, you know?"

She looked at him a long moment, as if debating with herself. "I'm a flyweight, Les," she said finally. "I fight other flyweights, just like in the men's division, you know? This is how big God made me, but you come watch me some night and you'll see it's plenty big enough."

She wasn't smiling, and somewhere on the free-floating periphery of his mind he realized he'd made a blunder. "Yeah," he said, "of course. Of course you are. Listen, I didn't mean to— but why boxing? Of all the things a woman could do."

"What? You think men have a patent on aggression? Or excellence?" She let her eyes sail out over the room, hard eyes, angry eyes, and then she came back to him. "Look, you hungry or what?"

Lester swirled the ice in his drink. It was time to defuse the situation, but quick. "Hey," he said, smiling for all he was worth. "I'd like to tell you I'm on a diet, but I like eating too much for that—and plus, I haven't had a thing since that crap they gave us on the plane, dehydrated chicken and rice that tasted like some sort of by-product of the vulcanizing process. So yeah, let's go for it."

"There's a place up the beach," she said, "in town. I hear it's pretty good—Los Crotos. Want to try it?"

"Sure," he said, but the deadness crept back into his legs. Up the beach? In town? It was dark out there and he didn't speak the language.

She was watching him. "If you don't want to, it's no big deal," she said, finishing off her drink and setting the glass down with a rattle of ice that sounded like nothing so much as loose teeth spat into a cup. "We can just eat here. The thing is, I've been here two days now and I'm a little bored with the menu—you know, fish, fish, and more fish. I was thinking maybe a steak would be nice."

"Sure," he said. "Sure, no problem."

And then they were out on the beach, Gina barefoot at his side, her heels swinging from one hand, purse from the other. The night was dense and sustaining, the lights muted, palms working slowly in the breeze, empty *palapas* lined along the high-water mark like the abandoned cities of a forgotten race. Lester shuffled through the deep sand, his outsized feet as awkward as snow-shoes, while children and dogs chased each other up and down the beach in a blur of shadow against the white frill of the surf and knots of people stood in the deeper shadows of the palms, laughing and talking till the murmur of conversation was lost in the next sequence of breakers pounding the shore. He wanted to say something, anything, but his brain was impacted and he couldn't seem to think, so they walked in silence, taking it all in.

When they got to the restaurant—an open-air place set just off a shallow lagoon that smelled powerfully of sea wrack and decay—he began to loosen up. There were tables draped in white cloth, the waiter was solicitous and grave and he accepted Lester's mangled Spanish with equanimity. Drinks appeared. Lester was in his element again. "So," he said, leaning into the table and trying to sound as casual as he could while Gina squeezed a wedge of lime into her drink and let her shoe dangle from one smooth slim foot, "you're not married, are you? I mean, I don't see a ring or anything. . . ."

Gina hunched her shoulders, took a sip of her drink—they were both having top-shelf Margaritas, blended—and gazed out on the dark beach. "I used to be married to a total idiot," she said, "but that was a long time ago. My manager, Gerry O'Connell— he's Irish, you know?—him and me had a thing for a while, but I don't know anymore. I really don't." She focussed on him. "What about you?"

He told her he was a widower and watched her eyes snap to attention. Women loved to hear that—it got all their little wheels and ratchets turning—because it meant he wasn't damaged goods, like all the other hairy-chested cretins out there, but tragic, just tragic, just tragic. She asked how it had happened, a sink of sympathy and morbid female curiosity, and he told her the story of the kid in the Suburban and the wet pavement and how the student volunteers were supposed to have a monitor with them at all times, but not April, because she just shrugged it off— she wanted an authentic experience, and that was what she got, all right. His throat seemed to thicken when he got to that part, the irony of it, and what with the cumulative weight of the cocktails, the reek of the lagoon, and the strangeness of the place— Mexico, his first day in Mexico—he nearly broke down. "I wasn't there for her," he said. "That's the bottom line. I wasn't there."

Gina was squeezing his hand. "You must have really loved her."

"Yeah," he said. "I did." And he had loved her, he was sure of it, though he had trouble picturing her now, her image drifting through his consciousness as if blown by a steady wind.

Another drink came. They ordered dinner, a respite from the intensity of what he was trying to convey, and then Gina told him her own tale of woe, the alcoholic mother, the brother shot in the face when he was mistaken for a gang member, how she'd excelled in high-school sports and had nowhere to go with it, two years at the community college and a succession of mind-numbing jobs till Gerry O'Connell plucked her from anonymity and made her into a fighter. "I want to be the best," she said. "Number One—and I won't settle for anything less."

"You're beautiful," he said.

She looked at him. Her drink was half gone. "I know," she said.

By the time they were finished with dinner and they'd had a couple of after-dinner drinks, he was feeling unbeatable again. It was quarter past eleven and the solicitous waiter wanted to go home. Lester wanted to go home, too—he wanted to take Gina up to his room and discover everything there was to know about her. He lurched suddenly to his feet and threw a fistful of money at the table. "Want to go?" he said, the words sticking to the roof of his mouth.

She rose unsteadily from her seat and leaned into him while she adjusted the strap of her right heel. "Think we should take a cab?" she said.

"A cab? We're just at the other end of the beach."

She was staring up at him, small as a child, her head thrown back to take in the spread and bulk of him. "Didn't you see that notice in your room—on the bathroom door? I mean, it sounds almost funny, the way they worded it, but still, I wonder."

"Notice? What notice?"

She fished around in her purse until she came up with a folded slip of paper. "Here," she said. "I wrote it down because it was so bizarre: 'The management regrets to inform you that the beach area is unsafe after dark because of certain criminal elements the local authorities are sadly unable to suppress and advises that all guests should take a taxi when returning from town.' "

"Are you kidding? Criminal elements? This place is a sleepy little village in the middle of nowhere—they ought to try the Tenderloin if they want to see criminal elements. And besides, besides"—he was losing his train of thought—"besides . . ."

"Yes?"

"There's nobody in the whole country taller than five-four, as far as I can see." He laughed. He couldn't help himself. *Criminal elements!* And he was still shaking his head as they stepped out into the night.

Call it hubris.

They hadn't gone two hundred yards, the night deepening, dogs howling in the hills, and every star set firmly in its track, when they were jumped. It was nothing like the way Lester had visualized it while stalking home after the bars closed on Twenty-fourth Street, half hoping some sorry shithead would come up to him so he could break him in two. There were no words, no warning, no "Give me your wallet" or "I've got a gun" or "This is a stickup." One minute he was trudging through the sand, a drunken arm draped hopefully over Gina's shoulder, and the next he was on the ground, two pairs of booted feet lashing diligently at his face and ribs while a whole fluttering rush of activity washed round him, as if a flock of birds had burst up off the ground in a panic. He heard a grunt, a curse, the unmistakable crack of bone and cartilage rearranging itself, and it was Gina, Gina the Puma, whaling away at the shadows with both fists as he shoved himself up out of the sand and the boots suddenly stopped kicking and fled.

"You all right?" she said, and he could hear her hard steady breathing over the hammering of the waves.

He was cursing into the night—"Sons of bitches! Motherfuckers! I'll kill you!"—but it was all bluster, and he knew it. Worse, so did she.

"Yeah," he said finally, his chest heaving, the booze and adrenaline pulsing in his temples till the blood vessels there felt like big green garden hoses crawling up both sides of his head. "Yeah, I'm O.K. . . . I took a few kicks in the face maybe . . . and I think— I think they got my wallet."

"Here," she said, her voice oddly calm, "are you sure?" And then she was crouching, feeling around in the sand with spread fingers.

He joined her, glad to be down on his hands and knees and relieved of the effort of holding himself up. His wallet? He didn't give a shit about any wallet. The sand was cool, and the regular thump of the waves conveyed itself to him in the most immediate and prescient way.

"Les?" She was standing now, obscuring the stars. He couldn't make out her face. "You sure you're all right?"

From a great reeling distance he heard himself say, "Yeah, I'm fine." Her voice was insistent, the voice of an intimate, a wife, a lover.

"Come on, Les, get up. You can't stay here. It's not safe."

"O.K.," he said. "Sure. Just give me a minute."

Then there was a brightness, a burning-hot soldered light fused to the cracks of the blinds, and he woke to find himself in his bed—his Mexican bed, in his Mexican hotel, in Mexico. Alone. Without Gina, that is. The first thing he did was check his watch. There it was, clinging like a manacle to his wrist, dividing his naked forearm from his meaty pale hand and indifferently announcing the time: two-thirty-two. All right. He heaved himself up to a sitting position, drained the plastic water bottle he discovered behind the tequila on the night table, and took a minute to assess the situation.

There was a rumor of pain between his ribs, where, he began to recall, two pairs of sharp-toed boots had repeatedly inserted themselves in the waning hours of the previous night, but that was nothing compared with his face. It seemed to ache all over, from his hairline to his jaw. He reached a hand to his cheek and felt a tenderness there, and then he worked his jaw till the pain became too much for him. His right eye was swollen closed, there was a drumming in his head and a vague nauseous feeling creeping up the back of his throat. To top it off, his wallet was missing.

Now he'd have to call up and cancel his credit cards, and he was a fool and an idiot and he cursed himself twice over, but it wasn't the end of the world—he had ten thin crisp hundreds hidden away in his carry-on bag, or his shaving kit, actually where no one would think to look for them. It could have been worse, he was thinking, but he couldn't get much beyond that. How had he managed to get himself back last night? Or had Gina managed it? The thought made him burn with shame.

He took a shower, clapped on a pair of coruscating silver-lensed sunglasses to mask the desecration of his eye, and limped down to the restaurant. She wasn't there, and that was all right for the moment—he needed time to pull himself together before he could face her. The waitress was there, though, eternally responsive to his needs, wearing another down-to-the-toes peasant dress, this time in a shade of blue so pale it barely registered. She smiled and chirped at him and he ordered two tall Smirnoff-and-*naranja* with soda cloob and three fried eggs with tortillas and a fiery serrano salsa that cleared his airways, no doubt about it. He ate and drank steadily, and when he looked up idly at the sea stretching beyond the veranda, he saw nothing but a desert of water. He had a third cocktail for equilibrium, then went down to the front desk and asked the attendant there if she knew which room Gina was staying in.

"Gina?" the woman echoed, giving him a blank look. "What family name, please?"

He had no idea. She'd told him, but it was gone now, obliterated by vodka, tequila, and half a dozen kicks to the head. All he could think of was her professional name. "The Puma," he tried. "Gina the Puma."

The woman's hair was pulled back in a bun, her blouse buttoned up to her throat. She studied him a long moment. "I'm sorry," she said. "I can't help you."

"Gina," he repeated, and his voice got away from him a bit. "How many Ginas could there be in this place, for Christ's sake?"

When she answered this time, she spoke in Spanish, and then she turned away.

He began a methodical search of the place, from pool to bar and back again, suddenly desperate. He had to explain last night to Gina, joke it away, rationalize, apologize, spin shit into gold; she had to understand that he was drunk and his judgment was impaired, and if the circumstances had been different he would have wiped the beach with those scumbags, he would have. Startled faces gaped up at him from the recliners round the pool, maids in pale-green uniforms flattened themselves to the walls. Then he was in the blast of the midday sun, searching through the *palapas* on the beach, hundreds of *palapas*, and practically every one with a sunburned tourist lounging beneath it. Soon he was sunburned himself, sweating rivulets and breathing hard, so he stripped off his shirt, threw himself into the waves, and came up dripping to the nearest unoccupied *palapa* and sent a skinny little girl scurrying away to provide him with a piss-warm beer.

Several piss-warm beers later, he began to feel like himself again—and so what if he'd lost his shirt somewhere in the surf? He was in Mexico and he was drunk and he was going to find Gina and make it up to her, ask her to dinner, take a cab—a whole fleet of cabs—and buy her all the steak and lobster she could hold. He drank a tequila with wedges of lime and some true, cold beers at a tourist bar, and when the shadows began to lengthen he decided to continue up the beach to see if she'd maybe taken one of the water taxis over to Puerto Ángel or Carizalillo and was only now coming back.

The sun was hanging on a string just over the horizon, pink and lurid, and the tourists were busy packing up their sun-block and towels and paperback novels while the dark people, the ones who lived here year-round and didn't know what a vacation was, began to drift out of the trees with their children and their dogs to reclaim their turf. He kept walking, intent on the way his toes grabbed and released the sand, and he'd got halfway to the boats before he realized he'd left his sunglasses somewhere. No matter. He never even broke stride. They were nothing to him, one more possession, one more thing he could slough off like so much dead skin, like April's desk and her clothes and the straw baskets and pottery she'd decorated the apartment with.

Besides, there was hardly any glare off the water now and these people, these coppery little grimacing Indians who seemed to sprout up all over the beach once the sun began to close down, they needed to see him, with his flaming belly and his crusted cheekbone and savage eye, because this was what their criminal elements had done to him and he was wearing the evidence of it like a badge. "Fuck you," he was muttering under his breath. "Fuck you all."

At some point, Lester looked up to orient himself and saw that he was just opposite the restaurant from last night. There it sat, squat among the trees, its lights reflected on the surface of the lagoon. A soft glow lit the bar, which he could just make out, fig- ures there, movement, cocktail hour. He had a sudden intimation that Gina was in there, her dark head bent over a table in back, a drunken intimation that counted for absolutely nothing, but he acted on it, sloshing through the fetid lagoon in his sandals and shorts, mounting the three steps from the beach, and drifting across the creaking floorboards to the bar.

It wasn't Gina seated at the table but a local woman, the pro- prietress no doubt, totting up figures in a ledger; she raised her head when he walked in, but looked right through him. There were three men at the bar, some sort of police, in black shirts and trousers, one of them wearing dark glasses though there was no practical reason to at this hour. They ignored him and went on smoking and talking quietly, in soft rapping voices. A plastic half-gallon jug of tequila stood before them on the bar, amid a litter of plates and three water glasses half-full of silvery liquid. Lester addressed the bartender. "Margarita rocks," he said. "With *hielo*."

He sipped his drink, profoundly drunk now, but drunk, for a reason. Two reasons. Or three. For one thing, he had pain to kill, physical pain, and for another he was on vacation, and if you can't be legitimately wasted on your vacation, then when can you be? The third reason was Gina. He'd come so close, and then he'd blown it. *Criminal elements.* He glanced up at the cops with an idle curiosity that turned sour almost immediately: Where were they when he'd needed them?

And then he noticed something that made his heart skip a beat: the boots. These guys were wearing boots, sharp-toed boots with silver toe caps, the only boots in town. Nobody in Puerto Escondido wore boots. They could barely afford sandals, fishermen who earned their living with a hook and thirty feet of line wrapped round an empty two-litre Pepsi bottle, maids and itinerant merchants, dirt farmers from the hills. Boots? They were as likely to have Armani blazers, silk shirts, and monogrammed boxer shorts. Understanding came down like a hammer. He had to find Gina.

Dusk now, children everywhere, dogs, fishermen up to their chests in the rolling water, bats swooping, sand fleas leaping away from the blind advance of his feet. The steady flow of alcohol had invigorated him—he was feeling no pain, none at all—though he realized he'd have to eat something soon, and clean himself up, especially if he was going to see Gina, because his whole body was seething and rushing, and everything, from the palms to the *palapas* to the rocks scattered along the shore, seemed to have grown fur. Or fuzz. Peach fuzz.

That was when he stepped in the hole and went down awkwardly on his right side, his face plowing a furrow in the loose sand, and the bad eye, wet with fluid, picking up a fine coating of sharp white granules. But it was no problem, no problem at all. He rolled over and lay on his back awhile, laughing softly to himself. *Criminal elements*, he thought, and he was speaking the thought aloud as people stepped around him in the sand. "Sure, sure. And I'm the Pope in Rome."

When he finally got back to the hotel courtyard, he hesitated. Just stood there glistening in the muted light like a statue erected in honor of the befuddled tourist. On the one hand, he was struck by the impulse to go back to his room, wash the grit from his body, do something with his hair, and fish another shirt out of his bag; on the other, he felt an equally strong urge to poke his head in the bar for a minute—just a minute—to see if Gina was there. Ultimately, it was no contest. There he went, feet thundering on the planks, the sand sparkling all over him as if he'd been dipped in sugar.

There. There was the waitress, giving him an odd look—a blend of hopefulness and horror—and the thicket of heads bent over plates and glasses, the air heavy as water, the bartender looking up sharply. Ever hopeful, Lester lurched out onto the floor.

This time he got lucky: Gina was sitting at a table just round the corner of the bar, the farthest table out on the veranda, her legs crossed at the knee, one shoe dangling from her toes. There was music playing somewhere, a faint hum of it leaking in out of the night, Mexican music, shot full of saccharine trumpets and weeping violins. It was a romantic moment, or it could have been. But Gina didn't see him coming—she was turned the other way, in profile, the sea crashing behind her, her hair hanging limp to her shoulders—and it wasn't till he'd rounded the end of the bar that he saw she wasn't alone. There was a man sitting across from her, a drink in one hand, cigarette in the other. Lester saw a dangle of red hair, muscles under a Lollapalooza T-shirt, the narrow face of an insect.

In the next instant he loomed up on the table, pulled out a chair, and dropped into it with a thump that reverberated the length of the dining room. "Gina, listen," he said, as if they were right in the middle of a conversation and the man with the insect face didn't exist, "about last night, and you're not going to believe this, but it was—"

And then he faltered. Gina's mouth was hanging open—and this was a mouth that could cushion any blow, a mouth that knew the taste of leather and the shock of the punch that came out of nowhere. "Christ, Les," she said. "What happened to you— you're a mess. Have you looked in the mirror?"

He watched her exchange a glance with the man across the table, and then he was talking again, trying to get it out, the night, the way they'd come at him, and they weren't just your average muggers, they were the law, for Christ's sake, and how could anybody expect him to defend her from that?

"Les," she was saying. "Les, I think you've had too much to drink."

"I'm trying to tell you something," he said, and his own voice sounded strange to him, distant and whining, the voice of a loser, a fat man, a maker of bad guesses and worse decisions.

That was when the red-haired man spoke up, his eyes twitching in his head. "Who is this jerk anyway?"

Gina—Gina the Puma—gave him a look that was like a left jab. "Shut up, Drew," she said. And then, turning back to Lester, "Les, this is Drew." She tried to inject a little air into her voice, though he could see she wasn't up to it. "Drew wants to know where he can get a good steak around here."

Drew slouched in his chair. He had nothing to say. Lester looked from Gina to Drew and back again. He was very far gone, he knew that, but still, even through his haze, he was beginning to see something in those two faces that shut him out, that slammed the door with a bang and turned the key in the lock.

He had no right to Gina or this table or this hotel, either. He couldn't even make it through the first round.

Gina's voice came to him as if from a great distance—"Les, really, maybe you ought to go and lie down for a while"—and then he was on his feet. He didn't say "Yes" or "No" or even "See you later"—he just turned away from the table, wove his way through the restaurant, down the stairs, and back out into the night.

It was fully dark now, black dark, and the shadows had settled under the skeletons of the trees. He wasn't thinking about Gina or Drew or even April and the kid in the Suburban. There was no justice, no revenge, no reason—there was just this, just the beach and the night and the criminal elements. And when he got to me place by the lagoon and the stink of decay rose to his nostrils, he went straight for the blackest clot of shadow and the rasping murmur at the center of it. "You!" he shouted, all the air raging in his lungs. "Hey, you!"

lifeguard

JOHN UPDIKE

beyond doubt, I am a splendid fellow. In the autumn, winter, and spring, I execute the duties of a student of divinity; in the summer I disguise myself in my skin and become a life-guard. My slightly narrow and gingerly hirsute but not necessarily unmanly chest becomes brown. My smooth back turns the colour of caramel, which, in conjunction with the whipped cream of my white pith helmet, gives me, some of my teenage satellites assure me, a delightfully edible appearance. My legs, which I myself can study, cocked as they are before me while I repose on my elevated wooden throne, are dyed a lustreless maple walnut that accentuates their articulate strength. Correspondingly, the hairs of my body are bleached blond, so that my legs have the pointed elegance of, within the flower, umber anthers dusted with pollen.

For nine months of the year, I pace my pale hands and burning eyes through immense pages of Biblical text barnacled with fudging commentary; through multi-volumed apologetics couched in a falsely friendly Victorian voice and bound in subtly abrasive boards of finely ridged, pre-faded red; through handbooks of liturgy and histories of dogma; through the bewildering duplicities of Tillich's divine politicking; through the suave table talk of Father D'Arcy, Étienne Gilson. Jacques Maritain, and other such moderns mistakenly put at their ease by the exquisite furniture and overstuffed larder of the hospitable St. Thomas; through the terrifying attempts of Kierkegaard, Berdyaev, and Barth to scourge God into being. I sway appalled on the ladder of minus signs by which theologians would surmount the void. I tiptoe like a burglar into the house of naturalism to steal the silver. An acrobat, I swing from wisp to wisp. Newman's iridescent cobwebs crush in my hands. Pascal's blackboard mathematics are erased by a passing shoulder. The cave drawings, astoundingly vital by candlelight, of those aboriginal magicians, Paul and Augustine, in daylight fade into mere anthropology. The diverting productions of literary flirts like Chesterton, Eliot, Auden, and Greene— whether they regard Christianity as a pastel forest designed for a fairyland romp or a deliciously miasmic pit from which chiaroscuro can be mined with mechanical buckets—in the end all infallibly strike, despite the comic variety of gongs and mallets, the note of the rich young man who on the coast of Judaea refused in dismay to sell all that he had.

Then, for the remaining quarter of the solar revolution, I rest my eyes on a sheet of brilliant sand printed with the runes of naked human bodies. That there is no discrepancy between my studies, that the texts of the flesh complement those of the mind, is the easy burden of my sermon.

On the back rest of my lifeguard's chair is painted a cross— true, a red cross, signifying bandages, splints, spirits of ammonia, and sunburn unguents. Nevertheless, it comforts me. Each morning, as I mount into my chair, my athletic and youthfully fuzzy toes expertly gripping the slats that make a ladder, it is as if I am climbing into an immense, rigid, loosely fitting vestment.

Again, in each of my roles I sit attentively perched on the edge of an immensity. That the sea, with its multiform and mysterious hosts, its savage and senseless rages, no longer comfortably serves as a divine metaphor indicates how severely humanism has corrupted the apples of our creed. We seek God now in flowers and good deeds, and the immensities of blue that surround the little scabs of land upon which we draw our lives to their unsatisfactory conclusions are suffused by science with vacuous horror. I myself can hardly bear the thought of stars, or begin to count the mortalines of coral. But from my chair the sea, slightly distended by my higher perspective, seems a misty old gentleman stretched at his ease in an immense armchair which has for arms the arms of this bay and for an antimacassar the freshly laundered sky. Sailboats float on his surface like idle and unrelated but benevolent thoughts. The soughing of the surf is the rhythmic lifting of his ripple-stitched vest as he breathes. Consider. We enter the sea with a shock; our skin and blood shout in protest. But, that instant, that leap, past, what do we find? Ecstasy and buoyance. Swimming offers a parable. We struggle and thrash, and drown; we succumb, even in despair, and float, and are saved.

With what timidity, with what a sense of trespass do I set forward even this obliquely a thought so official! Forgive me. I am not yet ordained; I am too disordered to deal with the main text. My competence is marginal, and I will confine myself to the gloss of flesh with which this particular margin, this one beach, is annotated each day.

Here the cinema of life is run backwards. The old are the first to arrive. They are idle, and have lost the gift of sleep. Each of our bodies is a clock that loses time. Young as I am, I can hear in myself the protein acids ticking; I wake at odd hours and in the shuddering darkness and silence feel my death rushing towards me like an express train. The older we get, and the fewer the mornings left to us, the more deeply dawn stabs us awake. The old ladies wear wide straw hats and, in their hats' shadows, smiles as wide, which they bestow upon each other, upon salty shells they discover in the morning-smooth sand, and even upon me, downy-eyed from my night of dissipation. The gentlemen are often incongruous; withered white legs support brazen barrel chests, absurdly potent, bustling with white froth. How these old roosters preen on their 'condition'! With what fatuous expertness they swim in the icy water—always, however, prudently parallel to the shore, at a depth no greater than their height.

Then come the middle-aged, burdened with children and aluminium chairs. The men are scarred with the marks of their vocation—the red forearms of the gasoline-station attendant, the pale X on the back of the overall-wearing mason or carpenter, the clammer's nicked ankles. The hair on their bodies has as many patterns as matted grass. The women are wrinkled but fertile, like the Iraqi rivers that cradled the seeds of our civilization. Their children are odious. From their gaunt faces leer all the vices, the greeds, the grating urgencies of the adult, unsoftened by maturity's reticence and fatigue. Except that here and there, a girl, the eldest daughter, wearing a knit suit striped horizontally with green, purple, and brown, walks slowly, carefully, puzzled by the dawn enveloping her thick smooth body, her waist not yet nipped but her throat elongated.

Finally come the young. The young matrons bring fat and fussing infants who gobble the sand like sugar who toddle blissfully into the surf and bring me bolt upright on my throne. My whistle tweets. The mothers rouse. Many of these women are pregnant again, and sluggishly lie in their loose suits like cows tranced in a meadow. They gossip politics, and smoke incessantly, and lift their troubled eyes in wonder as a trio of flat-stomached nymphs parades past. These maidens take all our eyes. The vivacious redhead, freckled and white-footed, pushing against her boy and begging to be ducked; the solemn brunette, transporting the vase of herself with held breath; the dimpled blonde in the bib and diapers of her Bikini, the lambent fuzz of her midriff shimmering like a cat's belly. Lust stuns me like the sun.

You are offended that a divinity student lusts? What prigs the unchurched are. Are not our assaults on the supernatural lascivious, a kind of indecency? If only you knew what de Sadian degradations, what frightful psychological spelunking, our gentle transcendentalist professors set us to, as preparation for our work, which is to shine in the darkness.

I feel that my lust makes me glow; I grow cold in my chair, like a torch of ice, as I study beauty. I have studied much of it, wearing all styles of bathing suit and facial expression, and have come to this conclusion; a woman's beauty lies, not in any exaggeration of the specialized zones, not in any general harmony that could be worked out by means of the *sectio aurea* or a similar aesthetic superstition; but in the arabesque of the spine. The curve by which the back modulates into the buttocks. It is here that grace sits and rides a woman's body.

I watch from my white throne and pity women, deplore the demented judgement that drives them towards the braggart muscularity of the mesomorph and the prosperous complacence of the endomorph when it is we ectomorphs who pack in our scrawny sinews and exacerbated nerves the most intense gift, the most generous shelter, of love. To desire a woman is to desire to save her. Anyone who has endured intercourse that was neither predatory nor hurried knows how through it we descend, with a partner, into the grotesque and delicate shadows that until then have remained locked in the most guarded recess of our soul: into this harbour we bring her. A vague and twisted terrain becomes inhabited; each shadow, touched by the exploration, blooms into a flower of act. As if we are an island upon which a woman, tossed by her labouring vanity and blind self-seeking, is blown, and there finds security, until, an instant before the anticlimax, Nature with a smile thumps down her trump, and the island sinks beneath the sea.

There is great truth in those motion pictures which are slandered as true neither to the Bible nor to life. They are—written though they are by demons and drunks—true to both. We are all Solomons lusting for Sheba's salvation. The God-filled man is filled with a wilderness that cries to be populated. The stony chambers need jewels, furs, tints of cloth and flesh, even though, as in Samson's case, the temple comes tumbling. Women are an alien race of pagans set down among us. Every seduction is a conversion.

Who has loved and not experienced that sense of rescue? It is not true that our biological impulses are tricked out with ribands of chivalry; rather, our chivalric impulses go clanking in encumbering biological armour. Eunuchs love. Children love. I would love.

My chief exercise, as I sit above the crowds, is to lift the whole mass into immortality. It is not a light task the throng is so huge, and its members so individually unworthy. No *memento mori* is so clinching as a photograph of a vanished crowd. Cheering Roosevelt, celebrating the Armistice, there it is, wearing its ten thousand straw hats and stiff collars, a fearless and wooden-faced bustle of life: it is gone. A crowd dies in the street like a derelict; it leaves no heir, no trace, no name. My own persistence beyond the last rim of time is easy to imagine: indeed, the effort of imagination lies the other way—to conceive of my ceasing. But when I study the vast tangle of humanity that blackens the beach as far as the sand stretches, absurdities crowd in on me. Is it as maiden, matron, or crone that the females will be eternalized? What will they do without children to watch and gossip to exchange? What of the thousand deaths of memory and bodily change we endure—can each be redeemed at a final Adjustments Counter? The sheer numbers involved make the mind scream. The race is no longer a tiny clan of simian aristocrats lording it over an ocean of grass; mankind is a plague racing like fire across the exhausted continents. This immense clot gathered on the beach, a fraction of a fraction—can we not say that this breeding swarm is its own immortality and end the suspense? The beehive in a sense survives; and is each of us not proved to be a hive, a galaxy of cells each of whom is doubtless praying, from its pew in our thumbnail or oesophagus, for personal resurrection? Indeed, to the cells themselves cancer may seem a revival of faith. No, in relation to other people oblivion is sensible and sanitary.

This sea of others exasperates and fatigues me most on Sunday mornings. I don't know why people no longer go to church—whether they have lost the ability to sing or the willingness to listen. From eight-thirty onwards they crowd in from the parking lot, ants each carrying its crumb of baggage, until by noon, when the remote churches are releasing their gallant and gaily dressed minority, the sea itself is jammed with hollow heads and thrashing arms like a great bobbing backwash of rubbish. A transistor radio somewhere in the sand releases in a thin, apologetic gust the closing peal of a transcribed service. And right here, here at the very height of torpo and confusion, I slump, my eyes slit, and the blurred forms of Protestantism's errant herd seem gathered by the water's edge in impassioned poses of devotion. I seem to be lying dreaming in the infinite rock of space before Creation, and the actual scene I see is a vision of impossibility: a Paradise. For had we existed before the gesture that split the firmament, could we have conceived of our most obvious possession, our most platitudinous blessing, the moment, the single ever-present moment that we perpetually bring to our lips brimful?

So: be joyful. Be Joyful is my commandment. It is the message I read in your jiggle. Stretch your skins like pegged hides curing in the miracle of the sun's moment. Exult in your legs' scissoring, your waist's swivel. Romp; eat the froth; be children. I am here above you; I have given my youth that you may do this. I wait. The tides of time have treacherous under-currents. You are borne continually towards the horizon. I have prepared myself; my muscles are instilled with everything that must be done. Someday my alertness will bear fruit; from near the horizon there will arise, delicious, translucent, like a green bell above the water, the call for help, the call, a call, it saddens me to confess, that I have yet to hear.

from **american beach**

RUSS RYMER

for most of the years I've known her, MaVynee Betsch has lived on a chaise longue on the beach in front of the house her great-grandfather built. The house is not one he would recognize. After his death, of old age and a tried heart in 1947, it fell out of the family, and has lost to successive renovations the formal white clapboard and latticework gingerbread and the dark, top-hung shutters over heavy sash windows that give it such an air of staid nobility in old photographs. The building has been streamlined: clad in plywood, stuccoed, and painted beige, with the sliding glass doors and weathered wooden deck that typify the standard-model modern vacation bungalow. The people who own it live in a distant corner of Georgia and come to relax on occasional summer days. When they're not around, MaVynee sets up her chaise on the wide porch and writes her letters and reads her books and presides over the panoramic ocean front of American Beach just as her great-grandfather, Abraham Lincoln Lewis, once presided.

She calls him Fafa, the man whom no adult not in the family would have thought of calling anything but "Mr. Lewis" when he was alive, the dark-skinned man with the peanut-shaped head and the soft, other-worldly voice and calm demeanor, whose unfathomable ocean of anger was never tossed by surface storms of temper, who came out of the turpentine farms and lumber mills and cigar factories of Reconstruction Florida to become the preeminent figure in the black economic life of that entire corner of the South.

MaVynee recalls him from her early years, his last. "Oh, that man," she told me one day. "There's no way to describe the effect he had on people just by walking into a room." She remembers him arriving at the beach house he had built with his fortune in the town built by his company, remembers how he wouldn't spend any time looking back up the hill at the results of all his labors but would stand on his porch in his suspenders and tie—while Mama Zone, his second wife, aired the house and his valet drew the bath and his chauffeur, Ollie, garaged the car—staring wordlessly out across the Atlantic as though by patience and penetrating gaze he could perceive something known to all, but hidden even from him.

"And what was he looking at?" MaVynee asked me one day, waving a braceleted arm out over the white sand and constant surf and the vast blue emptiness to the east. "Africa, baby! That's Africa out there. He was looking at where he was from!"

On her chaise longue on the beach, in front of the house that Fafa built but would no longer recognize, in the town he founded, which has now, in its central precincts, nearly fallen down, MaVynee lives in an edifice of memory, in the ruins of a history, with her gaze trained on a past she knows lies just beyond the horizon, invisible to common sight.

Occasionally she will be asked to lead a tour. A bus will pull into American Beach packed with students from a black college or a public high school, and MaVynee will narrate a ride through town, standing in the aisle with her back to the windshield as the diesel grumbles idly through tight streets. Sometimes, as once when the bus bore students from Bethune-Cookman College in

Daytona Beach, I'd take a seat. The Bethune-Cookman students were less impressed with their destination than with their guide, at least at first. MaVynee Betsch is nothing if not scenic. For tours, she wears her formal gown—a bright, crisp kente cloth wrapped into a skirt, under a draped felt serape. She ties a scarf of black lace tightly across her forehead, with a turquoise cloisonné butterfly perched in its meshes just between her eyebrows. Her great topiary circle of gray hair rises so high above her crown that on this day it bent against the ceiling of the bus; the mass of her hair disappears down the neck of her blouse and emerges at her waist to fill a hair net the size of a beach ball, which she cradles in the crook of her left arm. The hair is studded with buttons advertising liberal political causes.

On a visit to American Beach some years ago, when I had only heard of MaVynee's existence and doubted it, frankly, I interrupted a group of men working on a car in a driveway and asked them if they knew where the Beach Lady lived. (That was the name I'd been given.) "No," they answered; then I told them that she had big hair. "Oh, yeah," one of them said. "The lady with the fingernails." And sure enough, when I found her, on the porch of A. L. Lewis's house on Gregg Street, her fingers were amply endowed. The nails of her right hand were relatively short (for utility, I presumed). But those on her left hand extended almost to her ankles, spiraling around each other like the roots of some ambulatory mangrove. To protect them, she carries them in a plastic bag she grasps with her thumb. She lacquers them with Revlon. She was, on our first meeting, as exotic as she had been described, but no one had warned me of her most extraordinary feature, a voice of such vaulting, lilting clarity and speech of such evident culture that soon after she began to talk I had forgotten the strangeness of her appearance altogether. As I would find out, MaVynee, in her youth, had been an opera singer.

Now her voice began its work on the students. "When I was young," she began, enunciating into a microphone and steadying herself with a hip against the bus driver's shoulder, "were black people allowed to visit most Southern beaches?" She made a comic, exasperated face. "Unh-unh!" she cautioned, and let out with her favorite exclamation of extreme repudiation: *"No . . . way, . . . Jo . . . sé!* So what did we do? Well, my great-grandfather, A. L. Lewis, was president of the Afro-American Life Insurance Company in Jacksonville, which was the first—wait a minute, that's right—the *first* insurance company in the state of Florida. That's first, *period*, baby—black or white. And in the early 1930s, the company decided to build a resort where blacks could come, and this is it: American Beach."

The result of the Afro-American Life Insurance Company's initiative was once described to me by a service station owner in Fernandina, a white man named Topsy. He viewed it with an outsider's dispassionate objectivity. "It used to be on weekends we could only go so far down the beach," he said, "and then you'd look down there and as far as you could see were t-h-o-o-u-u-s-s-a-a-a-n-d-s of blacks. And if you got closer, you saw the buses, big Greyhounds all lined up side by side.

"They had the best beach," Topsy told me. "There was more going on."

It's the consensus locally that "they" had the best beach in general, cupped in the curve of the island, where the strand was widest, under the brow of the island's largest sand dune—a beach sequestered from the rest of the world by square mile upon square mile of undeveloped live oak and palmetto forest that stretched in all directions. And indeed, as MaVynee told the students, the buses came. They came for four decades, from the late 1930s into the 1970s, from Atlanta and Chicago and Birmingham and Charleston, arriving by caravan halfway through the summer nights, and the pocket hotels had bellhops to unload the luggage, and big-name bands and burlesque troupes played the clubs, and the restaurants were mobbed, and the motel was booked up years in advance, and the summer houses were inhabited by eminent people in the forefront of their generation in Jacksonville and the South—pioneering black dentists, doctors, lawyers, preachers, educators, undertakers, and, as you might expect, insurance company executives.

MaVynee can list the Beach's illustrious visitors—Cab Calloway, Ray Charles, Ossie Davis, Zora Neale Hurston, Joe Louis, Hank

Aaron, Paul Robeson, and Billy Eckstine among them—and she can call each house by its owner's name. Some of the names are contemporary—the actress Barbara Montgomery, of *Amem!* fame, Emory University psychology professor Eugene Emory, jazz drummer Billy Moore, Cleveland dramaturge Alexander Hickson, Jacksonville educator Emma Morgan, former Howard University dean Edna Calhoun, Florida State Senator Arnett Girardeau, Federal Judge Henry Adams, Florida Supreme Court Justice Leander Shaw, Jacksonville historians Camilla Thompson, Charlotte Stewart, and Hortense Gray, and television journalist Lydia Stewart. But the houses MaVynee holds in highest reverence are those whose names are old: the house built by Dr. Harry Richardson, Tuskegee educator and the first black graduate of Harvard Divinity School (whose wife, Selma, a former Tuskegee professor now nearing a hundred, still comes down from Atlanta); the house of Ida Guzman, also of Tuskegee, who was a friend of George Washington Carver; the house of Dr. I. E. Williams, medical director of the Afro-American Life Insurance Company, and his wife Arnolta, friend of W. E. B. Du Bois and honored by presidents as recent as Ronald Reagan; the house of I. H. Burney, a president of the Afro-American, and Miriam Burney, the first black woman to graduate from Mount Holyoke College; and the house of Gwen Sawyer-Cherry, the first black woman legislator in Florida.

That generation has largely died off, and the names were strange to the Bethune-Cookman students, staring from the windows of the only bus to come through in a very long time. As the bus crawled along the main street—Lewis Street—from its juncture with highway A1A, I thought how little had changed since my own first trip down Lewis Street fifteen years earlier, on a day when I was kiting down A1A headed for Jacksonville and stopped and doubled back because the name I had passed on the road sign—"American Beach"—was nowhere on my map. The acres of oak and palmetto jungle that once insulated the Beach are diminished now. Housing developments, like Summer Beach to the north, and golf resorts, like Amelia Island Plantation to the south, crowd it on all sides. But now, as before, American Beach's long straight narrow main street is a hallway to a hidden realm. It loiters past a small white wooden church and a score of modest brick or frame homes set on a wooded plateau, before reaching the flank of the great sand dune, which rises to its south. There the world ahead opens up and falls away to expose an enormous sand caldera, a nearly treeless, terraced amphitheater open to the sea.

The students seemed stunned by the view. Homes lined the terraced streets; the house closest to them, across Lewis Street from the dune, had dropped its balcony into the yard and was tumbling onto its face. In the bottom of the bowl of sand were a cluster of square buildings, a central grassy square, and a string of sentinel houses along the beach. The houses were kempt, generally. A couple were even new. But the largest, a concrete fantasy known as the Blue Palace, through the very center of which a driveway extended all the way onto the beach, was an empty cinder, filling with drifted sand. The commercial buildings, except for a low brick beachside bar called the Rendezvous, looked derelict, their windows missing and their doors boarded, the gay palm trees and inviting flowers painted on their walls fading from the punishment of too many summers. The effect from the crest of Lewis Street was of stumbling out of the forest onto a lost civilization and wondering at its apocalypse. It was that beautiful, that compellingly mysterious, and one had the impression that the sand walls of American Beach were like the murderous funnel of the doodle bug—that once having fallen into the vortex of the town's history, you might never again scramble back out.

One day on the beach, MaVynee was approached by a white woman out on her jaunty constitutional from a neighboring resort, who said to her, in an apparent effort to be helpful, "Why don't you people clean this place up?"

"Lady," MaVynee shot back, "I've been to Athens and I've been to Rome. You have your ruins. These are ours."

American Beach, for MaVynee, is in its entirety a shrine—its landscape no less than its buildings. Her walks around its streets are a solitary Panathenaic Procession. She calls the sand dune NaNa, the African name of affection for a female ancestor, and as it shadows with cloud or blossoms with springtime she observes its face with an intensity of concentration she might otherwise expend on a lover's face. "I have a spiritual connection with this beach," she told the students. "Maybe it's because my parents honeymooned here." Her soprano dropped into a suggestive throatiness worthy of Lauren Bacall. "I think I may have been conceived here!" she deadpanned and then grinned large, delighted to be both at home in her town and at home on a stage, albeit in the front of a bus. "I'm serious!" she shrieked as the students laughed. "I'm sure of it!"

Whether or not she was conceived there, American Beach would not be a good place for MaVynee Betsch to elude her identity. Its road signs read like a *dramatis personae* of her life and lineage. Of the eleven streets that cross or parallel Lewis Street, several— Waldron Street, Price Street, Lee Street, and Gregg Street—bear the surnames of men who huddled with A. L. Lewis in a church study in Jacksonville in 1901 to plan the formation of the burial society that became the Afro (as the company is known to its familiars). Several more, such as Ervin Street (after the Afro's first sales agent) and Burney Road (after one of its last presidents), are named for those who labored under Lewis to keep the enterprise going.

The other streets are kin. Julia Street is named after A. L. Lewis's mother, about whom MaVynee knows little except that she was born a slave and lived in the Florida Panhandle. James Street is named after James H. Lewis, A. L. Lewis's son, whose beach house still stands next to that of the patriarch and who succeeded him as president of the Afro and held that office into his senescence, retiring in 1967 to be nursed toward death by his daughter, Mary, and her daughter MaVynee—only to outlive the one and be reviled by the other, who calls him the Riverboat Gambler. "Whooo, God!" MaVynee burst out when I asked her if James H. Lewis the son was anything like A. L. Lewis the father. *"No . . . way, . . . Jo . . . sé!* I used to tease my grandfather that Fafa had a cold the day he was conceived! I damn sure did! Those two were as different physically as they were mentally, sexually, and spiritually."

Three blocks after James Street comes Leonard Street, honoring J. Leonard Lewis, who was James H. Lewis's son and became the Afro's legal counsel after graduation from New York University Law School; who competed with his brother-in-law John Betsch, MaVynee's father, to become the Riverboat Gambler's heir apparent; and who won the rivalry but never gained the Afro's presidency, dying shockingly young not long after his rival's own untimely death.

And then, up in the forest, shrouded in trees, comes Mary Avenue. MaVynee tells people that the name honors Mary McLeod Bethune, founder of Bethune-Cookman College, friend of her great-grandfather, and sales agent and later board member of the Afro-American Life Insurance Company. She tells them the street is also named for A. L. Lewis's first wife, and also for his granddaughter, Mary Lewis Betsch, who was the daughter of James H. Lewis, sister of J. Leonard, wife of John Betsch, and mother of three children: Johnny, Johnnetta, and the oldest, MaVynee. Mary Betsch was a graduate of Wilberforce University, in Ohio; after the death of her husband and brother, she left her college registrar's job to work as a bookkeeper at the Afro and rose to become its first female top administrator; she was the force behind the building of its new Jacksonville headquarters in the 1950s, and might have taken the company's helm herself—for she was decidedly tough enough—had she not had the tougher job of succoring her father, the aging ex-president, the Riverboat Gambler, in his ornery last days and administering to the broken health of her eldest daughter, who would never outlast her influence.

As MaVynee reads out the street names to students on her tours, Mary Avenue is the one she invokes most quietly or lingers over longest. She may pass it by without mentioning it at all, or she may tell them how Mary Betsch directed the church choir and infused her children with a love of music, how she brought the retail life of Jacksonville nearly to a halt over the matter of a broken watch, when a white jewelry store clerk had the temerity to summon her by her first name. And once in a while MaVynee tells the story of her mother on her deathbed, in 1975. MaVynee sat with her through that time, in the antiseptic, air-conditioned hospital room in Jacksonville that would contain their last concentrated intimacies before containing those of strangers, in an acute-care ward sealed away from anything to do with their lives. And then one day the air conditioner broke and the nurses threw open the windows. It was the last day of Mary's life. The breeze bore in the noise and heat of the city, and something else, too—the faint scent, from fifteen miles away, of salty ocean air. Mary Betsch turned her head on the pillow to face the breeze and for the first time in a long time her pain faded and her voice had a young wonder in it, as though she had glimpsed the shape of sanctuary in some sustaining memory. "The beach, MaVynee. The beach!" she whispered, and they were the last words she spoke to her daughter.

a change of scene

D AVID M ALOUF

I

having come like so many others for the ruins, they had been surprised to discover, only three kilometres away, this other survival from the past: a big old-fashioned hotel.

Built in florid neo-baroque, it dated from a period before the Great War when the site was much frequented by Germans, since it had figured, somewhat romanticized, in a passage of Hofmannsthal. The fashion was long past and the place had fallen into disrepair. One corridor of the main building led to double doors that were crudely boarded up, with warnings in four languages that it was dangerous to go on, and the ruined side-wings were given over to goats. Most tourists these days went to the Club Méditerranée on the other side of the bay. But the hotel still maintained a little bathing establishment on the beach (an attendant went down each morning and swept it with a rake) and there was still, on a cliff-top above zig-zag terraces, a pergolated belvedere filled with potted begonias, geraniums and dwarf citrus—an oasis of cool green that the island itself, at this time of year and this late in its history, no longer aspired to. So Alec, who had a professional interest, thought of the ruins as being what kept them here, and for Jason, who was five, it was the beach; but Sylvia, who quite liked ruins and wasn't at all averse to lying half-buried in sand while Jason paddled and Alec, at the entrance to the cabin, tapped away at his typewriter, had settled at first sight for the hotel.

It reminded her, a bit creepily, of pre-war holidays with her parents up on the Baltic—a world that had long ceased to exist except in pockets like this. Half-lost in its high wide corridors, among rococo doors and bevelled gilt-framed mirrors, she almost expected—the past was so vividly present—to meet herself, aged four, in one of the elaborate dresses little girls wore in those days. Wandering on past unreadable numbers she would come at last to a door that was familiar and would look in and find her grandmother, who was standing with her back to a window, holding in her left hand, so that the afternoon sun broke through it, a jar of homemade cherry syrup, and in her right a spoon. "Grandma," she would say, "the others are all sleeping. I came to you."

Her grandmother had died peacefully in Warsaw, the year the Germans came. But she was disturbed, re-entering that lost world, to discover how much of it had survived in her buried memory, and how many details came back now with an acid sweetness, like a drop of cherry syrup. For the first time since she was a child she had dreams in a language she hadn't spoken for thirty years—not even with her parents—and was surprised that she could find the words. It surprised her too that Europe—that dark side of her childhood—was so familiar, and so much like home.

She kept that to herself. Alec, she knew, would resent or be hurt by it. She had, after all, spent all but those first years in another place altogether, where her parents were settled and secure as they never could have been in Poland, and it was in that place, not in Europe, that she had grown up, discovered herself and married.

Her parents were once again rich, middle-class people, living in an open-plan house on the North Shore and giving *al fresco* parties at a poolside barbecue. Her father served the well-done steaks with an air of finding this, like so much else in his life, delightful but unexpected. He had not, as a boy in Lvov, had T-bone steaks in mind, nor even a dress factory in Marrickville. These were accidents of fate. He accepted them, but felt he was living the life of an imposter. It added a touch of humorous irony to everything he did. It was her mother who had gone over completely to the New World. She wore her hair tinted a pale mauve, made cheesecake with passion-fruit, and played golf. As for Sylvia, she was simply an odd sort of local. She had had no sense of a foreign past till she came back here and found how European she might be.

Her mother, if she had known the full extent of it, would have found her interest in the hotel "morbid", meaning Jewish. And it was perverse of her (Alec certainly thought so) to prefer it to the more convenient cabins. The meals were bad, the waiters clumsy and morose, with other jobs in the village or bits of poor land to tend. The plumbing, which looked impressive, all marble and heavy bronze that left a green stain on the porcelain, did not provide water. Alec had no feeling for these ruins of forty years ago. His period was that of the palace, somewhere between eleven and seven hundred BC, when the site had been inhabited by an unknown people, a client state of Egypt, whose language he was working on; a dark, death-obsessed people who had simply disappeared from the pages of recorded history, leaving behind them a few common artefacts, the fragments of a language, and this one city or fortified palace at the edge of the sea.

Standing for the first time on the bare terrace, which was no longer at the edge of the sea, and regarding the maze of open cellars, Alec had been overwhelmed. His eyes, roving over the level stones, were already recording the presence of what was buried here—a whole way of life, richly eventful and shaped by clear beliefs and rituals, that rose grandly for him out of low brick walls and a few precious scratches that were the symbols of corn, salt, water, oil and the names, or attributes, of gods.

What her eyes roamed over, detecting also what was buried, was Alec's face; reconstructing from what passed over features she thought she knew absolutely, in light and in darkness, a language of feeling that he, perhaps, had only just become aware of. She had never, she felt, come so close to what, outside their life together, most deeply touched and defined him. It was work that gave his life its high seriousness and sense of purpose, but he had never managed to make it real for her. When he talked of it he grew excited, but the talk was dull. Now, in the breathlessness of their climb into the hush of sunset, with the narrow plain below utterly flat and parched and the great blaze of the sea beyond, with the child dragging at her arm and the earth under their feet thick with pine-needles the colour of rusty blood, and the shells of insects that had taken their voice elsewhere—in the dense confusion of all this, she felt suddenly that she understood and might be able to share with him now the excitement of it, and had looked up and found the hotel, just the outline of it. Jason's restlessness had delayed for a moment her discovery of what it was.

They had been travelling all day and had come up here when they were already tired, because Alec, in his enthusiasm, could not wait. Jason had grown bored with shifting about from one foot to another and wanted to see how high they were.

"Don't go near the edge," she told the boy.

He turned away to a row of corn- or oil-jars, big enough each one for a man to crawl into, that were sunk to the rim in stone, but they proved, when he peered in, to be less interesting than he had hoped. No genii, no thieves. Only a coolness, as of air that had got trapped there and had never seeped away.

"It's cold," he had said, stirring the invisible contents with his arm.

But when Alec began to explain, in words simple enough for the child to understand, what the jars had been used for and how the palace might once have looked, his attention wandered, though he did not interrupt.

Sylvia too had stopped listening. She went back to her own discovery, the big silhouette of what would turn out later to be the hotel.

It was the child's tone of wonder that lingered in her mind: "It's cold." She remembered it again when they entered the grand but shabby vestibule of the hotel and she felt the same shock of chill as when, to humour the child, she had leaned down and dipped her arm into a jar.

"What is it?" Jason had asked.

"It's nothing."

He made a mouth, unconvinced, and had continued to squat there on his heels at the rim.

Alec had grown up on a wheat farm west of Gulgong. Learning early what it is to face bad seasons when a whole crop can fail, or bushfires, or floods, he had developed a native toughness that would, Sylvia saw from his father, last right through into old age. Failure for Alec meant a failure of nerve. This uncompromising view made him hard on occasion, but was the source as well of his golden rightness. Somewhere at the centre of him was a space where honour, fairness, hard work, the belief in a man's responsibility at least for his own fate—and also, it seemed, the possibility of happiness—were given free range; and at the clear centre of all there was a rock, unmoulded as yet, that might one day be an altar. Alec's deficiencies were on the side of strength, and it delighted her that Jason reproduced his father's deep blue eyes and plain sense of having a place in the world. She herself was too rawboned and intense. People called her beautiful. If she was it was in a way that had too much darkness in it, a mysterious rather than an open beauty. Through Jason she had turned what was leaden in herself to purest gold.

It was an added delight to discover in the child some openness to the flow of things that was also hers, and which allowed them, on occasion, to speak without speaking; as when he had said, up there on the terrace. "It's cold", at the very moment when a breath from the far-off pile that she didn't yet know was a hotel, had touched her with a premonitory chill.

They were close, she and the child. And in the last months before they came away the child had moved into a similar closeness with her father. They were often to be found, when they went to visit, at the edge of the patio swimming-pool, the old man reading to the boy, translating for him from what Alec called his "weirdo books", while Jason, in bathing-slip and sneakers, nodded, swung his plump little legs, asked questions, and the old man, with his glasses on the end of his nose and the book resting open a moment on his belly, considered and found analogies.

After thirty years in the garment trade her father had gone back to his former life and become a scholar.

Before the war he had taught philosophy. A radical free-thinker in those days, he had lately, after turning his factory over to a talented nephew, gone right back past his passion for Wittgenstein and the other idols of his youth, to what the arrogance of that time had made him blind to—the rabbinical texts of his fathers. The dispute, for example, between Rabbi Isserles of Cracow and Rabbi Luria of Ostrov that had decided at Posen, in the presence of the exorcist Joel Baal-Shem, miracle-worker of Zamoshel, that demons have no right over moveable property and may not legally haunt the houses of men.

Her father's room in their ranch-style house at St Ives was crowded with obscure volumes in Hebrew; and even at this distance from the Polish sixteenth century, and the lost communities of his homeland, the questions remained alive in his head and had come alive, in diminutive form, in the boy's. It was odd to see them out there in the hard sunlight of her mother's cactus garden, talking ghosts.

Her mother made faces. Mediaeval nonsense! Alec listened, in a scholarly sort of way, and was engaged at first, but found the whole business in the end both dotty and sinister, especially as it touched the child. He had never understood his father-in-law, and worried sometimes that Sylvia, who was very like him, might have qualities that would emerge in time and elude him. And now Jason! Was the old man serious, or was this just another of his playful jokes?

"No," Sylvia told him as they drove back in the dark, with Jason sleeping happily on the back seat, "it's none of the things you think it is. He's getting ready to die, that's all."

Alec restrained a gesture of impatience. It was just this sort of talk, this light and brutal way of dealing with things it might be better not to mention, that made him wonder at times if he really knew her.

"Well I hope he isn't scaring Jason, that's all."

"Oh fairy tales, ghost stories—that's not what frightens people."

"Isn't it?" said Alec. "Isn't it?"

II

they soon got to know the hotel's routine and the routine of the village, and between the two established their own. After a breakfast of coffee with condensed milk and bread and honey they made their way to the beach: Alec to work, and between shifts at the typewriter to explore the coastline with a snorkel, Sylvia and the child to laze in sand or water.

The breakfast was awful. Alec had tried to make the younger of the two waiters, who served them in the morning, see that the child at least needed fresh milk. For some reason there wasn't any, though they learned from people at the beach that the Cabins got it.

"No," the younger waiter told them, "no milk." Because there were no cows, and the goat's milk was for yogurt.

They had the same conversation every morning, and the waiter, who was otherwise slack, had begun to serve up the tinned milk with a flourish that in Alec's eye suggested insolence. As if to say: *There! You may be Americans* (which they weren't), *and rich* (which they weren't either) *but fresh milk cannot be had. Not on this island.*

The younger waiter, according to the manager, was a Communist. That explained everything. He shook his head and made a clucking sound. But the older waiter, who served them at lunch, a plump, grey-headed man, rather grubby, who was very polite and very nice with the child, was also a Communist, so it explained nothing. The older waiter also assured them there was no milk. He did it regretfully, but the result was the same.

Between them these two waiters did all the work of the hotel. Wandering about in the afternoon in the deserted corridors, when she ought to have been taking a siesta, Sylvia had come upon the younger one having a quiet smoke on a window-sill. He was barefoot, wearing a dirty singlet and rolled trousers. There was a pail of water and a mop beside him. Dirty water was slopped all over the floor. But what most struck her was the unnatural, fishlike whiteness of his flesh—shoulders, arms, neck—as he acknowledged her presence with a nod but without at all returning her smile.

Impossible, she had thought, to guess how old he might be. Twenty-eight or thirty he looked, but might be younger. There were deep furrows in his cheeks and he had already lost some teeth.

He didn't seem at all disconcerted. She had, he made it clear, wandered into *his* territory. Blowing smoke over his cupped hand (why did they smoke that way?) and dangling his bare feet, he gave her one of those frank, openly sexual looks that cancel all boundaries but the original one; and then, to check a gesture that might have made him vulnerable (it did—she had immediately thought, how boyish!) he glared at her. with the look of a waiter, or peasant, for a foreign tourist. His look had in it all the contempt of a man who knows where he belongs, and whose hands are cracked with labour on his own land, for a woman who has come sightseeing because she belongs nowhere.

Except, she had wanted to protest, it isn't like that at all. It is true I have no real place (and she surprised herself by acknowledging it) but I know what it is to have lost one. That place is gone and all its people are ghosts. I am one of them—a four-year-old in a pink dress with ribbons. I am looking for my grandmother. Because all the others are sleeping . . .

She felt differently about the young waiter after that, but it made no odds. He was just as surly to them at breakfast, and just as nasty to the child.

The bay, of which their beach was only an arc, was also used by fishermen, who drew their boats up on a concrete ramp beside the village, but also by the guests from the Cabins and by a colony of hippies who camped in caves at the wilder end.

The hippies were unpopular with the village people. The manager of the hotel told Sylvia that they were dirty and diseased, but they looked healthy enough, and once, in the early afternoon, when most of the tourists had gone in to sleep behind closed shutters, she had seen one of them, a bearded blond youth with a baby on his hip, going up and down the beach collecting litter. They were Germans or Dutch or Scandinavians. They did things with wire, which they sold to the tourists, and traded with the fishermen for octopus or chunks of tuna.

All day the fishermen worked beside their boats on the ramp: mending nets and hanging them from slender poles to dry, or cleaning fish, or dragging octopus up and down on the quayside to remove the slime. They were old men mostly, with hard feet, all the toes stubbed and blackened, and round little eyes. Sometimes, when the child was bored with playing alone in the wet sand, he would wander up the beach and watch them at their work. The quick knives and the grey-blue guts tumbling into the shallows were a puzzle to him, for whom fish were either bright objects that his father showed him when they went out with the snorkel or frozen fingers. The octopus too. He had seen lights on the water at night and his father had explained how the fishermen were using lamps to attract the creatures, who would swarm to the light and could be jerked into the dinghy with a hook. Now he crinkled his nose to see one of the fishermen whip a live octopus out of the bottom of the boat and turning it quickly inside-out, bite into the raw, writhing thing so that its tentacles flopped. He looked at Sylvia and made a mouth. These were the same octopus that, dried in the sun, they would be eating at tomorrow's lunch.

Because the bay opened westward, and the afternoon sun was stunning, their beach routine was limited to the hours before noon.

Quite early, usually just before seven, the young waiter went down and raised the striped canvas awning in front of their beach cabin and raked a few square metres of sand.

Then at nine a sailor came on duty on the little heap of rocks above the beach where a flagpole was set, and all morning he would stand there in his coarse white trousers and boots, with his cap tilted forward and strapped under his chin, watching for sharks. It was always the same boy, a cadet from the Training College round the point. The child had struck up a kind of friendship with him and for nearly an hour sometimes he would "talk" to the sailor, squatting at his feet while the sailor laughed and did tricks with a bit of cord. Once, when Jason failed to return and couldn't hear her calling, Sylvia had scrambled up the rockface to fetch him, and the sailor, who had been resting on his heel for a bit, had immediately sprung to his feet looking scared.

He was a stocky boy of eighteen or nineteen, sunburned almost to blackness and with very white teeth. She had tried to reassure him that she had no intention of reporting his slackness; but once he had snapped back to attention and then stood easy, he looked right through her. Jason turned on the way down and waved, but the sailor stood very straight against the sky with his trousers flapping and his eyes fixed on the sea, which was milky and thick with sunlight, lifting and lapsing in a smooth unbroken swell, and with no sign of a fin.

After lunch they slept. It was hot outside but cool behind drawn shutters. Then about five-thirty Alec would get up, climb the three kilometres to the palace, and sit alone there on the open terrace to watch the sunset. The facts he was sifting at the typewriter would resolve themselves then as luminous dust; or would spring up alive out of the deepening landscape in the cry of cicadas, whose generations beyond counting might go back here to beginnings. They were dug in under stones, or they clung with shrill tenacity to the bark of pines. It was another language. Immemorial Indecipherable.

Sylvia did not accompany him on these afternoon excursions, they were Alec's alone. They belonged to some private need. Stretched out in the darkened room she would imagine him up there, sitting in his shirtsleeves in the gathering dusk, the gathering voices exploring a melancholy he had only just began to perceive in himself and of which he had still not grasped the depths. He came back, after the long dusty walk, with something about him that was raw and in need of healing. No longer a man of thirty-seven—clever, competent, to whom she had been married now for eleven years—but a stranger at the edge of youth, who had discovered, tremblingly, in a moment of solitude up there, the power of dark.

It was the place. Or now, and here, some agent of himself that he had just caught sight of. Making love on the high bed, with the curtains beginning to stir against the shutters and the smell of sweat and pine-needles on him, she was drawn into some new dimension of his still mysterious being, and of her own. Something he had felt or touched up there, or which had touched him—his own ghost perhaps, an intense coolness—had brought him closer to her than ever before.

When it was quite dark at last, a deep blue dark, they walked down to one of the quayside restaurants.

There was no traffic on the promenade that ran along beside the water, and between seven and eight-thirty the whole town passed up and down between one headland and the other: family groups, lines of girls with their arms linked, boisterous youths in couples or in loose threes and fours, sailors from the Naval College, the occasional policeman. Quite small children, neatly dressed, played about among rope coils at the water's edge or fell asleep over the scraps of meals. Lights swung in the breeze, casting queer shadows, there were snatches of music. Till nearly one o'clock the little little port that was deserted by day quite hummed with activity.

When they came down on the first night, and found the crowds sweeping past under the lights, the child had given a whoop of excitement and cried: "Manifestazione!" It was, along with gelato, his only word of Italian.

Almost every day while they were in Italy, there had been a demonstration of one sort or another: hospital workers one day, then students, bank clerks, bus-drivers, even highschool kids and their teachers. Always with placards, loud-hailers, red flags and masses of grim-faced police. "Manifestazione," Jason had learned to shout the moment rounded a corner and found even a modest gathering; though it wasn't always true. Sometimes it was just a street market, or an assembly of men in business suits arguing about football or deciding the price of unseen commodities— olive or sheep or wheat. The child was much taken by the flags and the chanting in a language that made no sense. It was all play-like and good-humoured.

But once, overtaken by a fast-moving crowd running through from one street to the next, she had felt herself flicked by the edge of a wave that further back, or just ahead, might have the power to break her grip on the child's hand, or to sweep her off her feet or toss them violently in the air. It was only a passing vision, but she had felt things stir in her that she had long forgotten, and was disproportionately scared.

Here, however, the crowd was just a village population taking a stroll along the quay or gathering at café tables to drink ouzo and nibble side plates of miniature snails; and later, when the breeze came, to watch outdoor movies in the square behind the church.

It was pleasant to sit out by the water, to have the child along, and to watch the crowd stroll back and forth—the same faces night after night. They ate lobster, choosing one of the big bluish-grey creatures that crawled against the side of a tank, and slices of pink water-melon. If the child fell asleep Alec carried him home on his shoulder, all the way up the steps and along the zig-zag terraces under the moon.

III

one night, the fifth or sixth of their stay, instead of the usual movie there was a puppet-show.

Jason was delighted. They pushed their way in at the side of the crowd and Alec lifted the child on to his shoulders so that he had a good view over the heads of fishermen, sailors from the College and the usual assembly of village youths and girls, who stood about licking icecreams and spitting the shells of pumpkin-seeds.

The little wooden stage was gaudy; blue and gold. In front of it the youngest children squatted in rows, alternately round-eyed and stilled or squealing with delight or terror as a figure in baggy trousers, with a moustache and dagger, strutted up and down on the narrow sill—blustering, bragging, roaring abuse and lunging ineffectually at invisible tormentors, who came at him from every side. The play was both sinister and comic, the moustachioed figure both hero and buffoon. It was all very lively. Big overhead lights threw shadows on the blank wall of the church: pine branches, all needles, and once, swelling abruptly out of nowhere, a giant, as one of the village showoffs swayed aloft. For a moment the children's eyes were diverted by his antics. They cheered and laughed and, leaping up, tried to make their own shadows appear.

The marionette was not to be outdone. Improvising now, he included the insolent spectator in his abuse. The children subsided. There was more laughter and some catcalling, and when the foolish youth rose again he was hauled down, but was replaced, almost at once by another, whose voice drowned the puppet's violent squawking—then by a third. There was a regular commotion.

The little stage-man, maddened beyond endurance, raged up and down waving his dagger and the whole stage shook; over on the wings there was the sound of argument, and a sudden scuffling.

They could see very little of this from where they were pressed in hard against the wall, but the crowd between them and the far-off disturbance began to be mobile. It surged. Suddenly things were out of hand. The children in front, who were being crowded forward around the stage, took panic and began to wail for their parents. There were shouts, screams, the sound of hard blows. In less than a minute the whole square was in confusion and the church wall now was alive with big, ugly shadows that merged in waves of darkness, out of which heads emerged, fists poked up then more heads. Sylvia found herself separated from Alec by a dozen heaving bodies that appeared to be pulled in different directions and by opposing passions. She called out, but it was like shouting against the sea. Alec and Jason were nowhere to be seen.

Meanwhile the stage, with its gaudy trappings, had been struck away and the little blustering figure was gone. In its place an old man in a singlet appeared, black-haired and toothless, his scrawny body clenched with fury and his mouth a hole. He was scream- ing without change of breath in the same doll-like voice as the puppet, a high-pitched squawking that he varied at times with grunts and roars. He was inhabited now not only by the puppet's voice but by its tormentors' as well, a pack of violent spirits of opposing factions like the crowd, and was the vehicle first of one, then of another. His thin shoulders wrenched and jerked as if he too was being worked by strings. Sylvia had one clear sight of him before she was picked up and carried, on a great new surg- ing of the crowd, towards the back wall of one of the quayside restaurants, then down what must have been a corridor and on to the quay. In the very last moment before she was free, she saw before her a man covered with blood. Then dizzy from lack of breath, and from the speed with which all this had occurred, she found herself at the water's edge. There was air. There was the safe little bay. And there too were Alec and the boy.

They were badly shaken, but not after all harmed, and in just a few minutes the crowd had dispersed and the quayside was restored to its usual order. A few young men stood about in small groups, arguing or shaking their heads or gesticulating towards the square, but the affair was clearly over. Waiters appeared. They smiled, offering empty tables. People settled and gave orders. They too decided that it might be best, for the child's sake, if they simply behaved as usual. They ordered and ate.

They saw the young sailor who watched for sharks. He and a friend from the village were with a group of girls, and Jason was delighted when the boy recognized them and gave a smart, mock-formal salute. All the girls laughed.

It was then that Sylvia remembered the man she had seen with blood on him. It was the older waiter from the hotel.

"I don't think so," Alec said firmly. "You just thought it was because he's someone you know." He seemed anxious, in his cool, down-to-earth way, not to involve them, even tangentially, in what was a local affair. He frowned and shook his head: *not in front of the boy*.

"No, I'm sure of it," she insisted. "Absolutely sure."

But next morning, at breakfast, there he was quite unharmed, waving them towards their usual table.

"I must have imagined it after all," Sylvia admitted to herself. And in the clear light of day, with the breakfast tables gleaming white and the eternal sea on the window-frames, the events of the previous night did seem unreal.

There was talk about what had happened among the hotel people and some of the guests from the Cabins but nothing was clear. It was part of a local feud about fishing rights, or it was political—the puppet-man was a known troublemaker from another village—or the whole thing had no point at all; it was one of those episodes that explode out of nowhere in the electric south, having no cause and therefore requiring no explanation, but gathering up into itself all sorts of hostilities—personal, political, some with their roots in nothing more than youthful high-spirits and the frustrations and closeness of village life at the end of a hot spell. Up on the terraces women were carding wool. Goats nibbled among the rocks, finding rubbery thistles in impossible places. The fishermen's nets, black, brown, umber, were stretched on poles in the sun; and the sea, as if suspended between the same slender uprights, rose smooth, dark, heavy, fading where it imperceptibly touched the sky into mother-of-pearl.

But today the hippies did not appear, and by afternoon the news was abroad that their caves had been raided. In the early hours, before it was light, they had been driven out of town and given a firm warning that they were not to return.

The port that night was quiet. A wind had sprung up, and waves could be heard on the breakwater. The lights swayed overhead, casting uneasy shadows over the rough stones of the promenade and the faces of the few tourists who had chosen to eat. It wasn't cold, but the air was full of sharp little grits and the tablecloths had been damped to keep them from lifting. The locals knew when to come out and when not to. They were right.

The wind fell again overnight. Sylvia, waking briefly, heard it suddenly drop and the silence begin.

The new day was sparklingly clear. There was just breeze enough, a gentle lapping of air, to make the waves gleam silver at the edge of the sand and to set the flag fluttering on its staff, high up on the cliff where the sailor, the same one, was watching for sharks. Jason went to talk to him after paying his usual visit to the fishermen.

Keeping her eye on the child as he made his round of the beach, Sylvia read a little, dozed off, and must for a moment have fallen asleep where Jason had half-buried her in the sand. She was startled into uneasy wakefulness by a hard, clear, cracking sound that she couldn't account for, and was still saying to herself in the split-second of starting up, *Where am I? Where is Jason?*, when she caught, out of the heel of her eye, the white of his shorts where he was just making his way up the cliff face to his sailor; and in the same instant saw the sailor, above him, sag at the knees clutching with both hands at the centre of himself, then hang for a long moment in mid-air and fall.

In a flash she was on her feet and stumbling to where the child, crouching on all fours, had come to a halt, and might have been preparing, since he couldn't have seen what had happened, to go on.

It was only afterwards, when she had caught him in her arms and they were huddled together under the ledge, that she recalled how her flight across the beach had been accompanied by a burst of machine-gun fire from the village. Now, from the direction of the Naval College, came an explosion that made the earth shake.

None of this, from the moment of her sitting up in the sand till the return of her senses to the full enormity of the thing, had lasted more than a minute by the clock, and she had difficulty at first in convincing herself that she was fully awake. Somewhere in the depths of herself she kept starting up in that flash of time before the sailor fell, remarking how hot it was, recording the flapping of a sheet of paper in Alec's abandoned typewriter—he must have gone snorkelling or into the village for a drink—and the emptiness of the dazzling sea. *Where am I? Where is Jason?* Then it would begin all over again. It was in going over it the second time, with the child already safe in her arms, that she began to tremble and had to cover her mouth not to cry out.

Suddenly two men dropped into the sand below them. They carried guns. Sylvia and the child, and two or three others who must have been in the water, were driven at gun-point towards the village. There was a lot of gesticulation, and some muttering that under the circumstances seemed hostile, but no actual violence.

They were pushed, silent and unprotesting, into the crowded square. Alec was already there. They moved quickly together, too shocked to do more than touch briefly and stand quietly side by side.

There were nearly a hundred people crushed in among the pine trees, about a third of them tourists. It was unnaturally quiet, save for the abrupt starting up of the cicadas with their deafening beat; then, as at a signal, their abrupt shutting off again. Men with guns were going through the crowd, choosing some and pushing them roughly away towards the quay; leaving others. Those who were left stared immediately ahead, seeing nothing.

One of the first to go was the young waiter from the hotel. As the crowd gave way a little to let him pass, he met Sylvia's eye, and she too looked quickly away; but would not forget his face with the deep vertical lines below the cheekbones and the steady gaze.

There was no trouble. At last about twenty men had been taken and a smaller number of women. The square was full of open spaces. Their group, and the other groups of tourists, looked terribly exposed. Among these dark strangers involved in whatever business they were about—women in coarse black dresses and shawls, men in dungarees—they stood barefoot in briefs and bikinis, showing too much flesh, as in some dream in which they had turned up for an important occasion without their clothes. It was this sense of being both there and not that made the thing for Sylvia so frighteningly unreal. They might have been invisible. She kept waiting to come awake, or waiting for someone else to come awake and release her from a dream that was not her own, which she had wandered into by mistake and in which she must play a watcher's part.

Now one of the gunmen was making an announcement. There was a pause. Then several of those who were left gave a faint cheer.

The foreigners, who had understood nothing of what the gunman said, huddled together in the centre of the square and saw only slowly that the episode was now over; they were free to go. They were of no concern to anyone here. They never had been. They were, in their odd nakedness, as incidental to what had taken place as the pine trees, the little painted ikon in its niche in the church wall, and all those other mute, unseeing objects before whom such scenes are played.

Alec took her arm and they went quickly down the alley to the quay. Groups of armed men were there, standing about in the sun. Most of them were young, and one, a schoolboy in shorts with a machine-gun in his hand, was being berated by a woman who must have been his mother. She launched a torrent of abuse at him, and then began slapping him about the head while he cringed and protested, hugging his machine-gun but making no attempt to protect himself or move away.

IV

there had been a coup. One of the Germans informed them of it the moment they came into the lobby. He had heard it on his transistor. What they had seen was just the furthest ripple of it, way out at the edge. It had all, it seemed, been bloodless, or nearly so. The hotel manager, bland and smiling as ever, scouring his ear with an elongated finger-nail, assured them there was nothing to worry about. A change of government, what was that? They would find everything—the beach, the village—just the same, only more orderly. It didn't concern them.

But one of the Swedes, who had something to do with the legation, had been advised from the capital to get out as soon as possible, and the news passed quickly to the rest. Later that night a boat would call at a harbour further up the coast. The Club had hired a bus and was taking its foreign guests to meet it, but could not take the hotel people as well.

"What will we do?" Sylvia asked, sitting on the high bed in the early afternoon, with the shutters drawn and the village, as far as one could tell, sleeping quietly below. She was holding herself in.

"We must get that boat," Alec told her. They kept their voices low so as not to alarm the child. "There won't be another one till the end of the week."

She nodded. Alec would talk to the manager about a taxi.

She held on. She dared not think, or close her eyes even for a moment, though she was very tired. If she did it would start all over again. She would see the sailor standing white under the flagpole; then he would cover his belly with his hands and begin to fall. Carefully re-packing their cases, laying out shirts and sweaters on the high bed, she never allowed herself to evaluate the day's events by what she had seen. She clung instead to Alec's view, who had seen nothing; and to the manager's who insisted that except for a change in the administration two hundred miles away things were just as they had always been. The child, understanding that it was serious, played one of his solemn games.

When she caught him looking at her once he turned away and rolled his Dinky car over the worn carpet. "Hrummm, hrummm," he went. But quietly. He was being good.

Suddenly there was a burst of gunfire.

She rushed to the window, and pushing the child back thrust her face up close to the slats; but only a corner of the village was visible from here. The view was filled with the sea, which remained utterly calm. When the second burst came, rather longer than the first, she still couldn't tell whether it came from the village or the Naval College or from the hills.

Each time, the rapid clatter was like an iron shutter coming down. It would be so quick.

She turned away to the centre of the room, and almost immediately the door opened and Alec rushed in. He was flushed, and oddly, boyishly exhilarated. He had his typewriter under his arm.

"I'm all right," he said when he saw her face. "There's no fir-
ing in the village. It's back in the hills. I went to get my stuff."

There was something in him, some reckless pleasure in his
own daring, that scared her. She looked at the blue Olivetti, the
folder of notes, and felt for a moment like slapping him, as that
woman on the quay had slapped her schoolboy son—she was so
angry, so affronted by whatever it was he had been up to out
there, which had nothing to do with his typewriter and papers
and had put them all at risk.

"Don't be upset," he told her sheepishly. "It was nothing. There
was no danger." But his own state of excitement denied it. The
danger was in him.

The taxi, an old grey Mercedes, did not arrive till nearly eight.
Loaded at last with their luggage it bumped its way into the village.

The scene there was of utter confusion. The bus from the
Club, which should have left an hour before, was halted at the
side of the road and was being searched. Suitcases were strewn
about all over the pavements, some of them open and spilling
their contents, others, it seemed, broken or slashed. One of the
Club guests had been badly beaten. He was wandering up the
middle of the road with blood on his face and a pair of bent spectacles dangling from his ear, plaintively complaining. A woman
with grey hair was screaming and being pushed about by two
other women and a man—other tourists.

"Oh my God," Alec said, but Sylvia said nothing. When a boy
with a machine-gun appeared they got out quietly and stood at
the side of the car, trying not to see what was going on further
up the road, as if their situation was entirely different. Their suitcases were opened, their passports examined.

The two gunmen seemed undangerous. One of them laid his
hand affectionately on the child's head. Sylvia tried not to
scream.

At last they were told to get back into the car, given their passports, smiled at and sent on their way. The pretence of normali-
ty was terrifying. They turned away from the village and up the

dusty track that Alec had walked each evening to the palace. Thistles poked up in the moonlight, all silver barbs. Dust smoked among sharp stones. Sylvia sank back into the depths of the car and closed her eyes. It was almost over. For the first time in hours she felt her body relax in a sigh.

It was perhaps that same sense of relaxation and relief, an assurance that they had passed the last obstacle, that made Alec reckless again.

"Stop a minute," he told the driver.

They had come to the top of the ridge. The palace, on its high terrace, lay sixty or seventy metres away across a shallow gully.

"What is it?" Sylvia shouted, springing suddenly awake. The car had turned, gone on a little and stopped.

"No, it's nothing," he said. "I just wanted a last look."

"Alec—" she began as their headlamps flooded the valley. But before she could say more the lights cut the driver backed, turned, swung sharply on to the road and they were roaring away at a terrible speed into the moonless dark.

The few seconds of sudden illumination had been just enough to leave suspended back there—over the hastily covered bodies, with dust already stripping from them to reveal a cheek, a foot, the line of a rising knee—her long, unuttered cry.

She gasped and took the breath back into her. Jason, half-turned in the seat, was peering out of the back window. She dared not look at Alec.

The car took them fast round bend after bend of the high cliff road, bringing sickening views of the sea tumbling white a hundred feet below in a series of abrupt turns that took all the driver's attention and flung them about so violently in the back of the car that she and Jason had to cling to one another to stay upright. At last, still dizzy with flight, they sank down rapidly to sea level. The driver threw open the door of the car, tumbled out their luggage and was gone before Alec had even produced the money to pay.

"Alec—" she began.

"No," he said, "not now. Later."

There was no harbour, just a narrow stretch of shingle and a concrete mole. The crowd they found themselves among was packed in so close under the cliff that there was barely room to move. A stiff breeze was blowing and the breakers sent spray over their heads, each wave, as it broke on the concrete slipway, accompanied by a great cry from the crowd, a salty breath. They were drenched, cold, miserable. More taxis arrived. Then the bus. At last, after what seemed hours, a light appeared far out in the blackness and the ship came in, so high out of the water that it bounded on the raging surface like a cork.

"We're almost there," Alec said, "we're almost there," repeating the phrase from time to time as if there were some sort of magic in it.

The ship stood so high out of the water that they had to go in through a tunnel in the stern that was meant for motor vehicles. They jammed into the cavernous darkness, driven from behind by the pressure of a hundred bodies with their individual weight of panic, pushed in hard against suitcases, wooden crates hastily tied brown parcels, wire baskets filled with demented animals that squealed and stank. Coming suddenly from the cold outside into the closed space whose sides resounded with the din of voices and strange animal cries, was like going deep into a nightmare from which Sylvia felt she would never drag herself alive. The huge chamber steamed. She couldn't breathe. And all through it she was in terror of losing her grip on the child's hand, while in another part of her mind she kept telling herself: I should release him. I should let him go. Why drag *him* into this?

At last it was over. They were huddled together in a narrow place on the open deck, packed in among others; still cold, and wetter than ever now as the ship plunged and shuddered and the fine spray flew over them, but safely away. The island sank in the weltering dark.

"I don't think he saw, do you?" Alec whispered. He glanced at her briefly, then away. "I mean, it was all so quick."

He didn't really want her to reply. He was stroking the boy's soft hair where he lay curled against her. The child was sleeping. He cupped the blond head with his hand, and asked her to confirm that darkness stopped there at the back of it, where flesh puckered between bony knuckles, and that the child was unharmed. It was himself he was protecting. She saw that. And when she did not deny his view, he leaned forward across the child's body and pressed his lips, very gently, to her cheek.

Their heads made the apex of an unsteady triangle where they leaned together, all three, and slept. Huddled in among neighbours, strangers with their troubled dreams, they slept, while the ship rolled on into the dark.

the midnight love feast

MICHEL TOURNIER

HE: it was a bright September morning after an equinoctial tide which had given the bay a devastated, frantic, almost pathetic air. We were walking along a shore sparkling with mirrors of water which made the flatfish quiver; a shore strewn with unusual shellfish—whelks, cockles, ormers, clams. But we weren't in the mood for fishing, and spent most of our time looking over towards the south coast, which was shrouded in a milky fog. Yes, there was mystery in the air, almost tragedy, and I wasn't particularly surprised when you drew my attention to two human bodies clasped in each other's arms and covered in sand, about a hundred metres away. We immediately ran up to what we took to be drowned corpses. But they weren't drowned corpses covered in sand. They were two statues sculpted in sand, of strange and poignant beauty. The bodies were curled up in a slight depression, and encircled by a strip of grey, mudstained cloth, which added to their realism. One thought of Adam and Eve before God came and breathed the breath of life into their nostrils of clay. One also thought of the inhabitants of Pompeii whose bodies were fossilized under the hail of volcanic ash from Vesuvius. Or of the men of Hiroshima, vitrified by the explosion of the Atom Bomb. Their tawny faces, spangled with flakes of mica, were turned towards each other and separated by an impassable distance. Only their hands and legs were touching.

We stood for a moment in front of these recumbent figures, as if at the edge of a newly-opened grave. At this moment a strange sort of devil suddenly emerged from some invisible hole, barefoot and stripped to the waist, wearing frayed jeans. He began a graceful dance, making sweeping arm movements which seemed to be greeting us, and then to be bowing to the recumbent figures as a preliminary to picking them up and raising them to the heavens. The deserted, slack-water shore the pale light, this couple made of sand, this dancing madman—all of these things surrounded us with a melancholy, unreal phantasmagoria. And then the dancer came to a standstill, as if suddenly in a trance. After which he bowed, knelt, prostrated himself before us, or rather—as we realized—before an apparition that had loomed up behind us. We turned round. To the right, the Tomberlaine rock was emerging from the haze. But most impressive, suspended like a Saharan mirage above the clouds, was the pyramid of the abbey of Mont-Saint-Michel, with all its glistening pink roof-tiles and glinting stained-glass windows.

Time had stopped. Something had to happen to restart it. It was a few drops of water tickling my feet that did it. A foam-capped tongue licked my toes. Listening carefully, we could hear the incessant rustling of the sea that was stealthily creeping up on us. In less than an hour this immense area, now laid bare to the wind and sun, would be returned to the glaucous, merciful depths.

"But they'll be destroyed!" you exclaimed.

With a sad smile the dancer bowed, as a sign of approval. Then he sprang up and mimed the return of the tide, as if he wanted to accompany it, encourage it, even provoke it by his dance. African sorcerers do much the same when they want to induce rain or drive out demons. And the sea obeyed, first flowing round the edges of the depression in which the couple were lying, then

finding a breach that allowed through an innocent trickle of
water, then two, then three. The joined hands were the first
affected and they disintegrated, leaving in suspense stumps of
amputated wrists. Horrified, we watched the capricious and
inexorable dissolution of this couple which we persisted in feeling to be human, close to us, perhaps premonitory. A stronger
wave broke over the woman's head, carrying away half her face,
then it was the man's right shoulder that collapsed, and we
thought them even more touching in their mutilation.

A few minutes later we were obliged to beat a retreat and
abandon the sand basin with its swirling, frothy eddies. The
dancer came with us, and we discovered that he was neither mad
nor dumb. His name was Patricio Lagos and he came from Chile,
more precisely from Chiloe Island, where he was born, which is
off the south coast of Chile. It is inhabited by Indians adept in
exploiting the forests. He had studied dancing and sculpture at
the same time, in Santiago, and had then emigrated to the
Antipodes. He was obsessed by the problem of time. Dance, the
art of the moment, ephemeral by nature, leaves no trace and suf-
fers from its inability to become rooted in any kind of continuity Sculpture, the art of eternity, defies time by seeking out inde-
structible materials. But in so doing, what it finally finds is death,
for marble has an obvious funerary vocation. On the Channel
and Atlantic coasts, Lagos had discovered the phenomenon of
tides governed by the laws of astronomy. Now the tide gives a
rhythm to the shore dancer's games, and at the same time sug-
gests the practice of ephemeral sculpture.

"My sand sculptures live," he declared, "and the proof of this is
that they die. It's the opposite of the statuary in cemeteries, which
is eternal because it is lifeless."

And so he feverishly sculpted couples in the wet sand just
uncovered by the ebbing tide, and both his dancing and his sculpture stemmed from the same inspiration. It was important that his
work should be finished at the very moment of slack water, for
this must be a parenthesis of rest and meditation. But the great
moment was the return of the tide and the terrible ceremony of
the destruction of the work. A slow, meticulous, inexorable

destruction, governed by an astronomical destiny, and which should be encircled by a sombre, lyrical dance. "I celebrate the pathetic fragility of life," he said. That was when you asked him a question of prime importance to us, which he answered in what I considered an obscure, mysterious way.

SHE: Yes, I raised the question of silence. Because according to our customs, dance is accompanied by music, and in one way it is only music embodied, music made flesh. So there was something para-doxical and strange about the dance he was performing in silence round his recumbent sand-figures. But he unreservedly rejected the word silence. "Silence?" he said, "but there *is* no silence! Nature detests silence, as she abhors a vacuum. Listen to the shore at low tide: it babbles through the thousands of moist lips it half-opens to the skies. *Volubile.* When I was learning French, I fell in love with that graceful, ambiguous word. It is another name for bindweed, whose fragile, interminable stem twines round the sturdier plants it comes across, and it finally chokes them under its disordered profusion studded with white trumpets. The rising tide too is voluble. It entwines the chests and thighs of my clay lovers with its liquid tentacles. And it destroys them. It is the kiss of death. But the rising tide is also voluble in the childish babble it whispers as it flows over the ooze. It insinuates its salty tongues into the sands with moist sighs. It would like to speak. It is search-ing for its words. It's a baby burbling in its cradle."

And he stayed behind and left us, with a little farewell wave and a sad smile, when we reached the beach.

HE: He's a bit mad, your sculptor-dancer, but it's true that by crossing Normandy from east to west, by emigrating from the pebbles of Fécamp to the sands of Mont-Saint-Michel we changed ocean sounds. The waves on the shores of the Pays de Caux smash thousands of stones in a rocky pandemonium. Here, the tide murmurs as it advances with seagull's steps.

SHE: This false silence hasn't been good for you. In Fécamp I loved a taciturn man. You despised all the conventional chit-chat with which human relations surround themselves. Good-morning, good-evening, how are you, very well, and you? what filthy weather . . . You killed all that verbiage with a stern look. Here, you have become uncommunicative. There are grunts in your silences, grumbles in your asides.

HE: Just a moment! I never despised "what filthy weather!" I don't think it's a waste of time to talk about the weather. It's an important subject to seamen. For me, weather reports are lyric poetry. But that's just it. The words we use ought to accord with the sky and the sea. The words appropriate to Fécamp don't correspond to the air in Avranches. Here there is something like a soft, insidious appeal, a demand that I don't know how to satisfy.

SHE: Here we are separated by an immense shore of silence, to which every day brings its low tide. The great logorrhoea of May 1968 made me dream of laconic wisdom, of words that were weighed, and rare, but full of meaning. We are sinking into an oppressive mutism that is just as empty as the student verbosity.

HE: Make up your mind! Nowadays you never stop reproaching me for my silence. No attack is too aggressive for you, no matter how hurtful it might be.

SHE: It's to get a rise out of you. I want a crisis, an explosion, a domestic scene. What is a domestic scene? It's the woman's triumph. It's when the woman has finally forced the man out of his silence by her nagging. Then he shouts, he rages, he's abusive, and the woman surrenders to being voluptuously steeped in this verbal downpour.

HE: Do you remember what they say about the Comte de Carhaix-Plouguer? When they're in company, his wife and he look as if they are the perfect couple. They exchange as many words as are necessary not to arouse curiosity. Though not one more, it's true. Because it's only a façade. Having discovered that his wife was unfaithful to him, the Count communicated his decision never again to talk to her when they were alone—and that was the last time he spoke to her. The extraordinary thing is that in spite of this silence, he managed to have three children with her.

SHE: I have never been unfaithful to you. But I would like to remind you that you sometimes don't even grant me the minimum of words necessary to arouse people's curiosity. On Sundays, we usually lunch together in a restaurant on the coast. There are times when I am so ashamed of our silence that I move my lips soundlessly, to make the other customers think I'm talking to you.

HE: One morning, while we were having breakfast . . .

SHE: I remember. You were deep in your newspaper. You had disappeared behind the newspaper, which you were holding up like a screen. Could anyone be more boorish?

HE: You pressed the playback button on a little tape recorder you had just put down on the table. And then we heard a chorus of wheezing, rattling, gurgling, puffing and blowing and snoring, all of it orchestrated, rhythmic, returning to the point of departure with a reprise of the whole gamut. I asked you: "What's that?" And you answered: "It's you when you're asleep. That's all you have to say to me. So I record it." "I snore?" "Obviously you snore! But you don't realize it. Now you can hear it. That's progress, isn't it?"

SHE: I didn't tell you everything. Incited by you, by your nocturnal snoring, I made enquiries. There is always an old student lying dormant in me. I discovered a science, rhonchology, a definition of nocturnal snoring. This is it: "Respiratory sound during sleep, caused at the moment of inhalation by the vibration of the soft palate, due to the combined and simultaneous effect of the air entering through the nose and the air being drawn through the mouth." There. I might add that this vibration of the soft palate is very similar to that of the sail of a boat when it's flapping in the wind. As you see in both cases it's something to do with air.

HE: I appreciate this nautical aside, but I might remind you that I have never worked on a sailing boat.

SHE: As for the cures suggested by rhonchology, the most radical is tracheotomy; that's to say, opening an artificial orifice in the trachea so that breathing may be carried on outside the normal nasal passages. But there is also uvulo-palato-pharyngo-plastic-surgery—u.p.p.p.s. to initiates—which consists in resecting part of the soft palate including the uvula, so as to limit its vibratory potential.

HE: Young men ought to be told what they're letting themselves in for when they get married.

SHE: And vice versa! How could a girl ever suspect that the Prince Charming she loves makes a noise like a steam engine at night? Nevertheless, when she spends night after night by the side of a heavy snorer, she works out a rather bitter philosophy for herself.

HE: What does this rhonchological philosophy say?

SHE: That a couple is formed slowly over the years, and that with time the words they exchange take on increasing importance. At the beginning; deeds are enough. And then their dialogue becomes more extensive. It has to become deeper, too. Couples die from having no more to say to each other. My relations with a man are at an end on the evening when, coming back to him from a day spent elsewhere, I no longer want to tell him what I have done, or to hear him tell me how he has spent those hours away from me.

HE: It's true that I was never talkative. But it quite often happens that you interrupt one of my stories because it doesn't interest you.

SHE: Because you've already told it a hundred times.

HE: You made a diabolical suggestion on that subject one day, and I'm still wondering whether you were being serious. You suggested that I should number my stories. From then on, instead of telling you one from beginning to end with all the subtleties of the good story-teller, I should simply state its number, and you would understand at once. If I said 27, you would remember the story of my grandmother's dog which came aboard my trawler by mistake and returned to Fécamp a military hero. 71, and we would both have thought silently of the fidelity of those two gulls I saved and fed on one boat, and which knew how to find me on another vessel. 14, and my grandfather's odyssey during his one and only visit to Paris would have come to mind. So don't reproach me for my silence any more!

SHE: I know all your stories, and I even tell them better than you do. A good story-teller must be able to ring the changes.

HE: Not absolutely. Repetition is part of the game. There is a narrative ritual which children, for instance, respect. They are not concerned with novelty; they insist on the same story being told in the same words. The slightest change makes them leap up in indignation. In the same way, there is a ritual of daily life, of weeks, seasons, feast-days, years. A happy life is one that can cast itself in these moulds without feeling confined.

SHE: You're wrong to think that my idea of numbering your stories was only aimed at silencing you. I could just as well have used it to get you to talk. I would simply have said: 23. And you would straightaway have told me how you lived under siege in Le Havre from September 2nd to 13th, 1944. But I ask myself, honestly would I have the heart to listen to the same story told indefinitely in the same words? Would I have the childlike imagination needed for that?

HE: I'm quite sure you would. You're lying, or you're lying to yourself. And there's the other point of view: mine. There's a certain, very dangerous concept which is quite likely to kill off the dialogue between a couple: the concept of the *innocent ear*. If a man changes his woman, he does so in order to find in the new woman an innocent ear for his stories. Don Juan was nothing but an incorrigible braggart, *un hâbleur*—a word of Spanish origin meaning a glib talker. A woman only interested him for the length of time—short, alas, and increasingly short—that she had faith in his *hâbleries*. If he detected the shadow of a doubt in her gaze, it cast a glacial chill over his heart and his genitals. And then he would leave, he would go off to look elsewhere for the exquisite, warm credulity that alone gave their true weight to his *hâbleries*. All this proves the importance of words in the life of a couple. And anyway, when one of the two sleeps with a third person, we say that he "deceives" the other, which is to situate his betrayal in the domain of language. A man and a woman who never lied to each other and who immediately confessed all their betrayals would not be deceiving one another.

SHE: No doubt. But that would be a dialogue of cynics, and the wounds they inflicted on each other in the name of transparency would quite soon part them.

HE: Then people should lie?

SHE: Yes and no. Between the obscurity of lying and the transparency of cynicism, there is room for a whole range of light and shade in which the truth is known but not discussed, or else is deliberately ignored. In company, courtesy doesn't allow certain truths to be uttered bluntly. Why shouldn't there also be courtesy between couples? You're deceiving me. I'm deceiving you, but we don't want to know about it. The only valid intimacy is of a twilight nature. "Pull down the shade a little," as the charming Paul Géraldy said.

HE: Between couples, perhaps, but certainly not between women. There, the crudest cynicism is calmly displayed. Ladies, amongst yourselves, you are appalling gossips! I was waiting at the hairdresser's one day, on the side marked "Gentlemen", which was only separated from the ladies' salon by a half-partition. I was staggered by the complicity that united stylists, manicurists, shampoo girls and clients in a generalized babble in which the most intimate secrets of bodies and couples were laid bare without the slightest discretion.

SHE: And men in the company of other men keep such things to themselves, I suppose?

HE: More than you think. More than women do, in any case. Masculine vanity, which is generally too ridiculous, imposes a certain reticence on them in such matters. For instance, we aren't too fond of talking about our illnesses.

SHE: It's true that "intimate secrets", as you so delicately put it, don't amount to much for men. Everything always comes down to figures, with them. So many times or so many centimetres. Women's secrets are far more subtle and obscure! As for our complicity, it's a complicity of the oppressed, and hence universal, because women are everywhere subjected to men's whims. No man will ever know the depth of the feeling of complicity that can unite two women, even when they are perfect strangers to each other. I remember a visit to Morocco. I was the only woman in our little group. As so often in the South, we were approached by a very young boy who spontaneously invited us to come to his house for tea. The father received us, surrounded by his sons—three or four of them, I don't remember exactly. The youngest one must just have learnt to walk. There was a blanket over a doorway which no doubt led to the bedrooms. Every so often it moved surreptitiously, and a black eye could be seen peeping through. The mother, the daughters, the grandmother, the mother-in-law, confined to the inner rooms, were waiting, listening, spying. I remember the way the women had protested when a running-water tap was installed in their houses. For them, that was the end of their trips to the village fountain, and of the long, delightful chats with the other women that these trips occasioned. When we left, I passed a girl on her way home.

She smiled at me alone, because I was the only woman, and there was a world of warm fraternity in that smile. And when I say fraternity, I ought rather to say sorority, but the word doesn't exist in French.

HE: Perhaps because the thing itself is too rare to deserve a name.

SHE: It's principally because it's men who construct language. In a strange novel called *The Miracle of the Women's Island*, Gerhart Hauptmann invents his own version of the Robinson Crusoe story. He imagines that after a steamer has been shipwrecked, lifeboats exclusively occupied by women are cast up on a desert island. The result is a women's republic of about a hundred citizenesses.

HE: It must be hell!

SHE: Not at all. Quite the contrary! It's the great sorority. The idea Hauptmann champions is that if women fall out with one another, it's the fault of men. It is men who are the great sowers of discord among sisters, even among the sisterhood of nuns, whose shared confessor is a disruptive influence.

HE: Is that the miracle?

SHE: No. The miracle is that one day, after years of living in their happy sorority, one of the women discovers that she is inexplicably pregnant.

HE: The Holy Ghost, no doubt.

SHE: Everything might still be all right if she had given birth to a daughter. But the malignancy of fate saw to it that she had a son. The knell of the women's island had tolled. The virile virus was about to do its devastating work.

HE: In short, since you and I have the misfortune to belong to opposite sexes, since we have no more to say to each other, the only thing left for us to do is to separate. Let's at least do so with a flourish. We'll get all our friends together for a late-night dinner.

SHE: A *medianoche*, as the Spaniards call it.

HE: We'll choose the shortest night of the year so that our guests will leave as the sun is rising over the bay. We'll serve nothing but the produce of my foreshore fishing.

SHE: We'll talk to them, they'll talk to us, it will be a great palaver about the couple and love. Our *medianoche* will be a midnight love feast and a celebration of the sea. When all our guests have had their say, you will tap your knife on your glass and solemnly announce the sad news: "Oudalle and Nadège are separating because they don't get on any more. Sometimes they even have words. Then a disagreeable silence surrounds them . . ." And when the last guest has gone, we'll put a notice on the front door: FOR SALE, and we too will go our different ways.

And so it was. Invitations were sent out for the summer solstice to all Nadège and Oudalle's friends. Nadège reserved all the rooms in the three hotels in Avranches. Oudalle, with two of his fishing friends, prepared a memorable banquet of foreshore fish.

It was still light when the first guests arrived. These were the ones who had had the farthest to travel, as they had come all the way from Arles. Then, almost immediately, their nearest neighbours rang the bell, and it was half an hour before the next influx arrived. More and more came, all through the night, in a constant balletic flow of cars, just as Nadège and Oudalle had wished, for they hadn't prepared a formal dinner round a table but a permanent buffet from which all the guests could help themselves no matter when they arrived. To start with, there was poached crab, a consommé of mussels with croûtons, and smoked eel. Then hermit-crabs flambéed in whisky, and smoke-dried sea urchins. In keeping with tradition, they waited for the twelfth stroke of midnight to serve the *plat de rèsistance*—lobster Pompadour garnished with sea cucumbers. Then the night continued with octopus with paprika, paellas of cuttlefish, and a fricassee of wrasse. With the first glimmers of dawn the guests were brought ormers in white wine, sea-anemone fritters, and scallops in champagne. Thus, it was a true marine *medianoche* with neither vegetables, fruit nor sugar.

A group of guests had gathered on the high terrace whose piles reached out onto the shore itself. Neither Nadège nor Oudalle could have said whose idea it was to tell the first story. That one was lost in the night, as no doubt were the second and the third. But surprised by what was taking place in their house, they saw to it that the subsequent narratives were recorded and preserved. There were thus nineteen, and these narratives were sometimes tales which began with the magical and traditional "once upon a time", and sometimes short stories told in the first person, slices of life that were often raw and sordid. Nadège and Oudalle listened, astonished by these imaginary constructions they saw being built in their own house and which vanished as soon as the last word was uttered, giving way to other, equally ephemeral descriptions. They thought of Lagos's sand statues. They followed the slow work this succession of fictions was accomplishing in them. They had the feeling that the short stories—grimly realistic, pessimistic and demoralizing—were tending to further their separation and the break-up of their marriage, whereas on the contrary the tales—delectable, warm-hearted and tender—were working to bring them together. And while the short stories had at first commanded more attention by their weighty, melancholy truth, as the night wore on the tales gained in beauty and in strength, and finally reached the point of radiating an irresistible charm. In the first hours Ange Crevet, the humiliated child full of hatred, Ernest the poacher, the suicidal Théobald, and Blandine's frightful father, and Lucie, the woman without a shadow, and a few others—all this grey, austere crowd exuded an atmosphere of morose hatred. But soon Angus, King Faust the Wise Man, Pierrot with his Columbine, Adam the dancer and Eve the perfumed lady, the Chinese painter and his Greek rival, formed the scintillating procession of a new, young and eternal wedding. And it was above all the last tale, the one about the two banquets, that rescued, so it seemed daily conjugal life by elevating the actions repeated every day and every night to the level of a fervent intimate ceremony.

The solstice sun was setting the silhouette of Mont-Saint-Michel aglow when the last guest stood up to take his leave after having told, to his hosts alone, the most beautiful tale no doubt ever invented. The incoming tide was flowing under the open-work floor of the terrace. The shellfish caressed by the waves opened their valves and let out the mouthful of water they had been retaining during the arid hours. The thousands upon thousands of parched throats on the foreshore filled themselves with the briny fluid and began to whisper. The shore was stammering in search of a language, as Lagos had understood so well.

"You didn't stand up, you didn't tap your glass with your knife, and you didn't announce the sad news of our separation to our friends," said Nadège.

"Because the inevitability of our separation no longer seems so obvious to me since all those stories have entered my head," Oudalle replied.

"What we lacked, in fact, was a house of words to live in together. In former times, religion provided couples with an edifice that was at the same time real—the church—and imaginary, peopled with saints, illuminated with legends, resounding with hymns, which protected them from themselves and from outside aggression. We lacked this edifice. Our friends have provided us with all the materials for it. Literature as a panacea for couples in distress . . ."

"We were like two carps buried in the mud of our daily life," Oudalle concluded, ever true to his halieutic metaphors. "From now on we shall be like two trout quivering side by side in the fast-flowing waters of a mountain stream."

"Your seafood *medianoche* was exquisite," Nadège added. "I appoint you the head chef of my house. You shall be the high priest of my kitchens and the guardian of the culinary and manducatory rites that invest a meal with its spiritual dimension."

from **the autobiography of my mother**

JAMAICA KINCAID

in the moments when Philip was inside me, in those moments when the pleasure of his thrusts and withdrawals waned and I was not a prisoner of the most primitive and most essential of emotions, that thing silently, secretly, shamefully called sex, my mind turned to another source of pleasure. He was a man that was Philip's opposite. His name was Roland.

His mouth was like an island in the sea that was his face; I am sure he had ears and nose and eyes and all the rest, but I could see only his mouth, which I knew could do all the things that a mouth usually does, such as eat food, purse in approval or disapproval, smile, twist in thought: inside were his teeth and behind them was his tongue. Why did I see him that way, how did I come to see him that way? It was a mystery to me that he had been alive all along and that I had not known of his existence and I was perfectly fine—I went to sleep at night and I could wake up in the morning and greet the day with indifference if it suited me, I could comb my hair and scratch myself and I was still perfectly fine—and he was alive, sometimes living in a house next to mine, sometimes living in a house far away, and his existence was ordinary and perfect and parallel to mine, but I did not know of it, even though sometimes he was close enough to me for me to notice that he smelled of cargo he had been unloading; he was a stevedore.

His mouth really did look like an island, lying in a twig-brown sea, stretching out from east to west, widest near the center, with tiny, sharp creases, its color a shade lighter than that of the twig-brown sea in which it lay, the place where the two lips met disappearing into the pinkest of pinks, and even though I must have held his mouth in mine a thousand times, it was always new to me. He must have smiled at me, though I don't really know, but I don't like to think that I would love someone who hadn't first smiled at me. It had been raining, a heavy downpour, and I took shelter under the gallery of a dry-goods store along with some other people. The rain was an inconvenience, for it was not necessary; there had already been too much of it, and it was no longer only outside, overflowing in the gutters, but inside also, roofs were leaking and then falling in. I was standing under the gallery and had sunk deep within myself, enjoying completely the despair I felt at being myself. I was wearing a dress; I had combed my hair that morning; I had washed myself that morning. I was looking at nothing in particular when I saw his mouth. He was speaking to someone else, but he was looking at me. The someone else he was speaking to was a woman. His mouth then was not like an island at rest in a sea but like a small patch of ground viewed from high above and set in motion by a force not readily seen.

When he saw me looking at him, he opened his mouth wider, and that must have been the smile. I saw then that he had a large gap between his two front teeth, which probably meant that he could not be trusted, but I did not care. My dress was damp, my shoes were wet, my hair was wet, my skin was cold, all around me were people standing in small amounts of water and mud, shivering, but I started to perspire from an effort I wasn't aware I was making; I started to perspire because I felt hot, and I started to perspire because I felt happy. I wore my hair then in two plaits and the ends of them rested just below my collarbone; all the moisture in my hair collected and ran down my two plaits, as if they were two gutters, and the water seeped through my dress just below the collarbone and continued to run down my chest, only stopping at the place where the tips of my breasts met the fabric, revealing, plain as a new print, my nipples. He was looking at me and talking to someone else, and his mouth grew wide and narrow, small and large, and I wanted him to notice me, but there was so much noise: all the people standing in the gallery, sheltering themselves from the strong rain, had something they wanted to say, something not about the weather (that was by now beyond comment) but about their lives, their disappointments most likely, for joy is so short-lived there isn't enough time to dwell on its occurrence. The noise, which started as a hum, grew to a loud din, and the loud din had an unpleasant taste of metal and vinegar, but I knew his mouth could take it away if only I could get to it; so I called out my own name, and I knew he heard me immediately, but he wouldn't stop speaking to the woman he was talking to, so I had to call out my name again and again until he stopped, and by that time my name was like a chain around him, as the sight of his mouth was like a chain around me. And when our eyes met, we laughed, because we were happy, but it was frightening, for that gaze asked everything: who would betray whom, who would be captive, who would be captor, who would give and who would take, what would I do. And when our eyes met and we laughed at the same time, I said, "I love you, I love you," and he said, "I know." He did not say it out of vanity, he did not say it out of conceit, he only said it because it was true.

His name was Roland. He was not a hero, he did not even have a country; he was from an island, a small island that was between a sea and an ocean, and a small island is not a country. And he did not have a history; he was a small event in somebody else's history, but he was a man. I could see him better than he could see himself, and that was because he was who he was and I was myself, but also because I was taller than he was. He was unpolished, but he carried himself as if he were precious. His hands were large and thick, and for no reason that I could see he would spread them out in front of him and they looked as if they were the missing parts from a powerful piece of machinery; his legs were straight from hip to knee, and then from the knee they bent at an angle as if he had been at sea too long or had never learned to walk properly to begin with. The hair on his legs was tightly curled as if the hairs were pieces of thread rolled between the thumb and the forefinger in preparation for sewing, and so was the hair on his arms, the hair in his underarms, and the hair on his chest; the hair in those places was black and grew sparsely; the hair on his head and the hair between his legs was black and tightly curled also, but it grew in such abundance that it was impossible for me to move my hands through it. Sitting, standing, walking, or lying down, he carried himself as if he was something precious, but not out of vanity, for it was true, he was something precious; yet when he was lying on top of me he looked down at me as if I were the only woman in the world, the only woman he had ever looked at in that way—but that was not true, a man only does that when it is not true. When he first lay on top of me I was so ashamed of how much pleasure I felt that I bit my bottom lip hard—but I did not bleed, not from biting my lip, not then. His skin was smooth and warm in places I had not kissed him; in the places I had kissed him his skin was cold and coarse, and the pores were open and raised.

Did the world become a beautiful place? The rainy season eventually went away, the sunny season came, and it was too hot; the riverbed grew dry, the mouth of the river became shallow, the heat eventually became as wearying as the rain, and I would have wished it away if I had not become occupied with this other sensation, a sensation I had no single word for. I could feel myself full of happiness, but it was a kind of happiness I had never experienced before, and my happiness would spill out of me and run all the way down a long, long road and then the road would come to an end and I would feel empty and sad, for what could come after this? How would it end?

Not everything has an end, even though the beginning

changes. The first time we were in a bed together we were lying on a thin board that was covered with old cloth, and this small detail, evidence of our poverty—people in our position, a stevedore and a doctor's servant, could not afford a proper mattress—was a major contribution to my satisfaction, for it allowed me to brace myself and match him breath for breath. But how can it be that a man who can carry large sacks filled with sugar or bales of cotton on his back from dawn to dusk exhausts himself within five minutes inside a woman? I did not then and I do not now know the answer to that. He kissed me. He fell asleep. I bathed my face then between his legs; he smelled of curry and onions, for those were the things he had been unloading all day; other times when I bathed my face between his legs—for I did it often, I liked doing it—he would smell of sugar, or flour, or the large, cheap bolts of cotton from which he would steal a few yards to give me to make a dress.

What is the everyday? What is the ordinary? One day, as I was walking toward the government dispensary to collect some supplies—one of my duties as a servant to a man who was in love with me beyond anything he could help and so had long since stopped trying, a man I ignored except when I wanted him to please me—I met Roland's wife, face-to-face, for the first time. She stood in front of me like a sentry—stern, dignified, guarding the noble idea, if not noble ideal, that was her husband. She did not block the sun, it was shining on my right; on my left was a large black cloud; it was raining way in the distance; there was no rainbow on the horizon. We stood on the narrow strip of concrete that was the sidewalk. One section of a wooden fence that was supposed to shield a yard from passerby on the street bulged out and was broken, and a few tugs from any careless party would end its usefulness; in that yard a primrose bush bloomed unnaturally, its leaves too large, its flowers showy, and weeds were everywhere, they had prospered in all the wet. We were not alone. A man walked past us with a cutlass in his knapsack and a mistreated dog two steps behind him; a woman walked by with a large basket of food on her head; some children were walking home from school, and they were not walking together; a man was leaning out a window, spitting, he used snuff. I was wearing a pair of modestly high heels, red, not a color to wear to work in the middle of the day, but that was just the way I had been feeling, red with a passion, like that hibiscus that was growing under the window of the man who kept spitting from the snuff. And Roland's wife called me a whore, a slut, a pig, a snake, a viper, a rat, a lowlife, a parasite, and an evil woman. I could see that her mouth formed a familiar hug around these words—poor thing, she had been used to saying them. I was not surprised. I could not have loved Roland the way I did if he had not loved other women. And I was not surprised; I had noticed immediately the space between his teeth. I was not surprised that she knew about me; a man cannot keep a secret, a man always wants all the women he knows to know each other.

I believe I said this: "I love Roland; when he is with me I want him to love me; when he is not with me I think of him loving me. I do not love you. I love Roland." This is what I wanted to say, and this is what I believe I said. She slapped me across the face; her hand was wide and thick like an oar; she, too, was used to doing hard work. Her hand met the side of my face: my jawbone, the skin below my eye and under my chin, a small portion of my nose, the lobe of my ear. I was then a young woman in my early twenties, my skin was supple, smooth, the pores invisible to the naked eye. It was completely without bitterness that I thought as I looked at her face, a face I had so little interest in that it would tire me to describe it, Why is the state of marriage so desirable that all women are afraid to be caught outside it? And why does this woman, who has never seen me before, to whom I have never made any promise, to whom I owe nothing, hate me so much? She expected me to return her blow but, instead, I said, again completely without bitterness, "I consider it beneath me to fight over a man."

I was wearing a dress of light-blue Irish linen. I could not afford to buy such material, because it came from a real country, not a false country like mine; a shipment of this material in blue, in pink, in lime green, and in beige had come from Ireland, I suppose, and Roland had given me yards of each shade from the bolts. I was wearing my blue Irish-linen dress that day, and it was demure enough—a pleated skirt that ended quite beneath my knees, a belt at my waist, sleeves that buttoned at my wrists, a high neckline that covered my collarbone—but underneath my dress I wore absolutely nothing, no undergarments of any kind, only my stockings, given to me by Roland and taken from yet another shipment of dry goods, each one held up by two pieces of elastic that I had sewn together to make a garter. My declaration of what I considered beneath me must have enraged Roland's wife, for she grabbed my blue dress at the collar and gave it a huge tug, it rent in two from my neck to my waist. My breasts lay softly on my chest, like two small pieces of unrisen dough, unmoved by the anger of this woman; not so by the touch of her husband's mouth, for he would remove my dress, by first patiently undoing all the buttons and then pulling down the bodice, and then he would take one breast in his mouth, and it would grow to a size much bigger than his mouth could hold, and he would let it go and turn to the other one; the saliva evaporating from the skin on that breast was an altogether different sensation from the sensation of my other breast in his mouth, and I would divide myself in two, for I could not decide which sensation I wanted to take dominance over the other. For an hour he would kiss me in this way and then exhaust himself on top of me in five minutes. I loved him so. In the dark I couldn't see him clearly, only an outline, a solid shadow; when I saw him in the day-time he was fully dressed. His wife, as she rent my dress, a dress made of material she knew very well, for she had a dress made of the same material, told me his history: it was not a long one, it was not a sad one, no one had died in it, no land had been laid waste, no birthright had been stolen; she had a list, and it was full of names, but they were not the names of countries.

What was the color of her wedding day? When she first saw him was she overwhelmed with desire? The impulse to possess is alive in every heart, and some people choose vast plains, some people choose high mountains, some people choose wide seas, and some people choose husbands; I chose to possess myself. I resembled a tree, a tall tree with long, strong branches; I looked delicate, but any man I held in my arms knew that I was strong; my hair was long and thick and deeply waved naturally, and I wore it braided and pinned up, because when I wore it loose around my shoulders it caused excitement in other people— some of them men, some of them women, some of them it pleased, some of them it did not. The way I walked depended on who I thought would see me and what effect I wanted my walk to have on them. My face was beautiful, I found it so.

And yet I was standing before a woman who found herself unable to keep her life's booty in its protective sack, a woman whose voice no longer came from her throat but from deep within her stomach, a woman whose hatred was misplaced. I looked down at our feet, hers and mine, and I expected to see my short life flash before me; instead, I saw that her feet were without shoes. She did have a pair of shoes, though, which I had seen; they were white, they were plain, a round toe and flat laces, they took shoe polish well, she wore them only on Sundays and to church. I had many pairs of shoes, in colors meant to attract attention and dazzle the eye; they were uncomfortable, I wore them every day, I never went to church at all.

My strong arms reached around to caress Roland, who was lying on my back naked; I was naked also. I knew his wife's name, but I did not say it; he knew his wife's name, too, but he did not say it. I did not know the long list of names that were not countries that his wife had committed to memory. He himself did not know the long list of names; he had not committed this list to memory. This was not from deceit, and it was not from careless- ness. He was someone so used to a large fortune that he took it for granted; he did not have a bankbook, he did not have a ledger, he had a fortune—but still he had not lost interest in acquiring more. Feeling my womb contract, I crossed the room, still naked; small drops of blood spilled from inside me, evidence of my refusal to accept his silent offering. And Roland looked at me, his face expressing confusion. Why did I not bear his chil- dren? He could feel the times that I was fertile, and yet each month blood flowed away from me, and each month I expressed confidence at its imminent arrival and departure, and always I was overjoyed at the accuracy of my prediction. When I saw him like that, on his face a look that was a mixture—confusion, dumbfoundedness, defeat—I felt much sorrow for him, for his life was reduced to a list of names that were not countries, and to the number of times he brought the monthly flow of blood to a halt; his life was reduced to women, some of them beautiful, wearing dresses made from yards of cloth he had surreptitiously removed from the bowels of the ships where he worked as a stevedore.

At that time I loved him beyond words; I loved him when he was standing in front of me and I loved him when he was out of my sight. I was still a young woman. No small impressions, the size of a child's forefinger, had yet appeared on the soft parts of my body; my legs were long and hard, as if they had been made to take me a long distance; my arms were long and strong, as if prepared for carrying heavy loads. I was in love with Roland. He was a man. But who was he really? He did not sail the seas, he did not cross the oceans, he only worked in the bottom of vessels that had done so; no mountains were named for him, no valleys, no nothing. But still he was a man, and he wanted something beyond ordinary satisfaction—beyond one wife, one love, and one room with walls made of mud and roof of cane leaves, beyond the small plot of land where the same trees bear the same fruit year following year—for it would all end only in death, for though no history yet written had embraced him, though he could not identify the small uprisings within himself, though he would deny the small uprisings within himself, a strange calm would sometimes come over him, a cold stillness, and since he could find no words for it, he was momentarily blinded with shame.

One night Roland and I were sitting on the steps of the jetty, our backs facing the small world we were from, the world of sharp, dangerous curves in the road, of steep mountains of recent volcanic formations covered in a green so humble no one had ever longed for them, of 365 small streams that would never meet up to form a majestic roar, of clouds that were nothing but large vessels holding endless days of water, of people who had never been regarded as people at all; we looked into the night, its blackness did not come as a surprise, a moon full of dead white light traveled across the surface of a glittering black sky; I was wearing a dress made from another piece of cloth he had given me, another piece of cloth taken from the bowels of a ship without permission, and there was a false pocket in the skirt, a pocket that did not have a bottom, and Roland placed his hand inside the pocket, reaching all the way down to touch inside me; I looked at his face, his mouth I could see and it stretched across his face like an island and like an island, too, it held secrets and was dangerous and could swallow things whole that were much larger than itself; I looked out toward the horizon, which I could not see but knew was there all the same, and this was also true of the end of my love for Roland.

through the tunnel

Doris Lessing

going to the shore on the first morning of the vacation, the young English boy stopped at a turning of the path and looked down at a wild and rocky bay, and then over to the crowded beach he knew so well from other years. His mother walked on in front of him, carrying a bright striped bag in one hand. Her other arm, swinging loose, was very white in the sun. The boy watched that white naked arm, and turned his eyes, which had a frown behind them, towards the bay and back again to his mother. When she felt he was not with her, she swung around. "Oh, there you are, Jerry!" she said. She looked impatient, then smiled. "Why, darling, would you rather not come with me? Would you rather—" She frowned, conscientiously worrying over what amusements he might secretly be longing for, which she had been too busy or too careless to imagine. He was very familiar with that anxious, apologetic smile. Contrition sent him running after her. And yet, as he ran, he looked back over his shoulder at the wild bay; and all morning, as he played on the safe beach, he was thinking of it.

Next morning, when it was time for the routine of swimming and sunbathing, his mother said, "Are you tired of the usual beach, Jerry? Would you like to go somewhere else?"

"Oh, no!" he said quickly, smiling at her out of that unfailing impulse of contrition—a sort of chivalry. Yet, walking down the path with her, he blurted out, "I'd like to go and have a look at those rocks down there."

She gave the idea her attention. It was a wild-looking place, and there was no one there; but she said, "Of course, Jerry. When you've had enough, come to the big beach. Or just go straight back to the villa, if you like." She walked away, that bare arm, now slightly reddened from yesterday's sun, swinging. And he almost ran after her again, feeling it unbearable that she should go by herself, but he did not.

She was thinking, Of course he's old enough to be safe without me. Have I been keeping him too close? He mustn't feel he ought to be with me. I must be careful.

He was an only child, eleven years old. She was a widow. She was determined to be neither possessive nor lacking in devotion. She went worrying off to her beach.

As for Jerry, once he saw that his mother had gained her beach, he began the steep descent to the bay. From where he was, high up among red-brown rocks, it was a scoop of moving blueish green fringed with white. As he went lower, he saw that it spread among small promontories and inlets of rough, sharp rock, and the crisping, lapping surface showed stains of purple and darker blue. Finally, as he ran sliding and scraping down the last few yards, he saw an edge of white surf and the shallow, luminous movement of water over white sand, and, beyond that, a solid, heavy blue.

He ran straight into the water and began swimming. He was a good swimmer. He went out fast over the gleaming sand, over a middle region where rocks lay like discoloured monsters under the surface, and then he was in the real sea—a warm sea where irregular cold currents from the deep water shocked his limbs.

When he was so far out that he could look back not only on the little bay but past the promontory that was between it and the big beach, he floated on the buoyant surface and looked for his mother. There she was, a speck of yellow under an umbrella that looked like a slice of orange peel. He swam back to shore, relieved at being sure she was there, but all at once very lonely.

On the edge of a small cape that marked the side of the bay away from the promontory was a loose scatter of rocks. Above them, some boys were stripping off their clothes. They came running, naked, down to the rocks. The English boy swam towards them, but kept his distance at a stone's throw. They were of that coast; all of them were burned smooth dark brown and speaking a language he did not understand. To be with them, of them, was a craving that filled his whole body. He swam a little closer; they turned and watched him with narrowed, alert dark eyes. Then one smiled and waved. It was enough. In a minute, he had swum in and was on the rocks beside them, smiling with a desperate, nervous supplication. They shouted cheerful greetings at him; and then, as he preserved his nervous, uncomprehending smile, they understood that he was a foreigner strayed from his own beach, and they proceeded to forget him. But he was happy. He was with them.

They began diving again and again from a high point into a well of blue sea between rough, pointed rocks. After they had dived and come up, they swam around, hauled themselves up, and waited their turn to dive again. They were big boys—men, to Jerry. He dived, and they watched him; and when he swam around to take his place, they made way for him. He felt he was accepted and he dived again, carefully, proud of himself.

Soon the biggest of the boys poised himself, shot down into the water, and did not come up. The others stood about, watching. Jerry, after waiting for the sleek brown head to appear, let out a yell of warning; they looked at him idly and turned their eyes back towards the water. After a long time, the boy came up on the other side of a big dark rock, letting the air out of his lungs in a sputtering gasp and a shout of triumph. Immediately the rest of them dived in. One moment, the morning seemed full of chattering boys; the next, the air and the surface of the water were empty. But through the heavy blue, dark shapes could be seen moving and groping.

Jerry dived, shot past the school of underwater swimmers, saw a black wall of rock looming at him, touched it, and bobbed up at once to the surface, where the wall was a low barrier he could see across. There was no one visible; under him, in the water, the dim shapes of the swimmers had disappeared. Then one, and then another of the boys came up on the far side of the barrier of rock, and he understood that they had swum through some gap or hole in it. He plunged down again. He could see nothing through the stinging salt water but the blank rock. When he came up the boys were all on the diving rock, preparing to attempt the feat again. And now, in a panic of failure, he yelled up, in English, "Look at me! Look!" and he began splashing and kicking in the water like a foolish dog.

They looked down gravely, frowning. He knew the frown. At moments of failure, when he clowned to claim his mother's attention. It was with just this grave, embarrassed inspection that she rewarded him. Through his hot shame, feeling the pleading grin on his face like a scar that he could never remove, he looked up at the group of big brown boys on the rock and shouted *"Bonjour! Merci! Au revoir! Monsieur, monsieur!"* while he hooked his fingers round his ears and waggled them.

Water surged into his mouth; he choked, sank, came up. The rock, lately weighted with boys, seemed to rear up out of the water as their weight was removed. They were flying down past him now, into the water; the air was full of falling bodies. Then the rock was empty in the hot sunlight. He counted one, two, three . . .

At fifty, he was terrified. They must all be drowning beneath him, in the watery caves of the rock! At a hundred, he stared around him at the empty hillside, wondering if he should yell for help. He counted faster, faster, to hurry them up, to bring them to the surface quickly, to drown them quickly—anything rather than the terror of counting on and on into the blue emptiness of the morning. And then, at a hundred and sixty, the water beyond the rock was full of boys blowing like brown whales. They swam back to the shore without a look at him.

He climbed back to the diving rock and sat down, feeling the hot roughness of it under his thighs. The boys were gathering up their bits of clothing and running off along the shore to another promontory. They were leaving to get away from him. He cried openly, fists in his eyes. There was no one to see him, and he cried himself out.

It seemed to him that a long time had passed, and he swam out to where he could see his mother. Yes, she was still there, a yellow spot under an orange umbrella. He swam back to the big rock, climbed up, and dived into the blue pool among the fanged and angry boulders. Down he went, until he touched the wall of rock again. But the salt was so painful in his eyes that he could not see.

He came to the surface, swam to shore and went back to the villa to wait for his mother. Soon she walked slowly up the path, swinging her striped bag, the flushed, naked arm dangling beside her. "I want some swimming goggles," he panted, defiant and beseeching.

She gave him a patient, inquisitive look as she said casually, "Well, of course, darling."

But now, now, now! He must have them this minute, and no other time. He nagged and pestered until she went with him to a shop. As soon as she had bought the goggles, he grabbed them from her hand as if she were going to claim them for herself, and was off, running down the steep path to the bay.

Jerry swam out to the big barrier rock, adjusted the goggles, and dived. The impact of the water broke the rubber-enclosed vacuum, and the goggles came loose. He understood that he must swim down to the base of the rock from the surface of the water. He fixed the goggles tight and firm, filled his lungs, and floated, face down, on the water. Now he could see. It was as if he had eyes of a different kind—fish eyes that showed everything clear and delicate and wavering in the bright water.

Under him, six or seven feet down, was a floor of perfectly clean, shining white sand, rippled firm and hard by the tides. Two greyish shapes steered there, like long, rounded pieces of wood or slate. They were fish. He saw them nose towards each other, poise motionless, make a dart forward, swerve off, and come around again. It was like a water dance. A few inches above them the water sparkled as if sequins were dropping through it. Fish again—myriads of minute fish, the length of his fingernail—were drifting through the water, and in a moment he could feel the innumerable tiny touches of them against his limbs. It was like swimming in flaked silver. The great rock the big boys had swum through rose sheer out of the white sand—black, tufted lightly with greenish weed. He could see no gap in it. He swam down to its base.

Again and again he rose, took a big chestful of air, and went down. Again and again he groped over the surface of the rock, feeling it, almost hugging it in the desperate need to find the entrance. And then, once, while he was clinging to the black wall, his knees came up and he shot his feet out forward and they met no obstacle. He had found the hole.

He gained the surface, clambered about the stones that littered the barrier rock until he found a big one, and, with this in his arms, let himself down over the side of the rock. He dropped, with the weight, straight to the sandy floor. Clinging tight to the anchor of stone, he lay on his side and looked in under the dark shelf at the place where his feet had gone. He could see the hole. It was an irregular, dark gap; but he could not see deep into it. He let go of his anchor, clung with his hands to the edges of the hole, and tried to push himself in.

He got his head in, found his shoulders jammed, moved them in sidewise, and was inside as far as his waist. He could see nothing ahead. Something soft and clammy touched his mouth; he saw a dark frond moving against the greyish rock, and panic filled him. He thought of octopuses, of clinging weed. He pushed himself out backward and caught a glimpse, as he retreated, of a harmless tentacle of seaweed drifting in the mouth of the tunnel. But it was enough. He reached the sunlight, swam to shore, and lay on the diving rock. He looked down into the blue well of water. He knew he must find his way through that cave, or hole, or tunnel, and out the other side.

First, he thought, he must learn to control his breathing. He let himself down into the water with another big stone in his arms, so that he could lie effortlessly on the bottom of the sea. He counted. One, two, three. He counted steadily. He could hear the movement of blood in his chest. Fifty-one, fifty-two. . . . His chest was hurting. He let go of the rock and went up into the air. He saw that the sun was low. He rushed to the villa and found his mother at her supper. She said only "Did you enjoy yourself?" and he said "Yes."

All night the boy dreamed of the water-filled cave in the rock, and as soon as breakfast was over he went to the bay.

That night, his nose bled badly. For hours he had been under-water, learning to hold his breath, and now he felt weak and dizzy. His mother said, "I shouldn't overdo things, darling, if I were you."

That day and the next, Jerry exercised his lungs as if everything, the whole of his life, all that he would become, depended upon it. Again his nose bled at night, and his mother insisted on his coming with her the next day. It was a torment to him to waste a day of his careful self-training, but he stayed with her on that other beach, which now seemed a place for small children, a place where his mother might lie safe in the sun. It was not his beach.

He did not ask for permission, on the following day, to go to his beach. He went, before his mother could consider the com-plicated rights and wrongs of the matter. A day's rest, he discov-ered, had improved his count by ten. The big boys had made the passage while he counted a hundred and sixty. He had been counting fast, in his fright. Probably now, if he tried, he could get through that long tunnel, but he was not going to try yet. A curi-ous, most unchildlike persistence, a controlled impatience, made him wait. In the meantime, he lay underwater on the white sand, littered now by stones he had brought down from the upper air, and studied the entrance to the tunnel. He knew every jut and corner of it, as far as it was possible to see. It was as if he already felt its sharpness about his shoulders.

He sat by the clock in the villa, when his mother was not near, and checked his time. He was incredulous and then proud to find he could hold his breath without strain for two minutes. The words "two minutes," authorised by the clock, brought close the adventure that was so necessary to him.

In another four days, his mother said casually one morning, they must go home. On the day before they left, he would do it. He would do it if it killed him, he said defiantly to himself. But two days before they were to leave—a day of triumph when he increased his count by fifteen—his nose bled so badly that he turned dizzy and had to lie limply over the big rock like a bit of seaweed, watching the thick red blood flow on to the rock and trickle slowly down to the sea. He was frightened. Supposing he turned dizzy in the tunnel? Supposing he died there, trapped? Supposing—his head went around, in the hot sun, and he almost gave up. He thought he would return to the house and lie down, and next summer, perhaps, when he had another year's growth in him—*then* he would go through the hole.

But even after he had made the decision, or thought he had, he found himself sitting up on the rock and looking down into the water; and he knew that now, this moment, when his nose had only just stopped bleeding, when his head was still sore and throbbing—this was the moment when he would try. If he did not do it now, he never would. He was trembling with fear that he would not go; and he was trembling with horror at the long, long tunnel under the rock, under the sea. Even in the open sunlight, the barrier rock seemed very wide and very heavy; tons of rock pressed down on where he would go. If he died there, he would lie until one day—perhaps not before next year—those big boys would swim into it and find it blocked.

He put on his goggles, fitted them tight, tested the vacuum. His hands were shaking. Then he chose the biggest stone he could carry and slipped over the edge of the rock until half of him was in the cool enclosing water and half in the hot sun. He looked up once at the empty sky, filled his lungs once, twice, and then sank fast to the bottom with the stone. He let it go and began to count. He took the edges of the hole in his hands and drew himself into it, wriggling his shoulders in sidewise as he remembered he must, kicking himself along with his feet.

Soon he was clear inside. He was in a small rock-bound hole filled with yellowish-grey water. The water was pushing him up against the roof. The roof was sharp and pained his back. He pulled himself along with his hands—fast, fast—and used his legs as levers. His head knocked against something; a sharp pain dizzied him. Fifty, fifty-one, fifty-two. . . . He was without light, and the water seemed to press upon him with the weight of rock. Seventy-one, seventy-two . . . There was no strain on his lungs. He felt like an inflated balloon, his lungs were so light and easy, but his head was pulsing.

He was being continually pressed against the sharp roof, which felt slimy as well as sharp. Again he thought of octopuses, and wondered if the tunnel might be filled with weed that could tangle him. He gave himself a panicky, convulsive kick forward, ducked his head, and swam. His feet and hands moved freely, as if in open water. The hole must have widened out. He thought he must be swimming fast, and he was frightened of banging his head if the tunnel narrowed.

A hundred, a hundred and one . . . The water paled. Victory filled him. His lungs were beginning to hurt. A few more strokes and he would be out. He was counting wildly; he said a hundred and fifteen, and then, a long time later, a hundred and fifteen again. The water was a clear jewel-green all around him. Then he saw, above his head, a crack running up through the rock. Sunlight was falling through it, showing the clean, dark rock of the tunnel, a single mussel shell, and darkness ahead.

He was at the end of what he could do. He looked up at the crack as if it were filled with air and not water, as if he could put his mouth to it to draw in air. A hundred and fifteen, he heard himself say inside his head—but he had said that long ago. He must go on into the blackness ahead, or he would drown. His head was swelling, his lungs cracking. A hundred and fifteen, a hundred and fifteen pounded through his head, and he feebly clutched at rocks in the dark, pulling himself forward leaving the brief space of sunlit water behind. He felt he was dying. He was no longer quite conscious. He struggled on in the darkness between lapses into unconsciousness. An immense, swelling pain filled his head, and then the darkness cracked with an explosion of green light. His hands, groping forward, met nothing; and his feet, kicking back, propelled him out into the open sea.

He drifted to the surface, his face turned up to the air. He was gasping like a fish. He felt he would sink now and drown; he could not swim the few feet back to the rock. Then he was clutching it and pulling himself up onto it. He lay face down, gasping. He could see nothing but a red-veined, clotted dark. His eyes must have burst, he thought; they were full of blood. He tore off his goggles and a gout of blood went into the sea. His nose was bleeding, and the blood had filled the goggles.

He scooped up handfuls of water from the cool, salty sea, to splash on his face, and did not know whether it was blood or salt water he tasted. After a time, his heart quieted, his eyes cleared, and he sat up. He could see the local boys diving and playing half a mile away. He did not want them. He wanted nothing but to get back home and lie down.

In a short while, Jerry swam to shore and climbed slowly up the path to the villa. He flung himself on his bed and slept, waking at the sound of feet on the path outside. His mother was coming back. He rushed to the bathroom, thinking she must not see his face with bloodstains, or tearstains, on it. He came out of the bathroom, and met her as she walked into the villa, smiling, her eyes lighting up.

"Have a nice morning?" she asked, laying her hand on his warm brown shoulder a moment.

"Oh, yes, thank you," he said.

"You look a bit pale." And then, sharp and anxious, "How did you bang your head?"

"Oh, just banged it," he told her.

She looked at him closely. He was strained; his eyes were glazed-looking. She was worried. And then she said to herself, Oh, don't fuss! Nothing can happen. He can swim like a fish.

They sat down to lunch together.

"Mummy," he said, "I can stay underwater for two minutes—three minutes, at least." It came bursting out of him.

"Can you, darling?" she said. "Well, I shouldn't overdo it. I don't think you ought to swim any more today."

She was ready for a battle of wills, but he gave in at once. It was no longer of the least importance to go to the bay.

black boy

KAY BOYLE

at that time, it was the forsaken part, it was the other end of the city, and on early spring mornings there was no one about. By soft words, you could woo the horse into the foam, and ride her with the sea knee-deep around her. The waves came in and out there, as indolent as ladies, gathered up their skirts in their hands and, with a murmur, came tiptoeing in across the velvet sand.

The wooden promenade was high there, and when the wind was up the water came running under it like wild. On such days, you had to content yourself with riding the horse over the deep white drifts of dry sand on the other side of the walks; the horse's hoofs here made no sound and the sparks of sand stung your face in fury. It had no body to it, like the mile or two of sand packed hard that you could open out on once the tide was down.

My little grandfather, Puss, was alive then, with his delicate gart and ankles, and his belly pouting in his dove-gray clothes. When he saw from the window that the tide was sidling out, he put on his pearl fedora and came stepping down the street. For a minute, he put one foot on the sand, but he was not at ease there. On the boardwalk over our heads was some other kind of life in progress. If you looked up, you could see it in motion through the cracks in the timber: rolling chairs, and women in high heels proceeding, if the weather were fair.

"You know," my grandfather said, "I think I might like to have a look at a shop or two along the boardwalk." Or: "I suppose you don't feel like leaving the beach for a minute," or "If you would go with me, we might take a chair together, and look at the hats and the dresses and roll along in the sun."

He was alive then, taking his pick of the broad easy chairs and the black boys.

"There's a nice skinny boy," he'd say. "He looks as though he might put some action into it. Here you are, sonny. Push me and the little girl down to the Million Dollar Pier and back."

The cushions were red velvet with a sheen of dew over them. And Puss settled back on them and took my hand in his. In his mind there was no hesitation about whether he would look at the shops on one side, or out on the vacant side where there was nothing shining but the sea.

"What's your name, Charlie?" Puss would say without turning his head to the black boy pushing the chair behind our shoulders.

"Charlie's my name, sir," he'd answer with his face dripping down like tar in the sun.

"What's your name, sonny?" Puss would say another time, and the black boy answered:

"Sonny's my name, sir."

"What's your name, Big Boy?"

"Big Boy's my name."

He never wore a smile on his face, the black boy. He was thin as a shadow but darker, and he was pushing and sweating, getting the chair down to the Million Dollar Pier and back again, in and out through the people. If you turned toward the sea for a minute, you could see his face out of the corner of your eye, hanging black as a bat's wing, nodding and nodding like a dark heavy flower.

But in the early morning, he was the only one who came down onto the sand and sat under the beams of the boardwalk, sitting idle there with a languor fallen on every limb. He had long bones. He sat idle there, with his clothes shrunk up from his wrists and his ankles, with his legs drawn up, looking out at the sea.

"I might be a king if I wanted to be," was what he said to me.

Maybe I was twelve years old, or maybe I was ten when we used to sit eating dog biscuits together. Sometimes when you broke them in two, a worm fell out and the black boy lifted his sharp finger and flicked it carelessly from off his knee.

"I seen kings," he said, "with a kind of cloth over they heads, and kind of jewels-like around here and here. They weren't any blacker than me, if as black," he said. "I could be almost anything I made up my mind to be."

"King Nebuchadnezzar," I said. "He wasn't a white man."

The wind was off the ocean and was filled with alien smells. It was early in the day, and no human sign was given. Overhead were the green beams of the boardwalk and no wheel or step to sound it.

"If was a king," said the black boy with his biscuit in his fingers, "I wouldn't put much stock in hanging around here."

Great crystal jelly beasts were quivering in a hundred different colors on the wastes of sand around us. The dogs came, jumping them, and when they saw me still sitting still, they wheeled like gulls and sped back to the sea.

"I'd be traveling around," he said, "here and there. Now here, now there. I'd change most of my habits."

His hair grew all over the top of his head in tight dry rosettes. His neck was longer and more shapely than a white man's neck, and his fingers ran in and out of the sand like the blue feet of a bird.

"I wouldn't have much to do with pushing chairs around under them circumstances," he said. "I might even give up sleeping out here on the sand."

Or if you came out when it was starlight, you could see him sitting there in the clear white darkness. I could go and come as I liked, for whenever I went out the door, I had the dogs shouldering behind me. At night, they shook the taste of the house out of their coats and came down across the sand. There he was, with his knees up, sitting idle.

"They used to be all kinds of animals come down here to drink in the dark," he said. "They was a kind of a mirage came along and gave that impression. I seen tigers, lions, lambs, deer; I seen ostriches drinking down there side by side with each other. They's the Northern Lights gets crossed some way and switches the wrong picture down."

It may be that the coast has changed there, for even then it was changing The lighthouse that had once stood far out on the white rocks near the outlet was standing then like a lighted torch in the heart of the town. And the deep currents of the sea may have altered so that the clearest water runs in another direction, and houses may have been built down as far as where the brink used to be. But the brink was so perilous then that every word the black boy spoke seemed to fall into a cavern of beauty.

"I seen camels; I seen zebras," he said. "I might have caught any of one of them if I'd felt inclined."

The street was so still and wide then that when Puss stepped out of the house, I could hear him clearing his throat of the sharp salty air. He had no intention of soiling the soles of his boots, but he came down the street to find me.

"If you feel like going with me," he said, "we'll take a chair and see the fifty-seven varieties changing on the electric sign."

And then he saw the black boy sitting quiet. His voice drew up short on his tongue and he touched his white mustache.

"I shouldn't think it a good idea," he said, and he put his arm through my arm. "I saw another little oak not three inches high in the Jap's window yesterday. We might roll down the boardwalk and have a look at it. You know," said Puss, and he put his kid gloves carefully on his fingers, "that black boy might do you some kind of harm."

"What kind of harm could he do me?" I said.

"Well," said Puss with the garlands of lights hanging around him, "he might steal some money from you. He might knock you down and take your money away."

"How could he do that?" I said. "We just sit and talk there."
Puss looked at me sharply.

"What do you find to sit and talk about?" he said.

"I don't know," I said. "I don't remember. It doesn't sound like much to tell it."

The burden of his words was lying there on my heart when I woke up in the morning I went out by myself to the stable and led the horse to the door and put the saddle on her. If Puss were ill at ease for a day or two, he could look out the window in peace and see me riding high and mighty away. The day after tomorrow, I thought, or the next day, I'll sit down on the beach again and talk to the black boy. But when I rode out, I saw him seated idle there, under the boardwalk, heedless, looking away to the cool wide sea. He had been eating peanuts and the shells lay all around him. The dogs came running at the horse's heels, nipping the foam that lay along the tide.

The horse was as shy as a bird that morning, and when I drew her up beside the black boy, she tossed her head on high. Her mane went back and forth, from one side to the other, and a flight of joy in her limbs sent her forelegs like rockets into the air. The black boy stood up from the cold smooth sand, unsmiling, but a spark of wonder shone in his marble eyes. He put out his arm in the short tight sleeve of his coat and stroked her shivering shoulder.

"I was going to be a jockey once," he said, "but I changed my mind."

I slid down on one side while he climbed up the other.

"I don't know as I can ride him right," he said as I held her head. "The kind of saddle you have, it gives you nothing to grip your heels around. I ride them with their bare skin."

The black boy settled himself on the leather and put his feet in the stirrups. He was quiet and quick with delight, but he had no thought of smiling as he took the reins in his hands.

I stood on the beach with the dogs beside me, looking after the horse as she ambled down to the water. The black boy rode easily and straight, letting the horse stretch out and sneeze and canter. When they reached the jetty, he turned her casually and brought her loping back.

"Some folks licks hell out of their horses," he said. "I'd never raise a hand to one, unless he was to bite me or do something I didn't care for."

He sat in the saddle at ease, as though in a rocker, stroking her shoulder with his hand spread open, and turning in the stirrups to smooth her shining flank.

"Jockeys make a pile of money," I said.

"I wouldn't care for the life they have," said the black boy. "They have to watch their diet so careful."

His fingers ran delicately through her hair and laid her mane back on her neck.

When I was up on the horse again, I turned her toward the boardwalk.

"I'm going to take her over the jetty," I said. "You'll see how she clears it. I'll take her up under the boardwalk to give her a good start."

I struck her shoulder with the end of my crop, and she started toward the tough black beams. She was under it, galloping, when the dogs came down the beach like mad. They had chased a cat out of cover and were after it, screaming as they ran, with a wing of sand blowing wide behind them, and when the horse saw them under her legs, she jumped sidewise in sprightliness and terror and flung herself against an iron arch.

For a long time I heard nothing at all in my head except the melody of someone crying, whether it was my dead mother holding me in comfort, or the soft wind grieving over me where I had fallen. I lay on the sand asleep; I could feel it running with my tears through my fingers. I was rocked in a cradle of love, cradled and rocked in sorrow.

"Oh, my little lamb, my little lamb pie!" Oh, sorrow, sorrow, wailed the wind, or the tide, or my own kin about me. "Oh, lamb, oh, lamb!"

I could feel the long swift fingers of love untying the terrible knot of pain that bound my head. And I put my arms around him and lay close to his heart in comfort.

Puss was alive then, and when he met the black boy carrying me up to the house, he struck him square across the mouth.

the beach umbrella

CYRUS COLTER

the thirty-first street beach lay dazzling under a sky so blue that Lake Michigan ran to the horizon like a sheet of sapphire silk, studded with little barbed white sequins for sails; and the heavy surface of the water lapped gently at the boulder "sea wall" which had been cut into, graded, and sanded to make the beach. Saturday afternoons were always frenzied: three black lifeguards, giants in sunglasses, preened in their towers and chaperoned the bathers—adults, teen-agers, and children—who were going through every physical gyration of which the human body is capable. Some dove, swam, some hollered, rode inner tubes, or merely stood waistdeep and pummeled the water; others—on the beach—sprinted, did handsprings and somersaults, sucked Eskimo pies, or just buried their children in the sand. Then there were the lollers—extended in their languor under a garish variety of beach umbrellas.

Elijah lolled too—on his stomach in the white sand, his chin cupped in his palm; but under no umbrella. He had none. By habit, though, he stared in awe at those who did, and sometimes meddled in their conversation: "It's gonna be gettin' *hot* pretty soon—if it ain't careful," he said to a Bantu-looking fellow and his girl sitting near by with an older woman. The temperature was then in the nineties. The fellow managed a negligent smile. "Yeah," he said, and persisted in listening to the women. Buoyant still, Elijah watched them. But soon his gaze wavered, and then moved on to other lollers of interest. Finally he got up, stretched, brushed sand from his swimming trunks, and scanned the beach for a new spot. He started walking.

He was not tall. And he appeared to walk on his toes—his walnut-colored legs were bowed and skinny and made him hobble like a jerky little spider. Next he plopped down near two men and two girls—they were hilarious about something—sitting beneath a big purple-and-white umbrella. The girls, chocolate brown and shapely, emitted squeals of laughter at the wisecracks of the men. Elijah was enchanted. All summer long the rambunctious gaiety of the beach had fastened on him a curious charm, a hex, that brought him gawking and twiddling to the lake each Saturday. The rest of the week, save Sunday, he worked. But Myrtle, his wife, detested the sport and stayed away. Randall, the boy, had been only twice and then without little Susan, who during the summer was her mother's own midget reflection. But Elijah came regularly, especially whenever Myrtle was being evil, which he felt now was almost always. She was getting worse, too—if that was possible. The woman was money-*crazy*.

"You gotta sharp-lookin' umbrella there!" he cut in on the two laughing couples. They studied him— the abruptly silent way. Then the big-shouldered fellow smiled and lifted his eyes to their spangled roof. "Yeah? . . . Thanks," he said. Elijah carried on: "I see a lot of 'em out here this summer—much more'n last year." The fellow meditated on this, but was noncommittal. The others went on gabbing, mostly with their hands. Elijah, squinting in the hot sun, watched them. He didn't see how they could be married; they cut the fool too much, acted like they'd itched to get together for weeks and just now made it. He pondered going back in the water, but he'd already had an hour of that. His eyes traveled the sweltering beach. Funny about his folks: they were every shape and color a God-made human could be. Here was a real sample of variety—pink white to jetty black. Could you any longer call that a *race* of people? It was a complicated complication—for some real educated guy to figure out. Then another thought slowly bore in on him: the beach umbrellas blooming across the sand attracted people—slews of friends, buddies; and gals, too. Wherever the loudest-racket tore the air, a big red, or green, or yellowish umbrella—bordered with white fringe maybe—flowered in the middle of it all and gave shade to the happy good-timers.

Take, for instance, that tropical-looking pea-green umbrella over there, with the Bikini-ed brown chicks under it, and the portable radio jumping. A real beach party! He got up, stole over, and eased down in the sand at the fringe of the jubilation—two big thermos jugs sat in the shade and everybody had a paper cup in hand as the explosions of buffoonery carried out to the water. Chief provoker of mirth was a bulging-eyed old gal in a white bathing suit who, encumbered by big flabby overripe thighs, cavorted and pranced in the sand. When, perspiring from the heat, she finally fagged out, she flopped down almost on top of him. So far, he had gone unnoticed. But now, as he craned in at closer range, she brought him up: "Whatta *you* want, Pops?" She grinned, but with a touch of hostility.

Pops! Where'd she get that stuff? He was only forty-one, not a day older than that boozy bag. But he smiled. "Nothin'," he said brightly, "but you sure got one goin' here." He turned and viewed the noise-makers.

"An' you wanta get in on it!" she wrangled.

"Oh, I was just lookin'—"

"—You was just lookin'. Yeah, you was just lookin' at them young chicks there!" She roared a laugh and pointed at the sexy-looking girls under the umbrella.

Elijah grinned weakly.

"Beat it!" she catcalled, and turned back to the party.

He sat like a rock—the hell with her. But soon he relented, and wandered down to the water's edge—remote now from all inhospitality—to sit in the sand and hug his raised knees. Far out, the sailboats were pinned to the horizon and, despite all the close-in fuss, the wide miles of lake lay impassive under a blazing calm; far south and east down the long-curving lake shore, miles in the distance, the smoky haze of the Whiting plant of the Youngstown Sheet and Tube Company hung ominously in an otherwise bright sky. And so it was that he turned back and viewed the beach again—and suddenly caught his craving. Weren't they something—the umbrellas! The flashy colors of them! Yes . . . yes, he too must have one. The thought came slow and final, and scared him. For there stood Myrtle in his mind. She nagged him now night and day, and it was always money that got her started; there was never enough—for Susan's shoes, Randy's overcoat, for new kitchen linoleum, Venetian blinds, for a better car than the old Chevy. "I just don't understand you!" she had said only *night* before last. "Have you got any plans at all for your family? You got a family, you know. If you could only bear to pull yourself away from that deaf old tightwad out at that warehouse, and go get yourself a *real* job . . . But no! Not *you!*"

She was talking about old man Schroeder, who owned the warehouse where he worked. Yes, the pay could be better, but it still wasn't as bad as she made out. Myrtle could be such a fool sometimes. He had been with the old man nine years now; had started out as a freight handler, but worked up to doing inventories and a little paper work. True, the business had been going down recently, for the old man's sight and hearing were failing and his key people had left. Now he depended on *him*, Elijah—who of late wore a necktie on the job, and made his inventory rounds with a ball-point pen and clipboard. The old man was friendlier, too—almost "hat in hand" to him. He liked everything about the job now—except the pay. And that was only because of Myrtle. She just wanted so much; even talked of moving out of their rented apartment and buying out in the Chatham area. But one thing had to be said for her: she never griped about anything for herself; only for the family, the kids. Every payday he endorsed his check and handed it over to her, and got back in return only gasoline and cigarette money. And this could get

pretty tiresome. About six weeks ago he'd gotten a thirty-dollar-
a-month raise out of the old man, but that had only made her
madder than ever. He'd thought about looking for another job all
right; but where would he go to get another white-collar job?
There weren't many of them for him. *She* wouldn't care if he
went back to the steel mills, back to pouring that white-hot ore
out at Youngstown Sheet and Tube. It would be okay with *her*—
so long as his pay check was fat. But that kind of work was no
good, undignified; coming home on the bus you were always so
tired you went to sleep in your seat, with your lunch pail in your
lap.

Just then two wet boys, chasing each other across the sand,
raced by him into the water. The cold spray on his skin made him
jump, jolting him out of his thoughts. He turned and slowly
scanned the beach again. The umbrellas were brighter, gayer,
bolder than ever—each a hiving center of playful people. He
stood up finally, took a long last look, and then started back to
the spot where he had parked the Chevy.

The following Monday evening was hot and humid as Elijah sat
at home in their plain living room and pretended to read the
newspaper; the windows were up, but not the slightest breeze
came through the screens to stir Myrtle's fluffy curtains. At the
moment she and nine-year-old Susan were in the kitchen finishing the dinner dishes. For twenty minutes now he had sat waiting for the furtive chance to speak to Randall. Randall, at twelve,
was a serious, industrious boy, and did deliveries and odd jobs for
the neighborhood grocer. Soon he came through—intent,
absorbed—on his way back to the grocery store for another
hour's work.

"Gotta go back, eh, Randy?" Elijah said.

"Yes, sir." He was tall for his age, and wore glasses. He paused
with his hand on the doorknob.

Elijah hesitated. Better wait, he thought—wait till he comes
back. But Myrtle might be around then. Better ask him now. But
Randall had opened the door. "See you later, Dad," he said—and
left.

Elijah, shaken, again raised the newspaper and tried to read. He should have called him back, he knew, but he had lost his nerve—because he couldn't tell how Randy would take it. Fifteen dollars was nothing though, really—Randy probably had fifty or sixty stashed away somewhere in his room. Then he thought of Myrtle, and waves of fright went over him—to be even thinking about a beach umbrella was bad enough; and to buy one, especially now, would be to her some kind of crime; but to borrow even a part of the money for it from Randy . . . well, Myrtle would go out of her mind. He had never lied to his family before. This would be the first time. And he had thought about it all day long. During the morning, at the warehouse, he had gotten out the two big mail-order catalogues, to look at the beach umbrellas; but the ones shown were all so small and dinky-looking he was contemptuous. So at noon he drove the Chevy out to a sporting-goods store on West Sixty-third Street. There he found a gorgeous assortment of yard and beach umbrellas. And there he found his prize. A beauty, a big beauty, with wide red and white stripes, and a white fringe. But oh the price! Twenty-three dollars! And he with nine.

"What's the matter with you?" Myrtle had walked in the room. She was thin, and medium brown-skinned with a saddle of freckles across her nose, and looked harried in her sleeveless housedress with her hair unkempt.

Startled, he lowered the newspaper. "Nothing," he said.

"How can you read looking *over* the paper?"

"Was I?"

Not bothering to answer, she sank in a chair. "Susie," she called back into the kitchen, "bring my cigarettes in here, will you, baby?"

Soon Susan, chubby and solemn, with the mist of perspiration on her forehead, came in with the cigarettes. "Only three left, Mama," she said, peering into the pack.

"Okay," Myrtle sighed, taking the cigarettes. Susan started out. "Now, scour the sink good, honey—and then go take your bath. You'll feel cooler."

Before looking at him again, Myrtle lit a cigarette. "School starts in three weeks," she said, with a forlorn shake of her head. "Do you realize that?"

"Yeah? . . . Jesus, time flies." He could not look at her.

"Susie needs dresses, and a couple of pairs of *good* shoes—and she'll need a coat before it gets cold."

"Yeah, I know." He parred the arm of the chair.

"Randy—bless his heart—has already made enough to get most of *his* things. That boy's something; he's all business—I've never seen anything like it." She took a drag on her cigarette. "And old man Schroeder giving you a thirty-dollar raise! What was you thinkin' about? What'd you *say* to him?"

He did not answer at first. Finally he said, "Thirty dollars are thirty dollars, Myrtle. *You* know business is slow."

"*I'll* say it is! And there won't be any business before long—and then where'll you be? I tell you over and over again, you better start looking for something *now*! I been preachin' it to you for a year."

He said nothing.

"Ford and International Harvester are hiring every man they can lay their hands on! And the mills out in Gary and Whiting are going full blast—you see the red sky every night. The men make *good* money."

"They earn every nickel of it, too," he said in gloom.

"But they *get* it! Bring it home! It spends! Does that mean anything to you? Do you know what some of them make? Well, ask Hawthorne—or ask Sonny Milton. Sonny's wife says his checks some weeks run as high as a hundred sixty, hundred eighty, dollars. One week! Take-home pay!"

"Yeah? . . . And Sonny told me he wished he had a job like mine."

Myrtle threw back her head with a bitter gasp. "Oh-h-h, God! Did you tell him what you made? Did you tell him that?"

Suddenly Susan came back into the muggy living room. She went straight to her mother and stood as if expecting an award. Myrtle absently patted her on the side of the head. "Now, go and run your bath water, honey," she said.

Elijah smiled at Susan. "Susie," he said, "d'you know your

tummy is stickin' way out—you didn't eat too much, did you?"
He laughed.

Susan turned and observed him; then looked at her mother.
"No," she finally said.

"Go on, now, baby," Myrtle said. Susan left the room.

Myrtle resumed. "Well, there's no use going through all this
again. It's plain as the nose on your face. You got a family—a good
family, *I* think. The only question is, do you wanta get off your
hind end and do somethin' for it. It's just that simple."

Elijah looked at her. "You can talk real crazy sometimes,
Myrtle."

"I think it's that old man!" she cried, her freckles contorted.
"He's got you answering the phone, and taking inventory—
wearing a necktie and all that. You wearing a necktie and your
son mopping in a grocery store, so he can buy his own clothes."
She snatched up her cigarettes, and walked out of the room.

His eyes did not follow her, but remained off in space. Finally
he got up and went back into the kitchen. Over the stove the
plaster was thinly cracked, and, in spots, the linoleum had worn
through the pattern; but everything was immaculate. He opened
the refrigerator, poured a glass of cold water, and sat down at the
kitchen table. He felt strange and weak, and sat for a long time
sipping the water.

Then after a while he heard Randall's key in the front door,
sending tremors of dread through him. When Randall came into
the kitchen, he seemed to him as tall as himself; his glasses were
steamy from the humidity outside, and his hands were dirty.

"Hi, Dad," he said gravely without looking at him, and opened
the refrigerator door.

Elijah chuckled. "Your mother'll get after you about going in
there without washing your hands."

But Randall took out the water pitcher and closed the door.

Elijah watched him. Now was the time to ask him. His heart was
hammering. Go on—now! But instead he heard his husky voice
saying, "What'd they have you doing over at the grocery tonight?"

Randall was drinking the glass of water. When he finished he
said, "Refilling shelves."

"Pretty hot job tonight, eh?"

"It wasn't so bad." Randall was matter-of-fact as he set the empty glass over the sink, and paused before leaving.

"Well . . . you're doing fine, son. Fine. Your mother sure is proud of you . . ." Purpose had lodged in his throat.

The praise embarrassed Randall. "Okay, Dad," he said, and edged from the kitchen.

Elijah slumped back in his chair, near prostration. He tried to clear his mind of every particle of thought, but the images became only more jumbled, oppressive to the point of panic.

Then before long Myrtle came into the kitchen—ignoring him. But she seemed not so hostile now as coldly impassive, exhibiting a bravado he had not seen before. He got up and went back into the living room and turned on the television. As the TV-screen lawmen galloped before him, he sat oblivious, admitting the failure of his will. If only he could have gotten Randall to himself long enough—but everything had been so sudden, abrupt; he couldn't just ask him out of the clear blue. Besides, around him, Randall always seemed so busy, too busy to talk. He couldn't understand that; he had never mistreated the boy, never whipped him in his life; had shaken him a time or two, but that was long ago, when he was little.

He sat and watched the finish of the half-hour TV show. Myrtle was in the bedroom now. He slouched in his chair, lacking the resolve to get up and turn off the television.

Suddenly he was on his feet.

Leaving the television on, he went back to Randall's room in the rear. The door was open and Randall was asleep, lying on his back on the bed, perspiring, still dressed except for his shoes and glasses. He stood over the bed and looked at him. He was a good boy; his own son. But how strange—he thought for the first time—there was no resemblance between them. None whatsoever. Randy had a few of his mother's freckles on his thin brown face, but he could see none of himself in the boy. Then his musings were scattered by the return of his fear. He dreaded waking him. And he might be cross. If he didn't hurry, though, Myrtle or Susie might come strolling out any minute. His bones seemed rubbery from the strain. Finally he bent down and touched Randall's shoulder. The boy did not move a muscle, except to open his eyes. Elijah smiled at him. And he slowly sat up.

"Sorry, Randy—to wake you up like this."

"What's the matter?" Randall rubbed his eyes.

Elijah bent down again, but did not whisper. "Say, can you let me have fifteen bucks—till I get my check? I need to get some things—and I'm a little short this time." He could hardly bring the words up.

Randall gave him a slow, queer look.

"I'll get my check a week from Friday," Elijah said, ". . . and I'll give it back to you then—sure."

Now instinctively Randall glanced toward the door, and Elijah knew Myrtle had crossed his thoughts. "You don't have to mention anything to your mother," he said with casual suddenness.

Randall got up slowly off the bed, and, in his socks, walked to the little table where he did his homework. He pulled the drawer out, fished far in the back a moment, and brought out a white business envelope secured by a rubber band. Holding the envelope close to his stomach, he took out first a ten-dollar bill, and then a five, and sighing, handed them over.

"Thanks, old man," Elijah quivered, folding the money. "You'll get this back the day I get my check. . . . That's for sure."

"Okay," Randall finally said.

Elijah started out. Then he could see Myrtle on payday—her hand extended for his check. He hesitated, and looked at Randall, as if to speak. But he slipped the money in his trousers pocket and hurried from the room.

The following Saturday at the beach did not begin bright and sunny. By noon it was hot, but the sky was overcast and angry, the air heavy. There was no certainty whatever of a crowd, raucous or otherwise, and this was Elijah's chief concern as, shortly before twelve o'clock, he drove up in the Chevy and parked in the bumpy, graveled stretch of high ground that looked down eastward over the lake and was used for a parking lot. He climbed out of the car, glancing at the lake and clouds, and prayed in his heart it would not rain—the water was murky and restless, and only a handful of bathers had showed. But it was early yet. He stood beside the car and watched a bulbous, brown-skinned woman, in bathing suit and enormous straw hat, lugging a lunch basket down toward the beach, followed by her brood of children. And a fellow in swimming trunks, apparently the father, took a towel and sandals from his new Buick and called petulantly to his family to "just wait a minute, please." In another car, two women sat waiting, as yet fully clothed and undecided about going swimming. While down at the water's edge there was the usual cluster of dripping boys who, brash and boisterous, swarmed to the beach every day in fair weather or foul.

Elijah took off his shirt, peeled his trousers from over his swimming trunks, and started collecting the paraphernalia from the back seat of the car: a frayed pink rug filched from the house, a towel, sunglasses, cigarettes, a thermos jug filled with cold lemonade he had made himself, and a dozen paper cups. All this he stacked on the front fender. Then he went around to the rear and opened the trunk. Ah, there it lay—encased in a long, slim package trussed with heavy twine, and barely fitting athwart the spare tire. He felt prickles of excitement as he took the knife from the tool bag, cut the twine, and pulled the wrapping paper away. Red and white stripes sprang at him. It was even more gorgeous than when it had first seduced him in the store. The white fringe gave it style; the wide red fillets were cardinal and stark, and the white stripes glared. Now he opened it over his head, for the full thrill of its colors, and looked around to see if anyone else agreed. Finally after a while he gathered up all his equipment and headed down for the beach, his short, nubby legs seeming more bowed than ever under the weight of their cargo.

When he reached the sand, a choice of location became a pressing matter. That was why he had come early. From past observation it was clear that the center of gaiety shifted from day to day; last Saturday it might have been nearer the water, this Saturday, well back; or up, or down, the beach a ways. He must pick the site with care, for he could not move about the way he did when he had no umbrella; it was too noticeable. He finally took a spot as near the center of the beach as he could estimate, and dropped his gear in the sand. He knelt down and spread the pink rug, then moved the thermos jug over onto it, and folded the towel and placed it with the paper cups, sunglasses, and cigarettes down beside the jug. Now he went to find a heavy stone or brick to drive down the spike for the hollow umbrella stem to fit over. So it was not until the umbrella was finally up that he again had time for anxiety about the weather. His whole morning's effort had been an act of faith, for, as yet, there was no sun, although now and then a few azure breaks appeared in the thinning cloud mass. But before very long this brighter texture of the sky began to grow and spread by slow degrees, and his hopes quickened. Finally he sat down under the umbrella, lit a cigarette, and waited.

It was not long before two small boys came by—on their way to the water. He grinned, and called to them, "Hey, fellas, been in yet?"—their bathing suits were dry.

They stopped, and observed him. Then one of them smiled, and shook his head.

Elijah laughed. "Well, whatta you waitin' for? Go on in there and get them suits wet!" Both boys gave him silent smiles. And they fingered. He thought this a good omen—it had been different the Saturday before.

Once or twice the sun burst through the weakening clouds. He forgot the boys now in watching the skies, and soon they moved on. His anxiety was not detectable from his lazy posture under the umbrella, with his dwarfish, gnarled legs extended and his bare heels on the little rug. But then soon the clouds began to fade in earnest, seeming not to move away laterally, but slowly to recede unto a lucent haze, until at last the sun came through hot and bright. He squinted at the sky and felt delivered. They would come, the folks would come!—were coming now; the beach would soon be swarming. Two other umbrellas were up already, and the diving board thronged with wet, acrobatic boys. The lifeguards were in their towers now, and still another launched his yellow rowboat. And up on the Outer Drive, the cars one by one, were turning into the parking lot. The sun was bringing them out all right; soon he'd be in the middle of a field day. He felt a low-key, welling excitement, for the water was blue, and far out the sails were starched and white.

Soon he saw the two little boys coming back. They were soaked. Their mother—a thin, brown girl in a yellow bathing suit—was with them now, and the boys were pointing to his umbrella. She seemed dignified for her youth, as she gave him a shy glance and then smiled at the boys.

"Ah, ha!" he cried to the boys. "You've been in *now* all right!" And then laughing to her, "I was kiddin' them awhile ago about their dry bathing suits."

She smiled at the boys again. "They like for me to be with them when they go in," she said.

"I got some lemonade here," he said abruptly, slapping the thermos jug. "Why don't you have some?" His voice was anxious.

She hesitated.

He jumped up. "Come on, sit down." He smiled at her and stepped aside.

Still she hesitated. But her eager boys pressed close behind her. Finally she smiled and sat down under the umbrella.

"You fellas can sit down under there too—in the shade," he said to the boys, and pointed under the umbrella. The boys flopped down quickly in the shady sand. He starred at once serving them cold lemonade in the paper cups.

"Whew! I thought it was goin' to rain there for a while," he said, making conversation after passing out the lemonade. He had squatted on the sand and lit another cigarette. "Then there wouldn't a been much goin' on. But it turned out fine after all—there'll be a mob here before long."

She sipped the lemonade, but said little. He felt she had sat down only because of the boys, for she merely smiled and gave short answers to his questions. He learned the boys' names, Melvin and James; their ages, seven and nine, and that they were still frightened by the water. But he wanted to ask *her* name, and inquire about her husband. But he could not capture the courage.

Now the sun was hot and the sand was hot. And an orange-and-white umbrella was going up right beside them—two fellows and a girl. When the fellow who had been kneeling to drive the umbrella spike in the sand stood up, he was string-bean tall, and black, with his glistening hair freshly processed. The girl was a lighter brown, and wore a lilac bathing suit, and although her legs were thin, she was pleasant enough to look at. The second fellow was medium, really, in height, but short beside his tall, black friend. He was yellow-skinned, and fast getting bald, although still in his early thirties. Both men sported little shoestring mustaches.

Elijah watched them in silence as long as he could. "You picked the right spot all right!" he laughed at last, putting on his sunglasses.

"How come, man?" The tall, black fellow grinned, showing his mouthful of gold teeth.

"You see *every*body here!" happily rejoined Elijah. "They all come here!"

"Man, I been coming here for years," the fellow reproved, and sat down in his khaki swimming trunks to take off his shoes. Then he stood up. "But right now, in the water I goes." He looked down at the girl. "How 'bout you, Lois, baby?"

"No, Caesar," she smiled, "not yet; I'm gonna sit here awhile and relax."

"Okay, then—you just sit right there and relax. And Little Joe"—he turned and grinned to his shorter friend—"you sit there an' relax right along with her. You all can talk with this gentleman here"—he nodded at Elijah—"an' his nice wife." Then, pleased with himself, he trotted off toward the water.

The young mother looked at Elijah, as if he should have hastened to correct him. But somehow he had not wanted to. Yet too, Caesar's remark seemed to amuse her, for she soon smiled. Elijah felt the pain of relief—he did not want her to go; he glanced at her with a furtive laugh, and then they both laughed. The boys had finished their lemonade now, and were digging in the sand. Lois and Little Joe were busy talking.

Elijah was not quite sure what he should say to the mother. He did not understand her, was afraid of boring her, was desperate to keep her interested. As she sat looking out over the lake, he watched her. She was not pretty; and she was too thin. But he thought she had poise; he liked the way she treated her boys—tender, but casual; how different from Myrtle's frantic herding.

Soon she turned to the boys. "Want to go back in the water?" she laughed.

The boys looked at each other, and then at her. "Okay," James said finally, in resignation.

"Here, have some more lemonade," Elijah cut in.

The boys, rescued for the moment, quickly extended their cups. He poured them more lemonade, as she looked on smiling.

Now he turned to Lois and Little Joe sitting under their orange-and-white umbrella. "How 'bout some good ole cold lemonade?" he asked with a mushy smile. "I got plenty of cups." He felt he must get something going.

Lois smiled back, "No, thanks," she said, fluttering her long eyelashes, "not right now."

He looked anxiously at Little Joe.

"*I'll* take a cup!" said Little Joe, and turned and laughed to Lois: "Hand me that bag there, will you?" He pointed to her beach bag in the sand. She passed it to him, and he reached in and pulled out a pint of gin. "We'll have some *real* lemonade," he vowed, with a daredevilish grin.

Lois squealed with pretended embarrassment, "Oh. *Joe!*"

Elijah's eyes were big now; he was thinking of the police. But he handed Little Joe a cup and poured the lemonade, to which Joe added gin. Then Joe, grinning, thrust the bottle at Elijah. "How 'bout yourself, chief?" he said.

Elijah, shaking his head, leaned forward and whispered, "You ain't supposed to drink on the beach, y'know."

"*This* ain't a drink, man—it's a taste!" said Little Joe, laughing and waving the bottle around toward the young mother. "How 'bout a little taste for your wife here?" he said to Elijah.

The mother laughed and threw up both her hands. "No, not for me!"

Little Joe gave her a rakish grin. "What'sa matter? You *'fraid* of that guy?" He jerked his thumb toward Elijah. "You 'fraid of gettin' a whippin', eh?"

"No, not exactly," she laughed.

Elijah was so elated with her his relief burst up in hysterical laughter. His laugh became strident and hoarse and he could not stop. The boys gaped at him, and then at their mother. When finally he recovered, Little Joe asked him, "Whut's so funny 'bout *that*?" Then Little Joe grinned at the mother. "You beat *him* up *sometimes*, eh?"

This started Elijah's hysterics all over again. The mother looked concerned now, and embarrassed; her laugh was nervous and shadowed. Little Joe glanced at Lois, laughed, and shrugged his shoulders. When Elijah finally got control of himself again he looked spent and demoralized.

Lois now tried to divert attention by starting a conversation with the boys. But the mother showed signs of restlessness and seemed ready to go. At this moment Caesar returned. Glistening beads of water ran off his long, black body; and his hair was unprocessed now. He surveyed the group and then flashed a wide, gold-toothed grin. "One big, happy family, like I said." Then he spied the paper cup in Little Joe's hand. "What you got there, man?"

Little Joe looked down into his cup with a playful smirk. "Lemonade, lover boy, lemonade."

"Don't hand me that jive, Joey. You ain't never had any straight lemonade in your life."

This again brought uproarious laughter from Elijah. "I got the straight lemonade *here*!" He beat the thermos jug with his hand. "Come on—have some!" He reached for a paper cup.

"Why, sure," said poised Caesar. He held out the cup and received the lemonade. "Now, gimme that gin," he said to Little Joe. Joe handed over the gin, and Caesar poured three fingers into the lemonade and sat down in the sand with his legs crossed under him. Soon he turned to the two boys, as their mother watched him with amusement. "Say, ain't you boys goin' in any more? Why don't you tell your daddy there to take you in?" He nodded toward Elijah.

Little Melvin frowned at him. "My daddy's workin'," he said.

Caesar's eyebrows shot up. "Ooooh, la, la!" he crooned. "Hey, now!" And he turned and looked at the mother and then at Elijah, and gave a clownish little snigger.

Lois tittered before feigning exasperation at him. "There you go again," she said, "talkin' when you shoulda been listening."

Elijah laughed with the rest. But he felt deflated. Then he glanced at the mother, who was laughing too. He could detect in her no sign of dismay. Why then had she gone along with the gag in the first place, he thought—if now she didn't hate to see it punctured?

"Hold the phone!" softly exclaimed Little Joe. "Whut is *this*?" He was staring over his shoulder. Three women, young, brown, and worldly-looking, wandered toward them, carrying an assortment of beach paraphernalia and looking for a likely spot. They wore very scant bathing suits, and were followed, but slowly, by an older woman with big, unsightly thighs. Elijah recognized her at once. She was the old gal who, the Saturday before, had chased him away from her beach party. She wore the same white bathing suit, and one of her girls carried the pea-green umbrella.

Caesar forgot his whereabouts ogling the girls. The older woman, observing this, paused to survey the situation. "How 'bout along in here?" she finally said to one of the girls. The girl carrying the thermos jug set it in the sand so close to Caesar it nearly touched him. He was rapturous. The girl with the umbrella had no chance to put it up, for Caesar and Little Joe instantly encumbered her with help. Another girl turned on their radio, and grinning, feverish Little Joe started snapping his fingers to the music's beat.

Within a half hour, a boisterous party was in progress. The little radio, perched on a hump of sand, blared out hot jazz, as the older woman—whose name turned out to be Hattie—passed around some cold, rum-spiked punch; and before long she went into her dancing-prancing act—to the riotous delight of all, especially Elijah. Hattie did not remember him from the Saturday past, and he was glad, for everything was so different today! As different as milk and ink. He knew no one realized it, but this was *his* party really—the wildest, craziest, funniest, and best he had ever seen or heard of. Nobody had been near the water—except Caesar, and the mother and boys much earlier. It appeared Lois was Caesar's girl friend, and she was hence more capable of reserve in face of the come-on antics of Opal, Billie, and Quanita—Hattie's girls. But Little Joe, to Caesar's tortured envy, was both free and aggressive. Even the young mother, who now volunteered her name to be Mrs. Green, got frolicsome, and twice jabbed Little Joe in the ribs.

Finally Caesar proposed they all go in the water. This met with instant, tipsy acclaim; and Little Joe, his yellow face contorted from laughing, jumped up, grabbed Billie's hand, and made off with her across the sand. But Hattie would not budge. Full of rum, and stubborn, she sat sprawled with her flaccid thighs spread in an obscene V, and her eyes half shut. Now she yelled at her departing girls: "You all watch out, now! Dont'cha go in too far. . . . Just wade! None o' you can swim a lick!"

Elijah now was beyond happiness. He felt a floating, manic glee. He sprang up and jerked Mrs. Green splashing into the water, followed by her somewhat less ecstatic boys. Caesar had to paddle about with Lois and leave Little Joe unassisted to caper with Billie, Opal, and Quanita. Billie was the prettiest of the three, and, despite Hattie's contrary statement, she could swim; and Little Joe, after taking her out in deeper water, waved back to Caesar in triumph. The sun was brazen now, and the beach and lake thronged with a variegated humanity. Elijah, a strong, but awkward, country-style swimmer, gave Mrs. Green a lesson in floating on her back, and, though she too could swim, he often felt obligated to place both his arms under her young body and buoy her up.

And sometimes he would purposely let her sink to her chin, whereupon she would feign a happy fright and utter faint simian screeches. Opal and Quanita sat in the shallows and kicked up their heels at Caesar, who, fully occupied with Lois, was a grinning water-threshing study in frustration.

Thus the party went—on and on—till nearly four o'clock. Elijah had not known the world afforded such joy; his homely face was a wet festoon of beams and smiles. He went from girl to girl, insisting that she learn to float on his outstretched arms. Once begrudgingly Caesar admonished him, "Man, you gonna *drown* one o' them pretty chicks in a minute." And Little Joe bestowed his highest accolade by calling him "lover boy," as Elijah nearly strangled from laughter.

At last, they looked up to see old Hattie as she reeled down to the water's edge, coming to fetch her girls. Both Caesar and Little Joe ran out of the water to meet her, seized her by the wrists, and, despite her struggles and curses, dragged her in. "Turn me loose! You big galoots!" she yelled and gasped as the water hit her. She was in knee-deep before she wriggled and fought herself free and lurched out of the water. Her breath reeked of rum. Little Joe ran and caught her again, but she lunged backwards, and free, with such force she sat down in the wet sand with a thud. She roared a laugh now, and spread her arms for help, as her girls came sprinting and splashing out of the water and tugged her to her feet. Her eyes narrowed to vengeful, grinning slits as she turned on Caesar and Little Joe: "*I* know whut you two're up to!" She flashed a glance around toward her girls. "I been watchin' both o' you studs! Yeah, yeah, but your eyes may shine, an' your teeth may grit . . ." She went limp in a sneering, raucous laugh. Everybody laughed now—except Lois and Mrs. Green.

They had all come out of the water now, and soon the whole group returned to their three beach umbrellas. Hattie's girls immediately prepared to break camp. They took down their pea-green umbrella, folded some wet towels, and donned their beach sandals, as Hattie still bantered Caesar and Little Joe.

"Well, you sure had *yourself* a ball today," she said to Little Joe, who was sitting in the sand.

"Comin' back next Saturday?" asked grinning Little Joe.

"I jus' might at that," surmised Hattie. "We wuz here last Saturday."

"Good! Good!" Elijah broke in. "Let's *all* come back—next Saturday!" He searched every face.

"*I'll* be here," churned Little Joe, grinning to Caesar. Captive Caesar glanced at Lois, and said nothing.

Lois and Mrs. Green were silent. Hattie, insulted, looked at them and started swelling up. "Never mind," she said pointedly to Elijah, "you jus' come on anyhow. You'll run into a slew o' folks lookin' for a good time. You don't need no *certain* people." But a little later, she and her girl all said friendly goodbyes and walked off across the sand.

The party now took a sudden downturn. All Elijah's efforts at resuscitation seemed unavailing. The westering sun was dipping toward the distant buildings of the city, and many of the bathers were leaving. Caesar and Little Joe had become bored; and Mrs. Green's boys, whining to go, kept a reproachful eye on their mother.

"Here, you boys, take some more lemonade." Elijah said quickly, reaching for the thermos jug. "Only got a little left—better get while gettin's good!" He laughed. The boys shook their heads.

On Lois he tried cajolery. Smiling, and pointing to her wet, but trim bathing suit, he asked, "What color would you say that is?"

"Lilac," said Lois, now standing.

"It sure is pretty! Prettiest on the beach!" he whispered.

Lois gave him a weak smile. Then she reached down for her beach bag, and looked at Caesar.

Caesar stood up, "Let's cut," he turned and said to Little Joe, and began taking down their orange-and-white umbrella.

Elijah was desolate. "Whatta you goin' for? It's gettin' cooler! Now's the time to *enjoy* the beach!"

"I've got to go home," Lois said.

Mrs. Green got up now; her boys had started off already. "Just a minute, Melvin," she called, frowning. Then, smiling, she turned and thanked Elijah.

He whirled around to them all. "Are we comin' back next Saturday? Come on—let's all come back! Wasn't it great! It was *great*! Don't you think? Whatta you say?" He looked now at Lois and Mrs. Green.

"We'll see," Lois said, smiling. "Maybe."

"Can *you* come?" He turned to Mrs. Green.

"I'm not sure," she said. "I'll try."

"Fine! Oh, that's fine!" He turned on Caesar and Little Joe. "I'll be lookin' for you guys, hear?"

"Okay, chief," grinned Little Joe. "An' put somethin' in that lemonade, will ya?"

Everybody laughed . . . and soon they were gone.

Elijah slowly crawled back under his umbrella, although the sun's heat was almost spent. He looked about him. There was only one umbrella on the spot now, his own; where before there had been three. Cigarette butts and paper cups lay strewn where Hattie's girls had sat, and the sandy imprint of Caesar's enormous street shoes marked his site. Mrs. Green had dropped a bobby pin. He too was caught up now by a sudden urge to go. It was hard to bear much longer—the lonesomeness. And most of the people were leaving anyway He stirred and fidgeted in the sand, and finally started an inventory of his belongings . . . Then his thoughts flew home, and he reconsidered. Funny—he hadn't thought of home all afternoon. Where had the time gone anyhow? . . . It seemed he'd just pulled up in the Chevy and unloaded his gear; now it was time to go home again. Then the image of solemn Randy suddenly formed in his mind, sending waves of guilt through him. He forgot where he was as the duties of his existence leapt on his back—where would he ever get Randy's fifteen dollars? He felt squarely confronted by a great blank void. It was an awful thing he had done—all for a day at the beach . . . with some sporting girls. He thought of his family and felt tiny—and him itching to come back next Saturday! Maybe Myrtle was right about him after all. Lord, if she knew what he had done. . . .

He sat there for a long time. Most of the people were gone now. The lake was quiet save for a few boys still in the water. And the sun, red like blood, had settled on the dark silhouettes of the housetops across the city. He sat beneath the umbrella just as he had at one o'clock . . . and the thought smote him. He was jolted. Then dubious. But there it was—quivering, vital, swelling inside his skull like an unwanted fetus. So this was it! He mutinied inside. So he must sell it . . . his *umbrella*. Sell it for anything—only as long as it was enough to pay back Randy. For fifteen dollars even, if necessary. He was dogged; he couldn't do it; that wasn't the answer anyway. But the thought clawed and clung to him, rebuking and coaxing him by turns, until it finally became conviction. He must do it; it was the right thing to do; the only thing to do. Maybe then the awful weight would lift, the dull commotion in his stomach cease. He got up and started collecting his belongings; placed the thermos jug, sunglasses, towel, cigarettes, and little rug together in a neat pile, to be carried to the Chevy later. Then he turned to face his umbrella. Its red and white stripes stood defiant against the wide, churned-up sand. He stood for a moment mooning at it. Then he carefully let it down and, carrying it in his right hand, went off across the sand.

The sun now had gone down behind the vast city in a shower of crimson-golden glints, and on the beach only a few stragglers remained. For his first prospects, he approached two teen-age boys, but suddenly realizing they had no money, he turned away and went over to an old woman, squat and black, in street clothes—a spectator—who stood gazing eastward out across the lake. She held in her hand a little black book, with red-edged pages, which looked like the New Testament. He smiled at her. "Wanna buy a nice new beach umbrella?" He held out the collapsed umbrella toward her.

She gave him a beatific smile, but shook her head. "No, son," she said, "that ain't what *I* want." And she turned to gaze out on the lake again.

For a moment he still held the umbrella out, with a question mark on his face. "Okay, then," he finally said, and went on.

Next he hurried to the water's edge, where he saw a man and two women preparing to leave. "Wanna buy a nice new beach umbrella?" His voice sounded high-pitched, as he opened the umbrella over his head. "It's brand-new. I'll sell it for fifteen dollars—it cost a lot more'n that."

The man was hostile, and glared. Finally he said, "Whatta you take me for—a fool?"

Elijah looked bewildered, and made no answer. He observed the man for a moment. Finally he let the umbrella down. As he moved away, he heard the man say to the women, "It's hot—he stole it somewhere."

Close by, another man sat alone in the sand. Elijah started toward him. The man wore trousers, but was stripped to the waist, and bent over intent on some task in his lap. When Elijah reached him, he looked up from half a hatful of cigarette butts he was breaking open for the tobacco he collected in a little paper bag. He grinned at Elijah, who meant now to pass on.

"No, I ain't interested either, buddy," the man insisted as Elijah passed him. "Not me. I jus' got *outa* jail las' week—an' ain't goin' back for no umbrella." He laughed, as Elijah kept on.

Now he saw three women, still in their bathing suits, sitting together near the diving board. They were the only people he had not yet tried—except the one lifeguard left. As he approached them, he saw that all three wore glasses and were sedate. Some schoolteachers maybe, he thought, or office workers. They were talking—until they saw him coming; then they stopped. One of them was plump, but a smooth dark brown, and sat with a towel around her shoulders. Elijah addressed them through her: "Wanna buy a nice beach umbrella?" And again he opened the umbrella over his head.

"Gee! It's beautiful," the plump woman said to the others. "But where'd you get?" she suddenly asked Elijah, polite mistrust entering her voice.

"I bought it—just this week."

The three women looked at each other "Why do you want to sell it so soon, then?" a second woman said.

Elijah grinned. "I need the money."

"Well!" The plump woman was exasperated. "*No*, we don't want it." And they turned from him. He stood for a while, watching them; finally he let the umbrella down and moved on.

Only the lifeguard was left. He was a huge youngster, not over twenty, and brawny and black, as he bent over cleaning out his beached rowboat. Elijah approached him so suddenly he looked up startled.

"Would you be interested in this umbrella?" Elijah said, and proffered the umbrella. "It's brand-new—I just bought it Tuesday. I'll sell it cheap." There was urgency in his voice.

The lifeguard gave him a queer stare; and then peered off toward the Outer Drive, as if looking for help. "You're lucky as hell," he finally said. "The cops just now cruised by—up on the

Drive. I'd have turned you in so quick it'd made your head swim. Now you get the hell outa here." He was menacing.

Elijah was angry. "Whatta you mean? I *bought* this umbrella—it's mine."

The lifeguard took a step toward him. "I said you better get the hell outa here! An' I mean it! You thievin' bastard, you!"

Elijah, frightened now, gave ground. He turned and walked away a few steps; and then slowed up, as if an adequate answer had hit him. He stood for a moment. But finally he walked on, the umbrella drooping in his hand.

He walked up the gravelly slope now toward the Chevy, forgetting his little pile of belongings left in the sand. When he reached the car, and opened the trunk, he remembered; and went back down and gathered them up. He returned, threw them in the trunk and, without dressing, went around and climbed under the steering wheel. He was scared, shaken; and before starting the motor sat looking out on the lake. It was seven o'clock; the sky was waning pale, the beach forsaken, leaving a sense of perfect stillness and approaching night; the only sound was a gentle lapping of the water against the sand—one moderate *hallo-o-o-o* would have carried across to Michigan. He looked down at the beach. Where were they all now—the funny, proud, laughing people? Eating their dinners, he supposed, in a variety of homes. And all the beautiful umbrellas—where were they? Without their colors the beach was so deserted. Ah, the beach . . . after pouring hot ore all week out at the Youngstown Sheet and Tube, he would probably be too fagged out for the beach. But maybe he wouldn't—who knew? It was great while it lasted . . . great. And his umbrella . . . he didn't know what he'd do with that . . . he might never need it again. He'd keep it, though—and see. Ha! . . . hadn't he sweat to get it! . . . and they thought he had stolen it . . . stolen it . . . ah . . . and maybe they were right. He sat for a few moments longer. Finally he started the motor, and took the old Chevy out onto the Drive in the pink-hued twilight. But down on the beach the sun was still shining.

i read my
nephew stories

ETHAN MORDDEN

ok., what am I doing on a beach in Massachusetts? Simple: my brother Ken ran away from home when he was fifteen.

I not only have a brother who ran away from home but an aunt who committed suicide, a great-uncle who went to prison, and a cousin who dropped out and went to India. I'm still trying to get the rights to our saga back from the O'Neill estate.

Anyway, Ken not only ran away from home but never came back, which bewildered my younger brothers and me but which my other older brother Jim called A Very Outstanding Event. Jim and Ken stayed in contact, and I would receive periodic laconic reports. Now Ken was doing bits at Cinecittà, now he was a reporter for the International *Herald Tribune* in Paris. Presenting the news was Ken's forte, it seemed, for he stayed with it. He even came home to do it on American television.

This, to me, seemed unnaturally forgiving, as if James Joyce had gone home to Dublin to lick his lips at the sight of the

Martello Tower and cry out, "Champion!" Jim and I met Ken for lunch one day in New York; Ken was up for a transfer from New Orleans to New York. So many distances, voyages, in some people's lives. You notice this particularly if, like me, you stay in one place for entire epochs, enthusiastically resisting all opportunities to travel, even to Brooklyn for dinner.

Ken didn't land the New York job. He ended up in Boston, which he said he preferred. To what, I wonder. New York? Paris? His past? He was married and had a little boy, and that got me amazed. Here was a man, flesh of my flesh, only three years older than I, who had already set upon his course of leaving his mark upon the world—and I was still worrying over whether I would ever come upon a copy of the Capitol "Pal Joey" with the original cover. We were brothers, but we weren't entirely related, if you see what I mean.

It turned out that even a Boston television anchorman has to come to New York periodically for meetings, and lunch with Ken and Jim became a regular feature of my life. At one of these dates, looking toward the summer, Ken invited us up to stay with him on Martha's Vineyard. Jim said no, but I was curious. I wanted to see what else I wasn't entirely unrelated to, Ken's wife and son. I had a good time and went again the next year, and it became an annual visit—more than a visit: dues. After three or four of these trips, I felt certain that if I tried to stick out a summer without visiting the Kens they would hale me into court. I had become a participant in their season, a member of my own family.

A certain weekend would be assigned me, set aside, built around the things I was likely to do and say. Ken was a man of Significant Draw, so the trip's logistics had Major Appeal. Zesty, highly inflected metropolitan types, doing this important favor for a friend of a friend of a friend, would pick me up in front of my building, the car packed with cold collation, ambition, and wit. Crowded cars, rigid stages. This is travelling. I hate it but—sometimes—I do it. There was usually one guy too many (besides me), and someone would get stuck with a liverwurst sandwich, and one of the women would want to stop when no one else did, and one of the men would drop a truly ghastly ethnic slur of some kind. (No one would say anything, but the silence was a hiss.) Then, too, the car trip from Manhattan to outer New England must vie with the Damascus-Peking caravan line for density of tedium. Still, eventually I would land at the ferry slip, thinking of some story I might get out of the car people. Soon enough I would be standing on the boat, and I would see my brother and sister-in-law standing with my nephew. I would wave. My brother, whom I understood very well in our youth but now think of as This Guy I Know, or even (Hey) Mister, waves back. He is jaunty, confident, always taller than I remember. He's going to age poisonously well. He's even getting just a bit gray; good career move. My sister-in-law points me out to the little boy, and he'll gaze at me with wonder and suspicion and bashful delight.

So that's what I'm doing on a beach in Massachusetts: sitting in their kitchen at the "breakfast bar," finishing my morning coffee.

Curtain up, and my sister-in-law says, "I wish you and your brother got along better."

"We get along quite well for two people so near yet so far, don't you think?"

"I mean, I wish you acted as if you liked each other. I know you do like each other, of course." She rinses out the name mugs: Ken, Ellen, Toby. "It's just so nice to see him . . . relating?" A paper towel to dry the mugs. My sister-in-law is very neat; her theory of eating implements is, they're either in use or in the cupboards. None of that wet stuff hanging in the porte cochère, or whatever they call those plastic racks next to the sink. You wash it, you dry it. You're brothers, you relate.

"Ken really isn't a big relater," I say. "I expect the television camera has spoiled him. He's gotten so used to addressing a population he probably doesn't know how to talk to one person anymore."

My brother, I gather, is a very hot item among analysts of the 18-to-49 female demographics, but we never mention this to him, because he has fierce aplomb, always did. No wonder he left home without explaining why. Frankly, I don't think he ever did know how to talk to one person; anchormanning is perfect casting for him.

Still, he has what appears to be a highly socialized marriage: his wife likes everything about him, and his son is so young that his occasional testy rebellions pass for standard-make puerile mischief. I think there may be a problem on the brew there, but my sister-in-law sees the three of them as a gang of fun-loving pals. She is very proud of Ken's fame, too. She sends me his clippings. She used to accompany these with warm little notes, trying to explain why she is doing it. Then I told her that in publishing, where time is the first concern, we just write "F.Y.I." on something and send it off. Amused, she has made it a household joke: she will hand me a bowl of rice pudding, indicate the whipped cream with a spy's nod, and murmur, "F.Y.I., friend?"

Anyway, I already know why she is doing this: loyalty and love. She's terrific, but she feels too hard. "You know," she begins, "last night . . ." She looks away, looks back at me.

"O.K., yes," I say, "but please don't cry."

I always know when she will. It's not really crying; she leaks for joy. It's like those sudden, momentary thunder-showers in London, when you look up and see the sun right through the rain. It'll be over shortly. But you still get wet.

"It was just so nice to be all together," she says. "And Toby loves it when you read to him. He won't let anyone else, you know. We have so much trouble getting him to bed in the city. It's different when you're here."

"It's always different where I am. It's in my contract."

"Now, don't make a joke of it. It was so sweet. And I know you know that, so don't look away, either. You and Toby look so cute together, too. And you read so well." She is leaking.

"Toby and I aren't that great a team," I put in. "He's very tough for six. I only read to him so he won't grouch at me."

"Oh, that's not true." She gazes happily around the tidy summer kitchen: the mounted utensils, the standing machines, Toby's watercolors on the wall, Smurf stickers on the fridge, all their little heads carefully cut off. "Grouch at you? It's family! We've got to be our own best friends!"

"I wish you wouldn't enthuse just after breakfast."

"When he has a nightmare . . . Of course, he doesn't often. But when he does, do you know he speaks your name? As if he's worried about you? I've heard him."

"Toby speaks my name?"

"Not Toby. Your brother."

Alarmed, I head for the beach. There's not much else to do out here but eat, sleep, and bake on the sand. You'd think an anchorman would be at a loss here: nothing but individuals to swank around for, at, with. What a waste of an act.

And God knows Ken's got one. The first time we were alone together as adults—at lunch at my neighborhood joint, the Mayfair, at Fifty-third and First—he broke a copious silence by telling me a sure way to fascinate a woman: immediately after, read her a story. He recommended "The Velveteen Rabbit." He said the combination of the sweetness of the fairy tale and the tenderness of lovemaking overwhelms them. Wrong. It isn't the combination—it's the paradox of the aggressiveness of cock and the sudden sweetness of the storybook working for and against each other.

But he's definitely on to something here. Sometimes I try to visualize Ellen lying next to him, listening to him read "The Velveteen Rabbit." I can see it. I can see it more easily than I can see myself on this patch of beach among—forgive me, Ellen—strangers. Still, I'm a game guest. I bring a litre of Johnnie Walker Red. I make my own bed, first thing up, even before the toothpaste. I spell them in looking after Toby. I take us all out to dinner on my last night. And I read my nephew stories.

It started by chance. One evening after dinner three or four years ago, I happened to pick up an ancient Oz book lying next to me on the couch. As I leafed through it, Toby came up and said, "Mine."

His father looked over from six newspapers, including the Manchester *Guardian*. "No, Toby, that's mine," he said. But my name was written on the front free endpaper.

"Read," Toby urged me.

I demurred with some evasion, and he hit me.

"Better read to him," my newscaster brother said, not unamused.

I did read to him, and he listened carefully. All three of them do; and they watch me as they listen. It's like reading one's work in a bookstore. They even unplug the phone. After a while, Toby puts his head in my lap, and after a longer while he falls asleep. Then I carry him upstairs, and his parents follow, his mother to dote and his father to stand in the doorway, framed in the light from the hall as if he had moved from the news to a suspense series. It's film noir; it's coming too close. Sometimes Toby murmurs reproachful excerpts as I put him to bed—"Why didn't you tell me the secret?" or "You are not playing fairly." Surely these are not meant for me, precisely. Not precisely. By then, my brother has moved into the room to put his arms around my sister-in-law from behind. These soft noises there, as I tuck Toby in. He likes to be tightly wrapped, like a present. Then I turn to face them, hugged together as they are, and for a moment I fear they won't let me out of the room.

The beach is always quiet here, nearly deserted well up into a Saturday noontime. I open my spiral notebook and pursue the tale of the moment—about, as usual, things I have seen, done, said. I have got to try writing *fiction*: about the encounter of Nabokov and Tolstoy in Heaven, perhaps "The Goblin Who Missed Thanksgiving." I do not want to write anymore about people I know, people with feelings that I have been tricked into sharing. I should write books like those I read to Toby, set in fabulous places among bizarre creatures. You can say anything you want to in such tales and no reader will wonder who you are. You could be the Velveteen Rabbit.

My sister-in-law comes along after a bit with Toby and several tons of beach equipment. There are flagstaffs to stick in the sand and pails of two sorts, the metal kind decorated with merry scenes and the plastic kind with a side pocket for the toting of a shovel. There are rubber balls, a dead Slinky all coiled up in itself, picture books, drawing tablets, and remnants of a hundred miniature zoos, forts, shopping centers, and such, the pieces recombined in Toby's imagination to form the characters of some dire cosmopolitan epic.

I burrow deep into my notebook as my sister-in-law pulls out the old Modern Library Giant edition of "Ulysses," the orange jacket encased in plastic. She maintains the reading level of an academic but is hurt if you ask why she doesn't do something besides be married to my brother. Or she would be hurt if I dared ask. I've delved into "Ulysses" so often I recently took it up in Italian to keep the quest venturesome. "Ulisse," translated with astonishing resourcefulness by Giulio de Angelis. It comes complete with notes and commentary, just as I do. Yet my sister-in-law knows it better than I, can even recite the chapter titles in order. She holds absolutely still when she reads.

Toby ignores us, digging, patting, piling. A grand, circular moat. A lump of sand in the center. Flags at the perimeter. Soldiers, rustics, exotic animals, and Hollywood extraterrestrials lining up to get in. Toby growls to himself as he works, like a dog fussing at a sock. "I'm making a sand tower," he announces at one point.

When my sister-in-law excuses herself to ready dinner, Toby and I dart suspicious glances at each other. He waits till she disappears over the dunes, then says, "Do you want to help me dribble?"

"Sure."

He hands me a pail and leads the way to the sea. "Look out for octopus," he warns.

He's going to grouch at me, I know. He always does.

"You fill it with water," he says. "It has to be just right. Not like that!"

He keeps pushing me.

"Like this," he says.

It takes me eight dips to satisfy him; apparently the water has to fill the pail tight to the rim without spilling. How often in this life one must negotiate a walk along the blade when the topic at hand is absolutely nothing at all. How often one plays one's life for trivial stakes. With certain people, everything matters.

"Now, watch," says Toby.

This is dribbling: you ease the bottom end of the pail upward, leading the water to plop onto the sand, creating a mason's effect on the walls of your fortress. You decorate your power.

"Now you," says Toby, with a sense of challenge.

"Why don't you show me again? I don't have the feel of it yet."

Growling, he grabs my pail and throws it off to the side. "I didn't like that water," he explains.

I return to my story, a sad tale of growing up and pulling away in a small Southern town. Toby busies himself with his dribbling.

In the city, the scene is fury, speed, and ice, sheer ice. Holding your own, you may accidentally alienate one of the four or five most influential people in your professional or social or romantic life, and you may spend years working off the blunder. But on the beach nothing happens, and everything is forgivable. The happy time crawls past. You can't go wrong.

"Hey, Toby, what's on for dinner?" I ask.

Toby looks out at the sea. "No, there won't be any dinner for us at all. Can birds swim?"

"Why won't there be dinner?"

"My daddy is mad at Mommy, and they aren't going to feed us. I heard them crashing last night, so that means they're mad at someone. Do they like you?"

"Your mother does."

"Is she your sister?"

"No. Your dad is my brother."

"I don't think he likes us."

Toby's dog comes snorting up the beach from the west: a large terrier who moves with the frozen despair of an old man and the mild curiosity of a baby, named, by the child, with a child's logic, Tober.

"Get away, Tober!" Toby screeches. "Get away, you sneaky hound!"

The dog gently investigates the sea, sniffing at the waves. Ken cannot be far away. He is always walking the dog, possibly to see what stir he can inspire with his fame.

Possibly. This is a sophisticated beach, the cream of Boston hip (if there is such a thing). He would be in no danger from autograph crazies. But people would surely recognize him—"as seen on television," the ultimate American credential—and buzz like wasps in a pancake house.

I see my brother in the distance, walking slowly around the curl of a dune, his hands in the pockets of his shorts, the long-thighed light-brown kind you only see on straight men, brothers and fathers.

Tober noses up to Toby, who stares at him for a bit, then gives him a push.

"You aren't very nice to your pet," I venture.

"He comes around too much. And he snapped at the doorman. They bought a muzzle for him. But you know what? I hid it in my toy chest. Sometimes I wear it in my room. Tober isn't really mine anyway. He only likes my father."

My brother is almost upon us now.

"Hey, Tober," I call out. "Here, Tobes."

Tober looks at me, starts over, halts. It's not always easy to know what you're supposed to do in this family.

Toby eyes the beast with disgust. "Make him nap," he says.

And Ken arrives.

"How are you coming, my friend?" my brother asks me. He doesn't act like a newscaster but like a man who might know a few.

"I'm doing just fine."

"Good man. Toby, did you remember to put water in Tober's dish this morning?"

This means Toby didn't, but the boy has unconcernedly returned to his sand tower. "He didn't look thirsty."

"I hate to think that a poor dumb animal is going without water because a little boy was too lazy to bother with him."

Toby and I glance at the dog, quietly settled on his haunches, looking far out to sea. A handsome, suave animal, not the kind to dance on your leg or suddenly begin howling when company comes.

"He was naughty yesterday," says Toby. "So I'm not giving him water for a month."

Toby's father kneels to reason with his son. "Toby," he begins. "You can't punish a living creature by depriving it of food."

Toby looks down, but resolutely. "You took my allowance away," he says.

"That's just money."

"I was going to buy candy with it. Candy is food."

Toby's father grasps Toby's little child's shoulders and tells him, in the voice that tolerantly introduces those irritating responsible opinions of the opposing viewpoint, "Listen here, Toby, have I ever deprived you of nourishment? Have you ever gone hungry?"

"Yes."

"No, you haven't."

"Last week," Toby insists, "you didn't take me to the puppet play."

"That was nearly six months ago, first off, and second, if you remember, you weren't taken to the puppet show because you got chocolate all over the television screen."

Patricide.

"Toby," he goes on, "look at me when I talk to you."

My family is made of those who demand to be looked at when they talk to you and those who look away when they hear. My brother started as a looker-away; now he has to be looked at. No wonder he became a newscaster. An entire city must look at him when he talks. I visualize his television audience sitting before their sets in highchairs, wearing bibs discolored by strained prunes. Their faces are sad as they are reproached and reasoned with.

"Hey," I put in. "Why don't you tell Toby about the time I pushed you off the roof?"

My brother ignores this; Toby looks up.

"I think you'd better take Tober up to the house," my brother goes on, "and see if—"

"What roof? Our roof? Did he push you off that high?"

"Toby—"

Toby looks at me. "When did you push him? Was I there?"

"No. But I was thinking of you at the time."

"What's that supposed to mean?" my brother asks me. "We were kids then."

"I knew you'd have a child someday. I did it for him."

"Thanks a lot."

"He broke his arm," I tell Toby. "I broke your father's arm. He had to wear a cast for a month, and they threw him off the football team." I ask my brother, "Remember?"

"All right now, Toby, you march straight up to the house and assume some responsibility for Tober. He's your dog."

Toby claps his hands like a pasha, and Tober meticulously gets to his feet, capping the motion with an elegant stretch of his spine, from rigid neck to apologetic haunches.

"Tober, come here!" Toby screams. "You mental case!"

"Not so loud," my brother directs. "Go on up, now."

"Keep watch on my sand tower," Toby warns us. "Don't let the other people come and wreck it."

"There are no other people," my brother tells him—one of those apparently aimless statements, mere punctuation from the sound of them, that, on the contrary, burst from the heart. Who but a fifteen-year-old runaway would get so much out of the statement "There are no other people"?

As Toby and the dog proceed up the beach back to the house, I appear engrossed in my work. I am writing gibberish in order to look inaccessible; a useless defense against a man who remembers what you were like when you were eight.

"Ellen says you brought her a present," my brother offers. No one is inaccessible to a newsman. Impenetrable, maybe: but approachable, absolutely.

"I got both of you a present."

"A mayonnaise jar, was it? Sounds very handy."

"It doesn't just hold mayonnaise. It helps make it. The recipe is printed on the glass. Bloomingdale's."

"She really likes you, you know."

Out come the weapons. We estimate our worth in the quality of the people who like us—as witness the hearty bantering that goes on on news shows between the features and the commercial breaks. A Boston friend taped some of my brother's programs for me, and on one of them it seems to me—it *seems*—as if the other newspeople turn their backs on him and cut him out of their banter, leaving him to shift his papers and chuckle at imaginary colleagues out of camera range.

"Toby says you aren't going to give us dinner," I say, as my brother kicks shells and pebbles down at the waterline. "He heard you and Ellen quarrelling."

"Toby's doing a very awkward time nowadays. You shouldn't encourage him. It's hard enough to keep him in line without you telling him stories about brothers throwing each other off roofs."

"Why not? You did it to me and I did it to you. It was the great moment of my childhood. I wanted to share it with him."

My brother works his way onto the crest of the tide flat, kicking gusts of sand as he travels. "You know how easily he gets stirred up," he goes on.

"It's funny how cool you were as a child, and how high-strung Toby is. I wouldn't think passion would run in your family."

"He's just a kid so far." My brother is kicking up whole wads of sand now, aimlessly, business on his mind. "What'll you do with that writing piece when it's done? Does it go in *Granta*?"

"Why are you stamping around in the sand like that?"

He shrugged. "High spirits. Why even ask?"

"Because you've even kicked Toby's sand tower to bits."

My brother sees what he has done.

"I'd hate to be in your sneakers when Toby gets back and sees what you did," I tell him. "He takes his beach sports very seriously."

"So do you."

I have to laugh at that. "I envy Toby his enthusiasms," I say. "He gets such a thrill out of everything, whether he loves them or despises them. He *feels*. Were we ever like that? Puppet plays and candy?"

"I wasn't," my brother says.

"How come you ran away from us?" I suddenly ask. "Do you expect Toby to run away from you?"

He is speechless.

Barking and shouting from across the dunes signal the return of Toby and Tober. They race down to us like a circus on a four-a-day booking. Toby is heading for the water, but his father catches him as he passes, pulls him up, and tosses him into the air as easily. as if he were confetti. Toby says, "Daddy!" with delight as he comes down; only this, but this is enough.

I pet the panting dog.

"Toby," says the newscaster. "Listen to bad news. I wrecked your sand castle. Accidentally. I was kicking at the sand without thinking. I'm sorry."

Openmouthed, Toby turns to me.

"I didn't do it," I warn him.

"What if you get a spanking now?" Toby asks, turning to his father, looking up to find him, taking hold of his hand. "Or no dinner?"

"We don't punish anyone for accidents, Toby," his father lectures. "You know that."

"Yes," Toby agrees. "I have to go finger-paint."

"O.K." His father turns to me. "O.K., my friend?" (Why do *I* have to render an opinion?) My brother slaps Toby's behind lightly and the child runs up the beach, Tober dragging decorously after him.

O.K., he says. Look, don't waste a smile on me—but my brother does, a television smile suited to a quaint human-interest feature, perhaps a convention of street-food aficionados in South Boston. "See you at dinner," he says.

I go back to writing my story. Bits of the day flip into the text, a field expedient. Bits of everyday; it makes people nervous. "You snitched!" a bag lady cried at me once, on Park Avenue.

"No, I didn't," I said; but I was thinking of some story.

"You told how I made a commotion with a cigarillo in the no-smoking section of the Carnegie Cinema show!"

"Never."

"No?"

"No," I repeated.

She shrugged, looked away, and coughed. "So what happens next?"

On the beach, next is always a meal. You pay out a certain

number of minutes and then comes food, the four of us at table, all eyes aimed at some imagined central point of contact. When we gather at the board, I babble, dispersing the attacks. I am like a bag lady in the scattered energy of my references. I speak of Louise Brooks, of "The Egoist," of Schubert's song cycles. They nod. They ask Intelligent Questions. And they *are* intelligent—I mean, they read *Granta*. They feel they must encourage me, my sister-in-law because anyone she is related to becomes wonderful by rules of love loyalty, and my brother because it is not entirely useless, in his line of work, to be connected to a writer. Still, he'll never quite be able to see me as anything but an infant rebel, reckless, bold for his years, but ultimately ineffectual. He treats me like someone who may have to be soothed, even humored, perhaps disarmed, at any moment.

This only exacerbates my defiance, of course. From the moment I enter the house that my brother lives in—to my sister-in-law's welcoming half smile, as warm as one blanket too many on a surprisingly balmy November night—I am at war.

My brother cuts greens for his Caesar salad, which, for some reason, is genuinely cordon bleu. But, then, Ken was always a stickler for High Style in everything he did. I hear, from secure sources, that back in Boston notables of the local great world stare over his shoulder as he prepares it. Oh, it looks simple. Who can't make a salad? They can't—not like his salad, anyway. Theirs is correct; his is superb. They come back again and again to watch him, and he pays them no heed. He acts as if no one should be able to do what he does.

From Toby's room comes the festive din of medleys drawn from the Walt Disney versions of "Snow White," "Pinocchio," and "Alice in Wonderland" on a tape I made for him last year. Occasionally, Toby sings along. I idly glance in at the door. Toby and Tober are sitting on the floor, engrossed in the act of listening; both of them are wearing cowboy hats and neckerchiefs.

When I return to the kitchen, my sister-in-law hands me a glass of white wine. I take it outside to watch the sun burn red over the water. I try to think of my latest story and all this real life. How inconvenient that work merges with truth. I was planning to model myself on Evelyn Waugh, not Thomas Mann. Yet even Waugh turned Mann in the end. Writers have a hundred dodges but a thousand revelations. Every so often, some of my friends ask pettishly why I never write about them. "But I do," I respond, as nicely as possible. Then they grow uneasy.

Amazingly enough, I enjoy these summer visits up here, so far off my turf. I like the break it makes in my city rhythm, the sense the place gives me of owing nothing to everybody—professionally, of course. If only I owed nothing to absolutely anyone socially, emotionally, and historically, I would be white clean free.

A family forms around me as I sit on the deck. Something licks the back of my hand: Tober, on devotion patrol in his capacity as household devotee. My sister-in-law joins us. A breeze animates the scene. Now Toby is here, querulously asking about the parentage of Donald Duck's three nephews. He knows they have none to speak of, but he wants to see what he will be told. His father comes out, balancing his hand on Toby's head as the twilight deepens.

I do not need to look at them to know how it appears. She is gazing upon my brother and he is gazing down at the boy and the boy is gazing at all of us, one after the other. For a moment, I luxuriate in the sentimentality of knowing that, whatever else happens, he will be raised in love. How terrifyingly important that is. Then I feel manipulated by this frenzy of feeling and swear to avenge the dishonor by styling all three of them as villains in my most scabrous stories.

My brother takes my wineglass to refill it, and Toby sits next to me, holding a juice drink poured to resemble a cocktail. "Now you could tell me more about when you pushed my father off the roof," he says.

"I don't think I ought to."

"Why?"

"That's a good question."

"Then why did you tell me before, on the beach?"

"That's an even better one."

"Tell me a story anyway."

"Once upon a time," I begin—for these are the easiest stories to invent and the most comfortable to tell, set hundreds of years ago among perfect strangers—"there was a little boy who lived all by himself in a great sand tower in the middle of a forest."

"What was his name?" Toby asks.

"He had none. He had lived all alone as long as he could remember, so he had never needed a name. One day, a knight rode by on a beautiful black horse, and the knight was encased from head to foot in resplendent silver armor."

"What was the horse's name?" Toby asks.

"Toby, you shouldn't interrupt the storyteller," his mother gently chides, her doting look slipping from him to me and back.

"The knight's armor shone so brilliantly in the sunlight that the little boy, looking down from the window at the very top of his tower, could actually see himself. It was the first time he had ever done so, for there were no mirrors in his tower. None whatsoever. There was no thing to look into, no reflection—"

"Did he have Cinemax?" Toby asks, absently yawning.

"Hush. Now, the little boy was surprised to see the knight. But he was even more surprised to see himself. And from his window high above the forest he called down to the knight, 'Who are you?' "

"Here you go, my friend," says my brother, returning with refills of the drinks.

"But the knight thought the little boy was speaking to his own reflection, and so he said nothing. The little boy was consumed with wonder, for he suddenly realized that he must be lonely in his tower. He longed to go down and say hello to the knight and find out some things about the world. But there was no way down through the tower. Nor was there any way for the knight to climb up to him. The little boy felt very sad."

Toby stretches out with his head in my lap.

"The knight was sad, too, for he had been wandering in the forest for many days, having lost his way. He feared he might wander forever, for this forest was so big that no one who strayed into it from outside ever found his way out. But there was nothing for the knight to do but move on, and he spurred his horse to pursue his journey. The little boy again cried out, 'Who are you?' But the knight happened to be passing behind a great oak tree, which hid his armor from sight and thus cut off the boy's reflection. So this time the knight assumed he was being addressed, and he thought he should answer the question. He should tell the little boy who he was. . . ."

Toby has fallen asleep.

"This tyke is all tuckered out," I tell his parents. "He didn't even wait for dinner."

"Did Ken read to you?" my sister-in-law asks. "When you were boys?"

"He didn't have to. I wasn't grouchy."

"Did he?"

She is looking at him and he is looking at her.

"Well, my mother didn't, and my dad was away a lot. . . ." Now they are looking at me. "I suppose somebody had to do the reading."

She takes his hand. "*Did* he?"

"Please don't leak."

"Don't what?"

"When the little boy asked the knight who he was, what did the knight answer?" my brother asks.

I look at him for a moment. "He answered, 'I have the same name as you.'"

My brother frowns. "Unusual repartee."

Toby stirs in my arms.

"I have the same name," I observe, "as all of you."

My sister-in-law smiles. But my brother, puzzled once too often this day, looks at me as if he does not know who I am.

goodbye, my brother

JOHN CHEEVER

we are a family that has always been very close in spirit. Our father was drowned in a sailing accident when we were young, and our mother has always stressed the fact that our familial relationships have a kind of permanence that we will never meet with again. I don't think about the family much, but when I remember its members and the coast where they lived and the sea salt that I think is in our blood, I am happy to recall that I am a Pommeroy—that I have the nose, the coloring, and the promise of longevity—and that while we are not a distinguished family, we enjoy the illusion, when we are together, that the Pommeroys are unique. I don't say any of this because I'm interested in family history or because this sense of uniqueness is deep or important to me but in order to advance the point that we are loyal to one another in spite of our differences, and that any rupture in this loyalty is a source of confusion and pain.

We are four children; there is my sister Diana and the three men—Chaddy, Lawrence, and myself. Like most families in which the children are out of their twenties, we have been separated by business, marriage, and war. Helen and I live on Long Island now, with our four children. I teach in a secondary school, and I am past the age where I expect to be made headmaster— or principal, as we say—but I respect the work. Chaddy, who has done better than the rest of us, lives in Manhattan, with Odette and their children. Mother lives in Philadelphia, and Diana, since her divorce, has been living in France, but she comes back to the States in the summer to spend a month at Laud's Head. Laud's Head is a summer place on the shore of one of the Massachusetts islands. We used to have a cottage there, and in the twenties our father built the big house. It stands on a cliff above the sea and, excepting St. Tropez and some of the Apennine villages, it is my favorite place in the world. We each have an equity in the place and we contribute some money to help keep it going.

Our youngest brother, Lawrence, who is a lawyer, got a job with a Cleveland firm after the war, and none of us saw him for four years. When he decided to leave Cleveland and go to work for a firm in Albany, he wrote Mother that he would, between jobs, spend ten days at Laud's Head, with his wife and their two children. This was when I had planned to take my vacation—I had been teaching summer school—and Helen and Chaddy and Odette and Diana were all going to be there, so the family would be together. Lawrence is the member of the family with whom the rest of us have least in common. We have never seen a great deal of him, and I suppose that's why we still call him Tifty—a nickname he was given when he was a child, because when he came down the hall toward the dining room for breakfast, his slippers made a noise that sounded like "Tifty, tifty, tifty." That's what Father called him, and so did everyone else. When he grew older, Diana sometimes used to call him Little Jesus, and Mother often called him the Croaker. We had disliked Lawrence, but we looked forward to his return with a mixture of apprehension and loyalty, and with some of the joy and delight of reclaiming a brother.

Lawrence crossed over from the mainland on the four-o'clock boat one afternoon late in the summer, and Chaddy and I went down to meet him. The arrivals and departures of the summer ferry have all the outward signs that suggest a voyage—whistles, bells, hand trucks, reunions, and the smell of brine—but it is a voyage of no import, and when I watched the boat come into the blue harbor that afternoon and thought that it was completing a voyage of no import, I realized that I had hit on exactly the kind of observation that Lawrence would have made. We looked for his face behind the windshields as the cars drove off the boat, and we had no trouble in recognizing him. And we ran over and shook his hand and clumsily kissed his wife and the children. "Tifty!" Chaddy shouted. "Tifty!" It is difficult to judge changes in the appearance of a brother, but both Chaddy and I agreed, as we drove back to Laud's Head, that Lawrence still looked very young. He got to the house first, and we took the suitcases out of his car. When I came in, he was standing in the living room, talking with Mother and Diana. They were in their best clothes and all their jewelry, and they were welcoming him extravagantly, but even then, when everyone was endeavoring to seem most affectionate and at a time when these endeavors come easiest, I was aware of a faint tension in the room. Thinking about this as I carried Lawrence's heavy suitcases up the stairs, I realized that our dislikes are as deeply ingrained as our better passions, and I remembered that once, twenty-five years ago, when I had hit Lawrence on the head with a rock, he had picked himself up and gone directly to our father to complain.

I carried the suitcases up to the third floor, where Ruth, Lawrence's wife, had begun to settle her family. She is a thin girl, and she seemed very tired from the journey, but when I asked her if she didn't want me to bring a drink upstairs to her, she said she didn't think she did.

When I got downstairs, Lawrence wasn't around, but the others were all ready for cocktails, and we decided to go ahead. Lawrence is the only member of the family who has never enjoyed drinking. We took our cocktails onto the terrace, so that we could see the bluffs and the sea and the islands in the east, and that the return of Lawrence and his wife, their presence in the house, seemed to refresh our responses to the familiar view; it was as if the pleasure they would take in the sweep and the color of that coast, after such a long absence, had been imparted to us. While we were there, Lawrence came up the path from the beach.

"Isn't the beach fabulous, Tifty?" Mother asked. "Isn't it fabulous to be back? Will you have a Martini?"

"I don't care," Lawrence said. "Whiskey, gin—I don't care what I drink. Give me a little rum."

"We don't have any *rum*," Mother said. It was the first note of asperity. She had taught us never to be indecisive, never to reply as Lawrence had. Beyond this, she is deeply concerned with the propriety of her house, and anything irregular by her standards, like drinking straight rum or bringing a beer can to the dinner table, excites in her a conflict that she cannot, even with her capacious sense of humor, surmount. She sensed the asperity and worked to repair it. "Would you like some Irish, Tifty dear?" she said. "Isn't Irish what you've always liked? There's some Irish on the sideboard. Why don't you get yourself some Irish?" Lawrence said that he didn't care. He poured himself a Martini, and then Ruth came down and we went in to dinner.

In spite of the fact that we had, through waiting for Lawrence, drunk too much before dinner, we were all anxious to put our best foot forward and to enjoy a peaceful time. Mother is a small woman whose face is still a striking reminder of how pretty she must have been, and whose conversation is unusually light, but she talked that evening about a soil-reclamation project that is going on up-island. Diana is as pretty as Mother must have been; she is an animated and lovely woman who likes to talk about the dissolute friends that she has made in France, but she talked that night about the school in Switzerland where she had left her two children. I could see that the dinner had been planned to please Lawrence. It was not too rich, and there was nothing to make him worry about extravagance.

After supper, when we went back onto the terrace, the clouds held that kind of light that looks like blood, and I was glad that Lawrence had such a lurid sunset for his homecoming. When we had been out there a few minutes, a man named Edward Chester came to get Diana. She had met him in France, or on the boat home, and he was staying for ten days at the inn in the village. He was introduced to Lawrence and Ruth, and then he and Diana left.

"Is that the one she's sleeping with now?" Lawrence asked.

"What a horrid thing to say!" Helen said.

"You ought to apologize for that, Tifty," Chaddy said.

"I don't know," Mother said tiredly. "I don't know, Tifty. Diana is in a position to do whatever she wants, and I don't ask sordid questions. She's my only daughter. I don't see her often."

"Is she going back to France?"

"She's going back the week after next."

Lawrence and Ruth were sitting at the edge of the terrace, not in the chairs, not in the circle of chairs. With his mouth set, my brother looked to me then like a Puritan cleric. Sometimes, when I try to understand his frame of mind, I think of the beginnings of our family in this country, and his disapproval of Diana and her lover reminded me of this. The branch of the Pommeroys to which we belong was founded by a minister who was eulogized by Cotton Mather for his untiring abjuration of the Devil. The Pommeroys were ministers until the middle of the nineteenth century, and the harshness of their thought—man is full of misery, and all earthly beauty is lustful and corrupt—has been preserved in books and sermons. The temper of our family changed somewhat and became more lighthearted, but when I was of school age, I can remember a cousinage of old men and women who seemed to hark back to the dark days of the ministry and to be animated by perpetual guilt and the deification of the scourge. If you are raised in this atmosphere—and in a sense we were—I think it is a trial of the spirit to reject its habits of guilt, self-denial, taciturnity, and penitence, and it seemed to me to have been a trial of the spirit in which Lawrence had succumbed.

"Is that Cassiopeia?" Odette asked.

"No, dear," Chaddy said. "That isn't Cassiopeia."

"Who was Cassiopeia?" Odette said.

"She was the wife of Cepheus and the mother of Andromeda," I said.

"The cook is a Giants fan," Chaddy said. "She'll give you even money that they win the pennant."

It had grown so dark that we could see the passage of light through the sky from the lighthouse at Cape Heron. In the dark below the cliff, the continual detonations of the surf sounded. And then, as she often does when it is getting dark and she has drunk too much before dinner, Mother began to talk about the improvements and additions that would someday be made on the house, the wings and bathrooms and gardens.

"This house will be in the sea in five years," Lawrence said.

"Tifty the Croaker," Chaddy said.

"Don't call me Tifty," Lawrence said.

"Little Jesus," Chaddy said.

"The sea wall is badly cracked," Lawrence said. "I looked at it this afternoon. You had it repaired four years ago, and it cost eight thousand dollars. You can't do that every four years."

"Please, Tifty," Mother said.

"Facts are facts," Lawrence said, "and it's a damned-fool idea to build a house at the edge of the cliff on a sinking coastline. In my lifetime, half the garden has washed away and there's four feet of water where we used to have a bathhouse."

"Let's have a very *general* conversation." Mother said bitterly. "Let's talk about politics or the boat-club dance."

"As a matter of fact," Lawrence said, "the house is probably in some danger now. If you had an unusually high sea, a hurricane sea, the wall would crumble and the house would go. We could all be drowned."

"I can't *bear* it," Mother said. She went into the pantry and came back with a full glass of gin.

I have grown too old now to think that I can judge the sentiments of others, but I was conscious of the tension between Lawrence and Mother, and I knew some of the history of it. Lawrence couldn't have been more than sixteen years old when he decided that Mother was frivolous, mischievous, destructive, and overly strong. When he had determined this, he decided to separate himself from her. He was at boarding school then, and I remember that he did not come home for Christmas. He spent

Christmas with a friend. He came home very seldom after he had made his unfavorable judgment on Mother, and when he did come home, he always tried, in his conversation, to remind her of his estrangement. When he married Ruth, he did not tell Mother. He did not tell her when his children were born. But in spite of these principled and lengthy exertions he seemed, unlike the rest of us, never to have enjoyed any separation, and when they are together, you feel at once a tension, an unclearness.

And it was unfortunate, in a way, that Mother should have picked that night to get drunk. It's her privilege, and she doesn't get drunk often, and fortunately she wasn't bellicose, but we were all conscious of what was happening. As she quietly drank her gin, she seemed sadly to be parting from us; she seemed to be in the throes of travel. Then her mood changed from travel to injury, and the few remarks she made were petulant and irrelevant. When her glass was nearly empty, she stared angrily at the dark air in front of her nose, moving her head a little, like a fighter. I knew that there was not room in her mind then for all the injuries that were crowding into it. Her children were stupid, her husband was drowned, her servants were thieves, and the chair she sat in was uncomfortable. Suddenly she put down her empty glass and interrupted Chaddy, who was talking about baseball. "I know one *thing*," she said hoarsely. "I know that if there is an afterlife, I'm going to have a very different kind of family. I'm going to have nothing but fabulously rich, witty, and enchanting children." She got up and, starting for the door, nearly fell. Chaddy caught her and helped her up the stairs. I could hear their tender good-nights, and then Chaddy came back. I thought that Lawrence by now would be tired from his journey and his return, but he remained on the terrace, as if he were waiting to see the final malfeasance, and the rest of us left him there and went swimming in the dark.

When I woke the next morning, or half woke, I could hear the sound of someone rolling the tennis court. It is a fainter and a deeper sound than the iron buoy bells off the point—an unrhythmic iron chiming—that belongs in my mind to the

beginnings of a summer day, a good portent. When I went downstairs, Lawrence's two kids were in the living room, dressed in
ornate cowboy suits. They are frightened and skinny children.
They told me their father was rolling the tennis court but that
they did not want to go out because they had seen a snake under
the doorstep. I explained to them that their cousins—all the
other children—ate breakfast in the kitchen and that they'd better run along in there. At this announcement, the boy began to
cry. Then his sister joined him. They cried as if to go in the
kitchen and eat would destroy their most precious rights. I told
them to sit down with me. Lawrence came in, and I asked him if
he wanted to play some tennis. He said no, thanks, although he
thought he might play some singles with Chaddy. He was in the
right here, because both he and Chaddy play better tennis than
I, and he did play same singles with Chaddy after breakfast, but
later on, when the others came down to play family doubles,
Lawrence disappeared. This made me cross—unreasonably so, I
suppose—but we play darned interesting family doubles and he
could have played in a set for the sake of courtesy.

Late in the morning, when I came up from the court alone, I
saw Tifty on the terrace, prying up a shingle from the wall with
his jackknife. "What's the matter, Lawrence?" I said. "Termites?"
There are termites in the wood and they've given us a lot of
trouble.

He pointed out to me, at the base of each row of shingles, a
faint blue line of carpenter's chalk. "This house is about twenty-
two years old," he said. "These shingles are about two hundred
years old. Dad must have bought shingles from all the farms
around here when he built the place, to make it look venerable.
You can still see the carpenter's chalk put down where these
antiques were nailed into place."

It was true about the shingles, although I had forgotten it.
When the house was built, our father, or his architect, had ordered
it covered with lichened and weather-beaten shingles. I didn't follow Lawrence's reasons for thinking that this was scandalous.

"And look at these doors," Lawrence said. "Look at these doors
and window frames." I followed him over to a big Dutch door

that opens onto the terrace and looked at it. It was a relatively new door, but someone had worked hard to conceal its newness. The surface had been deeply scored with some metal implement, and white paint had been rubbed into the incisions to imitate brine, lichen, and weather rot. "Imagine spending thousands of dollars to make a sound house look like a wreck," Lawrence said. "Imagine the frame of mind this implies. Imagine wanting to live so much in the past that you'll pay men carpenters' wages to disfigure your front door." Then I remembered Lawrence's sensitivity to time and his sentiments and opinions about our feelings for the past. I had heard him say, years ago, that we and our friends and our part of the nation, finding ourselves unable to cope with the problems of the present, had, like a wretched adult, turned back to what we supposed was a happier and a simpler time, and that our taste for reconstruction and candlelight was a measure of this irremediable failure. The faint blue line of chalk had reminded him of these ideas, the scarified door had reinforced them, and now clue after clue presented itself to him—the stern light at the door, the bulk of the chimney, the width of the floorboards and the pieces set into them to resemble pegs. While Lawrence was lecturing me on these frailties, the others came up from the court. As soon as Mother saw Lawrence, she responded, and I saw that there was little hope of any rapport between the matriarch and the changeling. She took Chaddy's arm. "Let's go swimming and have Martinis on the beach," she said. "Let's have a *fabulous* morning."

The sea that morning was a solid color, like verd stone. Everyone went to the beach but Tifty and Ruth. "I don't mind *him*," Mother said. She was excited, and she tipped her glass and spilled some gin into the sand. "I don't mind *him*. It doesn't matter to me how *rude* and *horrid* and *gloomy* he is, but what I can't bear are the faces of his wretched little children, those fabulously unhappy little children." With the height of the cliff between us, everyone talked wrathfully about Lawrence; about how he had grown worse instead of better, how unlike the rest of us he was, how he endeavored to spoil every pleasure. We drank our gin; the abuse seemed to reach a crescendo, and then, one by one, we went swimming in the solid green water. But when we came out no one mentioned Lawrence unkindly; the line of abusive conversation had been cut, as if swimming had the cleansing force claimed for baptism. We dried our hands and lighted cigarettes, and if Lawrence was mentioned, it was only to suggest, kindly, something that might please him. Wouldn't he like to sail to Barin's cove, or go fishing?

And now I remember that while Lawrence was visiting us, we went swimming oftener than we usually do, and I think there was a reason for this. When the irritability that accumulated as a result of his company began to lessen our patience, not only with Lawrence but with one another, we would all go swimming and shed our animus in the cold water. I can see the family now, smarting from Lawrence's rebukes as they sat on the sand, and I can see them wading and diving and surface-diving and hear in their voices the restoration of patience and the rediscovery of inexhaustible good will. If Lawrence noticed this change—this illusion of purification—I suppose that he would have found in the vocabulary of psychiatry, or the mythology of the Atlantic, some circumspect name for it, but I don't think he noticed the change. He neglected to name the curative powers of the open sea, but it was one of the few chances for diminution that he missed.

The cook we had that year was a Polish woman named Anna Ostrovick, a summer cook. She was first-rate—a big, fat, hearty, industrious woman who took her work seriously. She liked to cook and to have the food she cooked appreciated and eaten, and whenever we saw her, she always urged us to eat. She cooked hot bread—crescents and brioches—for breakfast two or three times a week, and she would bring these into the dining room herself and say, "Eat, eat, eat!" When the maid took the serving dishes back into the pantry, we could sometimes hear Anna, who was standing there, say, "Good! They eat." She fed the garbage man, the milkman, and the gardener. "Eat!" she told them. "Eat, eat!" On Thursday afternoons, she went to the movies with the maid, but she didn't enjoy the movies, because the actors were all so thin. She would sit in the dark theatre for an hour and a half watching the screen anxiously for the appearance of someone who had enjoyed his food. Bette Davis merely left with Anna the impression of a woman who has not eaten well. "They are all so skinny," she would say when she left the movies. In the evenings, after she had gorged all of us, and washed the pots and pans, she would collect the table scraps and go out to feed the creation. We had a few chickens that year, and although they would have roosted by then, she would dump food into their troughs and urge the sleeping fowl to eat. She fed the songbirds in the orchard and the chipmunks in the yard. Her appearance at the edge of the garden and her urgent voice—we could hear her calling "Eat, eat, eat"—had become, like the sunset gun at the boat club and the passage of light from Cape Heron, attached to that hour. "Eat, eat, eat," we could hear Anna say. "Eat, eat . . ." Then it would be dark.

When Lawrence had been there three days, Anna called me into the kitchen. "You tell your mother," she said, "that *he* doesn't come into my kitchen. If *he* comes into my kitchen all the time, I go. *He* is always coming into my kitchen to tell me what a sad woman I am. He is always telling me that I work too hard and that I don't get paid enough and that I should belong to a union with vacations. Ha! He is so skinny but he is always coming into my kitchen when I am busy to pity me, but I am as good as him, I am as good as *anybody*, and I do not have to have people like that getting into my way all the time and feeling sorry for me. I am a famous and a wonderful cook and I have jobs everywhere and the only reason I come here to work this summer is because I was never before on an island, but I can have other jobs tomorrow, and if he is always coming into my kitchen to pity me, you tell your mother I am going. I am as good as *anybody* and I do not have to have that skinny all the time telling how poor I am."

I was pleased to find that the cook was on our side, but I felt that the situation was delicate. If Mother asked Lawrence to stay out of the kitchen, he would make a grievance out of the request. He could make a grievance out of anything, and it sometimes seemed that as he sat darkly at the dinner table, every word of disparagement, wherever it was aimed, came home to him. I didn't mention the cook's complaint to anyone, but somehow there wasn't any more trouble from that quarter.

The next cause for contention that I had from Lawrence came over our backgammon games.

When we are at Laud's Head, we play a lot of backgammon. At eight o'clock, after we have drunk our coffee, we usually get out the board. In a way, it is one of our pleasantest hours. The lamps in the room are still unlighted, Anna can be seen in the dark garden, and in the sky above her head there are continents of shadow and fire. Mother turns on the light and rattles the dice as a signal. We usually play three games apiece, each with the others. We play for money, and you can win or lose a hundred dollars on a game, but the stakes are usually much lower. I think that Lawrence used to play—I can't remember—but he doesn't play any more. He doesn't gamble. This is not because he is poor or because he has any principles about gambling but because he thinks the game is foolish and a waste of time. He was ready enough, however, to waste his time watching the rest of us play. Night after night, when the game began, he pulled a chair up beside the board, and watched the checkers and the dice. His expression was scornful, and yet he watched carefully. I wondered why he watched us night after night, and, through watching his face, I think that I may have found out.

Lawrence doesn't gamble, so he can't understand the excitement of winning and losing money. He has forgotten how to play the game, I think, so that its complex odds can't interest him. His observations were bound to include the facts that backgammon is an idle game and a game of chance, and that the board, marked with points, was a symbol of our worthlessness. And since he doesn't understand gambling or the odds of the game, I thought that what interested him must be the members of his family. One night when I was playing with Odette—I had won thirty-seven dollars from Mother and Chaddy—I think I saw what was going on in his mind.

Odette has black hair and black eyes. She is careful never to expose her white skin to the sun for long, so the striking contrast of blackness and pallor is not changed in the summer. She needs

and deserves admiration—it is the element that contents her—
and she will flirt, unseriously, with any man. Her shoulders were
bare that night, her dress was cut to show the division of her
breasts and to show her breasts when she leaned over the board
to play. She kept losing and flirting and making her losses seem
like a part of the flirtation. Chaddy was in the other room. She
lost three games, and when the third game ended, she fell back
on the sofa and, looking at me squarely, said something about
going out on the dunes to settle the score. Lawrence heard her. I
looked at Lawrence. He seemed shocked and gratified at the
same time, as if he had suspected all along that we were not playing for anything so insubstantial as money. I may be wrong, of
course, but I think that Lawrence felt that in watching our
backgammon he was observing the progress of a mordant tragedy
in which the money we won and lost served as a symbol for
more vital forfeits. It is like Lawrence to try to read significance
and finality into every gesture that we make, and it is certain of
Lawrence that when he finds the inner logic to our conduct, it
will be sordid.

Chaddy came in to play with me. Chaddy and I have never
liked to lose to each other. When we were younger, we used to
be forbidden to play games together, because they always ended
in a fight. We think we know each other's mettle intimately. I
think he is prudent; he thinks I am foolish. There is always bad
blood when we play anything—tennis or backgammon or soft-
ball or bridge—and it does seem at times as if we were playing
for the possession of each other's liberties. When I lose to
Chaddy, I can't sleep. All this is only half the truth of our competitive relationship, but it was the half-truth that would be discernible to Lawrence, and his presence at the table made me so
self-conscious that I lost two games. I tried not to seem angry
when I got up from the board. Lawrence was watching me. I
went out onto the terrace to suffer there in the dark the anger I
always feel when I lose to Chaddy.

When I came back into the room, Chaddy and Mother were
playing Lawrence was still watching. By his lights, Odette had lost
her virtue to me, I had lost my self-esteem to Chaddy, and now

I wondered what he saw in the present match. He watched rapt-ly, as if the opaque checkers and the marked board served for an exchange of critical power. How dramatic the board, in its ring of light, and the quiet players and the crash of the sea outside must have seemed to him! Here was spiritual cannibalism made visible; here, under his nose, were the symbols of the rapacious use human beings make of one another.

Mother plays a shrewd, an ardent, and an interfering game. She always has her hands in her opponent's board. When she plays with Chaddy, who is her favorite, she plays intently. Lawrence would have noticed this. Mother is a sentimental woman. Her heart is good and easily moved by tears and frailty, a characteris-tic that, like her handsome nose, has not been changed at all by age. Grief in another provokes her deeply, and she seems at times to be trying to divine in Chaddy some grief, some loss, that she can succor and redress, and so re-establish the relationship that she enjoyed with him when he was sickly and young. She loves defending the weak and the childlike, and now that we are old, she misses it. The world of debts and business, men and war, hunting and fishing has on her an exacerbating effect. (When Father drowned, she threw away his fly rods and his guns.) She has lectured us all endlessly on self-reliance, but when we come back to her for comfort and for help— particularly Chaddy—she seems to feel most like herself. I suppose Lawrence thought that the old woman and her son were playing for each other's soul.

She lost. "Oh *dear*," she said. She looked stricken and bereaved, as she always does when she loses. "Get me my glasses, get me my checkbook, get me something to drink." Lawrence got up at last and stretched his legs. He looked at us all bleakly. The wind and the sea had risen, and I thought that if he heard the waves, he must hear them only as a dark answer to all his dark questions; that he would think that the tide had expunged the embers of our picnic fires. The company of a lie is unbearable, and he seemed like the embodiment of a lie. I couldn't explain to him the simple and intense pleasures of playing for money, and it seemed to me hideously wrong that he should have sat at the edge of the board and concluded that we were playing for one another's soul. He walked restlessly around the room two or three times and then, as usual, gave us a parting shot. "I should think you'd go crazy," he said, "cooped up with one another like this, night after night. Come on, Ruth. I'm going to bed."

That night, I dreamed about Lawrence. I saw his plain face magnified into ugliness, and when I woke in the morning, I felt sick, as if I had suffered a great spiritual loss while I slept, like the loss of courage and heart. It was foolish to let myself be troubled by my brother. I needed a vacation. I needed to relax. At school, we live in one of the dormitories, we eat at the house table, and we never get away. I not only teach English winter and summer but I work in the principal's office and fire the pistol at track meets. I needed to get away from this and from every other form of anxiety, and I decided to avoid my brother. Early that day, I took Helen and the children sailing, and we stayed out until suppertime. The next day, we went on a picnic. Then I had to go to New York for a day, and when I got back, there was the costume dance at the boat club. Lawrence wasn't going to this, and it's a party where I always have a wonderful time.

The invitations that year said to come as you wish you were. After several conversations, Helen and I had decided what to wear. The thing she most wanted to be again, she said, was a bride, and so she decided to wear her wedding dress. I thought this was a good choice—sincere, lighthearted, and inexpensive. Her choice influenced mine, and I decided to wear an old football uniform. Mother decided to go as Jenny Lind, because there was an old Jenny Lind costume in the attic. The others decided to rent costumes, and when I went to New York, I got the clothes. Lawrence and Ruth didn't enter into any of this.

Helen was on the dance committee, and she spent most of Friday decorating the club. Diana and Chaddy and I went sailing. Most of the sailing that I do these days is in Manhasset, and I am used to setting a homeward course by the gasoline barge and the tin roofs of the boat shed, and it was a pleasure that afternoon, as we returned, to keep the bow on a white church spire in the village and to find even the inshore water green and clear. At the end of our sail, we stopped at the club to get Helen. The committee had been trying to give a submarine appearance to the ballroom, and the fact that they had nearly succeeded in accomplishing this illusion made Helen very happy. We drove back to Laud's Head. It had been a brilliant afternoon, but on the way home we could smell the east wind—the dark wind, as Lawrence would have said—coming in from the sea.

My wife, Helen, is thirty-eight, and her hair would be gray, I guess, if it were not dyed, but it is dyed an unobtrusive yellow—a faded color—and I think it becomes her. I mixed cocktails that night while she was dressing, and when I took a glass upstairs to her, I saw her for the first time since our marriage in her wedding dress. There would be no point in saying that she looked to me more beautiful than she did on our wedding day, but because I have grown older and have, I think, a greater depth of feeling, and because I could see in her face that night both youth and age, both her devotion to the young woman that she had been and the positions that she had yielded graciously to time, I think I have never been so deeply moved. I had already put on the football uniform, and the weight of it, the heaviness of the pants and the shoulder guards, had worked a change in me, as if in putting on these old clothes I had put off the reasonable anxieties and troubles of my life. It felt as if we had both returned to the years before our marriage, the years before the war.

The Collards had a big dinner party before the dance, and our family—excepting Lawrence and Ruth—went to this. We drove over to the club, through the fog, at about half past nine. The orchestra was playing a waltz. While I was checking my raincoat, someone hit me on the back. It was Chucky Ewing, and the funny thing was that Chucky had on a football uniform. This seemed comical as hell to both of us. We were laughing when we went down the hall to the dance floor. I stopped at the door to look at the party, and it was beautiful. The committee had hung fish nets around the sides and over the high ceiling. The nets on the ceiling were filled with colored balloons. The light was soft and uneven, and the people—our friends and neighbors—dancing in the soft light to "Three O'Clock in the Morning" made a pretty picture. Then I noticed the number of women dressed in white, and I realized that they, like Helen, were wearing wedding dresses. Patsy Hewitt and Mrs. Gear and the Lackland girl waltzed by, dressed as brides. Then Pep Talcott came over to where Chucky and I were standing. He was dressed to be Henry VIII, but he told us that the Auerbach twins and Henry Barrett and Dwight MacGregor were all wearing football uniforms, and that by the last count there were ten brides on the floor.

This coincidence, this funny coincidence, kept everybody laughing, and made this one of the most lighthearted parties we've ever had at the club. At first I thought that the women had planned with one another to wear wedding dresses, but the ones that I danced with said it was a coincidence and I'm sure that Helen had made her decision alone. Everything went smoothly for me until a little before midnight. I saw Ruth standing at the edge of the floor. She was wearing a long red dress. It was all wrong. It wasn't the spirit of the party at all. I danced with her, but no one cut in, and I was darned if I'd spend the rest of the night dancing with her and I asked her where Lawrence was. She said he was out on the dock, and I took her over to the bar and left her and went out to get Lawrence.

The east fog was thick and wet, and he was alone on the dock. He was not in costume. He had not even bothered to get himself up as a fisherman or a sailor. He looked particularly saturnine. The fog blew around us like a cold smoke. I wished that it had been a clear night, because the easterly fog seemed to play into my misanthropic brother's hands. And I knew that the buoys— the groaners and bells that we could hear then—would sound to him like half-human, half-drowned cries, although every sailor knows that buoys are necessary and reliable fixtures, and I knew that the foghorn at the lighthouse would mean wanderings and losses to him and that he could misconstrue the vivacity of the dance music. "Come on in, Tifty," I said, "and dance with your wife or get her some partners."

"Why should I?" he said. "Why should I?" And he walked to the window and looked in at the party. "Look at it," he said. "Look at that . . ."

Chucky Ewing had got hold of a balloon and was trying to organize a scrimmage line in the middle of the floor. The others were dancing a samba. And I knew that Lawrence was looking bleakly at the party as he had looked at the weather-beaten shingles on our house, as if he saw here an abuse and a distortion of time; as if in wanting to be brides and football players we exposed the fact that, the lights of youth having been put out in us, we had been unable to find other lights to go by and, destitute of faith and principle, had become foolish and sad. And that he was thinking this about so many kind and happy and generous people made me angry, made me feel for him such an unnatural abhorrence that I was ashamed, for he is my brother and a Pommeroy. I put my arm around his shoulders and tried to force him to come in, but he wouldn't.

I got back in time for the Grand March, and after the prizes had been given out for the best costumes, they let the balloons down. The room was hot, and someone opened the big doors onto the dock, and the easterly wind circled the room and went out, carrying across the dock and out onto the water most of the balloons. Chucky Ewing went running out after the balloons, and when he saw them pass the dock and settle on the water, he took off his football uniform and dove in. Then Eric Auerbach dove in and Lew Phillips dove in and I dove in, and you know how it is at a party after midnight when people start jumping into the water. We recovered most of the balloons and dried off and went on dancing, and we didn't get home until morning.

The next day was the day of the flower show. Mother and Helen and Odette all had entries. We had a pickup lunch, and Chaddy drove the women and children over to the show. I took a nap, and in the middle of the afternoon I got some trunks and a towel and, on leaving the house, passed Ruth in the laundry. She was washing clothes. I don't know why she should seem to have so much more work to do than anyone else, but she is always washing or ironing or mending clothes. She may have been taught, when she was young, to spend her time like this, or she may be at the mercy of an expiatory passion. She seems to scrub and iron with a penitential fervor, although I can't imagine what it is that she thinks she's done wrong. Her children were with her in the laundry. I offered to take them to the beach, but they didn't want to go.

It was late in August, and the wild grapes that grow profusely all over the island made the land wind smell of wine. There is a little grove of holly at the end of the path, and then you climb the dunes, where nothing grows but that coarse grass. I could hear the sea, and I remember thinking how Chaddy and I used to talk mystically about the sea. When we were young, we had decided that we could never live in the West because we would miss the sea. "It is very nice here," we used to say politely when we visited people in the mountains, "but we miss the Atlantic." We used to look down our noses at people from Iowa and Colorado who had been denied this revelation, and we scorned the Pacific. Now I could hear the waves, whose heaviness sounded like a reverberation, like a tumult, and it pleased me as it had pleased me when I was young, and it seemed to have a purgative force, as if it had cleared my memory of, among other things, the penitential image of Ruth in the laundry.

But Lawrence was on the beach. There he sat. I went in without speaking. The water was cold, and when I came out, I put on a shirt. I told him that I was going to walk up to Tanners Point, and he said that he would come with me. I tried to walk beside him. His legs are no longer than mine, but he always likes to stay a little ahead of his companion. Walking along behind him, looking at his bent head and his shoulders, I wondered what he could make of that landscape.

There were the dunes and cliffs, and then, where they declined, there were some fields that had begun to turn from green to brown and yellow. The fields were used for pasturing sheep, and I guess Lawrence would have noticed that the soil was eroded and that the sheep would accelerate this decay. Beyond the fields there are a few coastal farms, with square and pleasant buildings, but Lawrence could have pointed out the hard lot of an island farmer. The sea, at our other side, was the open sea. We always tell guests that there, to the east, lies the coast of Portugal, and for Lawrence it would be an easy step from the coast of Portugal to the tyranny in Spain. The waves broke with a noise like a "hurrah, hurrah, hurrah," but to Lawrence they would say *"Vale, vale."* I suppose it would have occurred to his baleful and incisive mind that the coast was terminal moraine, the edge of the prehistoric world, and it must have occurred to him that we walked along the edge of the known world in spirit as much as in fact. If he should otherwise have overlooked this, there were some Navy planes bombing an uninhabited island to remind him.

That beach is a vast and preternaturally clean and simple landscape. It is like a piece of the moon. The surf had pounded the floor solid, so it was easy walking, and everything left on the sand had been twice changed by the waves. There was the spine of a shell, a broomstick, part of a bottle and part of a brick, both of them milled and broken until they were nearly unrecognizable, and I suppose Lawrence's sad frame of mind—for he kept his head down—went from one broken thing to another. The company of his pessimism began to infuriate me, and I caught up with him and put a hand on his shoulder. "It's only a summer day, Tifty," I said. "It's only a summer day. What's the matter? Don't you like it here?"

"I don't like it here," he said blandly, without raising his eyes. "I'm going to sell my equity in the house to Chaddy. I didn't expect to have a good time. The only reason I came back was to say goodbye."

I let him get ahead again and I walked behind him, looking at his shoulders and thinking of all the goodbyes he had made. When Father drowned, he went to church and said goodbye to Father. It was only three years later that he concluded that Mother was frivolous and said goodbye to her. In his freshman year at college, he had been very good friends with his roommate, but the man drank too much, and at the beginning of the spring term Lawrence changed roommates and said goodbye to his friend. When he had been in college for two years, he concluded that the atmosphere was too sequestered and he said goodbye to Yale. He enrolled at Columbia and got his law degree there, but he found his first employer dishonest, and at the end of six months he said goodbye to a good job. He married Ruth in City Hall and said goodbye to the Protestant Episcopal Church; they went to live on a back street in Tuckahoe and said goodbye to the middle class. In 1938, he went to Washington to work as a government lawyer, saying goodbye to private enterprise, but after eight months in Washington he concluded that the Roosevelt administration was sentimental and he said goodbye to it. They left Washington for a suburb of Chicago, where he said goodbye to his neighbors, one by one, on counts of drunkenness, boorishness, and stupidity He said goodbye to Chicago and went to Kansas; he said goodbye to Kansas and went to Cleveland. Now he had said goodbye to Cleveland and come East again, stopping at Laud's Head long enough to say goodbye to the sea.

It was elegiac and it was bigoted and narrow, it mistook circumspection for character, and I wanted to help him. "Come out of it," I said. "Come out of it, Tifty."

"Come out of what?"

"Come out of this gloominess. Come out of it. It's only a summer day. You're spoiling your own good time and you're spoiling everyone else's. We need a vacation, Tifty. I need one. I need to rest. We all do. And you've made everything tense and unpleasant. I only have two weeks in the year. Two weeks. I need to have a good time and so do all the others. We need to rest. You think that your pessimism is an advantage, but it's nothing but an unwillingness to grasp realities."

"What are the realities?" he said. "Diana is a foolish and a promiscuous woman. So is Odette. Mother is an alcoholic. If she doesn't discipline herself, she'll be in a hospital in a year or two. Chaddy is dishonest. He always has been. The house is going to fall into the sea." He looked at me and added, as an afterthought, "You're a fool."

"You're a gloomy son of a bitch," I said. "You're a gloomy son of a bitch."

"Get your fat face out of mine," he said. He walked along.

Then I picked up a root and, coming at his back—although I have never hit a man from the back before—I swung the root, heavy with sea water, behind me, and the momentum sped my arm and I gave him, my brother, a blow on the head that forced him to his knees on the sand, and I saw the blood come out and begin to darken his hair. Then I wished that he was dead, dead and about to be buried, not buried but about to be buried, because I did not want to be denied ceremony and decorum in putting him away, in putting him out of my consciousness, and I saw the rest of us—Chaddy and Mother and Diana and Helen— in mourning in the house on Belvedere Street that was torn down twenty years ago, greeting our guest and our relatives at the door and answering their mannerly condolences with mannerly grief. Nothing decorous was lacking so that even if he had been murdered on a beach, one would feel before the tiresome ceremony ended that he had come into the winter of his life and that it was a law of nature, and a beautiful one, that Tifty should be buried in the cold, cold ground.

He was still on his knees. I looked up and down. No one had seen us. The naked beach, like a piece of the moon, reached to invisibility. The spill of a wave, in a glancing run, shot up to where he knelt. I would still have liked to end him, but now I had begun to act like two men, the murderer and the Samaritan. With a swift roar, like hollowness made sound, a white wave reached him and encircled him, boiling over his shoulders, and I held him against the undertow. Then I led him to a higher place. The blood had spread all through his hair, so that it looked black. I took off my shirt and tore it to bind up his head. He was conscious, and I didn't think he was badly hurt. He didn't speak. Neither did I. Then I left him there.

I walked a little way down the beach and turned to watch him, and I was thinking of my own skin then. He had got to his feet and he seemed steady. The daylight was still clear, but on the sea wind fumes of brine were blowing in like a light fog, and when I had walked a little way from him, I could hardly see his dark figure in this obscurity. All down the beach I could see the heavy salt air blowing in. Then I turned my back on him, and as I got near to the house, I went swimming again, as I seem to have done after every encounter with Lawrence that summer.

When I got back to the house, I lay down on the terrace. The others came back. I could hear Mother defaming the flower arrangements that had won prizes. None of ours had won anything. Then the house quieted, as it always does at that hour. The children went into the kitchen to get supper and the others went upstairs to bathe. Then I heard Chaddy making cocktails, and the conversation about the flower-show judges was resumed. Then Mother cried. "Tifty! Tifty! Oh, Tifty!"

He stood in the door, looking half dead. He had taken off the bloody bandage and he held it in his hand. "My brother did this," he said. "My brother did it. He hit me with a stone—something—on the beach." His voice broke with self-pity. I thought he was going to cry. No one else spoke. "Where's Ruth?" he cried. "Where's Ruth? Where in hell is Ruth? I want her to start packing. I don't have any more time to waste here. I have important things to do. I have *important* things to do." And he went up the stairs.

They left for the mainland the next morning, taking the six-o'clock boat. Mother got up to say goodbye, but she was the only one, and it is a harsh and an easy scene to imagine—the matriarch and the changeling, looking at each other with a dismay that would seem like the powers of love reversed. I heard the children's voices and the car go down the drive, and I got up and went to the window, and what a morning that was! Jesus, what a morning! The wind was northerly. The air was clear. In the early heat, the roses in the garden smelled like strawberry jam. While I was dressing, I heard the boat whistle, first the warning signal and then the double blast, and I could see the good people on the top deck drinking coffee out of fragile paper cups, and Lawrence at the bow, saying to the sea, *"Thalassa, thalassa,"* while his timid and unhappy children watched the creation from the encirclement of their mother's arms. The buoys would toll mournfully for Lawrence, and while the grace of the light would make it an exertion not to throw out your arms and swear exultantly, Lawrence's eyes would trace the black sea as it fell astern; he would think of the bottom, dark and strange, where full fathom five our father lies.

Oh, what can you do with a man like that? What can you do? How can you dissuade his eye in a crowd from seeking out the cheek with acne, the infirm hand; how can you teach him to respond to the inestimable greatness of the race, the harsh surface beauty of life; how can you put his finger for him on the obdurate truths before which fear and horror are powerless? The sea that morning was iridescent and dark. My wife and my sister were swimming—Diana and Helen—and I saw their uncovered heads, black and gold in the dark water. I saw them come out and I saw that they were naked, unshy, beautiful, and full of grace, and I watched the naked women walk out of the sea.

a floor of flounders

WHITNEY BALLIETT

last summer, I rented a small, hilltop house on Smithtown Bay, a serene, unassuming glacial dent about halfway out the north side of Long Island, and not long before returning to the city, I paid my first visit to Joe Molers. Visiting Joe Molers, according to my nearest neighbor, is a practically obligatory local custom. "Molers has an atmosphere about him," he told me. "An atmosphere of almost handmade stability and poise and satisfaction. Somewhere along the line what he was born and what he ought to be became what he is. I suppose it's because he found a vision that works. In 1907, when Molers was about eighteen, he came out here from New York for a couple of weeks with some sort of settlement house summer camp, and that was it. He became addicted to Smithtown Bay. Since then, one way or another, he has managed to spend five or six months a year camping on the bay. But I'm probably making him out eccentric and remote. Actually, he couldn't be more accessible. He's an attractive, hospitable man, an excellent Italian cook, and the best fisherman and hunter around here. He loves to talk and he plays good guitar and kazco. The best time to visit Joe is early morning or early evening. He lives by the sun, and during the day he's usually fishing or giving away the fish he doesn't need or walking on the beach or getting his water." My neighbor waggled his finger at me. "There are only two kinds of people in Smithtown—those who know Molers and those who don't."

I decided on early morning for my visit, and, after drinking some coffee, I started down the hill toward Molers' camp. During the night, the wind had swung around and was blowing hard out of the northwest. The sky was clean and the light startling. A rug of dew covered the ground, and it was chilly. Down in the Sound, the water was black and covered with whitecaps. The sand flats—a smooth toast color—caught the light and threw it against the bluffs that march long the western curve of the bay. A couple of clammers, were already out. At the bottom of the hill, the marsh grass bordering the Nissequogue River, which curves past my house and empties into the sound just past Molers' camp, moved in long, steady rollers. A night heron struggled up from the grass, was pitched on one wing by the wind, squawked, and flew heavily into the trees. I walked went past a small town beach and reached the lee of the long, low dune on which Molers' camp is built. The wind vanished, and the sun felt hot on my back. The marsh grass, already faintly rusted, blew soundlessly on my left, and beyond, the river curled like smoke toward Smithtown, some four or five miles upstream. I found myself on a narrow path still wet from the tide. Hundreds of tiny, perfect holes dotted it, and as I thundered along, fiddler crabs, their claws cocked, poured out of the holes, hesitated, and slid into the grass. A hundred yards beyond the town beach, I saw the first signs of Molers' place. The growth along the spine of the dune—mostly wracked cedars, beach plum bushes, cat briar, and poison ivy— had gradually become impenetrable, until it appeared to cluster tightly around two flat roofs. The river, parting the marsh grass, had come inshore and lay beside an immaculate beach, about fifty yards long. Four gray boats—rowboats and duck-and-goose boats—were moored to stout poles driven into the sand. The beach had been freshly raked into currentlike patterns. A duckboard-topped table stood back from the water, and beside it, a trough of deep sand led up between beach-plum bushes. I started up the trough, which moved treacherously like a treadmill, and near the top called out Molers' name. Silence, and then a muffled: "Yoh, yoh." The path broke into a clearing, covered with more raked sand and filled with blinding sunlight. For a second or two, I didn't see Molers standing in the door of his shack. A stocky, short man, with bowed legs and a barrel chest, he was dressed in a tight wool shirt, a brown cardigan, bathing trunks, and ankle boots with no socks. A knitted cap was pulled low on his head. He looked like Pablo Picasso—leathery and gnomish and solid. He had a can of condensed milk in one hand and, suspended from the other, a half-empty jug of water. "Hello. Some day," he said, raising the milk and the water toward me in greeting. Molers' voice was hoarse, and his eyes, narrow and slightly slanted above high cheekbones, were puffy from sleep. I introduced myself. "Well, come in," he said, turning and disappearing into the house. "I'm just setting up to eat. Unfold one of those camp chairs in the corner and make yourself comfortable. Have you et yet?" I said I'd had coffee and didn't eat much in the morning. "Is that right? You better have some of my pancakes, which I call bullets. I'm just going to work on the batter. I cook them about an inch or more thick, and it's like bread inside, but light. Not the wet cardboard you get in a restaurant." I sat down and watched Molers start his batter. "For some reason, people who don't know me so well bring presents to the camp, and they've always things I don't use—candy, wine or beer, even cigarettes and cigars." Molers turned and smiled, showing perfect teeth. "A while back, a summer lady lives up the river came with her kids and brought this package covered in tin foil. She said she'd baked it for me. After she left, I opened it, and I thought, what the hell is this? It was hard and heavy and dark-looking. A friend of mine dropped by the camp just then and I showed it to him. He didn't know what it was either, so we cut it open and ate some and he said maybe it was some sort of Jewish rye. It didn't have any taste and an hour later it was still sitting in your stomach. So I sliced up the rest of it and put it outside and the birds ate it. Birds will eat anything, I guess." Molers laughed, and breaking two eggs into a shallow saucer, beat them with a fork. Then he sifted four teaspoons of baking soda, a teaspoon of salt, four tablespoons of sugar, and a cup of flour into a bowl. A cup of water, the eggs, and some shortening followed, and Molers stirred the batter with a long wooden spoon, slowly adding a second cup of water. He stirred steadily for a minute or so, rocking back and forth, his knees slightly bent. "Now that will have to sit while the griddle heats. Did you ever see a griddle like that? I bought it thirty years ago for eighteen dollars from the New Jersey Gas and Electric." Molers stepped over to a two-burner kerosene stove, pried up the griddle's pail-like handle, and held it up. It resembled a sawed-off hat box, and was hollow underneath. The hollow was fitted with a perforated cone to distribute the heat evenly. With a faint "ooch," he banged the griddle back on the stove, and, in easy, non-stop motions, pulled a long table out from the wall. It was covered with gleaming white oilcloth, and he set it with gleaming white plates and cups. He told me to pull up to the table, and before I could say anything, emptied two fried eggs and a couple of strips of bacon onto my plate. "These'll freshen up your appetite. I only eat twice a day, but I don't know a man who can eat more than me. I have my second meal— spaghetti or stuffed eggplant or fish—about three or four o'clock in the afternoon. I was a machinist for fifty years and since I retired eight years ago, I've been living winters on Staten Island. I take the ferryboat over to the city every morning at ten and I eat my first meal about eleven, usually at a place near Eighth Avenue and Twenty-third, where I can get a big vegetable plate. At six, I eat again in a Horn-Hardack's. The tray's not big enough for the food I put on it and the girls who work there generally joke me about it. I'm five feet nothing in height but I never gain a pound. I retired from a place that makes zippers and umbrellas near Union Square, and I don't miss it. When I get off the ferry, sometimes I walk straight up to a Hundred and Twenty-fifth. Or sometimes I take a subway into the eighties or nineties, and walk over to Central Park, look into the Natural History, and walk down until I hit a Horn–Hardack's. When the weather is bad, I go to the movies. I saw sixty a couple of winters back. The east side is warmer than the west side in winter, so I'm usually over east. There's not a piece of New York I don't know. I've got a few friends live in the city, but I never visit them. Just the same as I don't visit anyone out here. I don't like to go in anybody's home. It looks to me you're intruding. It makes me feel funny. You've been there an hour or two and the first thing you know there's nothing else to talk about. You get nervous and leave. Which destroys the visit—so why go in the first place? I like people—in my own place. There's usually friends at the camp every weekend, and now in the cool weather I have to go to work and start my spaghetti parties. Six or seven of them. The Meyers and the Lanes and the Keetons and the Schechtars from over on your side of the river and some people to the other side, like Fred Cavi, who taught me to read for the guitar and is an A-1 musician. My spaghetti takes me three or four hours to make. First, meatballs the size of your fist, and made of pork and beef, chopped salami, parsley, pinoli nuts, flour, and eight or nine eggs. Then the sauce—a number two can of plum tomatoes, a can of Campbell's tomato soup, beef stock, a couple of cloves of garlic, pepper, oregano, sugar, Parmesan cheese, and vinegar, and simmer it. When the bubbles in the sauce are clear, I put in the meatballs, and simmer it some more. I used to watch my mother cook. She cooked all day. She had to. There were eight of us—three brothers, three sisters, me, and my father. I don't think my mother made spaghetti as good as mine. But I never beat her eggplant. Here, try a couple of bullets." Molers dumped two fat white cakes, three or four inches across, on my plate. "Break one. Look inside. Touch it. Just like cake." I broke one open—it *was* cake— and ate it. It was delicious. I told Molers and he put two more bullets on my plate. I criss-crossed my hands and said that was fine, and he shrugged and put his own plate on the table. There were three fried eggs, a pile of bacon, and seven bullets on it. Pulling a bell of concentration over him, Molers began to eat, and I sat back and looked around the shack. It was about twelve feet square, high ceilinged, and painted a fresh, pale green. There were four small windows. Their frames, a glistening dark green, had the sculptured quality of many layers of paint. Each window was propped open by a dark-green piece of broomstick. Against the wall where we were sitting there were a tiny clothes closet and an open steamer trunk, piled neatly with dry goods. A color photograph of the American flag, out from an old Sunday newspaper, was tacked above the lid of the trunk, and beside it, on a shelf, a black-faced alarm clock stared out from its box. Two stoves—the kerosene one and a gasoline four-burner—took up most of the south wall. Through the door in the east wall, which had two small portable ovens stacked against it, I could see most of the clearing in front of the shack—brilliant sand, a white, metal-topped kitchen table, listing slightly to the right, and a squat cedar tree. Beyond the cedar, a high bank shut out the sound. Behind me, on the north wall, sea-going shelves held Molers' crockery and cutlery. Three gasoline lanterns with spotless chimneys hung from a cross-tie. The floorboards were scrubbed white. The room had the quiet, explosive air of polished brass. Molers mopped up his yoke with his last bullet, sat back, and patted his stomach. "Have another bullet. Have two more bullets. There's plenty." I shook my head, Molers got up, and, with another stream of quick, seamless motions, cleared the table, filled a big pot at the back of the house with hot water, ritually washed the dishes, wiped the table, and slammed it back against the wall.

I went outside and sat on a bench next to the stoop. It was hot and still. Two gulls, driven from the flats by the tide, rode swells of wind. Across the clearing, a clump of poison ivy looked beady and luxuriant. Molers appeared from behind the shack, a broom in hand and with five sharp strokes swept a shovelful of sand out of the house. "The sand flows around this place like water," he said. "I bring it up from the sound side—about two hundred and fifty buckets a summer—and dump it here. People track it into the shack, I sweep it out, and then they track it down to the river side, which gets about a foot high every year. I'm very patient in doing things right. But it gets my goat when things—not people—go wrong. If it's an engine, or something like that, I lose my temper and smash it. I go to work and smash it and it relieves me right away." Molers sank onto a camp chair, and pulling off his sweater, revealed knotted arms topped by biceps the size of ten-pin balls. "I've had this camp since 1929. When I first came out from New York, I was a squatter over in Sunken Meadow, where the state park is now, about a mile up toward Huntington. When I saw the clear water and all the fish and the space and the air you could breathe, it changed my life. For the next twenty years—excepting a year I was a cook in the army in the War—I camped in tents and a couple of one-room bungalows on what used to be Bacon's estate. Then Smithtown took over that particular stretch, and since I'd been there so long, they said you choose another place over in Short Beach. This is it. I pay the town ten dollars a season, but I never know year to year if they're going to put hot dog stands or something along the beach and say, 'Ok, Joe. Out.' I don't own any of this except what I have in the shack. I built the shack with a couple of my brothers. Last year, for the first time, I had to put new shingles on the south side. It gets hot there and the sun wore the old shingles as thin as paper. That cedar used to shade the entire shack, but now it's dying. It must be my feet walking around it all these years that's killing it. Things change. The fishing and hunting there used to be around here! One night, oh, maybe forty years ago, I was out with a light in my boat. The water was shallow and I came upon a sandy place completely covered with flounders. A floor of flounders, about two city blocks square. Just lying there in my light on the bottom. God, one of them must have been two-and-a-half feet long, and it took me three throws with a six-prong spear to bring it up. It was like spearing a doormat. I had the first outboard on the river, and for twenty years the fastest. Now you've got so many boats and so many people there aren't enough fish to go around. I used to catch fifty and sixty fish an hour. I've got a snap inside showing me standing next to a pile of dog fish that reaches my waist. The fish I've given away would feed me two or three life-times. The same with eels, which are the most delicate and choice eating I know. Clean off the slime, which scares some people, cut the eel in slices, dip them in flour, and fry them. But I don't eel much at night now. It gets chilly out there and at my age you have to take it more careful. I've been sick but once in my life—rabbit fever. The hunting's gone, too. I used to see deer right here on the beach in the fall and sea turtles coming up to lay their eggs, and I've shot and trapped fox and possums and raccoons and of course rabbits and even weasels and such. Once I read in the paper where President Hoover was going south to trap possums, so *I* went out in the meadow and got one. I cleaned it and put it in a pot and invited a bunch here and told them I'd shot the biggest rabbit I ever saw and they better help me eat it. They did, and about halfway through I asked one of them—he was a great big state trooper, I think—what he thought he was eating. He looked at me funny, and said, 'Why, rabbit, Joe, right?' I said, 'No, possum' He was chewing on a leg, and he took it out of his mouth, and said, 'Well, damn it,' and threw the leg on the table. Then he collected himself and smiled and finished the leg and said he never knew possum was so flavorful. I still shoot black duck and geese and a coot once in a while. A friend come to the camp late one afternoon years ago and said he was hungry and there was a big goose out on the river. I got my gun and we untied a boat and went upstream. It was getting dark when we found him, but we sat and waited, in case he'd start up. Five minutes, ten, then up he went and blam! I started the engine and went ever and picked him out of the water, and Jesus H. Mackerel, my heart turned. It was a swan. Well, I knew you can't shoot swans and I felt nervous and bad about it. But we couldn't just throw it in the reeds, so took it back to the camp and cleaned it and hung it from the cedar for a while and then cooked it. I et one leg and a wing and my friend et the other leg and wing. Then he said, 'Joe, slice me a little of that breast just to taste, and I'm through!' I wasn't exactly starved myself anymore. I sliced him a piece and he et it and said it was the finest meat he ever had. Half an hour later, we finished both sides of the breast and that bird must have weighed twenty pounds. I've often thought since do guilty people eat more than ordinary."

Molers sighed, grimaced at the sun, and took off his cap. A thin cloud of white hair sprang up. He clamped the cap on the back of his head and stood up, slapping both thighs. "Would you like to see the camp? I've got some friends from New York that are supposed to arrive around now and I've got to go to work and fix a couple of eggplants." The paths around the camp—narrow, clean, sandy, and hidden by cat briars, Virginia creepers, and bittersweet—form a lopsided fish backbone that runs east–west. At its center are the shack and the clearing. West of the shack, a main path runs about twenty feet. Two short arms shoot off to the south and come out on sandy platforms above the river. On one of them, an open barrel sunk into the sand and half-filled with big stones, serves as a drain for dishwater and the like. Beyond that, the main path turns right and into a small garden, laid out on a raised bank. I counted at least two dozen ripe tomatoes. East from the shack, the main path meanders, passing a wooden platform that Molers used to pitch a tent on for guests. Opposite this, two more arms lead down to the river edge. The main path ends, after a final twist, in a small clearing that conceals a handsome outhouse. Molers led the way back to the shack, and then pointed toward the sound. "Let's go up to the sun parlor for a minute and look at the sea." At the top of a steep path, hidden behind the cedar, the wind hit us, snapping our clothes like flags. Six wooden steps led down to an enormous beach, and on the right the path wound in a perfect S to the sun parlor—four white posts covered with white canvas. It had white benches on three sides, white railings, and a sand floor, taken up largely by a beach chair, which, wrapped in canvas and tied with rope, looked disconcertingly like a sailor in his shroud. "In nice weather," Molers shouted in the wind, "I used to sit in the parlor a lot and think. Last winter, they dredged the river and put all the spill in front here and made this beach. Before, the parlor looked right over the water. Now, it looks over this Sahara. In fifty years, this will wash away and then I suppose they'll dredge and put it back to wash away again. At night, the waves sounded like they were right under the shack."

Back in the clearing, Molers opened a wire-fronted cabinet fastened to the north side of the shack in the shade and took out two big eggplants. "I keep flour and vegetables and fruit here," he said, "and my butter and milk and water down here." Molers bent over, grunted, and opened a sizable trap door flush with the sand. A white wooden box, about three feet all around, was filled with eggs, butter, and gallon jugs of water. "I can keep anything cold twenty-four hours. I get my water at Lane's pump house at the foot of your hill—about thirty-five gallons every couple of days. I take a boat, and with the way the tides are now, go right over the road and up to the pump. I pick up my dry goods at a little grocery up the river, which is as close as I ever get to town." Molers dropped the eggplants on the table in the clearing, brought a bowl and a knife from the shack, and, still standing, went to work. The wind shook the top of the cedar, and a foot or so behind Molers, a song sparrow landed and poked at a piece of stale bread. The sun, well up now, worked away at the new shingles. A deep blue shadow lay under the table. Molers smiled at his eggplant. "This is just as beautiful as the world could make it, this place. How many times I went to this foreman, that foreman in April, and told him, 'Well, I'm going on my vacation now.' 'Fine.' 'I'll see you in five months.' 'Five months,' they'd yell. 'This man is crazy.' 'Five months. I'll be back in December. You got a job open, I'll take it. If not, I'll go someplace else.' Maybe it was the taste of country I got in New York as a kid that set me in this direction. My father—he was a shoemaker—brought me over from Naples when I was four. We lived in Greenwich Village near what was Cottage Place, which had frame houses and grass and trees. I used to go over to a crik that ran into the Hudson and watch the crab fisherman—two of them in a boat with a big pot of boiling water. They'd scoop the crabs—blueshells they were— off the surface and throw them in the pot. If they saw me, they'd toss me a claw or a leg. On Sundays, we'd run all the way to Central Park, rolling a big hoop. I recall farms and fields. Or we would go swimming on South Beach on Staten Island. The water was filthy, even in those days. But there was the Irish element, too, used to pick me up and turn me upside down I was so small. And the smells and the dead horses in the streets. We moved to Brooklyn after my oldest brother was killed. He was sitting up on the roof of our building one afternoon with another fellow. It was hot and clear and—Jesus, just like that!—he was

hit by a lightning bolt. It never touched the other man." Molers
scooped the egg plant filling into the bowl, and diced it carefully. "When I started coming out here, I left my real name
behind—Edward Louis Dagostino. My sisters nicknamed me Joe
from a little ditty they teased me with, 'Joe, Joe, catch my toe,
catch my toe,' and Molers came from Molers barber school
where you could get a free haircut from one of the students. My
hair got pretty long once, and I went to a barbershop and had a
haircut, but the next day I got razzed: 'Yah, Joe's been to Molers,
Joe's been to Molers.' So I came out here Joe Molers. Even my
sisters and brothers call me Joe Molers. All of them got married
and had children, except me. I looked, but no woman would
agree to this life. In 1922, I went with a Quaker girl who worked
over the river at King's Park hospital. I asked her to marry me,
but she didn't care for the camping. So I never married, and I'm
not sorry. I'd probably have six kids breaking my neck, or else I'd
be six feet down. I have two hundred dollars a month—social
security and a World War One pension, and a few war bonds.
When I get off the ferry at the Battery in the winter, I look up
at the city, the right side, the left side, and it excites me because I
can go wherever I please." Molers laughed. "No wife would stand
my bed anyway. I sleep on the table we had breakfast off of. I put
a couple of army blankets on it, a thin mattress and another blanket, and come November, I wear a sweater, a pair of socks, and a
cup. In the old days, I slept on the bare table, but I guess my bones
are getting soft. You can't be lonely when you see the things I've
seen here. I was sitting out late one October night, just looking,
and suddenly the northern lights started up. Well, I'd never seen
them before, and I thought what in the name of heaven is happening. Lights dancing and waving—red, blue, green, white. I was
shivering with what was happening in that sky."

Molers looked up. "You hear something? That must be them."
He shook the last of the eggplant filling into the bowl, piled the
husks on top, and put the bowl in the outside cabinet. He was
wiping the table when the bushes parted on the river side, and
two women—big, blond, and laughing—came into the clearing.
One of them carried a suitcase and the other a huge box of gro-

ceries. An embarrassed looking boy of about fourteen or fifteen brought up the rear.

"Joe! How are you, dear?" the woman with the suitcase said. "Joe, you look marvellous. That's just what you were doing the last time I saw you—wiping that table."

"Well, I'm damned," Molers said, seizing the box of groceries, putting it on the table, and kissing both women. "Where you been, where you been? I haven't seen you since—when was it— way back early last season. I thought you weren't coming this year."

"I've been to India and Japan, Joe, and I just got back," the woman with the suitcase said. The other woman smiled and nodded vigorously.

"India!" Molers looked bewildered. "India. Did you hear that?" Molers grasped my arm. "This is Mrs. Ullman, Mrs. Mildred Ullman, and that's her boy, and this is Mrs. Celia Quinlan. Friends from New York."

We shook hands and Mrs. Ullman said: "Joe, didn't you hear us? We stood across the river and shouted at you for an hour to come and get us. Like you did last time. We shouted till we got cold and then we got in the car and drove all the way up to Smithtown and back down this side of the river. Eleven miles. Then we lugged all this stuff down the beach. Didn't you hear us?"

"No, no, not a word. Too much wind. Did you hear anything?" Molers asked me. I shook my head. "Well, never mind. You're here. Put on some bathing suits around back and some sweaters and we'll go out on the river and see if the blues are running."

learning to swim

GRAHAM SWIFT

mrs. Singleton had three times thought of leaving her husband. The first time was before they were married, on a charter plane coming back from a holiday in Greece. They were students who had just graduated. They had rucksacks and faded jeans. In Greece they had stayed part of the time by a beach on an island. The island was dry and rocky with great grey and vermilion coloured rocks and when you lay on the beach it seemed that you too became a hot, basking rock. Behind the beach there were eucalyptus trees like dry, leafy bones, old men with mules and gold teeth, a fragrance of thyme, and a café with melon seeds on the floor and a jukebox which played bouzouki music and songs by Cliff Richard. All this Mr. Singleton failed to appreciate. He'd only liked the milk-warm, clear blue sea, in which he'd stayed most of the time as if afraid of foreign soil. On the plane she'd thought: He hadn't enjoyed the holiday, hadn't liked Greece at all. All that sunshine. Then she'd thought she ought not to marry him.

Though she had, a year later.

The second time was about a year after Mr. Singleton, who was a civil engineer, had begun his first big job. He became a junior partner in a firm with a growing reputation. She ought to have been pleased by this. It brought money and comfort; it enabled them to move to a house with a large garden, to live well, to think about raising a family. They spent weekends in country hotels. But Mr. Singleton seemed untouched by this. He became withdrawn and incommunicative. He went to his work austere-faced. She thought: He likes his bridges and tunnels better than me.

The third time, which was really a phase, not a single moment, was when she began to calculate how often Mr. Singleton made love to her. When she started this it was about once every fortnight on average. Then it became every three weeks. The interval had been widening for some time. This was not a predicament Mrs. Singleton viewed selfishly. Love-making had been a problem before, in their earliest days together, which, thanks to her patience and initiative, had been overcome. It was Mr. Singleton's unhappiness, not her own, that she saw in their present plight. He was distrustful of happiness as some people fear heights or open spaces. She would reassure him, encourage him again. But the averages seemed to defy her personal effort: once every three weeks, once every month . . . She thought: Things go back to as they were.

But then, by sheer chance, she became pregnant.

Now she lay on her back, eyes closed, on the coarse sand of the beach in Cornwall. It was hot and, if she opened her eyes, the sky was clear blue. This and the previous summer had been fine enough to make her husband's refusal to go abroad for holidays tolerable. If you kept your eyes closed it could be Greece or Italy or Ibiza. She wore a chocolate-brown bikini, sun-glasses, and her skin, which seldom suffered from sunburn, was already beginning to tan. She let her arms trail idly by her side, scooping up little handfuls of sand. If she turned her head to the right and looked towards the sea she could see Mr. Singleton and their son Paul standing in the shallow water. Mr. Singleton was teaching Paul to swim. "Kick!" he was saying. From here, against the gentle waves, they looked like no more than two rippling silhouettes.

"Kick!" said Mr. Singleton, "Kick!" He was like a punisher, administering lashes.

She turned her head away to face upwards. If you shut your eyes you could imagine you were the only one on the beach; if you held them shut you could be part of the beach. Mrs. Singleton imagined that in order to acquire a tan you had to let the sun make love to you.

She dug her heels in the sand and smiled involuntarily.

When she was a thin, flat-chested, studious girl in a grey school uniform Mrs. Singleton had assuaged her fear and desperation about sex with fantasies which took away from men the brute physicality she expected of them. All her lovers would be artists. Poets would write poems to her, composers would dedicate their works to her. She would even pose, naked and immaculate, for painters, who having committed her true, her eternal form to canvas, would make love to her in an impalpable, ethereal way, under the power of which her bodily and temporal self would melt away, perhaps for ever. These fantasies (for she had never entirely renounced them) had crystallized for her in the image of a sculptor, who from a cold intractable piece of stone would fashion her very essence—which would be vibrant and full of sunlight, like the statues they had seen in Greece.

At university she had worked on the assumption that all men lusted uncontrollably and insatiably after women. She had not yet encountered a man who, whilst prone to the usual instincts, possessing moreover a magnificent body with which to fulfill them, yet had scruples about doing so, seemed ashamed of his own capacities. It did not matter that Mr. Singleton was reading engineering, was scarcely artistic at all, or that his powerful physique was unlike the nebulous creatures of her dreams. She found she loved this solid man-flesh. Mrs. Singleton had thought she was the shy, inexperienced, timid girl. Overnight she discovered that she wasn't this at all. He wore tough denim shirts, spoke and smiled very little and had a way of standing very straight and upright as if he didn't need any help from anyone. She had to educate him into moments of passion, of self-forgetfulness which made her glow with her own achievement. She was happy because she had not thought she was happy and she believed she could make someone else happy. At the university girls were starting to wear jeans, record-players played the Rolling Stones and in the hush of the Modern Languages Library she read Leopardi and Verlaine. She seemed to float with confidence in a swirling, buoyant element she had never suspected would be her own.

"Kick!" she heard again from the water.

Mr. Singleton had twice thought of leaving his wife. Once was after a symphony concert they had gone to in London when they had not known each other very long and she still tried to get him to read books, to listen to music, to take an interest in art. She would buy concert or theatre tickets, and he had to seem pleased. At this concert a visiting orchestra was playing some titanic, large-scale work by a late nineteenth-century composer. A note in the programme said it represented the triumph of life over death. He had sat on his plush seat amidst the swirling barrage of sound. He had no idea what he had to do with it or the triumph of life over death. He had thought the same thought about the rapt girl on his left, the future Mrs. Singleton, who now and then bobbed, swayed or rose in her seat as if the music physically lifted her. There were at least seventy musicians on the platform. As the piece worked to its final crescendo the conductor, whose arms were flailing frantically so that his white shirt back appeared under his flying tails, looked so absurd Mr. Singleton thought he would laugh. When the music stopped and was immediately supplanted by wild cheering and clapping he thought the world had gone mad. He had struck his own hands together so as to appear to be sharing the ecstasy. Then, as they filed out, he had almost wept because he felt like an insect. He even thought she had arranged the whole business so as to humiliate him.

He thought he would not marry her.

The second time was after they had been married some years. He was one of a team of engineers working on a suspension bridge over an estuary in Ireland. They took it in turns to stay on the site and to inspect the construction work personally. Once he had to go to the very top of one of the two piers of the bridge to examine work on the bearings and housing for the main over-head cables. A lift ran up between the twin towers of the pier amidst a network of scaffolding and power cables to where a working platform was positioned. The engineer, with the super-visor and the foreman, had only to stay on the platform from where all the main features of construction were visible. The men at work on the upper sections of the towers, specialists in their trade, earning up to two hundred pounds a week—who balanced on precarious cat-walks and walked along exposed reinforcing girders—often jibed at the engineers who never left the plat-form. He thought he would show them. He walked out on to one of the cat-walks on the outer face of the pier where they were fitting huge grip-bolts. This was quite safe if you held on to the rails but still took some nerve. He wore a check cheese-cloth shirt and his white safety helmet. It was a grey, humid August day. The cat-walk hung over greyness. The water of the estuary was the colour of dead fish. A dredger was chugging near the base of the pier. He thought, I could swim the estuary; but there is a bridge. Below him the yellow helmets of workers moved over the girders for the roadway like beetles. He took his hands from the rail. He wasn't at all afraid. He had been away from his wife all week. He thought: She knows nothing of this. If he were to step out now into the grey air he would be quite by himself, no harm would come to him . . .

Now Mr. Singleton stood in the water, teaching his son to swim. They were doing the water-wings, exercise. The boy wore a pair of water-wings, red underneath, yellow on top, which bal-looned up under his arms and chin. With this to support him, he would splutter and splash towards his father who stood facing him some feet away. After a while at this they would try the same procedure, his father moving a little nearer, but without the water-wings, and this the boy dreaded. "Kick!" said Mr. Singleton. "Use your legs!" He watched his son draw painfully towards him. The boy had not yet grasped that the body natural-ly floated and that if you added to this certain mechanical effects, you swam. He thought that in order to swim you had to make as much frantic movement as possible. As he struggled towards Mr. Singleton his head, which was too high out of the water, jerked messily from side to side, and his eyes which were half closed swivelled in every direction but straight ahead. "Towards me!" shouted Mr. Singleton. He held out his arms in front of him for Paul to grasp. As his son was on the point of clutching them he would step back a little, pulling his hands away, in the hope that the last desperate lunge to reach his father might really teach the boy the art of propelling himself in water. But he sometimes wondered if this were his only motive.

"Good boy. Now again."

At school Mr. Singleton had been an excellent swimmer. He had won various school titles, broken numerous records and competed successfully in ASA championships. There was a period between the ages of about thirteen and seventeen which he remembered as the happiest in his life. It wasn't the medals and trophies that made him glad, but the knowledge that he didn't have to bother about anything else. Swimming vindicated him. He would get up every morning at six and train for two hours in the baths, and again before lunch; and when he fell asleep, exhausted, in French and English periods in the afternoon, he didn't have to bother about the indignation of the masters—lank, ill-conditioned creatures—for he had his excuse. He didn't have to bother about the physics teacher who complained to the headmaster that he would never get the exam results he needed if he didn't cut down his swimming, for the headmaster (who was an advocate of sport) came to his aid and told the physics teacher not to interfere with a boy who was a credit to the school. Nor did he have to bother about a host of other things which were supposed to be going on inside him, which made the question of what to do in the evening, at week-ends, fraught and tantalizing, which drove other boys to moodiness and recklessness. For once in the cool water of the baths, his arms reaching, his eyes fixed on the blue marker line on the bottom, his ears full so that he could hear nothing around him, he would feel quite by himself, quite sufficient. At the end of races, when for one brief instant he clung panting alone like a survivor to the finishing rail which his rivals had yet to touch, he felt an infinite peace. He went to bed early, slept soundly, kept to his training regimen; and he enjoyed this Spartan purity which disdained pleasure and disorder. Some of his school mates mocked him—for not going to dances on Saturdays or to pubs, under age, or the Expresso after school. But he did not mind. He didn't need them. He knew they were weak. None of them could hold out, depend on themselves, spurn comfort if they had to. Some of them would go under in life. And none of them could cleave the water as he did or possessed a hard, stream-lined, perfectly tuned body as he did.

Then, when he was nearly seventeen all this changed. His father, who was an engineer, though proud of his son's trophies, suddenly pressed him to different forms of success. The head-master no longer shielded him from the physics master. He said: "You can't swim into your future." Out of spite perhaps or an odd consistency of self-denial, he dropped swimming altogether rather than cut it down. For a year and a half he worked at his maths and physics with the same single-mindedness with which he had perfected his sport. He knew about mechanics and engi-neering because he knew how to make his body move through water. His work was not merely competent but good. He got to university where he might have had the leisure, if he wished, to resume his swimming. But he did not. Two years are a long gap in a swimmer's training; two years when you are near your peak can mean you will never get back to your true form. Sometimes he went for a dip in the university pool and swam slowly up and down amongst practicing members of the university team, whom perhaps he could still have beaten, as a kind of relief.

Often, Mr. Singleton dreamt about swimming. He would be moving through vast expanses of water, an ocean. As he moved it did not require any effort at all. Sometimes he would go for long distances under water, but he did not have to bother about breath-ing. The water would be silvery-grey. And as always it seemed that as he swam he was really trying to get beyond the water, to put it behind him, as if it were a veil he were parting and he would emerge on the other side of it at last, on to some pristine shore, where he would step where no one else had stepped before.

When he made love to his wife her body got in the way; he wanted to swim through her.

Mrs. Singleton raised herself, pushed her sun-glasses up over her dark hair and sat with her arms stretched straight behind her back. A trickle of sweat ran between her breasts. They had developed to a good size since her schoolgirl days. Her skinniness in youth had stood her in good stead against the filling out of middle age, and her body was probably more mellow, more lithe and better proportioned now than it had ever been. She looked at Paul and Mr. Singleton half immersed in the shallows. It seemed to her that her husband was the real boy, standing stubbornly upright with his hands before him, and that Paul was some toy being pulled and swung relentlessly around him and towards him as though on some string. They had seen her sit up. Her husband waved, holding the boy's hand, as though for the two of them. Paul did not wave; he seemed more concerned with the water in his eyes. Mrs. Singleton did not wave back. She would have done if her son had waved. When they had left for their holiday Mr. Singleton had said to Paul, "You'll learn to swim this time. In salt water, you know, it's easier." Mrs. Singleton hoped her son wouldn't swim; so that she could wrap him, still, in the big yellow towel when he came out, rub him dry and warm, and watch her husband stand apart, his hands empty.

She watched Mr. Singleton drop his arm back to his side. "If you wouldn't splash it wouldn't go in your eyes," she just caught him say.

The night before, in their hotel room, they had argued. They always argued about half way through their holidays. It was symbolic, perhaps, of that first trip to Greece, when he had somehow refused to enjoy himself. They had to incur injuries so that they could then appreciate their leisure, like convalescents. For the first four days or so of their holiday Mr. Singleton would tend to be moody, on edge. He would excuse this as "winding down," the not-to-be-hurried process of dispelling the pressures of work Mrs. Singleton would be patient. On about the fifth day Mrs. Singleton would begin to suspect that the winding down would never end and indeed (which she had known all along) that it was not winding down at all—he was clinging, as to a defence to his bridges and tunnels; and she would show her resentment. At this point Mr. Singleton would retaliate by an attack upon her indolence.

Last night he had called her "flabby." He could not mean, of course, "flabby-bodied" (she could glance down, now, at her still-flat belly), though such a sensual attack, would have been simpler, almost heartening, from him. He meant "flabby of attitude." And what he meant by this, or what he wanted to mean, was that *he* was not flabby; that he worked, facing the real world, erecting great solid things on the face of the land, and that, whilst he worked, he disdained work's rewards—money, pleasure, rich food, holidays abroad—that he hadn't "gone soft," as she had done since they graduated eleven years ago, with their credentials for the future and their plane tickets to Greece. She knew this toughness of her husband was only a cover for his own failure to relax and his need to keep his distance. She knew that he found no particular virtue in his bridges and tunnels (it was the last thing he wanted to do really—build); it didn't matter if they were right or wrong, they were there, he could point to them as if it vindicated him—just as when he made his infrequent, if seismic, love to her it was not a case of enjoyment or satisfaction; he just did it.

It was hot in their hotel room. Mr. Singleton stood in his blue pyjama bottoms, feet apart, like a PT instructor.

"Flabby? What do you mean—'flabby'!?" she had said, looking daunted.

But Mrs. Singleton had the advantage whenever Mr. Singleton accused her in this way of complacency, of weakness. She knew he only did it to hurt her, and so to feel guilty, and so to feel the remorse which would release his own affection for her, his vulnerability, his own need to be loved. Mrs. Singleton was used to this process, to the tenderness that was the tenderness of successively opened and reopened wounds. And she was used to being the nurse who took care of the healing scars. For though Mr. Singleton inflicted the first blow he would always make himself more guilty than he made her suffer, and Mrs. Singleton, though in pain herself, could not resist wanting to clasp and cherish her husband, wanting to wrap him up safe when his own weakness and submissiveness showed and his body became liquid and soft against her; could not resist the old spur that her husband was unhappy and it was for her to make him happy. Mr. Singleton was extraordinarily lovable when he was guilty. She would even have yielded indefinitely, foregoing her own grievance, to this extreme of comforting him for the pain he caused her, had she not discovered, in time, that this only pushed the process a stage further. Her forgiveness of him became only another level of comfort, of softness he must reject. His flesh shrank from her restoring touch.

She thought: Men go round in circles, women don't move.

She kept to her side of the hotel bed, he, with his face turned, to his. He lay like a person washed up on a beach. She reached out her hand and stroked the nape of his neck. She felt him tense. All this was a pattern.

"I'm sorry," he said, "I didn't mean—"

"It's all right, it doesn't matter."

"Doesn't it matter?" he said.

When they reached this point they were like miners racing each other for deeper and deeper seams of guilt and recrimination.

But Mrs. Singleton had given up delving to rock bottom. Perhaps it was five years ago when she had thought for the third time of leaving her husband, perhaps long before that. When they were students she'd made allowances for his constraints, his reluctances. An unhappy childhood perhaps, a strict upbringing. She thought his inhibition might be lifted by the sanction of marriage. She'd thought, after all, it would be a good thing if he married her. She had not thought what would be good for her. They stood outside Gatwick Airport, back from Greece, in the grey, wet August light. Their tanned skin had seemed to glow. Yet she'd known this mood of promise would pass. She watched him kick against contentment, against ease, against the long, glittering lifeline she threw to him; and, after a while, she ceased to try to haul him in. She began to imagine again her phantom artists. She thought: People slip off the shores of the real world, back into dreams. She hadn't "gone soft," only gone back to herself. Hidden inside her like treasure there were lines of Leopardi, of Verlaine her husband would never appreciate. She thought, he doesn't need me, things run off him, like water. She even thought that her husband's neglect in making love to her was not a problem he had but a deliberate scheme to deny her. When Mrs. Singleton desired her husband she could not help herself. She would stretch back on the bed with the sheets pulled off like a blissful nude in a Modigliani. She thought this ought to gladden a man. Mr. Singleton would stand at the foot of the bed and gaze down at her. He looked like some strong, chaste knight in the legend of the Grail. He would respond to her invitation, but before he did so there would be this expression, half stern, half innocent, in his eyes. It was the sort of expression that good men in books and films are supposed to make to prostitutes. It would ensure that their love-making was marred and that afterward it would seem as if he had performed something out of duty that only she wanted. Her body would feel like stone. It was at such times, when she felt the cold, dead-weight feel of abused happiness, that Mrs. Singleton most thought she was through with Mr. Singleton. She would watch his strong, compact torso already lifting itself off the bed. She would think: He thinks he is tough, contained in himself, but he won't see what I offer him, he doesn't see how it is I who can help him.

Mrs. Singleton lay back on her striped towel on the sand. Once again she became part of the beach. The careless sounds of the seaside, of excited children's voices, of languid grownups', of wooden bats on balls, fluttered over her as she shut her eyes. She thought: It is the sort of day on which someone suddenly shouts, "Someone is drowning."

When Mrs. Singleton became pregnant she felt she had out-manoeuvred her husband. He did not really want a child (it was the last thing he wanted, Mrs. Singleton thought, a child), but he was jealous of her condition, as of some achievement he himself could attain. He was excluded from the little circle of herself and her womb, and, as though to puncture it, he began for the first time to make love to her of a kind where he took the insistent initiative. Mrs. Singleton was not greatly pleased. She seemed

buoyed up by her own bigness. She noticed that her husband
began to do exercises in the morning, in his underpants, press-
ups, squat-jumps, as if he were getting in training for something.
He was like a boy. He even became, as the term of her pregnan-
cy drew near its end, resilient and detached again, the virile father
waiting to receive the son (Mr. Singleton knew it would be a son,
so did Mrs. Singleton) that she, at the appointed time, would
deliver him. When the moment arrived he insisted on being present so as to prove he wasn't squeamish and to make sure he
wouldn't be tricked in the transaction. Mrs. Singleton was not
daunted. When the pains became frequent she wasn't at all afraid.
There were big, watery lights clawing down from the ceiling of
the delivery room like the lights in dentists' surgeries. She could
just see her husband looking down at her. His face was white and
clammy. It was his fault for wanting to be there. She had to push,
as though away from him. Then she knew it was happening. She
stretched back. She was a great surface of warm, splitting rock
and Paul was struggling bravely up into the sunlight. She had to
coax him with her cries. She felt him emerge like a trapped survivor. The doctor groped with rubber gloves. "There we are," he
said. She managed to look at Mr. Singleton. She wanted suddenly to put him back inside for good where Paul had come from.
With a fleeting pity she saw that this was what Mr. Singleton
wanted too. His eyes were half closed. She kept hers on him. He
seemed to wilt under her gaze. All his toughness and control were
draining from him and she was glad. She lay back triumphant and
glad. The doctor was holding Paul; but she looked, beyond, at Mr.
Singleton. He was far away like an insect. She knew he couldn't
hold out. He was going to faint. He was looking where her legs
were spread. His eyes went out of focus. He was going to faint,
keel over, right there on the spot.

Mrs. Singleton grew restless, though she lay unmoving on the
beach. Wasps were buzzing close to her head, round their picnic
bag. She thought that Mr. Singleton and Paul had been too long
at their swimming lesson. They should come out. It never struck
her, hot as she was, to get up and join her husband and son in the
sea. Whenever Mrs. Singleton wanted a swim she would wait

until there was an opportunity to go in by herself; then she would wade out, dip her shoulders under suddenly and paddle about contentedly, keeping her hair dry, as though she were soaking herself in a large bath. They did not bathe as a family; nor did Mrs. Singleton swim with Mr. Singleton—who now and then, too, would get up by himself and enter the sea, swim at once about fifty yards out, then cruise for long stretches, with a powerful crawl or butterfly, back and forth across the bay. When this happened Mrs. Singleton would engage her son in talk so he would not watch his father. Mrs. Singleton did not swim with Paul either. He was too old now to cradle between her knees in the very shallow water, and she was somehow afraid that while Paul splashed and kicked around her he would suddenly learn how to swim. She had this feeling that Paul would only swim while she was in the sea, too. She did not want this to happen, but it reassured her and gave her sufficient confidence to let Mr. Singleton continue his swimming lessons with Paul. These lessons were obsessive, indefatigable. Every Sunday morning at seven, when they were at home, Mr. Singleton would take Paul to the baths for yet another attempt. Part of this, of course, was that Mr. Singleton was determined that his son should swim; but it enabled him also to avoid the Sunday morning languor: extra hours in bed, leisurely love-making.

Once, in a room at college, Mr. Singleton had told Mrs. Singleton about his swimming, about his training sessions, races; about what it felt like when you could swim really well. She had run her fingers over his long, naked back.

Mrs. Singleton sat up and rubbed sun-tan lotion on to her thighs. Down near the water's edge, Mr. Singleton was standing about waist deep, supporting Paul who, gripped by his father's hands, water wings still on, was flailing, face down, at the surface. Mr. Singleton kept saying, "No, keep still." He was trying to get Paul to hold his body straight and relaxed so he would float. But each time as Paul nearly succeeded he would panic, fearing his father would let go, and thrash wildly. When he calmed down and Mr. Singleton held him, Mrs. Singleton could see the water running off his face like tears.

Mrs. Singleton did not alarm herself at this distress of her son. It was a guarantee against Mr. Singleton's influence, an assurance that Paul was not going to swim; nor was he to be imbued with any of his father's sullen hardiness. When Mrs. Singleton saw her son suffer, it pleased her and she felt loving towards him. She felt that an invisible thread ran between her and the boy which commanded him not to swim, and she felt that Mr. Singleton knew that it was because of her that his efforts with Paul were in vain. Even now, as Mr. Singleton prepared for another attempt, the boy was looking at her smoothing the suntan oil on to her legs.

"Come on, Paul," said Mr. Singleton. His wet shoulders shone like metal.

When Paul was born it seemed to Mrs. Singleton that her life with her husband was dissolved, as a mirage dissolves, and that she could return again to what she was before she knew him. She let her staved-off hunger for happiness and her old suppressed dreams revive. But then they were not dreams, because they had a physical object and she knew she needed them in order to live. She did not disguise from herself what she needed. She knew that she wanted the kind of close, even erotic relationship with her son that women who have rejected their husbands have been known to have. The kind of relationship in which the son must hurt the mother, the mother the son. But she willed it, as if there would be no pain. Mrs. Singleton waited for her son to grow. She trembled when she thought of him at eighteen or twenty. When he was grown he would be slim and light and slender like a boy even though he was a man. He would not need strong body because all his power would be inside. He would be all fire and life in essence. He would become an artist, a sculptor. She would pose for him naked (she would keep her body trim for this), and he would sculpt her. He would hold the chisel. His hands would guide the cold metal over the stone and its blows would strike sunlight.

Mrs. Singleton thought: All the best statues they had seen in Greece seemed to have been dredged up from the sea.

She finished rubbing the lotion on to her insteps and put the cap back on the tube. As she did so she heard something that made her truly alarmed. It was Mr. Singleton saying, "That's it, that's the way! At last! Now keep it going!" She looked up. Paul was in the same position as before but he had learnt to make slower, regular motions with his limbs and his body no longer sagged in the middle. Though he still wore the water-wings he was moving, somewhat laboriously, forwards so that Mr. Singleton had to walk along with him; and at one point Mr. Singleton removed one of his hands from under the boy's ribs and simultaneously looked at his wife and smiled. His shoulders flashed. It was not a smile meant for her. She could see that. And it was not one of her husband's usual, infrequent, rather mechanical smiles. It was the smile a person makes about some joy inside, hidden and incommunicable.

"That's enough," thought Mrs. Singleton, getting to her feet, pretending not to have noticed, behind her sun-glasses, what had happened in the water. It *was* enough: They had been in the water for what seemed like an hour. He was only doing it because of their row last night, to make her feel he was not out-matched by using the reserve weapon of Paul. And, she added with relief to herself, Paul still had the water-wings and one hand to support him.

"That's enough now!" she shouted aloud, as if she were slightly, but not ill-humouredly, peeved at being neglected. "Come on in now!" She had picked up her purse as a quickly conceived ruse as she got up, and as she walked towards the water's edge she waved it above her head. "Who wants an ice-cream?"

Mr. Singleton ignored his wife. "Well done, Paul," he said. "Let's try that again."

Mrs. Singleton knew he would do this. She stood on the little ridge of sand just above where the beach, becoming fine shingle, shelved into the sea. She replaced a loose strap of her bikini over her shoulder and with a finger of each hand pulled the bottom half down over her buttocks. She stood feet apart, slightly on her toes, like a gymnast. She knew other eyes on the beach would be on her. It flattered her that she—and her husband, too—received admiring glances from those around. She thought, with relish for the irony: Perhaps they think we are happy, beautiful people. For all her girlhood diffidence, Mrs. Singleton enjoyed displaying her attractions and she liked to see other people's pleasure. When she lay sunbathing she imagined making love to all the moody, pubescent boys on holiday with their parents, with their slim waists and their quick heels.

"See if you can do it without me holding you," said Mr. Singleton. "I'll help you at first." He stooped over Paul. He looked like a mechanic making final adjustments to some proto-type machine.

"Don't you want an ice-cream then, Paul?" said Mrs. Singleton. "They've got those chocolate ones."

Paul looked up. His short wet hair stood up in spikes. He looked like a prisoner offered a chance of escape, but the plastic water-wings, like some absurd pillory, kept him fixed.

Mrs. Singleton thought: He crawled out of me; now I have to lure him back with ice-cream.

"Can't you see he was getting the hang of it?" Mr. Singleton said. "If he comes out now he'll—"

"Hang of it! It was you. You were holding him all the time."

She thought: Perhaps I am hurting my son.

Mr. Singleton glared at Mrs. Singleton. He gripped Paul's shoulders. "You don't want to get out now, do you Paul?" He looked suddenly as if he really might drown Paul rather than let him come out.

Mrs. Singleton's heart raced. She wasn't good at rescues, at resuscitations. She knew this because of her life with her husband.

"Come on, you can go back in later," she said.

Paul was a hostage. She was playing for time, not wanting to harm the innocent.

She stood on the sand like a marooned woman watching for ships. The sea, in the sheltered bay, was almost flat calm. A few, glassy waves idled in but were smoothed out before they could break. On the headlands there were outcrops of scaly rocks like basking lizards. The island in Greece had been where Theseus left Ariadne. Out over the blue water, beyond the heads of bobbing swimmers, seagulls flapped like scraps of paper.

Mr. Singleton looked at Mrs. Singleton. She was a fussy mother daubed with Ambre Solaire, trying to bribe her son with silly ice-creams; though if you forgot this she was a beautiful, tanned girl, like the girls men imagine on desert islands. But then, in Mr. Singleton's dreams, there was no one else on the untouched shore he ceaselessly swam to.

He thought, if Paul could swim, then I could leave her.

Mrs. Singleton looked at her husband. She felt afraid. The water's edge was like a dividing line between them which marked off the territory in which each existed. Perhaps they could never cross over.

"Well, I'm getting the ice-creams: you'd better get out."

She turned and paced up the sand. Behind the beach was an ice-cream van painted like a fairground.

Paul Singleton looked at his mother. He thought: She is deserting me—or I am deserting her. He wanted to get out to follow her. Her feet made puffs of sand which stuck to her ankles, and you could see all her body as she strode up the beach. But he was afraid of his father and his gripping hands. And he was afraid of his mother, too. How she would wrap him, if he came out, in the big yellow towel like egg yolk, how she would want him to get close to her smooth, sticky body, like a mouth that would swallow him. He thought: The yellow towel humiliated him, his father's hands humiliated him. The water-wings humiliated him: You put them on and became a puppet. So much of life is humiliation. It was how you won love. His father was taking off the water-wings like a man unlocking a chastity belt. He said: "Now try the same, coming towards me." His father stood some feet away from him. He was a huge, straight man, like the pier of a bridge. "Try." Paul Singleton was six. He was terrified of water. Every time he entered it he had to fight down fear. His father never realized this. He thought it was simple; you said: "Only water, no need to be afraid." His father did not know what fear was; the same as he did not know what fun was. Paul Singleton hated water. He hated it in his mouth and in his eyes. He hated the chlorine smell of the swimming baths, the wet, slippery tiles, the echoing whoops and screams. He hated it when his father read to him from *The Water Babies*. It was the only story his father read, because, since he didn't know fear or fun, he was really sentimental. His mother read lots of stories. "Come on then. I'll catch you." Paul Singleton held out his arms and raised one leg. This was the worst moment. Perhaps having no help was most humiliating. If you did not swim you sank like a statue. They would drag him out, his skin streaming. His father would say: "I didn't mean . . ." But if he swam his mother would be forsaken. She would stand on the beach with chocolate ice-cream running down her arm. There was no way out; there were all these things to be afraid of and no weapons. But then, perhaps he was not afraid of his mother nor his father, nor of water, but of something else. He had felt it just now—when he'd struck out with rhythmic, reaching strokes and his feet had come off the bottom and his father's hand had slipped from under his chest: as if he had mistaken what his fear was; as if he had been unconsciously pretending, even to himself, so as to execute some plan. He lowered his chin into the water. "Come on!" said Mr. Singleton. He launched himself forward and felt the sand leave his feet and his legs wriggle like cut ropes. "There," said his father as he realized. "There!" His father stood like a man waiting to clasp a lover; there was a gleam on his face. "Towards me! Towards me!" said his father suddenly. But he kicked and struck, half in panic, half in pride, away from his father, away from the shore, away, in this strange new element that seemed all his own.

from **the stranger**

A LBERT C AMUS

i had a hard time waking up on Sunday, and Marie had to call me and shake me. We didn't eat anything, because we wanted to get to the beach early. I felt completely drained and I had a slight headache. My cigarette tasted bitter. Marie made fun of me because, she said, I had on a "funeral face." She had put on a white linen dress and let her hair down. I told her she was beautiful and she laughed with delight.

On our way downstairs we knocked on Raymond's door. He told us he'd be right down. Once out in the street, because I was so tired and also because we hadn't opened the blinds, the day, already bright with sun, hit me like a slap in the face. Marie was jumping with joy and kept on saying what a beautiful day it was. I felt a little better and I noticed that I was hungry. I told Marie, who pointed to her oilcloth bag where she'd put our bathing suits and a towel. I just had to wait and then we heard Raymond shutting his door. He had on blue trousers and a white short-sleeved shirt. But he'd put on a straw hat, which made Marie laugh, and his forearms were all white under the black hairs. I found it a little repulsive. He was whistling as he came down the stairs and he seemed very cheerful. He said "Good morning, old man" to me and called Marie "mademoiselle."

The day before, we'd gone to the police station and I'd testified that the girl had cheated on Raymond. He'd gotten off with a warning. They didn't check out my statement. Outside the front door we talked about it with Raymond, and then we decided to take the bus. The beach wasn't very far, but we'd get there sooner that way. Raymond thought his friend would be glad to see us get there early. We were just about to leave when all of a sudden Raymond motioned to me to look across the street. I saw a group of Arabs leaning against the front of the tobacconist's shop. They were staring at us in silence, but in that way of theirs, as if we were nothing but stones or dead trees. Raymond told me that the second one from the left was his man, and he seemed worried. But, he added, it was all settled now. Marie didn't really understand and asked us what was wrong. I told her that they were Arabs who had it in for Raymond. She wanted to get going right away. Raymond drew himself up and laughed, saying we'd better step on it.

We headed toward the bus stop, which wasn't far, and Raymond said that the Arabs weren't following us. I turned around. They were still in the same place and they were looking with the same indifference at the spot where we'd just been standing. We caught the bus. Raymond, who seemed very relieved, kept on cracking jokes for Marie. I could tell he liked her, but she hardly said anything to him. Every once in a while she'd look at him and laugh.

We got off in the outskirts of Algiers. The beach wasn't far from the bus stop. But we had to cross a small plateau which overlooks the sea and then drops steeply down to the beach. It was covered with yellowish rocks and the whitest asphodels set against the already hard blue of the sky. Marie was having fun scattering the petals, taking big swipes at them with her oilcloth bag. We walked between rows of small houses behind green or white fences, some with their verandas hidden behind the tamarisks, others standing naked among the rocks. Before we reached the edge of the plateau, we could already see the motionless sea and, farther out, a massive, drowsy-looking promontory in the clear water. The faint hum of a motor rose up to us in the still air. And way off, we saw a tiny trawler moving, almost imperceptibly, across the dazzling sea. Marie gathered some rock irises. From the slope leading down to the beach, we could see that there were already some people swimming.

Raymond's friend lived in a little wooden bungalow at the far end of the beach. The back of the house rested up against the rocks, and the pilings that held it up in front went straight down into the water. Raymond introduced us. His friend's name was Masson. He was a big guy, very tall and broad-shouldered, with a plump, sweet little wife with a Parisian accent. Right off he told us to make ourselves at home and said that his wife had just fried up some fish he'd caught that morning. I told him how nice I thought his house was. He told me that he spent Saturdays and Sundays and all his days off there. "With my wife, of course," he added. Just then his wife was laughing with Marie. For the first time maybe, I really thought I was going to get married.

Masson wanted to go for a swim, but his wife and Raymond didn't want to come. The three of us went down to the beach and Marie jumped right in. Masson and I waited a little. He spoke slowly, and I noticed that he had a habit of finishing everything he said with "and I'd even say." when really it didn't add anything to the meaning of his sentence. Referring to Marie, he said, "She's stunning, and I'd even say charming." After that I didn't pay any more attention to this mannerism of his, because I was absorbed by the feeling that the sun was doing me a lot of good. The sand was starting to get hot underfoot. I held back the urge to get into the water a minute longer, but finally I said to Masson, "Shall we?" I dove in. He waded in slowly and started swimming only when he couldn't touch bottom anymore. He did the breast stroke, and not too well, either, so I left him and joined Marie. The water was cold and I was glad to be swimming. Together again, Marie and I swam out a ways, and we felt a closeness as we moved in unison and were happy.

Out in deeper water we floated on our backs and the sun on my upturned face was drying the last of the water trickling into my mouth. We saw Masson making his way back to the beach to stretch out in the sun. From far away he looked huge. Marie wanted us to swim together. I got behind her to hold her around the waist. She used her arms to move us forward and I did the kicking. The little splashing sound followed us through the morning air until I got tired. I left Marie and headed back, swimming smoothly and breathing easily. On the beach I stretched out on my stomach alongside Masson and put my face on the sand. I said it was nice and he agreed. Soon afterwards Marie came back. I rolled over to watch her coming. She was glistening all over with salty water and holding her hair back. She lay down right next to me and the combined warmth from her body and from the sun made me doze off.

Marie shook me and told me that Masson had gone back up to the house, that it was time for lunch. I got up right away because I was hungry, but Marie told me I hadn't kissed her since that morning. It was true, and yet I had wanted to. "Come into the water," she said. We ran and threw ourselves into the first little waves. We swam a few strokes and she reached out and held on to me. I felt her legs wrapped around mine and I wanted her.

When we got back, Masson was already calling us. I said I was starving and then out of the blue he announced to his wife that he liked me. The bread was good; I devoured my share of the fish. After that there was some meat and fried potatoes. We all ate without talking. Masson drank a lot of wine and kept filling my glass. By the time the coffee came, my head felt heavy and I smoked a lot. Masson, Raymond, and I talked about spending August together at the beach, sharing expenses. Suddenly Marie said, "Do you know what time it is? It's only eleven-thirty!" We were all surprised, but Masson said that we'd eaten very early and that it was only natural because lunchtime was whenever you were hungry. For some reason that made Marie laugh. I think she'd had a little too much to drink. Then Masson asked me if I wanted to go for a walk on the beach with him. "My wife always takes a nap after lunch. Me, I don't like naps. I need to walk. I tell her all the time it's better for her health. But it's her business." Marie said she'd stay and help Madame Masson with the dishes. The little Parisienne said that first they'd have to get rid of the men. The three of us went down to the beach.

The sun was shining almost directly overhead onto the sand, and the glare on the water was unbearable. There was no one left on the beach. From inside the bungalows bordering the plateau and jutting out over the water, we could hear the rattling of plates and silverware. It was hard to breathe in the rocky heat rising from the ground. At first Raymond and Masson discussed people and things I didn't know about. I gathered they'd known each other for a long time and had even lived together at one point. We headed down to the sea and walked along the water's edge. Now and then a little wave would come up higher than the others and wet our canvas shoes. I wasn't thinking about anything, because I was half asleep from the sun beating down on my bare head.

At that point Raymond said something to Masson which I didn't quite catch. But at the same time I noticed, at the far end of the beach and a long way from us, two Arabs in blue overalls coming in our direction. I looked at Raymond and he said, "It's him." We kept walking. Masson asked how they'd managed to follow us all this way. I thought they must have seen us get on the bus with a beach bag, but I didn't say anything.

The Arabs were walking slowly, but they were already much closer. We didn't change our pace, but Raymond said, "If there's any trouble. Masson, you take the other one. I'll take care of my man. Meursault, if another one shows up, he's yours." I said, "Yes," and Masson put his hands in his pockets. The blazing sand looked red to me now. We moved steadily toward the Arabs. The distance between us was getting shorter and shorter. When we were just a few steps away from each other, the Arabs stopped. Masson and I slowed down. Raymond went right up to his man. I couldn't hear what he said to him, but the other guy made a move as though he were going to butt him. Then Raymond struck the first blow and called Masson right away. Masson went for the one that had been pointed out as his and hit him twice, as hard as he could. The

Arab fell flat in the water, facedown, and lay there for several seconds with bubbles bursting on the surface around his head. Meanwhile Raymond had landed one too, and the other Arab's face was bleeding. Raymond turned to me and said. "Watch this. I'm gonna let him have it now." I shouted, "Look out, he's got a knife!" But Raymond's arm had already been cut open and his mouth slashed. Masson lunged forward. But the other Arab had gotten back up and gone around behind the one with the knife. We didn't dare move. They started backing off slowly, without taking their eyes off us, keeping us at bay with the knife. When they thought they were far enough away, they took off running as fast as they could while we stood there motionless in the sun and Raymond clutched at his arm dripping with blood.

Masson immediately said there was a doctor who spent his Sundays up on the plateau. Raymond wanted to go see him right away. But every time he tried to talk the blood bubbled in his mouth. We steadied him and made our way back to the bungalow as quickly as we could. Once there, Raymond said that they were only flesh wounds and that he could make it to the doctor's. He left with Masson and I stayed to explain to the women what had happened. Madame Masson was crying and Marie was very pale. I didn't like having to explain to them, so I just shut up, smoked a cigarette, and looked at the sea.

Raymond came back with Masson around one-thirty. His arm was bandaged up and he had an adhesive plaster on the corner of his mouth. The doctor had told him that it was nothing, but Raymond looked pretty grim. Masson tried to make him laugh. But he still wouldn't say anything. When he said he was going down to the beach, I asked him where he was going. He said he wanted to get some air. Masson and I said we'd go with him. But that made him angry and he swore at us. Masson said not to argue with him. I followed him anyway.

We walked on the beach for a long time. By now the sun was overpowering. It shattered into little pieces on the sand and water. I had the impression that Raymond knew where he was going, but I was probably wrong. At the far end of the beach we finally came to a little spring running down through the sand

behind a large rock. There we found our two Arabs. They were
lying down, in their greasy overalls. They seemed perfectly calm
and almost content. Our coming changed nothing. The one who
had attacked Raymond was looking at him without saying anything. The other one was blowing through a little reed over and
over again, watching us out of the corner of his eye. He kept
repeating the only three notes he could get out of his instrument.

The whole time there was nothing but the sun and the silence,
with the low gurgling from the spring and the three notes. Then
Raymond put his hand in his hip pocket, but the others didn't
move, they just kept looking at each other. I noticed that the toes
on the one playing the flute were tensed. But without taking his
eyes off his adversary, Raymond asked me, "Should I let him have
it?" I thought that if I said no he'd get himself all worked up and
shoot for sure. All I said was, "He hasn't said anything yet. It'd be
pretty lousy to shoot him like that." You could still hear the sound
of the water and the flute deep within the silence and the heat.
Then Raymond said, "So I'll call him something and when he
answers back, I'll let him have it." I answered, "Right. But if he
doesn't draw his knife, you can't shoot." Raymond started getting
worked up. The other Arab went on playing, and both of them
were watching every move Raymond made. "No," I said to
Raymond, "take him on man to man and give me your gun. If the
other one moves in, or if he draws his knife, I'll let him have it."

The sun glinted off Raymond's gun as he handed it to me. But
we just stood there motionless, as if everything had closed in
around us. We stared at each other without blinking, and everything came to a stop there between the sea, the sand, and the sun,
and the double silence of the flute and the water. It was then that
I realized that you could either shoot or not shoot. But all of a
sudden, the Arabs, backing away, slipped behind the rock. So
Raymond and I turned and headed back the way we'd come. He
seemed better and talked about the bus back.

I went with him as far as the bungalow, and as he climbed the
wooden steps, I just stood there at the bottom, my head ringing
from the sun, unable to face the effort it would take to climb the
wooden staircase and face the women again. But the heat was so

intense that it was just as bad standing still in the blinding stream falling from the sky. To stay or to go, it amounted to the same thing. A minute later I turned back toward the beach and started walking.

There was the same dazzling red glare. The sea gasped for air with each shallow, stifled little wave that broke on the sand. I was walking slowly toward the rocks and I could feel my forehead swelling under the sun. All that heat was pressing down on me and making it hard for me to go on. And every time I felt a blast of its hot breath strike my face, I gritted my teeth, clenched my fists in my trouser pockets, and strained every nerve in order to overcome the sun and the thick drunkenness it was spilling over me. With every blade of light that flashed off the sand, from a bleached shell or a piece of broken glass, my jaws tightened. I walked for a long time.

From a distance I could see the small, dark mass of rock surrounded by a blinding halo of light and sea spray. I was thinking of the cool spring behind the rock. I wanted to hear the murmur of its water again, to escape the sun and the strain and the women's tears, and to find shade and rest again at last. But as I got closer, I saw that Raymond's man had come back.

He was alone. He was lying on his back, with his hands behind his head, his forehead in the shade of the rock, the rest of his body in the sun. His blue overalls seemed to be steaming in the heat. I was a little surprised. As far as I was concerned, the whole thing was over, and I'd gone there without even thinking about it.

As soon as he saw me, he sat up a little and put his hand in his pocket. Naturally, I gripped Raymond's gun inside my jacket. Then he lay back again, but without taking his hand out of his pocket. I was pretty far away from him, about ten meters or so. I could tell he was glancing at me now and then through half-closed eyes. But most of the time, he was just a form shimmering before my eyes in the fiery air. The sound of the waves was even lazier, more drawn out than at noon. It was the same sun, the same light still shining on the same sand as before. For two hours the day had stood still; for two hours it had been anchored in a sea of molten lead. On the horizon, a tiny steamer went by, and I made out the black dot from the corner of my eye because I hadn't stopped watching the Arab.

It occurred to me that all I had to do was turn around and that would be the end of it. But the whole beach, throbbing in the sun, was pressing on my back. I took a few steps toward the spring. The Arab didn't move. Besides, he was still pretty far away. Maybe it was the shadows on his face, but it looked like he was laughing. I waited. The sun was starting to burn my cheeks, and I could feel drops of sweat gathering in my eyebrows. The sun was the same as it had been the day I'd buried Maman, and like then, my forehead especially was hurting me, all the veins in it throbbing under the skin. It was this burning, which I couldn't stand anymore, that made me move forward. I knew that it was stupid, that I wouldn't get the sun off me by stepping forward. But I took a step, one step, forward. And this time, without getting up, the Arab drew his knife and held it up to me in the sun. The light shot off the steel and it was like a long flashing blade cutting at my forehead. At the same instant the sweat in my eyebrows dripped down over my eyelids all at once and covered them with a warm, thick film. My eyes were blinded behind the curtain of tears and salt. All I could feel were the cymbals of sunlight crashing on my forehead and, indistinctly, the dazzling spear flying up from the knife in front of me. The scorching blade slashed at my eyelashes and stabbed at my stinging eyes. That's when everything began to reel. The sea carried up a thick, fiery breath. It seemed to me as if the sky split open from one end to the other to rain down fire. My whole being tensed and I squeezed my hand around the revolver. The trigger gave; I felt the smooth underside of the butt; and there, in that noise, sharp and deafening at the same time, is where it all started. I shook off the sweat and sun. I knew that I had shattered the harmony of the day, the exceptional silence of a beach where I'd been happy. Then I fired four more times at the motionless body where the bullets lodged without leaving a trace. And it was like knocking four quick times on the door of unhappiness.

the duel

Takeshi Kaiko

at the beach, two men were sitting on the coral reef. Beside them were two open lunch boxes on a spread cloth. The younger man occasionally nibbled a piece of fried chicken, while sipping local sake made from black molasses. The older man hugged his long legs, gazing into the horizon across the sea. He drank tea from the thermos bottle and ate sushi. The sky was filled with the characteristic tropical light that was clear, yet hazy at this hour, and its luminosity spread over the entire sky. The vast expanse of the East China Sea, streaked with blues, aquamarines, indigos, was at low ebb, smoothly sensuous, almost lascivious. The only sound was the water caressing and lapping innumerable tiny pores of the reef below their hips. There was no human shadow, no house on the spacious atoll. No cans, bottles, vinyl trash. No footprints, no fingerprints. The young man had been gently rocked by the lapping sound in his body ever since he reached the edge of the water.

Sea water had settled in pools here and there in the dents of the reef. The young man cautiously bent over the puddle, but the countless, tiny tropical fish fled in all directions, frightened by his shadow. Over the calcified bed of fish and insect debris, some fish emitted gleaming light, some wiggled suggestively, some others disappeared, spreading a tiny curtain of sand dust. The young man deliberately dropped a piece of chicken into the pool, instantly causing a commotion in the water. As the white piece glided down the clear aquamarine water, the yellow, the red, the violet flashed and vanished and the chicken was gone instantaneously. A tiny scorpion fish appeared from behind a rock, swaying lazily, its tentacle fins fully spread like peacock feathers. Finding nothing, the little creature swayed back to its rock, disappointed. The young man chuckled or burst out laughing each time he dropped the chicken pieces. Intermittently he threw a jigger or two of sake after them.

The older had thick eyebrows, a strong jaw, and large eyes. From time to time, he pulled out a letter from his coat pocket and read it in silence. A smile spread on his pale, hollow cheeks. His wife had written him a love poem in ancient Manyo style. As he was leaving home with his visitor that morning, she had handed each man a lacquered lunch box. In each she had enclosed a poem and instructed them not to open their lunch until they reached the beach. It seemed his wife wrote poems in the kitchen, while frying chicken or making sushi. The young man had opened his box as soon as they reached the beach and discovered a sheet of letter paper above the wrapped chicken pieces. The poem was written in antiquated but skillful calligraphy, as if challenging him. It was about the queen of all South Sea fishes welcoming the visitor to the island. The older man's lunch box seemed to have contained a love poem for her husband. "Don't read it on the way," his wife had said smiling. "You must wait until you get to the shore. Then you will want to come straight home in the evening." She had stood at the gate, waving goodbye to the departing men.

The strong, luxuriant sun began to lose its sharp edge, and a soft haze spread over the late afternoon sky. A harbinger of evening began to flow out of the lingering clouds and to permeate the atmosphere almost audibly like mysterious whispering. The offshore aquamarine grew pale while the blues and indigos deepened. Still constantly washing the reef, the sea was somehow growing desolate. The young man stopped playing with the fish and sipped sake, gazing into the ocean. As the sunlight waned, the alcohol seemed to grow heavy, irritating. It was time to stop. He had been able to maintain his freshness all afternoon, sitting on the ancient reef. If he continued to drink until evening, he would grow stale, trouble by words, sentences. But he rolled yet another drop or two of sake on his already coarsened and swollen tongue as though forcing down bitter medicine.

The older man looked at his watch and said, "It's about time we went. The snakeman must be waiting. You've got to see it at least once for the experience. The man said he would choose the best, both the snake and the mongoose. It's like a cockfight. The battle is short but ferocious."

"Does the mongoose always win?"

"Not necessarily. Seven or eight out of ten, yes—but sometimes he loses. This is like *a coup de main*. The duel is settled by the point of the sword. When the swords clash, the fight is already over. The mongoose targets the upper jaw of the snake to make sure of his victory. His instinct tells him that the fangs are there. He's never been taught, but he knows where the right spot is. Once he bites into the jaw, he hangs on for dear life and chews it up until the snake's neck is broken. If he misses the jaw, the mongoose loses. If he bites into the body or tail of the snake, the fangs will get him in a second."

"It's like the duel of Ganryujima!"

"Even if the mongoose wins, if his mouth is hurt while chewing the snake head, the poison will get to him and he will die within twenty-four hours. So, you don't know whether he is the real winner or not until the day after, so says the snakeman."

The older man continued his explanation, closing his lunch box. A *habu* snake is believed to be myopic and astigmatic. Waving his tongue, he senses the delicate stir in the air as an enemy approaches, and his unique apparatus detects the enemy's heat radiation. He strikes suddenly. He contracts his body into an S, and, pivoting on the third of his body on the ground, flies with the remaining two thirds. With his mouth open wide and baring scythelike fangs, he whips the air, half blind, yet with a deadly accuracy. He drives his fangs into the enemy, pours out one gram of venom, and instantly backs away. One gram of the deadly poison is said to be sufficient to kill thousands of rabbits. A *habu* can kill human beings and dogs; it can swallow eels, blue jays, frogs, black hares, field rats, long-haired rats, rocks, and occasionally, his own kind.

A *habu*'s parents disappear promptly the minute an egg hatches. The baby snake must find his own food from the day he is born, but he already possesses enough poison to kill a man. A solitary creature, a *habu* acts alone and ubiquitously. He slithers through the night, swims noiselessly across a swamp, traverses a valley, and sneaks into a town, creeps into a toilet, a boot, a kitchen, a charcoal sack, anything. Sometimes he creeps into a public bath and into a woman's clothes basket there, because he likes dark, warm, damp places. Once captured and put in a locked box, he will refuse to eat or drink, his blind eyes wide open and gaping. He will ignore a rat thrown into the box, keeping his mouth closed for six months or a year. With his eyes shining gold in the sun, or gleaming like dull copper in the dark, he will hold his head high and die of starvation.

The young man exclaimed, "What a magnificent creature!"

The older man nodded. "So, a *habu* is a desperado that can kill men and horses. As the saying goes: If his teacher comes, he will stab the teacher; if his father crosses his path, he will kill his father, too. But the mongoose is just as much of a scamp and kills snakes and rats, chickens and hens. In Okinawa, a mongoose gouged out a sleeping baby's eyes. Whether he is starved or full, he will rip the throat of an opponent. So, you might say they are a good match. The funny thing is that each one uses only one weapon. The mongoose attacks the jaw of a snake, and the snake can, if he wants to, wrap himself around the mongoose and strangle him, but he won't. A snake uses only his fangs. If the mongoose bites first, he just writhes helplessly."

The two men picked up their lunch boxes and stood. They

began to trudge over the large reef toward the beach. The sky and the ocean were utterly tranquil. Only the sound of the lapping water droned. The breeze was tempered now by a few cold streaks of air. The acrid odors of seaweeds, some putrid, some fresh, hung heavily in the lagoon. The two men climbed the slope, crept through a long, low, serpentine wall of dark banyan trees entangled with a clump of pines, and entered the village. Looking back at the edge of the village toward the atoll, they found the field of rocks sparkling green and white in the softening sun. Already everything had been erased. Traces of two men eating, talking, and laughing there all afternoon were gone. The sky, sea, reef, all stood silently as they did two thousand years ago.

Walking through the forest, the older man called, "Hoot, hoot!"

Soon there was a response. Hoot, hoot! The birdcall followed the man, who continued to hoot while walking. Sometimes the hoots seemed to go astray, probably blocked by trees; still they followed the two men.

The young man stopped and cried out, "An owl! An owl is crying!"

The older man smiled. "I have a genius for doing things that bring no money."

He continued to hoot as he walked.

The owl followed him, calling from tree branches, but it finally stopped at the border of the village and, hooting two or three grudging cries, flew away to the deeper part of the forest.

There was a vacant lot in the midst of closely built matchbox shacks. Boxes with metal screens like chicken coops stood in the center of the lot, and a man in a white coat was waiting beside them, holding a stick in his hand. As soon as the two men walked up to him, he began to talk. He was a man of medium height with a ruddy face and sharp eyes. He spoke in a mellow, experienced voice, showing the differences of genitalia on several male and female snakes preserved in alcohol jars. Then, from one of the boxes, he hooked a snake with the tip of a wire and swiftly caught its narrow neck with his bare hand. The snake opened its wide mouth fully and the white, translucent, sharp fangs jutted out from the sheath folds like hypodermic needles. The man put the snake's head against the edge of the wooden box, and the viper angrily bit into the wood, grating its surface. Instantly, liquid shot from its mouth and trickled down the box. Incongruous with its gigantic, triangular head in the ugly color of dirt, and inconsistent with its ferocious gold eyes, wet flesh like the inside of a little girl's crotch suddenly exposed itself under the sun. The mouth orifice was covered with gleaming pink-white membrane. Delicate red and blue distal blood vessels ran through the virginal flesh folds inside. It was moist, clean, white, tender, and fragile. The young man was fascinated. He felt an urge to caress it with his fingers, feel the tension and wetness of the white flesh, and trace the suction of the soft resilient folds into the deep interior. He wanted to fondle the translucent, strong, sharp fangs, too.

What's wrong with me? Am I exhausted? So run-down?

The box was partitioned with a screen divider. In one section was a snake, in the other a mongoose. The snake was slithering, scraping the wooden floor, ceaselessly forming and untangling the S shape. Her head erect and darting swiftly to left and right, she flickered her black tongue continually. She crawled up the dividing metal screen and groped about the screen mesh with her tongue. Her myopic eyes goggling toward the shining mist, she seemed to wonder what this strange vibration and heat could be that came through the air. Her whiplike forebody quivered, stretching and contracting, while her hind half, swinging aimlessly, stored up energy. Beyond the shiny fog was a small quadruped with the body of a weasel and the face of a rat, making light footstep noises as it scampered to right and left. Small red eyes shining, his soft, buff-colored back undulating, the little animal pivoted on his thick tail and stood on his hind legs. Pulling his forelegs to his breast as if beckoning, he squeaked sharply two, three times as though grinding teeth. The young man bent forward in spite of himself, and the animal's small threatening face looked up. Malevolence and cruelty unimaginable from such a small, lovable body flashed in the red eyes. The single-minded bloodthirstiness made its head something mean and base. The young man involuntarily stepped back and turned away.

"Are you ready?" The snakeman's voice was ominous. "Let's go!" He pulled up the divider. A buff color flashed into the box. The mongoose had darted to the snake's head, dug into it; already his small, white teeth were crunching. Wearing the mongoose on her head, the snake rolled and wriggled and contracted her long body like a corkscrew, but she never tried to wrap around the mongoose. As the older man had described, her only weapon was the fangs, and her defeat had become decisive at the first moment. Silently, she writhed and thrashed about, trying to free herself from the animal. The mongoose's eyes flared and his small, angular, blood-covered head rolled with the snake, but he hung on fast to the slippery body of the snake with his black claws while continuing chomping.

(Forestall, give all to the first moment. Once into the enemy's vitals, never let go! Hang on to the end! Crush! Chew!) The heavy but sharp crunching noise of breaking bones continued for a while. The triangle head lost its shape and the eyes were smashed. Fresh blood spurted, and long fangs protruded helplessly from the upper jaw. Turning his face sideways, the mongoose bit into the white flesh at the root of the fangs and continued to munch. The fangs broke off and fell to the floor. They shined dully in the blood puddle in the evening sun. The mangled head of the snake gaped like a dark vermilion hole. Her body stirred spasmodically, shrinking and stretching, but finally lay long in the pool of blood. Once she lost her head, she was like a decorative cord with its tassle severed. The mouth hung gaping, crushed shapelessly. The white, voluptuous body continued to bleed slowly. His body shivering, the mongoose jutted out his angular face and began to lap up blood and munch noisily on the delicate female body of the snake. He sipped, licked his paws, tore off a mouthful of flesh, chewed.

The two men left the area in silence, shoulder to shoulder. The poverty-stricken houses, like barnacle clusters, stood in the resounding explosion of the setting subtropical sun, and the perfect moment of the day inflamed the sky and the road. The young man stopped and lit a cigarette. Although he had been drinking all afternoon, he felt no trace of the blue flame of alcohol. A thirst slowly spread throughout his body.

"They don't wrestle," he commented, his voice a little hoarse.

The older man's eyes were somber, virile. He smiled deeply. "No mercy allowed."

Trailing a long shadow on the barren road, the older man hung his head low and spoke again. "No mercy allowed."

At last, the young man thought, *I have taken my first step on this island*.

great barrier reef

DIANE JOHNSON

the motel had smelled of cinder block and cement floor, and was full of Australian senior citizens off a motor coach, but when we woke up in the morning a little less jet-lagged, and from the balcony could see the bed of a tidal river, with ibis and herons poking along the shallows, and giant ravens and parrots in the trees—trees strangling with Monstera vines, all luridly beautiful—we felt it would be all right. But then, when we went along to the quay, I felt it wouldn't. The ship, the Dolphin, was smaller than one could have imagined. Where could sixteen passengers possibly sleep? Brown stains from rusted drainspouts spoiled the hull. Gray deck paint splattered the ropes and ladders, orange primer showed through the chips. Wooden crates of lettuce and cabbages and a case of peas in giant tin cans were stacked on the deck. This cruise had been J.'s idea, so I tried not to seem reproachful, or shocked at the tiny, shabby vessel. But I am not fond of travel in the best of circumstances—inconvenient displacements punctuated by painful longings to be home. For J., travel is natural opium.

J. was on his way to a meeting in Singapore of the International Infectious Disease Council, a body of eminent medical specialists from different lands who are charged with making decisions about diseases. Should the last remaining smallpox virus be destroyed? What was the significance of a pocket of polio in Sri Lanka? Could leprosy be finished off with a full-bore campaign in the spring? Was tuberculosis on the way back now via AIDS? What about measles in the Third World? I had not realized until I took up with J. that these remote afflictions were still around, let alone that they killed people in the millions. A professor of medicine, J. did research on things that infected the lungs.

He had always longed to visit the Great Barrier Reef, and afterward would give some lectures in Sydney and Wellington, and we planned to indulge another whim en route—skiing in New Zealand in the middle of summer, just to say we'd skied in August and as a bribe to me to come along, for I will go anywhere to ski, it is the one thing. For me the voyage was one of escape from California after some difficult times, and was to be—this was unspoken by either of us—a sort of trial honeymoon (though we were not married) on which we would discover whether we were suited to live together by subjecting ourselves to that most serious of tests, travelling together.

A crewman named Murray, a short, hardy man with a narrow Scots face and thick Aussie accent, showed us our stateroom. It had been called a stateroom in the brochure. Unimaginably small. J. couldn't stand up all the way in it. Two foam mattresses on pallets suspended from the wall, and a smell. The porthole was seamed with salt and rust. Across the passage, the door of another stateroom was open, but that one was a large, pretty room, with mahogany and nautical brass fittings and a desk, and the portholes shone. It was the one, certainly, that had been pictured in the brochure.

"This one here, the Royal, was fitted for Prince Charles, Prince of Wales, when he come on this voyage in 1974," Murray said.

"How do you book the Royal?" I asked.

"First come, first served," Murray said. Australian, egalitarian, opposed to privilege.

Up on deck, thinking of spending five days on the Dolphin, I began to be seized by feelings of panic and pain I couldn't explain. They racketed about in my chest, my heart beat fast, I felt as if a balloon were inflating inside me, squeezing up tears and pressing them out of my eyes and thrusting painful words up into my throat, where they lodged. What was the matter with me? Usually I am a calm person (I think); five days is not a lifetime; the aesthetics of a mattress—or its comfort—is not a matter for serious protests. A smell of rotten water sloshing somewhere inside the hull could be gotten used to. Anyone could eat tinned peas five days and survive, plenty of people in the world were glad to get tinned peas. I knew all that. I knew I wasn't reacting appropriately, and was sorry for this querulous fit of passion. Maybe it was only jet lag.

All the same, I said to J., "I just can't," and stared tragically at the moorings. He knew, of course, that I could and probably would, but he maintained an attitude of calm sympathy.

"You've been through a rough time," he said. "It's the court thing you're really upset about." Maybe so. The court thing, a draining and frightening custody suit, had only been a week ago, and now here we were a hemisphere away.

The other passengers came on board, one by one or two by two. Cases clattered on the metal gangs. To me, only one person looked possible—a tall, handsome, youngish man with scholarly spectacles and a weathered yachting cap. The rest were aged and fat, plain, wore shapeless brown or navy-blue coat-sweaters buttoned over paunches, had gray perms and bald spots, and they all spoke in this accent I disliked, as if their towels had been slammed in doors. They spoke like cats, I thought: *eeeooow*. Fat Australians, not looking fond of nature, why were they all here?

"Why are these people here?" I complained to J. "What do they care about the Great Barrier Reef?"

"It's a wonder of the world, anyone would want to see it," J. said, assuming the same dreamy expression he always wore when talking or thinking about the Great Barrier Reef, so long the object of his heart.

I hated all the other passengers. On a second inspection, besides the youngish man, only a youngish couple, Dave and Rita, looked promising, but then I was infuriated to learn that Dave and Rita were Americans—we hadn't come all this way to be cooped up for five days in a prison of an old Coast Guard cutter with other Americans—and, what was worse, Rita and Dave had drawn the Prince Charles cabin, and occupied it as if by natural right, Americans expecting and getting luxury.

Of course, I kept these overwrought feelings to myself. No Australian complained. None appeared unhappy with the ship; no satirical remark, no questioning comment marred their apparent delight with the whole shipshape of things—the cabins, even the appalling lunch, which was under way as soon as the little craft set out, pointing itself east, toward the open sea, from Mackay Harbor.

After we lost sight of land, my mood of desperate resentment did not disappear, as J. had predicted, but deepened. It was more than the irritability of a shallow difficult person demanding comfort, it was a failure of spirit, inexplicable and unwarranted on this bright afternoon. How did these obese Australian women these stiff old men, clamber so uncomplainingly belowdecks to their tiny cells, careen along the railings, laughing crazily as they tripped on ropes? Doubtless one would fall and the voyage would be turned back. When I thought of the ugliness of the things I had just escaped from—the unpleasant divorce, the custody battle, the hounding of lawyers and strangers—only to find myself in such a place as this, really unmanageable emotions made me turn my face away from the others.

Dinner was tinned peas, and minted lamb overdose to a gray rag, and potatoes. J. bought a bottle of wine from the little bar, which the deckhand Murray nimble leaped behind, transforming himself into waiter or bartender as required. We sat with the promising young man, Mark, and offered him some wine, but he said he didn't drink wine. He was no use; he was very, very prim, a bachelor civil servant from Canberra, with a slight stammer, only handsome and young by some accident, and would someday be old without changing, would still be taking lonely cruises, eating minted lamb, would still be unmarried and reticent. He had no conversation, had never been anywhere, did not even know what we wanted from him. Imagining his life, I thought about how sad it was to be him, hoping for whatever he hoped for but not hoping for the right things, content to eat these awful peas, doomed by being Australian, and even while I pitied him I found him hopeless. Even J., who could talk to anyone, gave up trying to talk to him, and, feeling embarrassed to talk only to each other as if he weren't there, we fell silent and stared out the windows at the rising moon along the black horizon of the sea.

There didn't seem a way, in the tiny cabin, for two normal-sized people to exist, let alone to make love; there was no space that could accommodate two bodies in any position. Our suitcases filled half the room. With our summer clothing, our proper suits to wear in Wellington and Sydney, and bulky ski clothes of quilted down, we were ridiculously encumbered with baggage. It seemed stupid now. We were obliged to stow our bags and coats precariously on racks overhead, our duffelbags sleeping at the feet of our bunks like lumpy interloper dogs. J. took my hand comfortingly in the dark, across the space between the two bunks, before he dropped off to sleep; I lay awake, seized with a terrible fit of traveller's panic, suffocating with fearful visions of fire, of people in prison cells or confined in army tanks, their blazing bodies emerging screaming from the holds of ships to writhe doomed on the ground, their stick limbs ringed in flame, people burned in oil splashed on them from the holds of rusted ships, and smells of underground, smells of sewers, the slosh of engine fuel from the hell beneath.

As is so often the traveller's fate, nothing on the cruise was as promised or as we had expected. The seedy crew of six had tourist-baked smiles and warmed-over jokes. There was a little faded captain who climbed out of his tower to greet us now and then, and a sort of Irish barmaid, Maureen, who helped Murray serve the drinks. The main business of the passage seemed not to be the life of the sea or the paradise of tropical birds on Pacific shores or the balmy water but putting in at innumerable islands to look at souvenir shops. J., his mind on the Great Barrier Reef, which we were expected to reach on the fourth day, sweetly bore in all, the boredom and the endless stops at each little island, but I somehow couldn't conquer my petulant dislike.

It fastened, especially, on our shipmates. Reluctantly, I learned their names, in order to detest them with more precision: Don and Donna from New Zealand, Priscilla from Adelaide—portly, harmless old creatures, as J. pointed out. Knowing that the derisive remarks that sprang to my lips only revealed me as petty and complaining to good-natured J., I didn't speak them aloud. But it seemed to me that these Australians only wanted to travel to rummage in the souvenir shops, though these were all alike from island to island: Daydream Island, Hook Island—was this a cultural or a generation gap? I brooded on the subject of souvenirs: why they should exist, why people should want them, by what law they were made ugly—shells shaped like toilets, a row of swizzlesticks in the shapes of women's silhouetted bodies, thin, fatter, fat, with bellies and breasts increasingly sagging as they graduated from "Sweet Sixteen" to "Sixty." I was unsettled to notice that the one depicting a woman of my age had a noticeably thickened middle. I watched a man buy a fat one and hand it to his wife. "Here, Mother, this one's you," he said. Laughter a form of hate. It was not a man from our ship, luckily, or I would have pushed him overboard. I brooded on my own complicity in the industry of souvenirs, for didn't I buy them myself? The things I bought—the tasteful (I liked to think) baskets and elegant textiles I was always carting home—were these not just a refined form of souvenir for a more citified sort of traveller?

Statuettes of drunken sailors, velvet pictures of island maidens, plastic seashell lamps made in Taiwan. What contempt the people who think up souvenirs have for other people! Yet our fellow-passengers plunked down money with no feeling of shame. They never walked on the sand or looked at the colors of the bright patchwork birds rioting in the palm trees. Besides us, only the other Americans, Rita and Dave, did this. It was Dave who found the perfect helmet shell, a regular treasure, the crew assured them, increasingly rare protected even—you weren't supposed to carry them away, but who was looking? I wanted it to have been J. who got it.

Each morning, each afternoon, we stopped at another island. This one was Daydream Island. "It's lovely, isn't it, dear?" Priscilla said to me. "People like to see a bit of a new place, the shopping, they have different things to make it interesting." But it wasn't different, it was the same each day: the crew hands the heavy, sacklike people, grunting, down into rowboats, and hauls them out onto a sandy slope of beach. Up they trudge toward a souvenir shop. This one had large shells perched on legs, and small shells pasted in designs on picture frames, and earrings made of shells, and plastic buckets, and plastic straw hats surrounded with fringe, and pictures of hula dancers.

"I don't care, I do hate them," I ranted passionately to J. "I'm right to hate them. They're what's the matter with the world, they're ugly consumers, they can't look at a shell unless it's coated in plastic, they never look at the sea—why are they here? Why don't they stay in Perth and Adelaide—you can buy shells there, and swizzlesticks in the shape of hula girls." Of course J. hadn't any answer for this, of course I was right.

I wandered onto a stretch of beach and took off my shoes, planning to wade. Whenever I was left alone I found myself harking back to the court hearing, my recollections just as sharp and painful as a week ago. I couldn't keep from going over and over my ordeal, and thinking of my hated former husband, or not really him so much as his lawyer, Waxman, a man in high-heeled boots and aviator glasses. I imagined him here in these waters. He has fallen overboard off the back of the ship. I am the only one to notice, and I have the power to cry out for his rescue but I don't. Our eyes meet; he is down in the water, still wearing the glasses. I imagine his expression of surprise when he realizes that I'm not going to call for help. What for him had been a mere legal game, a job, would cost him his life. He had misjudged me. The ship speeds along. We are too far away to hear his cries.

It was the third day, and we had set down at Happy Island. Here we had to wade across a sandbar. This island had goats grazing. "This is the first we've gotten wet," I bitterly complained. We stood in ankle-deep water amid queer gelatinous seaweed. I had wanted to swim, to dive, to sluice away the court and the memories, but hadn't been permitted to, because these waters, so innocently beautiful, so seductively warm, were riddled with poisonous creatures, deadly toxims and sharks.

"Be careful not to pick up anything that looks like this," Murray warned, showing us a harmless-looking little shell. "The deadly cone shell. And the coral, be careful a' that, it scratches like hell. One scratch can take over a year to heal. We have some ointment on board, be sure to tell one of the crew if you scratch yourself."

From here, I looked back at the ship, and, seeing the crew watching us, I suddenly saw ourselves, the passengers, with the crew's eyes: we were a collection of thick bodies, mere cargo to be freighted around, slightly volatile, likely to ferment, like damp grain and to give trouble—difficult cargo that boozed, send you scurrying unreasonably on tasks, got itself cut on coral, made you laugh at its jokes. I could see that the crew must hate us.

Yet, a little later, I came upon Murray tying on a fishhook for old George, whose fingers were arthritic. Murray was chatting to him with a natural smile. I studied them. Perhaps Murray by himself was a man of simple good nature, but the rest, surely, hated us. The captain, staring coolly out from his absurd quarterdeck, made no pretense of liking us, seemed always to be thinking of something else, not of this strange Pacific civilization of Quonset huts and rotting landing barges and odd South Sea denizens strangely toothless, beyond dentistry, beyond fashion, playing old records over and over on P.A. systems strung through the palms. You felt the forlornness of these tacky little islands that should have been beautiful and serene. I even wondered if we would ever get back to America. Not that I wanted to. America was smeared with horrible memories, scenes of litigation. Why shouldn't J. and I simply stay here? Why, more important, was I not someone who was able, like the lovely goat that grazed on the slope near here, to gaze at the turquoise sea and enjoy the sight of little rose-colored parrots wheeling in the air? Why was I not, like a nice person, simply content to *be*, to enjoy beauty and inner peace? Instead I must suffer, review, quiver with fears and rages—the fault, I saw, was in myself, I was a restless, peevish, flawed person. How would I be able to struggle out of this frame of mind? Slipping on the sandy bank, I frightened the little goat.

By the third day I began to notice a sea change in our shipmates, who had begun in sensible gabardines and print dresses, but now wore violently floral shirts and dresses, and were studded with shells—wreaths of shells about their necks and at their ears, hats embroidered with crabs and gulls. By now I knew a bit more about them. They were all travellers. George and Nettie, Fred and Polly had been friends for forty years, and spent a part of each year, now that they were all retired, travelling in Europe in their caravans. Dave and Rita were both schoolteachers, and Rita raised Great Danes. Priscilla was going along on this cruise with her brother Albert, because Albert had just lost his wife. Mark was taking his annual vacation. Don and Donna were thinking of selling their Auckland real-estate business, buying a sailboat to live on, and circumnavigating the globe. J. told me that George was a sensitive and sweet man who had lived his whole life in Australia, and only now in his retirement had begun to see something of the world. "And he says that the most beautiful place on earth is some place near Split, in Yugoslavia, and if I take you there, my darling, will you for God's sake cheer up now?" But I couldn't.

Tonight we were dining ashore, in a big shed on Frenchie's Island, a shabby tin building. Music was already playing on loudspeakers. Groups of people from other ships, or hotels, strolled around carrying drinks. A smell of roasted sausages, someone singing "Waltzing Matilda" in the kitchen at the back. The

Dolphin passengers were lined up at the bar and in the souvenir shop. In the big hangar of a room little tables encircled a dance floor, and at one end a microphone stood against a photo mural of the South Seas, as if the real scene outdoors were not sufficiently evocative. The sun lowered across the pink water, setting in the east, and the water in the gentle lagoon was as warm as our blood. "I wish a hurricane would come and blow it all away," I said to J.

When the diners had tipped their paper plates into a bin, they began to sing old American songs. Sitting outside, I could hear Maureen singing "And Let Her Sleep Under the Bar." Then came canned music from a phonograph, and people began to dance—the ones who were not too decrepit. I tried to hear only the chatter of the monkeys or parrots in the palm trees, innocent creatures disturbed by the raucous humans. J. was strangely cheerful and shot some pool with a New Zealander, causing me all of a sudden to think, with a chill of disapproval, that J. possibly was an Australian at heart and that I ought not to marry him or I would end up in a caravan in Split. His good looks and professional standing were only a mask that concealed . . . simplicity.

It didn't surprise me that people liked the handsome and amiable J.; it didn't even surprise me that they seemed to like me. I had concealed my tumult of feelings, and I was used to being treated by other people with protective affection, if only because I am small. This in part explained why the courtroom, and its formal process of accusation, its focus on me as a stipulated bad person, had been such a shock. It was as if a furious mob had come to smash with sticks the porcelain figure of my self. I had a brief intimation that the Australians, with their simple friendliness, could put me back together if I would let them, but I would rather lie in pieces for a while.

The moon was full and golden. "What a beautiful beautiful night," said Nettie from Perth, the wife of George, coming out onto the beach. Who could disagree? Not even I. The ship on the moonlit water lapped at anchor, resting, awaiting them, looking luxurious and serene. J. came out and showed us the Southern

Cross. At first I couldn't see it, all constellations look alike to
me—I have never been able to see the bears or belts or any of it.
But now, when J. turned my chin, I did see it, and it did look like
a cross.

In the night I had another dream, in which the lawyer had said,
"Isn't it true that you have often left your children while you
travel?" He had been looking not at me but at a laughing audience. He was speaking over a microphone. The audience wore
fringed hats of plastic straw.

"Not willingly, no," I said. "Not often."

"How many times did you go on trips last year and leave them
at home?"

"Oh, six, I don't know."

"That's not often?"

"Just a day or two each time. A man takes a business trip, you
don't call it 'leaving,' or 'often.'" But I was not allowed to speak
or explain.

"We're looking at how often you are in fact away from your
children."

Here I had awakened, realizing that it was all true, it wasn't just
a dream, it was what had happened—not, of course, the audience
in plastic hats. Even though in the end I had been vindicated in
the matter of the children, I still felt sticky with the encumbrance
of their father's hate. All I had wanted was to be free, and now I
was so soiled with words spoken at me, about me, by strangers,
by lawyers I had never seen before, who had never seen me. It
didn't seem fair that you could not prevent being the object of
other people's emotions, you were not safe anywhere from their
hate—or from their love, for that matter. You were never safe
from being invaded by their feelings when you wanted only to
be rid of them, free, off, away.

In the morning I had wanted to swim, to bathe in the sea, to
wash all this stuff off, splash; my longing must have been clear,
because Cawley, the other deckhand, laughed at me. "Not here
you don't, love," he said. "There's sharks here as long as a boat."

The captain, Captain Clarke, made one of his few visits. He had kept aloof in the pilot cabin above, though he must have slipped down to the galley to eat, or maybe the crew took him his food up there. Now he invited his passengers two by two to the bridge. When people were tapped, they hauled themselves up the metal ladder, steadied by Cawley or Murray, then would come down looking gratified. Albert, who went up alone, suggested that he had helped avoid a navigational accident.

J. and I were invited on the morning of the fourth day, the day we were to arrive at the reef itself in the late afternoon. I went up despite myself. Captain Clarke was a thin, red-haired man sitting amid pipes and instruments. He let us take the wheel, and showed us the red line that marked our route through the labyrinth of islands on the chart. His manner was grave, polite, resigned. No doubt these visits were dictated by the cruise company.

"But there are thousands of islands between here and the Great Barrier Reef!" said J., studying the charts.

"Souvenir shops on every one," I couldn't help saying. J. fastened me with a steady look in which I read terminal exasperation.

"These islands are not all charted," said the Captain. "The ones that are were almost all charted by Captain Cook himself, after he ran aground on one in 1770. He was a remarkable navigator. He even gave names to them all. But new ones are always being found. I've always hoped to find one myself."

"What would you name it?" J. asked.

"I would give it my name, or, actually, since there is already a Clarke Island, I would name it for my wife, Laura—Laura Clarke Island—or else for Alison my daughter."

"Do you keep your eyes open for one?"

"I mean to get one," he said.

When we went down to the deck again, Maureen was gazing at the waves. "It's getting choppy," she observed, unnecessarily, for the boat had begun to rear up like a prancing horse.

"Right, we probably won't make it," Murray agreed.

"What do you mean?" I asked, alarmed by the tinge of satisfaction that underlay their sorry looks.

"To the reef. No point in going if the sea's up, like it's coming up—washed right up, no use going out there. If it's like this, we put in at Hook Island instead."

Astonished, I looked around to see if J., or anyone else, was listening. No, or not worried—would just as soon have Hook Island. They continued to knit and read along the deck, which now began to heave more forcefully, as if responding to the desire of the crew to return to port without seeing the great sight.

"How often does it happen that you don't go to the reef?" I asked Murray, heart thundering. The point of all this, and J.'s dream, was to go to the reef, and now they were casually dismissing the possibility.

"Oh, it happens more often than not. This time of year, you know. Chancy, the nautical business is."

"Come out all this way and not see it?" I insisted, voice rising.

"Well, you can't see it if the waves are covering it up, can you? You can bump your craft into it, but you can't see it. Can you?"

"I don't know," I cried. "I don't even know what it is." But the shape of things was awfully clear; given the slightest excuse, the merest breeze or ripple, the Dolphin would not take us to the Great Barrier Reef, and perhaps had never meant to. I thought in panic of not alerting J., but then I rushed to tell him. He put down his book, his expression aghast, and studied the waves.

The midday sky began to take on a blush of deeper blue, and now that our attention was called to it, the sea seemed to grow dark and rough before our eyes. Where moments before it had been smooth enough to row, we now began to pitch. The report of the prow smacking the waves made me think of cannons, of Trafalgar. In defiance of the rocking motion, the Australian passengers began to move around the cabin and along the deck, gripping the railings, looking trustfully at the sky and smiling. Their dentures were white as teacups.

"Christ," said Murray, "one of these bloody old fools will break a hip. Folks, why don't you sit down?" Obediently, like children, the Australians went inside the main cabin and sat in facing rows of chairs. Despite the abrupt change in the weather, the ship continued its course out to sea. J. and I anchored ourselves in the prow, leaning against the tool chest, resolutely watching the horizon, not the bounding deck beneath our feet—a recommended way to avoid seasickness. In twenty minutes the sea had changed altogether, from calm to a thing that threw the little ship in the air. We felt as if we were slithering along the back of a sea monster that was toiling beneath us.

Soon the dread spectre of seasickness was among us. The Captain, rusty-haired, pale-eyed, as if his eyes had been bleached with sea wind, climbed off the bridge and glanced inside the cabin at his passengers.

"Oh, please, they want to go, they'll be all right," I called to him, but the words were swept off by the wind. The others were so occupied with the likelihood of nausea that they hadn't grasped that the ship might turn back, and they seemed rather to be enjoying the drama of getting seasick. Every few minutes someone would get up, totter out to the rail, retch over it, and return to the laughter and commiseration of the others. The friendly thing was to be sick, so I was contrarily determined not to be, and J. was strong by nature. One of the Australians, Albert, gave us a matey grin as he lurched over our feet toward a bucket. I looked disgustedly away, but J. wondered aloud if he should be helping these old folks.

"Of course, they'll use this as an excuse for not going," I was saying bitterly. These barfing Australian senior citizens would keep us from getting to the Great Barrier Reef. My unruly emotions, which had been milder today, now plumped around in my bosom like the boat smacking on the waves. J. watched the Australians screaming with laughter and telling each other, "That's right, barf in the bin."

"This is a rough one," Albert said, and pitched sharply against the cabin, so that J. leaped up to catch him. Murray, tightening ropes, called for him to go back inside.

"Tossed a cookie meself." He grinned at J. and me.

"We don't think it's so rough," I said.

"I've seen plenty rougher," Murray agreed. "Bloody hangover is my problem."

When the Captain leaned out to look down at the deck below

him, I cried, "Oh, we just have to go to the reef, we have to! Oh, please!"

"What's the likelihood this sea will die down?" J. shouted to the Captain. The Captain shrugged. I felt angry at J. for the first time, as if he were a magnet. It was unfair, I knew, to say it was J.'s fault—the storm, the tossing sea, the Dolphin, and, of course, the rest. J. who had signed us up for this terrible voyage, during which we would be lost at sea, before reaching the Great Barrier Reef, whatever it was, and who had caused the sea to come up like this. All J.'s fault. If I ever saw the children again it would be a miracle—or else they would be saying in after years, Our mother perished on the high seas somewhere off Australia. What would they remember of me? The sight of the boiling waves, now spilling over the bow, now below us, made me think of throwing myself in—just an unbidden impulse trailing into my mind, the way I half thought, always, of throwing my keys or my sunglasses off bridges. Of course I wouldn't do it.

The ship pitched, thrust, dove through the waters. Yet we had not turned back. "Whoooeee," the Aussies were screaming inside the lounge. Life was like this, getting tossed around, and then, right before the real goal is reached, something, someone, impedes you.

"J., don't let them turn back," I said again, for the tenth time, putting all the imperative passion I could into my voice. Without hearing me, J. was already climbing the ladder to the bridge. I looked at my fingers whitely gripping the rope handle on the end of the tool chest. A bait locker slid across the deck, back, across, back, and once, upon the impact of a giant wave, a dead fish stowed in it sloshed out onto the deck. Then, in the wind, I heard Murray's thin voice call out, "It's all right, love, we're going to the reef! The Captain says we're going to the reef!"

As abruptly as the storm had started, it subsided meekly, the sky once more changed color, now to metallic gray, lighter at the horizon, as if it were dawn. Ahead of us an indistinguishable shape lay in the water like the back of a submerged crocodile, a vast bulk under the surface. The Captain had stopped the engines, and we drifted in the water. "The reef, the reef!" cried the Australians, coming out on deck. I shouted, too. The crew began to busy themselves with readying the small boats, and the other passengers came boisterously out of the cabin, as if nothing had been wrong. "Ow," they said, "that was a bit of a toss."

"You'll have two hours on the reef, not more," the Captain told us before we climbed again into the rowboats. "Because of the tide. If you get left there at high tide, if we can't find you, well, we don't come back. Because you wouldn't be there." The Australians laughed at this merry joke.

J. handed me out of the boat and onto the reef. My first step on it shocked me. For I had had the idea of coral, hard and red, a great lump of coral sticking out of the ocean, a jagged thing that would scratch you if you fell on it, that you could carve into formations dictated by your own mind. We had heard it was endangered, and I had imagined its destruction by divers with chisels, carrying off lumps at a time.

Instead it was like a sponge. It sank underfoot, it sighed and sucked. Looking down, I could see that it was entirely alive, made of eyeless formations of cabbagey creatures sucking and opening and closing, yearning toward tiny ponds of water lying on the pitted surface, pink, green, gray, viscous, silent. I moved, I put my foot here, then hurriedly there, stumbled, and gashed my palm against something rough.

"Where should you step? I don't want to step on the things," I gasped.

"You have to. Just step as lightly as you can," J. said.

"It's alive, it's all alive!"

"Of course. It's coral, it's alive, of course," J. said. He had told me there were three hundred and fifty species of living coral here, along with the calcareous remains of tiny polyzoan and hydrozoan creatures that helped to form a home for others. Anemones, worms, gastropods, lobsters, crayfish, prawns, crown of thorns, other starfish, hydrocorals, the red Lithothamnion algae, the green Halimeda.

"Go on, J., leave me," I said, seeing that he wanted to be alone to have his own thoughts about all this marine life, whatever it meant to him. It meant something. His expression was one of rapture. He smiled at me and wandered off.

I had my Minox, but I found the things beneath my feet too fascinating to photograph. Through the viewer of my camera they seemed pale and far away. At my feet, in astonishing abundance, they went on with their strange life. I hated to tread on them, so stood like a stork and aimed the camera at the other passengers.

These were proceeding cautiously, according to their fashion, over the delicate surface—Mark in his yachting cap, with his camera, alone; the Kiwis in red tropical shirts more brilliant than the most bright-hued creatures underfoot; even the crew, with insouciant expressions, protectively there to save their passengers from falls or from strange sea poisons that darted into the inky ponds from the wounded life beneath our feet. For the first time, I felt, seeing each behaving characteristically, that I liked them all, and even that I liked them, or at least that I liked it that I understood what they would wear and do. Travellers like myself.

I watched J. kneeling in the water to peer into the centers of the mysterious forms. Almost as wonderful as this various life was J.'s delight. He was as dazzled as if we had walked on stars, and, indeed, the sun shining on the tentacles, wet petals, filling the spongy holes made things sparkle like a strange underfoot galaxy. He appeared as a long, sandy-haired, handsome stranger separate, unknowable. I, losing myself once more in the patterns and colors, thought of nothing, was myself as formless and uncaring as the coral, all my unruly bad-natured passions leaching harmlessly into the sea leaving a warm sensation of blankness and ease. I thought of the Hindu doctrine of *ahimsa*, of not harming living things, and I was not harming them, I saw—neither by stepping on them nor by leaving my anger and tears and the encumbrances of real life with them. For me the equivalent of J.'s happiness was this sense of being cured of a poisoned spirit.

At sunset we headed landward into the sun, a strange direction to a Californian, for whom all sunsets are out at sea. We would arrive at Mackay at midnight—it also seemed strange that a voyage that had taken four days out would take only six hours back, something to do with the curve of the continental shelf. A spirit of triumph imbued our little party—we had lived through storms and reached a destination. People sat in the lounge labelling their film.

Maureen came along and reminded us that as this was our last night on board, there would be a fancy-dress party. When we had read this in the brochure, I had laughed. It had seemed absurd that such a little ship would give itself great liner airs. J. and I had not brought costumes. In our cabin, I asked him what he meant to wear. Since my attitude had been so resolutely one of non-compliance, he seemed surprised that I was going to participate in the dressing up. "I know it's stupid, but how can we not?" I said. "It would be so churlish, with only sixteen of us aboard."

J. wore his ski pants, which were blue and tight, with a towel cape, and called himself Batman. I wore his ski parka, a huge, orange, down-filled garment. The others were elaborately got up, must have brought their masks and spangles with them. Rita wore a black leotard and had painted cat whiskers on her face, and Dave had a Neptune beard. Nettie wore a golden crown, and Don a harlequin suit, half purple, half green. I drew to one side and sat on the table with my feet drawn up inside J.'s parka, chin on my knees, watching the capers that now began. "Me? I am a pumpkin," I explained, when they noticed the green ribbon in my hair, my stem. It wasn't much of a costume, but it was all I could think of, and they laughed forgivingly and said that it looked cute.

J. won a prize, a bottle of beer, for the best paper cutout of a cow. I was surprised, watching him making meticulous little snips with the scissors, to see how a cow shape emerged under his hands, with a beautiful, delicate udder and teats, and knobs of horn. I had not thought that J. would notice a cow.

"I have an announcement," Mark said, in a strangely loud and shaky voice, one hand held up, his other hand nervously twisting his knotted cravat. The theme of his costume was not obvious.

"Excuse me, an announcement." The others smiled and shushed. "I've had word frommy friend—a few months ago I had the honor to assist a friend with his astronomical observations, and I've just had word that he—we—that the comet we discovered has been accepted by the international commission. It will bear his name, and, as I had the honor to assist, I'll be mentioned, too. Only a little comet, of course, barely a flash in the sky. There are millions of them, of course. There are millions of them, but—" A cheer, toasts. Mark bought drinks for everybody. The crew bought drinks for the guests, dishing up from behind the little bar with the slick expertise of landside bartenders. They seemed respectful at Mark's news. I raised my glass with the rest and felt ashamed at the way I had despised Mark's life—indeed, a nice life, spent exploring the heavens with a friend. How had I thought him friendless, this nice-looking young man?

"Split, Yugoslavia, is the most beautiful place on earth," George was telling me. "Like a travel poster. I've been almost everywhere by now except China, but there, at Split, my heart stopped." My attention was reclaimed from my own repentant thoughts; for a second I had been thinking that he was describing a medical calamity, and I had been about to say "How terrible!"

But no, he was describing a moment, an epiphany, the experience of beauty. He had the long, bald head of a statesman, but he was a farmer, now retired, from Perth. I was ashamed that it had taken me so long to see that the difference between Americans and Australians was that Americans were tired and bored, while for Australians, stuck off at the edge of the world, all was new, and they had the energy and spirit to go off looking for abstractions like beauty, and comets.

"Let me get you another one of those," George said, taking my wineglass, for a pumpkin cannot move.

"How long have you been married?" asked Nettie, smiling at me. I considered, not knowing whether I wanted to shock them by admitting that we were not married at all. "Two years," I said.

"Really?" Nettie laughed. "We all thought you was newly-weds." Her smile was sly.

I felt myself flush inside the hot parka. The others had thought all my withdrawn unfriendliness was newlywed shyness and the preoccupations of love. They were giving me another chance.

"It seems like it." I laughed. I would never marry J., I thought. He was too good-natured to be saddled with a cross person like me. And yet now I wasn't cross, was at ease and warm with affection for the whole company. Don and Donna were buying champagne all around, and the crew, now that they were about to be rid of this lot of passengers, seemed sentimental and sorry, as if we had been the nicest most amusing passengers ever. The prize for the best costume was to be awarded by vote. People wrote on bits of paper and passed them to Maureen, who sat on the bar and sorted them. There was even a little mood of tension, people wanting to win.

"And the prize for the best costume"— she paused portentously—"goes to the pumpkin!" My shipmates beamed and applauded. In the hot parka I felt myself grow even warmer with shame and affection. People of good will and good sense, and I had allowed a snobbish mood of acedia to blind me to it. Their white, untroubled smiles.

In a paper parcel was a key ring with a plastic-covered picture of the Dolphin, and the words "Great Barrier Reef" around the edge of it. I was seized by a love for it, would always carry it, I decided, if only as a reminder of various moral lessons I thought myself to have learned, and as a reminder of certain bad things about my own character.

"Thank you very much," I said. "I'll always keep it. And I'll always remember the Dolphin and all of you"—for I thought, of course, that I would. J. was looking at me with a considering air, as if to inspect my sincerity. But I was sincere.

"I know I've been a pig," I apologised to him later, as we gathered our things in the stateroom. "These people are really very sweet."

"I wonder if you'd feel like that if you hadn't gotten the prize," he said, peevishly. I was surprised at his tone. Of course, it wasn't the prize—only a little key chain, after all—that had cured me, but the process of the voyage, and the mysterious power of distant places to dissolve the problems the traveller has brought along. Looking at J., I could see that, for his part, he was happy but let down, as if the excitement and happiness of seeing the reef at last, and no doubt the nuisance of my complaining, had worn him out for the moment, and serious thoughts of his coming confrontations with malaria and leprosy and pain and sadness were returning, and what he needed was a good night's sleep.

perfection

V L A D I M I R   N A B O K O V

now then, here we have two lines," he would say to David in a cheery, almost rapturous voice as if to have two lines were a rare fortune, something one could be proud of. David was gentle but dullish. Watching David's ears evolve a red glow, Ivanov foresaw he would often appear in David's dreams, thirty or forty years hence: human dreams do not easily forget old grudges.

Fair-haired and thin, wearing a yellow sleeveless jersey held close by a leather belt, with scarred naked knees and a wrist-watch whose crystal was protected by a prison-window grating, David sat at the table in a most uncomfortable position, and kept tapping his teeth with the blunt end of his fountain pen. He was doing badly at school, and it had become necessary to engage a private tutor.

"Let us now turn to the second line," Ivanov continued with the same studied cheeriness. He had taken his degree in geography but his special knowledge could not be put to any use: dead riches, a highborn pauper's magnificent manor. How beautiful, for instance, are ancient charts! Viatic maps of the Romans, elongated, ornate, with snakelike marginal stripes representing canal-shaped seas; or those drawn in ancient Alexandria, with England and Ireland looking like two little sausages; or again, maps of medieval Christendom, crimson-and-grass-colored, with the paradisian Orient at the top and Jerusalem—the world's golden navel—in the center. Accounts of marvelous pilgrimages: that travelling monk comparing the Jordan to a little river in his native Chernigov, that envoy of the Tsar reaching a country where people strolled under yellow parasols, that merchant from Tver picking his way through a dense *"zhengel,"* his Russian for "jungle," full of monkeys, to a torrid land ruled by a naked prince. The islet of the known universe keeps growing: new hesitant contours emerge from the fabulous mists, slowly the globe disrobes—and lo, out of the remoteness beyond the seas, looms South America's shoulder and from their four corners blow fat-cheeked winds, one of them wearing spectacles.

But let us forget the maps. Ivanvo had many other joys and eccentricities. He was lanky, swarthy, none too young, with a permanent shadow cast on his face by a black beard that had once been permitted to grow for a long time, and had then been shaven off (at a barbershop in Serbia, his first stage of expatriation): the slightest indulgence made that shadow revive and begin to bristle. Throughout a dozen years of émigré life, mostly in Berlin, he had remained faithful to starched collars and cuffs; his deteriorating shirts had an outdated tongue in front to be buttoned to the top of his long underpants. Of late he had been obliged to wear constantly his old formal black suit with braid piping along the lapels (all his other clothes having rotted away); and occasionally, on an overcast day, in a forbearing light, it seemed to him that he was dressed with sober good taste. Some sort of flannel entrails were trying to escape from his necktie, and he was forced to trim off parts of them, but could not bring himself to excise them altogether.

He would set out for his lesson with David at around three in the afternoon, with a somewhat unhinged, bouncing gait, his head held high. He would inhale avidly the young air of the early summer, rolling his large Adam's apple, which in the course of the morning had already fledged. On one occasion a youth in leather leggings attracted Ivanov's absent gaze from the opposite sidewalk by means of a soft whistle, and, throwing up his own chin, kept it up for a distance of a few steps: thou shouldst correct thy fellow man's oddities. Ivanov, however, misinterpreted that didactic mimicry and, assuming that something was being pointed out to him overhead, looked trustingly even higher than was his wont—and, indeed, three lovely cloudlets, holding each other by the hand, were drifting diagonally across the sky; the third one fell slowly behind, and its outline, and the outline of the friendly hand still stretched out to it, slowly lost their graceful significance.

During those first warm days everything seemed beautiful and touching: the leggy little girls playing hopscotch on the sidewalk, the old men on the benches, the green conferu that sumptuous lindens scattered every time the air stretched its invisible limbs. He felt lonesome and stifled in black. He would take off his hat and stand still for a moment looking around. Sometimes, as he looked at a chimney sweep (that indifferent carrier of other people's luck, whom women in passing touched with superstitious fingers), or at an airplane overtaking a cloud, Ivanov daydreamed about the many things that he would never get to know closer, about professions that he would never practice, about a parachute, opening like a colossal corolla, or the fleeting, speckled world of automobile racers, about various images of happiness, about the pleasures of very rich people amid very picturesque natural surroundings. His thought fluttered and walked up and down the glass pane which for as long as he lived would prevent him from having direct contact with the world. He had a passionate desire to experience everything, to attain and touch everything, to let the dappled voices, the bird calls, filter through his being and to enter for a moment into a passerby's soul as one enters the cool shade of a tree. His mind would be preoccupied with unsolvable problems: How and where do chimney sweeps wash after work? Has anything changed about that forest road in Russia that a moment ago he had recalled so vividly?

When, at last, late as usual, he went up in the elevator, he would have a sensation of slowly growing, stretching upward, and, after his head had reached the sixth floor, of pulling up his legs like a swimmer. Then, having reverted to normal length, he would enter David's bright room.

During lessons David liked to fiddle with things but otherwise remained fairly attentive. He had been raised abroad and spoke Russian with difficulty and boredom, and, when faced with the necessity of expressing something important, or when talking to his mother, the Russian wife of a Berlin businessman, would immediately switch to German. Ivanov, whose knowledge of the local language was poor, expounded mathematics in Russian, while the textbook was, of course, in German, and this produced a certain amount of confusion. As he watched the boy's ears, edged with fair down, he tried to imagine the degree of tedium and detestation he must arouse in David, and this distressed him. He saw himself from the outside—a blotchy complexion, a *feu du rasoir*, a shiny black jacket, stains on its sleeve cuffs—and caught his own falsely animated tone, the throat-clearing noises he made, and even that sound which could not reach David—the blundering but dutiful beat of his long-ailing heart. The lesson came to an end, the boy would hurry to show him something, such as an automobile catalogue, or a camera, or a cute little screw found in the street—and then Ivanov did his best to give proof of intelligent participation—but, alas, he never had been on intimate terms with the secret fraternity of man-made things that goes under the name technology, and this or that inexact observation of his would make David fix him with puzzled pale-gray eyes and quickly take back the object which seemed to be whimpering in Ivanov's hands.

And yet David was not untender. His indifference to the unusual could be explained—for I, too, reflected Ivanov, must have appeared to be a stolid and dryish lad, I who never shared with anyone my loves, my fancies and fears. All that my childhood expressed was an excited little monologue addressed to itself. One might construct the following syllogism: a child is the most perfect type of humanity; David is a child; David is perfect.

With such adorable eyes as he has, a boy cannot possibly keep thinking only about the prices of various mechanical gadgets or about how to save enough trading stamps to obtain fifty pfennigs' worth of free merchandise at the store. He must be saving up something else too: bright childish impressions whose paint remains on the fingertips of the mind. He keeps silent about it just as I kept silent. But if several decades later—say, in 1970 (how they resemble telephone numbers, those distant years!), he will happen to see again that picture now hanging above his bed— Bonzo devouring a tennis ball—what a jolt he will feel, what light, what amazement at his own existence. Ivanov was not entirely wrong, David's eyes, indeed, were not devoid of a certain dreaminess; but it was the dreaminess of concealed mischief.

Enters David's mother. She has yellow hair and a high-strung temperament. The day before she was studying Spanish; today she subsists on orange juice. "I would like to speak to you. Stay seated, please. Go away, David. The lesson is over? David, go. This is what I want to say. His vacation is coming soon. It would be appropriate to take him to the seaside. Regrettably, I shan't be able to go myself. Would you be willing to take him along? I trust you, and he listens to you. Above all, I want him to speak Russian more often. Actually, he's nothing but a little *Sportsmann* as are all modern kids. Well, how do you look at it?"

With doubt. But Ivanov did not voice his doubt. He had last seen the sea in 1912, eighteen years ago when he was a university student. The resort was Hungerburg in the province of Estland. Pines, sand, silvery-pale water far away—oh, how long it took one to reach it, and then how long it took it to reach up to one's knees! It would be the same Baltic Sea, but a different shore. However, the last time I went swimming was not at Hungerburg but in the river Luga. Muzhiks came running out of the water, frog-legged, hands crossed over their private parts: *pudor agrestis*. Their teeth chattered as they pulled on their shirts over their wet bodies. Nice to go bathing in the river toward evening, especially under a warm rain that makes silent circles, each spreading and encroaching upon the next, all over the water. But I like to feel underfoot the presence of the bottom. How hard to put on again one's socks and shoes without muddying the soles of one's feet! Water in one's ear: keep hopping on one foot until it spills out like a tickly tear.

The day of departure soon came. "You will be frightfully hot in those clothes," remarked David's mother by way of farewell as she glanced at Ivanov's black suit (worn in mourning for his other defunct things). The train was crowded, and his new, soft collar (a slight compromise, a summer treat) turned gradually into a tight clammy compress. Happy David, his hair neatly trimmed, with one small central tuft playing in the wind, his open-necked shirt aflutter, stood, at the corridor window, peering out, and on curves the semicircles of the front cars would become visible, with the heads of passengers who leaned on the lowered frames. Then the train, its bell ringing, its elbows working ever so rapidly, straightened out again to enter a beech forest.

The house was located at the rear of the little seaside town, a plain two-storied house with red-currant shrubs in the yard, which a fence separated from the dusty road. A tawny-bearded fisherman sat on a log, slitting his eyes in the low sun as he tarred his net. His wife led them upstairs. Terra-cotta floors, dwarf furniture. On the wall, a fair-sized fragment of an airplane propeller: "My husband used to work at the airport." Ivanov unpacked his scanty linen, his razor, and a dilapidated volume of Pushkin's works in the Panafidin edition. David freed from its net a varicolored ball that went jumping about and from sheer exuberance only just missed knocking a horned shell off its shelf. The landlady brought tea and some flounder. David was in a hurry. He could not wait to get a look at the sea. The sun had already begun to set.

When they came down to the beach after a fifteen-minute walk, Ivanov instantly became conscious of an acute discomfort in his chest, a sudden tightness followed by a sudden void, and out on the smooth, smoke-blue sea a small boat looked black and appallingly alone. Its imprint began to appear on whatever he looked at, then dissolved in the air. Because now the dust of twilight dimmed everything around, it seemed to him that his eyesight was dulled, while his legs felt strangely weakened by the squeaky touch of the sand. From somewhere came the playing of an orchestra, and its every sound, muted by distance, seemed to be corked up; breathing was difficult. David chose a spot on the beach and ordered a wicker cabana for next day. The way back was uphill; Ivanov's heart now drifted away, then hurried back to perform anyhow what was expected of it, only to escape again, and through all this pain and anxiety the nettles along the fences smelled of Hungerburg.

David's white pajamas. For reasons of economy Ivanov slept naked. At first the earthen cold of the clean sheets made him feel even worse, but then repose brought relief. The moon groped its way to the wash-stand, selected there one facet of a tumbler, and started to crawl up the wall. On that and on the following nights, Ivanov thought vaguely of several matters at once, imagining among other things that the boy who slept in the bed next to his was his own son. Ten years before, in Serbia, the only woman he had ever loved—another man's wife—had become pregnant by him. She suffered a miscarriage and died the next night, deliring and praying. He would have had a son, a little fellow about David's age. When in the morning David prepared to pull on his swimming trunks, Ivanov was touched by the way his café-au-lait tan (already acquired on a Berlin lakeside) abruptly gave way to a childish whiteness below the waist. He was about to forbid the boy to go from house to beach with nothing on but those trunks, and was a little taken aback, and did not immediately give in, when David began to argue, with the whining intonations of German astonishment, that he had done so at another resort and that everyone did it. As to Ivanov, he languished on the beach in the sorrowful image of a city dweller. The sun, the sparkling blue, made him seasick. A hot tingling ran over the top of his head under his fedora, he felt as if he were being roasted alive, but he would not even dispense with his jacket, not only because as is the case with many Russians, it would embarrass him to "appear in his braces in the presence of ladies," but also because his shirt was too badly frayed. On the third day he suddenly gathered up his courage and, glancing furtively around from under his brows, took off his shoes. He settled at the bottom of a crater dug by David, with a newspaper sheet spread under his elbow, and listened to the tight snapping of the gaudy flags, or else peered over the sandy brink with a kind of tender envy at a thousand brown corpses felled in various attitudes by the sun; one girl was especially magnificent, as if cast in metal, tanned to the point of blackness, with amazingly light eyes and with fingernails as pale as a monkey's. Looking at her he tried to imagine what it felt like to be so sunbaked.

On obtaining permission for a dip, David would noisily swim off while Ivanov walked to the edge of the surf to watch his charge and to jump back whenever a wave spreading farther than its predecessors threatened to douse his trousers. He recalled a fellow student in Russia, a close friend of his, who had the knack of pitching pebbles so as to have them glance off the water's surface two, three, four times, but when he tried to demonstrate it to David, the projectile pierced the surface with a loud plop, and David laughed, and made a nice flat stone perform not four but at least six skips.

A few days later, during a spell of absentmindedness (his eyes had strayed, and it was too late when he caught up with them), Ivanov read a postcard that David had begun writing to his mother and had left lying on the window ledge. David wrote that his tutor was probably ill for he never went swimming. That very day Ivanov took extraordinary measures: he acquired a black bathing suit and, on reaching the beach, hid in the cabana, undressed gingerly, and pulled on the cheap shop-smelling stockinet garment. He had a moment of melancholy embarrassment when, pale-skinned and hairy-legged, he emerged into the sunlight. David, however, looked at him with approval. "Well!" exclaimed Ivanov with devil-may-care jauntiness, "here we go!" He went in up to his knees, splashed some water on his head, then walked on with outspread arms, and the higher the water rose, the deadlier became the spasm that contracted his heart. At last, closing his ears with his thumbs, and covering his eyes with the rest of his fingers, he immersed himself in a crouching position. The stabbing chill compelled him to get promptly out of the water. He lay down on the sand, shivering and filled to the brim of his being with ghastly, unresolvable anguish. After a while the sun warmed him, he revived, but from then on forswore sea bathing. He felt too lazy to dress; when he closed his eyes tightly, optical spots glided against a red background, Martian canals kept intersecting, and, the moment he parted his lids, the wet silver of the sun started to palpitate between his lashes.

The inevitable took place. By evening, all those parts of his body that had been exposed turned into a symmetrical archipelago of fiery pain. "Today, instead of going to the beach, we shall take a walk in the woods," he said to the boy on the morrow. "*Ach, nein,*" wailed David. "Too much sun is bad for the health," said Ivanov. "Oh, please!" insisted David in great dismay. But Ivanov stood his ground.

The forest was dense. Geometrid moths, matching the bark in coloration, flew off the tree trunks. Silent David walked reluctantly. "We should cherish the woods," Ivanov said in an attempt to divert his pupil. "It was the first habitat of man. One fine day man left the jungle of primitive intimations for the sunlit glade of reason. Those bilberries appear to be ripe, you have my permission to taste them. Why do you sulk? Try to understand: one should vary one's pleasures. And one should not overindulge in sea bathing. How often it happens that a careless bather dies of sun stroke or heart failure!"

Ivanov rubbed his unbearably burning and itching back against a tree trunk and continued pensively: "While admiring nature at a given locality, I cannot help thinking of countries that I shall never see. Try to imagine, David, that this is not Pomerania but a Malayan forest.

Look about you: you'll presently see the rarest of birds fly past, Prince Albert's paradise bird, whose head is adorned with a pair of long plumes consisting of blue oriflammes." "*Ach, quatsch,*" responded David dejectedly.

"In Russian you ought to say '*erundá.*' Of course, it's nonsense, we are not in the mountains of New Guinea. But the point is that with a bit of imagination—if, God forbid, you were someday to go blind or be imprisoned, or were merely forced to perform, in appalling poverty, some hopeless, distasteful task, you might remember this walk we are taking today in an ordinary forest as if it had been—how shall I say?—fairy-tale ecstasy."

At sundown dark-pink clouds fluffed out above the sea. With the dulling of the sky they seemed to rust, and a fisherman said it would rain tomorrow, but the morning turned out to be marvelous and David kept urging his tutor to hurry, but Ivanov was not feeling well; he longed to stay in bed and think of remote and vague semievents illumined by memory on only one side, of some pleasant smoke-gray things that might have happened once upon a time, or drifted past quite close to him in life's field of vision, or else had appeared to him in a recent dream. But it was impossible to concentrate on them, they all somehow slipped away to one side, half-turning to him with a kind of friendly and mysterious slyness but gliding away relentlessly, as do those transparent little knots that swim diagonally in the vitreous humor of the eye. Alas, he had to get up, to pull on his socks, so full of holes that they resembled lace mittens. Before leaving the house he put on David's dark-yellow sunglasses—and the sun swooned amid a sky dying a turquoise death, and the morning light upon the porch steps acquired a sunset tinge. David, his naked back amber-colored, ran ahead, and when Ivanov called to him, he shrugged his shoulders in irritation. "Do not run away," Ivanov said wearily. His horizon was narrowed by the glasses, he was afraid of a sudden automobile.

The street sloped sleepily toward the sea. Little by little his eyes became used to the glasses, and he ceased to wonder at the sunny day's khaki uniform. At the turn of the street he suddenly half-remembered something—something extraordinarily comforting and strange—but it immediately dissolved, and the turbulent sea air constricted his chest. The dusky flags flapped excitedly, pointing all in the same direction, though nothing was happening there yet. Here is the sand, here is the dull splash of the sea. His ears felt plugged up, and when he inhaled through the nose a rumble started in his head, and something bumped into a membranous dead end. I've lived neither very long nor very well, reflected Ivanov. Still it would be a shame to complain; this alien world is beautiful, and I would feel happy right now if only I could recall that wonderful, wonderful—what? What was it?

He lowered himself onto the sand. David began busily repairing with a spade the sand wall where it had crumbled slightly. "Is it hot or cool today?" asked Ivanov. "Somehow I cannot decide." Presently David threw down the spade and said, "I'll go for a swim." "Sit still for a moment," said Ivanov. "I must gather my thoughts. The sea will not run away." "*Please* let me go!" pleaded David.

Ivanov raised himself on one elbow and surveyed the waves. They were large and humpbacked; nobody was bathing at that spot; only much farther to the left a dozen orange-capped heads bobbed and were carried off to one side in unison. "Those waves," said Ivanov with a sigh, and then added: "You may paddle a little, but don't go beyond a *sazhen*. A *sazhen* equals about two meters."

He sank his head, propping one cheek, grieving, computing indefinite measures of life, of pity, of happiness. His shoes were already full of sand, he took them off with slow hands, then was again lost in thought, and again those evasive little knots began to swim across his field of vision—and how he longed, how he longed to recall—A sudden scream. Ivanov stood up.

Amid yellow-blue waves, far from the shore, flitted David's face, and his open mouth was like a dark hole. He emitted a spluttering yell, and vanished. A hand appeared for a moment and vanished too. Ivanov threw off his jacket. "I'm coming," he shouted. "I'm coming. Hold on!" He splashed through the water, lost his footing, his ice-cold trousers stuck to his shins. It seemed to him that David's head came up again for an instant. Then a wave surged, knocking off Ivanov's hat, blinding him; he wanted to take off his glasses, but his agitation, the cold, the numbing weakness, prevented him from doing so. He realized that in its retreat the wave had dragged him a long way from the shore. He started to swim trying to catch sight of David. He felt enclosed in a tight painfully cold sack, his heart was straining unbearably. All at once a rapid something passed through him, a flash of fingers rippling over piano keys—and *this* was the very thing he had been trying to recall throughout the morning. He came out on a stretch of sand. Sand, sea, and air were of an odd, faded, opaque tint, and everything was perfectly still. Vaguely he reflected that twilight must have come, and that David had perished a long time ago, and he felt what he knew from earthly life—the poignant heat of tears. Trembling and bending toward the ashen sand, he wrapped himself tighter in the black cloak with the snake-shaped brass fastening that he had seen on a student friend, a long, long time ago, on an autumn day—and he felt so sorry for David's mother, and wondered what would he tell her. It is not my fault, I did all I could to save him, but I am a poor swimmer, and I have a bad heart, and he drowned. But there was something amiss about these thoughts, and when he looked around once more and saw himself in the desolate mist all alone with no David beside him, he understood that if David was not with him, David was not dead.

Only then were the clouded glasses removed. The dull mist immediately broke, blossomed with marvelous colors, all kinds of sounds burst forth—the rote of the sea, the clapping of the wind, human cries—and there was David standing, up to his ankles in bright water, not knowing what to do, shaking with fear, not daring to explain that he had not been drowning, that he had struggled in jest—and farther out people were diving, groping through the water, then looking at each other with bulging eyes, and diving anew, and returning empty-handed, while others shouted to them from the shore, advising them to search a little to the left; and a fellow with a Red Cross armband was running along the beach, and three men in sweaters were pushing into the water a boat grinding against the shingle; and a bewildered David was being led away by a fat woman in a pince-nez, the wife of a veterinarian, who had been expected to arrive on Friday but had had to postpone his vacation, and the Baltic Sea sparkled from end to end, and, in the thinned-out forest, across a green country road, there lay, still breathing, freshly cut aspens; and a youth, smeared with soot, gradually turned white as he washed under the kitchen tap, and black parakeets flew above the eternal snows of the New Zealand mountains; and a fisherman, squinting in the sun, was solemnly predicting that not until the ninth day would the waves surrender the corpse.

from **turtle turtle**

M O N I C A   W E S O L O W S K A

chucho was needed back at the beach by his Mamá, but his hands on the oars didn't move. Now was the time of year for turtles and he wanted, please, to be the first to spot one. Eduardo had told him that in the old days thousands would roll in, like shiny boulders, to pave the beach from end to end; Eduardo had said the squeaking of their flippers on the sand had been worse than the sounds inland of traffic jams and grackles in the trees; Eduardo had said he'd moved back to Mexico, to this very beach, for the taste of turtle eggs.

Chucho suspected Eduardo was teasing. Eduardo knew how Chucho felt about turtles. Some people said he only felt that way since he'd been hired by the students from the university. Those people said a job like that should go to someone more deserving than a skinny fifteen-year-old boy. But Eduardo knew that Chucho had been picked because it wasn't for money that he wanted to stay up nights guarding turtles' nests from poachers. Turtles had always interested him for the homes they carried on their backs, but the students had made him excited about more. They'd taught him that turtles had for millions of years traveled millions of miles to return to this cove every year; and that the male turtles, after hatching, never came back to land; and that, to see a male turtle you had to catch one in the water having sex. They said male turtles got so crazy about sex, they'd try to mate with anything that moved, even a plastic buoy, or even each other. Chucho held his breath and scanned the surface of the ocean, but it remained flat and gray, like a highway, speckled with pelicans and seagulls instead of busses.

He pulled in the oars and lay back in the boat.

"Why don't you take your sister?" Mamá would say if he were walking to the store, or, "Where's your sweetie? Don't you have a sweetie?" someone would ask if he spent too long listening to the radio in the truck, but when he took the boat to try and spot turtles for the students, no one bothered him about being alone and sometimes he thought he'd just keep rowing North. Maybe the turtles were lost. Maybe only ten had come last year because the rest were stuck on some island and he would find them and bring them back. Or maybe he would reach the United States first. It would be no problem, if the ocean stayed like this—like the foot of a mother on a cradle, Eduardo might say Eduardo had strange ways of describing ordinary things which he put into songs. Eduardo said he'd sung these songs in Canada—with a band—and everyone had called him Eddie!

Two airplanes entered the sky above the boat, from opposite sides, and Chucho waved. Of course, he'd rather go by plane. He waved again, in case someone was looking down. The sharp white lines the planes dragged behind them crossed and spread into a fuzzy, pink-tinged X. The last time he'd seen this happen, he'd been with Eddie who'd said there was an expression in English about X showing the spot. Eddie said the X proved this was the best place on earth But that wasn't fair. Eddie had been born in the city, and he'd traveled all over Mexico, including here, before Chucho was even born, and he'd already been around the world and got a fancy nickname to prove he wasn't like people here.

Of course, Mamá said Chucho was nickname enough for any boy already named Jesús Juan JosJ Juárez, but he liked other names.

"Choose," he had said, "between Brad, Eric, and Chuck," the names he remembered from three Australian friends who had stayed for months perfecting their tans.

But she didn't choose. She didn't even try to pronounce the names and so he told her that someday, over the border, everyone would call him Big Chuck, and she would have to, too. He also told her he loved what he remembered of America, that huge room his father had with nothing but a TV and a carpet, blue and wide like the ocean without waves.

"Impossible," Mamá said. She said he'd been too young to remember and that he should not want to go back to the place that had nearly destroyed her and her children.

But Juan wasn't destroyed. Juan was a painter in Los Angeles and he said everyone who lived there long enough grew little white wings, including his wife, who also had an American passport, which she passed around when they came to visit, and a thing in her womb to make children when she wanted (the nurse had said it was okay, because she had prayed, but still Juan said not to tell Mamá) but even more fantastic than all of this was what Juan had told him late at night (after Chucho had been out with the hippies in the ocean; sometimes he wondered if the whole night was a dream) about the houses he painted, palaces full of paintings and statues of naked people, and a bed full of water which Juan just had to try. He was lying on it when the owner came home but the owner wasn't mad. No, the owner said he should keep lying on it, so he lay on it, and it felt like lying in a boat—with even the sound of waves—and then he remembered home, and the owner saw him remembering home and asked if he wanted to remember home with him, and so they took off their clothes and it felt good, like with a woman, but different. And then they put on their clothes, and Juan finished painting, and he helped the man hang up all his art again and he got his money and went home to his wife that he loved. That was a good man, he said, because he told his friends to call Juan when they needed paint jobs.

And then Juan said to Chucho, "When are you going to make Mamá happy and find a girl to marry like me?"

Chucho sat up, remembering she was waiting for him.

Along the horizon, the clouds that had been as flat and gray as railroad ties were turning purple against the setting sun, and pink, like ribs on the grill. Mamá had wanted him to drive her into town before dark to see the doctor for more herbs. She might be standing now, looking at the sun from the edge of her palapa and yelling, "Chucho, Chucho," and then "Jesús" when he didn't appear. There would be no time to eat. She should have let Eduardo drive her Eduardo was wooing her, so everybody said. For her land, some of them said. Which is really owned by her husband-in-America, they said. That's still more than Eduardo owns. What good is traveling the world if you come back with only a guitar and an ex-wife and child in Canada? they said.

He dipped the oars and pulled, and the ocean shuddered through him. If he had arms as long as oars, how far he could go, plucking fish from down deep whenever he was hungry. He dipped and pulled and thought if he had legs as long as a boat, he could step from here onto the beach and beyond to Mexico City and then Toronto. From here, the shore was nothing more than a yellow rind fringed with gray-green palms so dense the palapas and hammocks and tourists and Fantas and corns-on-the-cob were invisible as if he had come by accident to an undiscovered island . . . until he saw the pink hotel.

He loved that place, even if Eduardo called it a cockroach and cursed its city-owners for abandoning it half-built; he loved to take the path to it in the dark, climb to the roofless second floor, pick out a star and make love to it. It was almost as private as a boat, nothing but four pink walls on the top of a cliff, nothing between him and his star but steel rebar trembling up from the rough cement with desire for a third floor, a fourth floor, for ceilings and beds—unless tourists had come before him and strung their hammocks from the rebar, or built a fire.

The time with the fire, he'd stayed because they'd offered him tequila. He'd taken small sips at first, cautious because of what Mamá said it did to lonely men, but he must have had more considering what happened next. The hippies had shed their clothes around the fire, scaled the ladder, raced each other down the cliff—Chucho right behind them, trying not to watch their butts jiggling like boiled eggs—and into the water. Too soon, a girl got knocked down and swallowed water and started coughing, louder than the surf, and everyone came and stood around her naked, retching body. Of course, he'd seen men vomit before, but never a woman kneeling with her hair tangled down her naked back Grotesque, he had thought, and left, but he couldn't shake the feeling of racing blind into the night water, of his skin dissolving in the dark, of his soul seeping huge into the world.

The next day he went back but they'd left only blackened tree limbs, an empty bottle of tequila, a guitar pick, and a pair of women's lace underpants. He'd picked the underpants up with the end of a stick, the way you'd carry a dead snake to shake at your sisters, and thrown them out a window. They were light and blew around the pink place for days until he got sick of it and threw them into the sea. And what happened to them then? Did they wash up on the beach in some other country? Did other countries have beaches? Of course. The students had told him their work would only make a difference if there were an international collaboration. Imagine that Beaches all over the world, with people on them, connected by this ocean full of turtles.

He stood up suddenly but it wasn't a turtle he'd spotted, just tourists in the water, two men, no, a man with a woman, and he sat back down. He tried to pay attention to rowing, to fill his mind with the shifting slap of waves on shore, but as he got closer to the tourists, the shadow of his boat on the backs of their heads made them turn to look. The girl began to swim beside him like a dolphin. Earlier he'd seen her spinning, round and round, saying "It's paradise" until she got dizzy and fell down. So stupid. Why did they come here and call this paradise when the paradise was there, where they came from, where there were jobs painting rich people's houses and . . . but he was close enough to shore to jump out.

He jumped down into the water as the girl jumped up from it, and their eyes met and flicked away. He reached for the towrope. Maybe in America he'd have a girl like her, he thought, hair short like a boy's, but then, as the roughness of sand catching the bottom of the boat traveled up the rope, the man reached the shallows and jumped up, and up, and up, to become twice the size of Chucho.

The rope slackened for a beat.

Then the boat lifted and rushed past Chucho towards the shore. He stumbled after it and ran past it up the sand. He leaned with all his muscle away from the boat and plodded with it up the beach, staring at the line between wet and dry sand that was his destination, but what he felt was the long path of hair down the man's middle, rough and wet like the rope in his hand.

He forced himself to stop at the dead turtle that lay where he'd left it for the students to examine after he'd found it that morning, belly up, headless, surrounded now by vultures. He flung the end of his rope at the birds, but they only lifted their wings halfway and hopped, they cocked their heads; they plunged their beaks back in. Someone squealed. He turned to see the man catching the girl from behind, the girl bending under him, both of them continuing to walk as if they had become the belly and back of some giant, eight-limbed turtle, and then he heard his mother calling, "Chucho, Chucho" and "Jesús" and he stood waiting for her, please, to call him Chuck.

from **cannery row**

JOHN STEINBECK

doc was collecting marine animals in the Great Tide Pool on the tip of the Peninsula. It is a fabulous place: when the tide is in, a wave-churned basin, creamy with foam, whipped by the combers that roll in from the whistling buoy on the reef. But when the tide goes out the little water world becomes quiet and lovely. The sea is very clear and the bottom becomes fantastic with hurrying, fighting, feeding, breeding animals. Crabs rush from frond to frond of the waving algae. Starfish squat over mussels and limpets, attach their million little suckers and then slowly lift with incredible power until the prey is broken from the rock. And then the starfish stomach comes out and envelops its food. Orange and speckled and fluted nudibranchs slide gracefully over the rocks, their skirts waving like the dresses of Spanish dancers. And black eels poke their heads out of crevices and wait for prey. The snapping shrimps with their trigger claws pop loudly. The lovely, colored world is glassed over. Hermit crabs like frantic children scamper on the bottom sand. And now one, finding an empty snail shell he likes better than his own, creeps out, exposing his soft body to the enemy for a moment, and then pops into the new shell. A wave breaks over the barrier, and churns the glassy water for a moment and mixes bubbles into the pool, and then it clears and is tranquil and lovely and murderous again. Here a crab tears a leg from his brother. The anemones expand like soft and brilliant flowers, inviting any tired and perplexed animal to lie for a moment in their arms, and when some small crab or little tide-pool Johnnie accepts the green and purple invitation, the petals whip in, the stinging cells shoot tiny narcotic needles into the prey and it grows weak and perhaps sleepy while the searing caustic digestive acids melt its body down.

Then the creeping murderer, the octopus, steals out, slowly, softly, moving like a gray mist, pretending now to be a bit of weed, now a rock, now a lump of decaying meat while its evil goat eyes watch coldly. It oozes and flows toward a feeding crab, and as it comes close its yellow eyes burn and its body turns rosy with the pulsing color of anticipation and rage. Then suddenly it runs lightly on the tips of its arms, as ferociously as a charging cat. It leaps savagely on the crab, there is a puff of black fluid, and the struggling mass is obscured in the sepia cloud while the octopus murders the crab. On the exposed rocks out of water, the barnacles bubble behind their closed doors and the limpets dry out. And down to the rocks come the black flies to eat anything they can find. The sharp smell of iodine from the algae, and the lime smell of calcareous bodies and the smell of powerful protean, smell of sperm and ova fill the air. On the exposed rocks the starfish emit semen and eggs from between their rays. The smells of life and richness, of death and digestion, of decay and birth, burden the air. And salt spray blows in from the barrier where the ocean waits for its rising-tide strength to permit it back into the Great Tide Pool again. And on the reef the whistling buoy bellows like a sad and patient bull.

In the pool Doc and Hazel worked together. Hazel lived in the Palace Flophouse with Mack and the boys. Hazel got his name in as haphazard a way as his life was ever afterward. His worried mother had had seven children in eight years. Hazel was the eighth, and his mother became confused about his sex when he was born. She was tired and run down anyway from trying to feed and clothe seven children and their father. She had tried every possible way of making money—paper flowers, mushrooms at home, rabbits for meat and fur—while her husband from a canvas chair gave her every help his advice and reasoning and criticism could offer. She had a great aunt named Hazel who was reputed to carry life insurance. The eighth child was named Hazel before the mother got it through her head that Hazel was a boy and by that time she was used to the name and never bothered to change it. Hazel grew up—did four years in grammar school, four years in reform school, and didn't learn anything in either place. Reform schools are supposed to teach viciousness and criminality but Hazel didn't pay enough attention. He came out of reform school as innocent of viciousness as he was of fractions and long division. Hazel loved to hear conversation but he didn't listen to words—just to the tone of conversation. He asked questions, not to hear the answers but simply to continue the flow. He was twenty-six—dark-haired and pleasant, strong, willing, and loyal. Quite often he went collecting with Doc and he was very good at it once he knew what was wanted. His fingers could creep like an octopus, could grab and hold like an anemone. He was sure-footed on the slippery rocks and he loved the hunt. Doc wore his rain hat and high rubber boots as he worked but Hazel sloshed about in tennis shoes and blue jeans. They were collecting starfish. Doc had an order for three hundred.

Hazel picked a nobby purplish starfish from the bottom of the pool and popped it into his nearly full gunny sack. "I wonder what they do with them," he said.

"Do with what?" Doc asked.

"The starfish," said Hazel. "You sell 'em. You'll send out a barrel of 'em. What do the guys do with 'em? You can't eat 'em."

"They study them," said Doc patiently and he remembered that he had answered this question for Hazel dozens of times before. But Doc had one mental habit he could not get over. When anyone asked a question, Doc thought he wanted to know the answer. That was the way with Doc. *He* never asked unless he wanted to know and he could not conceive of the brain that would ask without wanting to know. But Hazel, who simply wanted to hear talk, had developed a system of making the answer to one question the basis of another. It kept conversation going.

"What do they find to study?" Hazel continued. "They're just starfish. There's millions of 'em around. I could get you a million of 'em."

"They're complicated and interesting animals," Doc said a little defensively. "Besides, these are going to the Middle West to Northwestern University."

Hazel used his trick. "They got no starfish there?"

"They got no ocean there," said Doc.

"Oh!" said Hazel and he cast frantically about for a peg to hang a new question on. He hated to have a conversation die out like this. He wasn't quick enough. While he was looking for a question Doc asked one. Hazel hated that, it meant casting about in his mind for an answer and casting about in Hazel's mind was like wandering alone in a deserted museum. Hazel's mind was choked with uncatalogued exhibits. He never forgot anything but he never bothered to arrange his memories. Everything was thrown together like fishing tackle in the bottom of a rowboat, hooks and sinkers and line and lures and gaffs all snarled up.

Doc asked, "How are things going up at the Palace?"

Hazel ran his fingers through his dark hair and he peered into the clutter of his mind. "Pretty good," he said. "That fellow Gay is moving in with us I guess. His wife hits him pretty bad. He don't mind that when he's awake but she waits 'til he gets to sleep and then hits him. He hates that. He has to wake up and beat her up and then when he goes back to sleep she hits him again. He don't get any rest so he's moving in with us."

"That's a new one," said Doc. "She used to swear out a warrant and put him in jail."

"Yeah!" said Hazel. "But that was before they built the new jail in Salinas. Used to be thirty days and Gay was pretty hot to get out, but this new jail—radio in the tank and good bunks and the sheriff's a nice fellow. Gay gets in there and he don't want to come out. He likes it so much his wife won't get him arrested any more. So she figured out this hitting him while he's asleep. It's nerve racking, he says. And you know as good as me—Gay never did take any pleasure beating her up. He only done it to keep his self-respect. But he gets tired of it. I guess he'll be with us now."

Doc straightened up. The waves were beginning to break over the barrier of the Great Tide Pool. The tide was coming in and little rivers from the sea had begun to flow over the rocks. The wind blew freshly in from the whistling buoy and the barking of sea lions came from around the point. Doc pushed his rain hat on the back of his head. "We've got enough starfish," he said and then went on, "Look, Hazel, I know you've got six or seven undersized abalones in the bottom of your sack. If we get stopped by a game warden, you're going to say they're mine, on my permit—aren't you?"

"Well—hell," said Hazel.

"Look," Doc said kindly. "Suppose I get an order for abalones and maybe the game warden thinks I'm using my collecting permit too often. Suppose he thinks I'm eating them."

"Well—hell," said Hazel.

"It's like the industrial alcohol board. They've got suspicious minds. They always think I'm drinking the alcohol. They think that about everyone."

"Well, ain't you?"

"Not much of it," said Doc. "That stuff they put in it tastes terrible and it's a big job to redistill it."

"That stuff ain't so bad," said Hazel. "Me and Mack had a snort of it the other day. What is it they put in?"

Doc was about to answer when he saw it was Hazel's trick again. "Let's get moving," he said. He hoisted his sack of starfish on his shoulder. And he had forgotten the illegal abalones in the bottom of Hazel's sack.

Hazel followed him up out of the tide pool and up the slippery trail to solid ground. The little crabs scampered and skittered out of their way. Hazel felt that he had better cement the grave over the topic of the abalones.

"That painter guy came back to the Palace," he offered.

"Yes?" said Doc.

"Yeah! You see, he done all our pictures in chicken feathers and now he says he got to do them all over again with nutshells. He says he changed his—his med—medium."

Doc chuckled. "He still building his boat?"

"Sure," said Hazel. "He's got it all changed around. New kind of a boat. I guess he'll take it apart and change it. Doc—is he nuts?"

Doc swung his heavy sack of starfish to the ground and stood panting a little. "Nuts?" he asked. "Oh, yes, I guess so. Nuts about the same amount we are, only in a different way."

Such a thing had never occurred to Hazel. He looked upon himself as a crystal pool of clarity and on his life as a troubled glass of misunderstood virtue. Doc's last statement had outraged him a little. "But that boat—" he cried. "He's been building that boat for seven years that I know of. The blocks rotted out and he made concrete blocks. Every time he gets it nearly finished he changes it and starts over again. I think he's nuts. Seven years on a boat."

Doc was sitting on the ground pulling off his rubber boots. "You don't understand," he said gently. "Henri loves boats but he's afraid of the ocean."

"What's he want a boat for then?" Hazel demanded.

"He likes boats," said Doc. "But suppose he finishes his boat. Once it's finished people will say, 'Why don't you put it in the water?' Then if he puts it in the water, he'll have to go out in it, and he hates the water. So you see, he never finishes the boat—so he doesn't ever have to launch it."

Hazel had followed this reasoning to a certain point but he abandoned it before it was resolved, not only abandoned it but searched for some way to change the subject. "I think he's nuts," he said lamely.

On the black earth on which the ice plants bloomed, hundreds of black stink bugs crawled. And many of them stuck their tails up in the air. "Look at all them stink bugs," Hazel remarked, grateful to the bugs for being there.

"They're interesting," said Doc.

"Well, what they got their asses up in the air for?"

Doc rolled up his wool socks and put them in the rubber boots and from his pocket he brought out dry socks and a pair of thin moccasins. "I don't know why," he said. "I looked them up recently—they're very common animals and one of the commonest things they do is put their tails up in the air. And in all the books there isn't one mention of the fact that they put their tails up in the air or why."

Hazel turned one of the stink bugs over with the toe of his wet tennis shoe the shining black beetle strove madly with floundering legs to get upright again. "Well, why do *you* think they do it?"

"I think they're praying," said Doc.

"What!" Hazel was shocked.

"The remarkable thing," said Doc, "isn't that they put their tails up in the air—the really incredibly remarkable thing is that we find it remarkable. We can only use ourselves as yardsticks. If we did something as inexplicable and strange we'd probably be praying—so maybe they're praying."

"Let's get the hell out of here," said Hazel.

the lady with
the pet dog

Anton Chekhov

a new person, it was said, had appeared on the esplanade: a lady with a pet dog. Dmitry Dmitrich Gurov, who had spent a fortnight at Yalta and had got used to the place, had also begun to take an interest in new arrivals. As he sat in Vernet's confectionery shop, he saw, walking on the esplanade, a fair-haired young woman of medium height, wearing a beret; a white Pomeranian was trotting behind her.

And afterwards he met her in the public garden and in the square several times a day. She walked alone, always wearing the same beret and always with the white dog; no one knew who she was and everyone called her simply "the lady with the pet dog."

"If she is here alone without husband or friends," Gurov reflected, "it wouldn't be a bad thing to make her acquaintance."

He was under forty, but he already had a daughter twelve years old, and two sons at school. They had found a wife for him when he was very young, a student in his second year, and by now she seemed half as old again as he. She was a tall, erect woman with dark eyebrows, stately and dignified and, as she said of herself, intellectual. She read a great deal, used simplified spelling in her letters, called her husband, not Dmitry, but Dimitry, while he privately considered her of limited intelligence, narrow-minded, dowdy, was afraid of her, and did not like to be at home. He had begun being unfaithful to her long ago—had been unfaithful to her often and, probably for that reason, almost always spoke ill of women, and when they were talked of in his presence used to call them "the inferior race."

It seemed to him that he had been sufficiently tutored for bitter experience to call them what he pleased, and yet he could not have lived without "the inferior race" two days together. In the company of men he was and ill at ease, he was chilly and uncommunicative with them; but when he was among women he felt free, and knew what to speak to them about and how to comport himself; and even to be silent with them was no strain on him. In his appearance, in his character, in his whole make-up there was something attractive and elusive that disposed women in his favor and allured them. He knew that, and some force seemed to draw him to them, too.

Oft-repeated and really bitter experience had taught him long ago that with decent people—particularly Moscow people—who are irresolute and slow to move, every affair which at first seems a light and charming adventure inevitably grows into a whole problem of extreme complexity, and in the end a painful situation is created. But at every new meeting with an interesting woman this lesson of experience seemed to slip from his memory, and he was eager for life, and everything seemed so simple and diverting.

One evening while he was dining in the public garden the lady in the beret walked up without haste to take the next table. Her expression, her gait, her dress, and the way she did her hair told him that she belonged to the upper class, that she was married, that she was in Yalta for the first time and alone, and that she was bored there. The stories told of the immorality in Yalta are to a great extent untrue; he despised them, and knew that such stories were made up for the most part by persons who would have been glad to sin themselves if they had had the chance; but when the lady sat down at the next table three paces from him, he recalled these stories of easy conquests, of trips to the mountains, and the tempting thought of a swift, fleeting liaison, a romance with an unknown woman of whose very name he was ignorant suddenly took hold of him.

He beckoned invitingly to the Pomeranian, and when the dog approached him, shook his finger at it. The Pomeranian growled; Gurov threatened it again.

The lady glanced at him and at once dropped her eyes.

"He doesn't bite," she said and blushed.

"May I give him a bone?" he asked; and when she nodded he inquired affably, "Have you been in Yalta long?"

"About five days."

"And I am dragging out the second week here."

There was a short silence.

"Time passes quickly, and yet it is so dull here!" she said, not looking at him.

"It's only the fashion to say it's dull here. A provincial will live in Belyov or Zhizdra and not be bored, but when he comes here it's 'Oh, the dullness! Oh, the dust!' One would think he came from Granada."

She laughed. Then both continued eating in silence, like strangers, but after dinner they walked together and there sprang up between them the light banter of people who are free and contented, to whom it does not matter where they go or what they talk about. They walked and talked of the strange light on the sea: the water was a soft, warm, lilac color, and there was a golden band of moonlight upon it. They talked of how sultry it was after a hot day. Gurov told her that he was a native of Moscow, that he had studied languages and literature at the university, but had a post in a bank; that at one time he had trained to become an opera singer but had given it up, that he owned two houses in Moscow. And he learned from her that she had grown up in Petersburg, but had lived in S—— since her marriage two years previously, that she was going to stay in Yalta for about another month, and that her husband, who needed a rest, too, might perhaps come to fetch her. She was not certain whether her husband was a member of a Government Board or served on a Zemstvo Council, and this amused her. And Gurov learned too that her name was Anna Sergeyevna.

Afterwards in his room at the hotel he thought about her— and was certain that he would meet her the next day. It was bound to happen. Getting into bed he recalled that she had been a schoolgirl only recently, doing lessons like his own daughter; he thought how much timidity and angularity there was still in her laugh and her manner of talking with a stranger. It must have been the first time in her life that she was alone in a setting in which she was followed, looked at, and spoken to for one secret purpose alone, which she could hardly fail to guess. He thought of her slim, delicate throat, her lovely gray eyes.

"There's something pathetic about her, though," he thought, and dropped off.

II

a week had passed since they had struck up an acquaintance. It was a holiday. It was close indoors, while in the street the wind whirled the dust about and blew people's hats off. One was thirsty all day, and Gurov often went into the restaurant and offered Anna Sergeyevna a soft drink or ice cream. One did not know what to do with oneself.

In the evening when the wind had abated they went out on the pier to watch the steamer come in. There were a great many people walking about the dock; they had come to welcome someone and they were carrying bunches of flowers. And two peculiarities of a festive Yalta crowd stood out: the elderly ladies were dressed like young ones and there were many generals.

Owing to the choppy sea, the steamer arrived late, after sunset, and it was a long time tacking about before it put in at the pier. Anna Sergeyevna peered at the steamer and the passengers through her lorgnette as though looking for acquaintances, and whenever she turned to Gurov her eyes were shining. She talked a great deal and asked questions jerkily, forgetting the next moment what she had asked; then she lost her lorgnette in the crush.

The festive crowd began to disperse; it was now too dark to see people's faces; there was no wind any more, but Gurov and Anna Sergeyevna still stood as though waiting to see someone else come off the steamer. Anna Sergeyevna was silent now, and sniffed her flowers without looking at Gurov.

"The weather has improved this evening," he said. "Where shall we go now? Shall we drive somewhere?"

She did not reply.

Then he looked at her intently, and suddenly embraced her and kissed her on the lips, and the moist fragrance of her flowers enveloped him; and at once he looked round him anxiously, wondering if anyone had seen them.

"Let us go to your place," he said softly. And they walked off together rapidly.

The air in her room was close and there was the smell of the perfume she had bought at the Japanese shop. Looking at her, Gurov thought: "What encounters life offers!" From the past he preserved the memory of carefree, good-natured women whom love made gay and who were grateful to him for the happiness he gave them, however brief it might be; and of women like his wife who loved without sincerity, with too many words, affectedly, hysterically, with an expression that it was not love or passion that engaged them but something more significant; and of two or three others, very beautiful, frigid women, across whose faces would suddenly fit a rapacious expression—an obstinate desire to take from life more than it could give, and these were women no longer young, capricious, unreflecting, domineering, unintelligent, and when Gurov grew cold to them their beauty aroused his hatred, and the lace on their lingerie seemed to him to resemble scales.

But here there was the timidity, the angularity of inexperienced youth, a feeling of awkwardness; and there was a sense of embarrassment, as though someone had suddenly knocked at the door. Anna Sergeyevna, "the lady with the pet dog," treated what had happened in a peculiar way, very seriously, as though it were her fall—so it seemed, and this was odd and inappropriate. Her features drooped and faded, and her long hair hung down sadly on either side of her face; she grew pensive and her dejected pose was that of a Magdalene in a picture by an old master.

"It's not right," she said. "You don't respect me now, you first of all."

There was a watermelon on the table. Gurov cut himself a slice and began eating it without haste. They were silent for at least half an hour.

There was something touching about Anna Sergeyevna; she had the purity of a well-bred, naive woman who has seen little of life. The single candle burning on the table barely illumined her face, yet it was clear that she was unhappy.

"Why should I stop respecting you, darling?" asked Gurov. "You don't know what you're saying."

"God forgive me," she said, and her eyes filled with tears. "It's terrible."

"It's as though you were trying to exonerate yourself."

"How can I exonerate myself? No. I am a bad, low woman; I despise myself and I have no thought of exonerating myself. It's not my husband but myself I have deceived. And not only just now; I have been deceiving myself for a long time. My husband may be a good, honest man, but he is a flunkey! I don't know what he does, what his work is, but I know he is a flunkey! I was twenty when I married him. I was tormented by curiosity; I wanted something better. 'There must be a different sort of life,' I said to myself. I wanted to live! To live, to live! Curiosity kept eating at me—you don't understand it, but I swear to God I could no longer control myself; something was going on in me: I could not be held back. I told my husband I was ill, and came here. And here I have been walking about as though in a daze, as though I were mad; and now I have become a vulgar, vile woman whom anyone may despise."

Gurov was already bored with her; he was irritated by her naive tone, by her repentance, so unexpected and so out of place; but for the tears in her eyes he might have thought she was joking or play-acting.

"I don't understand, my dear," he said softly. "What do you want?"

She hid her face on his breast and pressed close to him.

"Believe me, believe me, I beg you," she said, "I love honesty and purity, and sin is loathsome to me; I don't know what I'm doing. Simple people say, 'The Evil One has led me astray.' And I may say of myself now that the Evil One has led me astray."

"Quiet, quiet," he murmured.

He looked into her fixed, frightened eyes, kissed her, spoke to her softly and affectionately, and by degrees she calmed down, and her gaiety returned; both began laughing.

Afterwards when they went out there was not a soul on the esplanade. The town with its cypresses looked quite dead, but the sea was still sounding as it broke upon the beach; a single launch was rocking on the waves and on it a lantern was blinking sleepily.

They found a cab and drove to Oreanda.

"I found out your surname in the hall just now: it was written on the board—von Dideritz," said Gurov. "Is your husband German?"

"No; I believe his grandfather was German, but he is Greek Orthodox himself."

At Oreanda they sat on a bench not far from the church, looked down at the sea, and were silent. Yalta was barely visible through the morning mist; white clouds rested motionlessly on the mountaintops. The leaves did not stir on the trees, cicadas twanged, and the monotonous muffled sound of the sea that rose from below spoke of the peace, the eternal sleep awaiting us. So it rumbled below when there was no Yalta, no Oreanda here; so it rumbles now, and it will rumble as indifferently and as hollowly when we are no more. And in this constancy, in this complete indifference to the life and death of each of us, there lies, perhaps, a pledge of our eternal salvation, of the unceasing advance of life upon earth, of unceasing movement towards perfection. Sitting beside a young woman who in the dawn seemed so lovely, Gurov, soothed and spellbound by these magical surroundings—the sea, the mountains, the clouds, the wide sky—thought how everything is really beautiful in this world when one reflects:

everything except what we think or do ourselves when we forget the higher aims of life and our own human dignity.

A man strolled up to them—probably a guard—looked at them and walked away. And this detail, too, seemed so mysterious and beautiful. They saw a steamer arrive from Feodosia, its lights extinguished in the glow of dawn.

"There is dew on the grass," said Anna Sergeyevna, after a silence.

"Yes, it's time to go home."

They returned to the city.

Then they met every day at twelve o'clock on the esplanade, lunched and dined together, took walks, admired the sea. She complained that she slept badly, that she had palpitations, asked the same questions, troubled now by jealousy and now by the fear that he did not respect her sufficiently. And often in the square or the public garden, when there was no one near them, he suddenly drew her to him and kissed her passionately. Complete idleness, these kisses in broad daylight exchanged furtively in dread of someone's seeing them, the heat, the smell of the sea, and the continual flitting before his eyes of idle, well-dressed, well-fed people worked a complete change in him; he kept telling Anna Sergeyevna how beautiful she was, how seductive, was urgently passionate; he would not move a step away from her, while she was often pensive and continually pressed him to confess that he did not respect her, did not love her in the least, and saw in her nothing but a common woman. Almost every evening rather late they drove somewhere out of town, to Oreanda or to the waterfall; and the excursion was always a success, the scenery invariably impressed them as beautiful and magnificent.

They were expecting her husband, but a letter came from him saying that he had eye-trouble, and begging his wife to return home as soon as possible. Anna Sergeyevna made haste to go.

"It's a good thing I am leaving," she said to Gurov. "It's the hand of Fate!"

She took a carriage to the railway station, and he went with her. They were driving the whole day. When she had taken her place in the express, and when the second bell had rung, she said, "Let me look at you once more—let me look at you again. Like this."

She was not crying but was so sad that she seemed ill and her face was quivering.

"I shall be thinking of you—remembering you," she said. "God bless you; be happy. Don't remember evil against me. We are parting forever—it has to be, for we ought never to have met. Well, God bless you."

The train moved off rapidly, its lights soon vanished, and a minute later there was no sound of it, as though everything had conspired to end as quickly as possible that sweet trance, that madness. Left alone on the platform, and gazing into the dark distance, Gurov listened to the twang of the grasshoppers and the hum of the telegraph wires, feeling as though he had just waked up. And he reflected, musing, that there had now been another episode or adventure in his life, and it, too, was at an end, and nothing was left of it but a memory. He was moved, sad, and slightly remorseful: this young woman whom he would never meet again had not been happy with him; he had been warm and affectionate with her, but yet in his manner, his tone, and his caresses there had been a shade of light irony, the slightly coarse arrogance of a happy male who was, besides, almost twice her age. She had constantly called him kind, exceptional, high-minded; obviously he had seemed to her different from what he really was, so he had involuntarily deceived her.

Here at the station there was already a scent of autumn in the air; it was a chilly evening.

"It is time for me to go north, too," thought Gurov as he left the platform. "High time!"

III

at home in Moscow the winter routine was already established: the stoves were heated, and in the morning it was still dark when the children were having breakfast and getting ready for school, and the nurse would light the lamp for a short time. There were frosts already. When the first snow falls, on the first day the sleighs are out, it is pleasant to see the white earth, the white roofs; one draws easy, delicious breaths, and the season brings back the days of one's youth. The old limes and birches, white with hoar-frost, have a good-natured look; they are closer to one's heart than cypresses and palms, and near them one no longer wants to think of mountains and the sea.

Gurov, a native of Moscow, arrived there on a fine frosty day, and when he put on his fur coat and warm gloves and took a walk along Petrovka, and when on Saturday night he heard the bells ringing, his recent trip and the places he had visited lost all charm for him. Little by little he became immersed in Moscow life, greedily read three newspapers a day, and declared that he did not read the Moscow papers on principle. He already felt a longing for restaurants, clubs, formal dinners, anniversary celebrations, and it flattered him to entertain distinguished lawyers and actors, and to play cards with a professor at the physicians' club. He could eat a whole portion of meat stewed with pickled cabbage and served in a pan, Moscow style.

A month or so would pass and the image of Anna Sergeyevna, it seemed to him, would become misty in his memory, and only from time to time he would dream of her touching smile as he dreamed of others. But more than a month went by, winter came into its own, and everything was still clear in his memory as though he had parted from Anna Sergeyevna only yesterday. And his memories glowed more and more vividly. When in the evening stillness the voices of his children preparing their lessons reached his study, or when he listened to a song or to an organ playing in a restaurant, or when the storm howled in the chimney, suddenly everything would rise up in his memory: what had happened on the pier and the early morning with the mist on the mountains, and the steamer coming from Feodosia, and the kisses. He would pace about his room a long time, remembering and smiling; then his memories passed into reveries, and in his imagination the past would mingle with what was to come. He did not dream of Anna Sergeyevna, but she followed him about everywhere and watched him. When he shut his eyes he saw her before him as though she were there in the flesh, and she seemed to him lovelier, younger, tenderer than she had been, and he imagined himself a finer man than he had been in Yalta. Of evenings she peered out at him from the bookcase, from the fireplace, from the corner—he heard her breathing, the caressing rustle of her clothes. In the street he followed the women with his eyes, looking for someone who resembled her.

Already he was tormented by a strong desire to share his memories with someone. But in his home it was impossible to talk of his love, and he had no one to talk to outside; certainly he could not confide in his tenants or in anyone at the bank. And what was there to talk about? He hadn't loved her then, had he? Had there been anything beautiful, poetical, edifying, or simply interesting in his relations with Anna Sergeyevna? And he was forced to talk vaguely of love, of women, and no one guessed what he meant; only his wife would twitch her black eyebrows and say, "The part of a philanderer does not suit you at all, Dimitry."

One evening, coming out of the physicians' club with an official with whom he had been playing cards, he could not resist saying:

"If you only knew what a fascinating woman I became acquainted with at Yalta!"

The official got into his sledge and was driving away, but turned suddenly and shouted:

"Dmitry Dmitrich!"

"What is it?"

"You were right this evening: the sturgeon was a bit high."

These words, so commonplace, for some reason moved Gurov to indignation, and struck him as degrading and unclean. What savage manners, what mugs! What stupid nights, what dull, humdrum days! Frenzied gambling, gluttony, drunkenness, continual talk always about the same things! Futile pursuits and conversations always about the same topics take up the better part of one's time, the better part of one's strength, and in the end there is left a life clipped and wingless, an absurdness, and there is no escaping or getting away from it—just as though one were in a madhouse or a prison.

Gurov, boiling with indignation, did not sleep all night. And he had a headache all the next day. And the following nights too he slept badly; he sat up in the bed, thinking, or paced up and down his room. He was fed up with his children, fed up with the bank; he had no desire to go anywhere or to talk of anything.

In December during the holidays he prepared to take a trip and told his wife he was going to Petersburg to do what he could for a young friend—and he set off for S— What for? He did not know, himself. He wanted to see Anna Sergeyevna and talk with her, to arrange a rendezvous if possible.

He arrived at S— in the morning, and at the hotel took the best room, in which the floor was covered with gray army cloth, and on the table there was an inkstand, gray with dust and topped by a figure on horseback, its that in its raised hand and its head broken off. The porter gave him the necessary information: von Dideritz lived in a house of his own on Staro-Goncharnaya Street, not far from the hotel: he was rich and lived well and kept his own horses; everyone in the town knew him. The porter pronounced the name: "Dridiritz."

Without haste Gurov made his way to Staro-Goncharnaya Street and found the house. Directly opposite the house stretched a long gray fence studded with nails.

"A fence like that would make one run away," thought Gurov, looking now at the fence, now at the windows of the house.

He reflected: this was a holiday, and the husband was apt to be at home. And in any case, it would be tactless to go into the house and disturb her. If he were to send her a note, it might fall into her husband's hands and that might spoil everything. The best thing was to rely on chance. And he kept walking up and down the street and along the fence, waiting for the chance. He saw a beggar go in at the gate and heard the dog attack him; then an hour later he heard a piano, and the sound came to him faintly and indistinctly. Probably it was Anna Sergeyevna playing. The front door opened suddenly, and an old woman came out, followed by the familiar white Pomeranian. Gurov was on the point of calling to the dog, but his heart began beating violently and in his excitement he could not remember the Pomeranian's name.

He kept walking up and down, and hated the grey fence more and more, and by now he thought irritably that Anna Sergeyevna had forgotten him, and was perhaps already diverting herself with another man, and that that was very natural in a young woman who from morning till night had to look at that damn fence. He went back to his hotel room and sat on the couch for a long while, not knowing what to do, then he had dinner and a long nap.

"How stupid and annoying all this is!" he thought when he woke and looked at the dark windows: it was already evening. "Here I've had a good sleep for some reason. What am I going to do at night?"

He sat on the bed, which was covered with a cheap gray blanket of the kind seen in hospitals, and betwitted himself in his vexation:

"So there's your lady with the pet dog. There's your adventure. A nice place to cool your heels in."

That morning at the station a playbill in large letters had caught his eye. *The Geisha* was to be given for the first time. He thought of this and drove to the theater.

"It's quite possible that she goes to first nights," he thought.

The theater was full. As in all provincial theaters, there was a haze above the chandelier, the gallery was noisy and restless; in the front row, before the beginning of the performance the local dandies were standing with their hands clasped behind their backs; in the Governor's box the Governor's daughter, wearing a boa, occupied the front seat, while the Governor himself hid modestly behind the portiere and only his hands were visible; the curtain swayed; the orchestra was a long time tuning up. While the audience were coming in and taking their seats, Gurov scanned the faces eagerly.

Anna Sergeyevna, too, came in. She sat down in the third row, and when Gurov looked at her his heart contracted, and he understood clearly that in the whole world there was no human being so near, so precious, and so important to him; she, this little, undistinguished woman, lost in a provincial crowd, with a vulgar lorgnette in her hand, filled his whole life now, was his sorrow and his joy, the only happiness that he now desired for himself, and to the sounds of the bad orchestra, of the miserable local violins, he thought how lovely she was. He thought and dreamed.

A young man with small side-whiskers, very tall and stooped, came in with Anna Sergeyevna and sat down beside her; he nodded his head at every step and seemed to be bowing continually. Probably this was the husband whom at Yalta, in an access of bitter feeling, she had called a flunkey. And there really was in his lanky figure, his side-whiskers, his small bald patch, something of a flunkey's retiring manner; his smile was mawkish, and in his buttonhole there was an academic badge like a waiter's number.

During the first intermission the husband went out to have a smoke; she remained in her seat. Gurov, who was also sitting in the orchestra, went up to her and said in a shaky voice, with a forced smile:

"Good evening!"

She glanced at him and turned pale, then looked at him again in horror, unable to believe her eyes, and gripped the fan and the lorgnette tightly together in her hands, evidently trying to keep herself from fainting. Both were silent. She was sitting, he was standing, frightened by her distress and not daring to take a seat beside her. The violins and the flute that were being tuned up sang out. He suddenly felt frightened: it seemed as if all the people in the boxes were looking at them. She got up and went hurriedly to the exit; he followed her, and both of them walked blindly along the corridors and went up and down stairs, and figures in the uniforms prescribed for magistrates, teachers, and officials of the Department of Crown Lands, all wearing badges, flitted before their eyes, as did also ladies, and fur coats on hangers; they were conscious of drafts and the smell of stale tobacco. And Gurov, whose heart was beating violently, thought:

"Oh, Lord! Why are these people here and this orchestra!"

And at that instant he suddenly recalled how when he had seen Anna Sergeyevna off at the station he had said to himself that all was over between them and that they would never meet again. But how distant the end still was!

On the narrow, gloomy staircase over which it said "To the Amphitheatre," she stopped.

"How you frightened me!" she said, breathing hard, still pale and stunned. "Oh, how you frightened me! I am barely alive. Why did you come? Why?"

"But you do understand, Anna, do understand—" he said hurriedly, under his breath. "I implore you, do understand—"

She looked at him with fear, with entreaty, with love; she looked at him intently, to keep his features more distinctly in her memory.

"I suffer so," she went on, not listening to him. "All this time I have been thinking of nothing but you; I live only by the thought of you. And I wanted to forget, to forget; but why, oh, why have you come?"

On the landing above them two high school boys were looking down and smoking, but it was all the same to Gurov; he drew Anna Sergeyevna to him and began kissing her face and her hands.

"What are you doing, what are you doing!" she was saying in horror, pushing him away. "We have lost our senses. Go away today; go away at once— I conjure you by all that is sacred, I implore you— People are coming this way!"

Someone was walking up the stairs.

"You must leave," Anna Sergeyevna went on in a whisper. "Do you hear, Dmitry Dmitrich? I will come and see you in Moscow. I have never been happy; I am unhappy now, and I never, never, shall be happy, never! So don't make me suffer more! I swear I'll come to Moscow. But now let us part. My dear, good, precious one, let us part!"

She pressed his hand and walked rapidly downstairs, turning to look round at him, and from her eyes he could see that she really was unhappy. Gurov stood for a while, listening, then when all grew quiet, he found his coat and left the theater.

IV

and Anna Sergeyevna began coming to see him in Moscow. Once every two or three months she left S——, telling her husband that she was going to consult a doctor about a woman's ailment from which she was suffering—and her husband did and did not believe her. When she arrived in Moscow she would stop at the Slavyansky Bazar Hotel, and at once send a man in a red cap to Gurov. Gurov came to see her, and no one in Moscow knew of it.

Once he was going to see her in this way on a winter morning (the messenger had come the evening before and not found him in). With him walked his daughter, whom he wanted to take to school: it was on the way. Snow was coming down in big wet flakes.

"It's three degress above zero, and yet it's snowing," Gurov was saying to his daughter. "But this temperature prevails only on the surface of the earth; in the upper layers of the atmosphere there is quite a different temperature."

"And why doesn't it thunder in winter, papa?"

He explained that, too. He talked, thinking all the while that he was on his way to a rendezvous, and no living soul knew of it, and probably no one would ever know. He had two lives: an open one, seen and known by all who needed to know it, full of conventional truth and conventional falsehood, exactly like the lives of his friends and acquaintances; and another life that went on in secret. And through some strange, perhaps accidental, combination of circumstances, everything that was of interest and importance to him, everything that was essential to him, everything about which he felt sincerely and did not deceive himself, everything that constituted the core of his life, was going on concealed from others; while all that was false, the shell in which he hid to cover the truth—his work at the bank, for instance, his discussions at the club, his references to the "inferior race," his appearances at anniversary celebrations with his wife—all that went on in the open. Judging others by himself, he did not believe what he saw, and always fancied that every man led his real, most interesting life under cover of secrecy as under cover of night. The personal life of every individual is based on secrecy, and perhaps it is partly for that reason that civilized man is so nervously anxious that personal privacy should be respected.

Having taken his daughter to school, Gurov went on to the Slavyansky Bazar Hotel. He took off his fur coat in the lobby, went upstairs, and knocked gently at the door. Anna Sergeyevna, wearing his favorite gray dress, exhausted by the journey and by waiting, had been expecting him since the previous evening. She was pale, and looked at him without a smile, and he had hardly entered when she flung herself on his breast. Their kiss was a long, lingering one, as though they had not seen one another for two years.

"Well, darling, how are you getting on there?" he asked. "What news?"

"Wait; I'll tell you in a moment—I can't speak."

She could not speak; she was crying. She turned away from him, and pressed her handkerchief to her eyes.

"Let her have her cry; meanwhile I'll sit down," he thought, and he seated himself in an armchair.

Then he rang and ordered tea, and while he was having his tea she remained standing at the window with her back to him. She was crying out of sheer agitation, in the sorrowful consciousness that their life was so sad; that they could only see each other in secret and had to hide from people like thieves! Was it not a broken life?

"Come, stop now, dear!" he said.

It was plain to him that this love of theirs would not be over soon, that the end of it was not in sight. Anna Sergeyevna was growing more and more attached to him. She adored him, and it was unthinkable to tell her that their love was bound to come to an end some day; besides, she would not have believed it!

He went up to her and took her by the shoulders, to fondle her and say something diverting, and at that moment he caught sight of himself in the mirror.

His hair was already beginning to turn gray. And it seemed odd to him that he had grown so much older in the last few years, and lost his looks. The shoulders on which his hands rested were warm and heaving. He felt compassion for this life, still so warm and lovely, but probably already about to begin to fade and wither like his own. Why did she love him so much? He always seemed to women different from what he was and they loved in him not himself, but the man whom their imagination created and whom they had been eagerly seeking all their lives; and afterwards, when they saw their mistake, they loved him nevertheless. And not one of them had been happy with him. In the past he had met women, come together with them parted from them, but he had never once loved; it was anything you please, but not love. And only now when his head was gray he had fallen in love, really, truly—for the first time in his life.

Anna Sergeyevna and he loved each other as people do who are very close and intimate, like man and wife like tender friends; it seemed to them that Fate itself had meant them for one another, and they could not understand why he had a wife and she a husband; and it was as though they were a pair of migratory birds, male and female, caught and forced to live in different cages. They forgave each other what they were ashamed of in their past, they forgave everything in the present, and felt that this love of theirs had altered them both.

Formerly in moments of sadness he had soothed himself with whatever logical arguments came into his head, but now he no longer cared for logic; he felt profound compassion, he wanted to be sincere and tender.

"Give it up now, my darling," he said. "You've had your cry; that's enough. Let us have a talk now, we'll think up something."

Then they spent a long time taking counsel together, they talked of how to avoid the necessity for secrecy, for deception, for living in different cities, and not seeing one another for long stretches of time. How could they free themselves from these intolerable fetters?

"How? How?" he asked, clutching his head. "How?"

And it seemed as though in a little while the solution would be found, and then a new and glorious life would begin; and it was clear to both of them that the end was still far off, and that what was to be most complicated and difficult for them was only just beginning.

J.G. BALLARD was born in Shanghai in 1930. His many novels include *Empire of the Sun* and *The Drowned World*. He lives in Shepperton, England.

WHITNEY BALLIETT has written about jazz for *The New Yorker* for forty years. He has also written about the incomparable sounds and smells and sights of certain marshes and harbors and beaches. "A Floor of Flounders" appears here in print for the first time.

KAY BOYLE (1903–1992) was a short-story writer, novelist, poet, and essayist who published about fifty books, including several volumes of poetry. She twice won O. Henry awards for her short fiction, collections of which include *Fifty Stories* and *Life Being the Best and Other Stories*.

T. CORAGHESSAN BOYLE is the author of seven novels, including *World's End*, winner of the PEN/Faulkner Award. His short fiction regularly appears in major American magazines, and he was the recipient of the 1999 PEN/Malamud Award for Excellence in Short Fiction. He lives in Santa Barbara, California.

ALBERT CAMUS (1913–1960) was an Algerian-born French philosopher, novelist, dramatist, and journalist. His book *The Stranger*, first published in France in 1942 and in English in 1946, is one of the most widely read novels of the twentieth century. He was awarded the Nobel Prize for Literature in 1957.

RACHEL CARSON (1907–1964), a writer and marine biologist, wrote four books: *Under the Sea-Wind, The Sea Around Us, The Edge of the*

Sea, and, in 1962, *Silent Spring,* which spurred revolutionary changes in government policy toward the environment and was instrumental in launching the environmental movement.

JOHN CHEEVER (1912–1982) is the author of seven collections of stories and five novels. His first novel, *The Wapshot Chronicle,* won the 1958 National Book Award. In 1965 he received the Howells Medal for Fiction and in 1978 he won the National Book Critics Circle Award and the Pulitzer Prize. Shortly before his death in 1982, he was awarded the National Medal for Literature.

ANTON PAVLOVICH CHEKHOV (1860–1904) began to write short stories and humorous pieces for magazines while he was a medical student, and he continued to write for the rest of his life while working as a family doctor. His many short stories are still widely read today, while his plays, including *The Seagull, Uncle Vanya, Three Sisters,* and *The Cherry Orchard,* are among the finest in the modern repertory.

CYRUS COLTER, a lawyer, was born in 1910 in Noblesville, Indiana and began to write in his mid-fifties. In 1970, when he was sixty years old, he published his first book, the short story collection *The Beach Umbrella.* Since then he has published one other collection of stories and five novels. He is an emeritus professor at Northwestern University, where he held the Chester D. Tripp Chair in the Humanities.

DIANE JOHNSON is the author of thirteen books, including *Persian Nights, Health and Happiness, Lying Low, The Shadow Knows, Burning,* and *Le Divorce,* a National Book Award Finalist for 1997. Her most recent novel is *Le Mariage.* She divides her time between San Francisco and Paris.

TAKESHI KAIKO (1930–1989), born in Osaka, Japan, is the author of more than forty books that include short stories, fiction, nonfiction, history, and essays. Among his books translated into English are *Darkness in Summer* and *Into a Black Sun.* He was awarded the Kawabata Prize for his short stories.

JAMAICA KINCAID was born in St. John's, Antigua, in the West Indies. She is the author of, among other books, *Annie John, The Autobiography of My Mother, At the Bottom of the River,* and *My Garden Book.* She lives in Vermont with her husband and children, and she teaches at Harvard University.

DORIS LESSING is the author of more than thirty books that include novels, stories, reportage, poems, plays, and memoirs. Her most recent books are *Mara and Dann: An Adventure* and *Walking in the Shade: 1949 to 1962.* She lives in England.

DAVID MALOUF is the author of nine novels including *The Great World,* which in 1991 won the Commonwealth Writer's Prize and the Prix Fèmina Etranger. In 1994 *Remembering Babylon* received the *Los Angeles Times* Book Award for Fiction and the International IMPAC Dublin Literary Award. He divides his time between Tuscany and Australia.

ETHAN MORDDEN is the author of more than twenty-five books of fiction and nonfiction, including the novel *How Long Has This Been Going On?* and a decade-by-decade series on twentieth-century Broadway musicals that includes *Beautiful Mornin', Coming Up Roses,* and *Make-Believe.*

VLADIMIR NABOKOV (1899–1977) was born in St. Petersburg, Russia. His family fled to Germany in 1919, during the Bolshevik Revolution. He studied French and Russian at Trinity College in Cambridge, then lived in Berlin and Paris, where he launched a brilliant literary career. In 1940 he moved to the United States and achieved renown as a novelist, poet, critic, and translator. He taught literature at Wellesley, Stanford, Cornell, and Harvard. In 1961 he moved to Montreux, Switzerland, where he died in 1977.

RUSS RYMER is a journalist who has written for *The New Yorker, Harper's,* and *The New York Times.* He is the author of two books, *Genie,* nominated for the National Book Critics Circle Award, and *American Beach,* from which the selection here is excerpted. He lives in Los Angeles, California.

JOHN STEINBECK (1902–1968) is the author of over twenty books. He was awarded a Pulitzer Prize in 1940 and the Nobel Prize in Literature in 1962.

GRAHAM SWIFT was born in 1949 in London, where he still resides. He is the author of *Learning to Swim,* a collection of short stories, and six novels: *The Sweet-Shop Owner; Shuttlecock,* which received the Geoffrey Faber Memorial Prize; *Waterland,* which won the Guardian Fiction Award, the Winifred Holtby Memorial Prize and the Italian Premio Grinzane Cavour; *Out of This World; Ever After,* which won the French Prix du Meilleur Livre Etranger; and *Last Orders,* which was awarded the Booker Prize.

MICHEL TOURNIER was born in Paris in 1924 and is the author of many novels, short stories, essays, and works for children. His first novel, *Friday,* was awarded the Grand Prix du Roman by the Académie Française; his second novel, *The Ogre,* was awarded the Prix Goncourt.

JOHN UPDIKE, born in 1932 in Shillington, Pennsylvania, is the author of fifty-one books, including collections of short stories, poems, and criticisms. His novels have won the Pulitzer Prize (twice), the National Book Award, the National Book Critics Circle Award, the Rosenthal Award, and the Howells Medal. His most recent books include *Gertrude and Claudius* and *More Matter.*

MONICA WESOLOWSKA has fiction forthcoming in *Best New American Voices 2000.* Her work has also appeared in *The Writing Path II: Poetry and Prose from Writers' Conferences* and *The Berkeley Poetry Review.* In 1998–99, she was a fiction fellow at the Fine Arts Work Center in Provincetown, Massachusetts. She lives in her hometown of Berkeley, California.

about the editors

LENA LENČEK and **GIDEON BOSKER** specialize in popular culture and have cowritten more than ten books, including *Making Waves: Swimsuits and the Undressing of America; The Beach: The History of Paradise on Earth,* a *New York Times* Notable Book for 1998; and, most recently, *Beaches,* a photographic survey of the world's most beautiful beaches. Lenček is professor of Russian and the humanities at Reed College, and Bosker, a physician, is an assistant clinical professor of medicine at Yale University School of Medicine. They live in Portland, Oregon.

acknowledgments

few of life's hedonistic moments have such a palpable and enduring half-life as the pleasure of reading on the beach—about the beach. For giving us the excuse and opportunity to do both, we thank Matthew Lore, editor with a mission, whose impeccable taste and unerring eye inspired and guided this project through all phases, from inception to completion.

To friends, colleagues, relatives, and acquaintances—Rado Lenček, Grant Mainland, Peter Steinberger, Ottomar Rudolf, Michael Kunichika, John Van Sternen, Lexi Krock, Olivia Goldschmidt, and Aaron Baker—our fervent thanks for sharing their favorite shore stories. We are grateful to Richard Pine, our agent, for his steady support in this and other projects, and for being the human equivalent of Scuba.

For helping make our study and love for the beach a continuing work-in-progress, we would like to thank Wendy Wolf, Bill LeBlond, and Sarah Malarkey, who have encouraged us to keep probing into the sands of civilization and all its contents.

We acknowledge a great debt of gratitude to all who opened our eyes to the miracles, mischief, madness and the artistic and cultural depths of the beach: to Adrian Zecha, François Richil, Peter Wynn, Michael DiLenardo, all of Aman Resorts; to James B. Sherwood and Dr. Shirley Sherwood, Dr. Natale Rusconi, Vicki Keith, Patricia Harper, of Orient-Express Hotels, and Bruce Good, of the Cunard and Seabourn Line.

The tsunami wave of appreciation, however, goes to the authors and publishers who graciously granted us permission to reprint the stories here included. Without their cooperation, this book would simply not have been. Thanks to Shawneric Hachey for his expertise and efforts on the permissions front.

For the dreamy cover image of the Atlantic beach at low tide, we thank Joel Meyerowitz. For permission to use her evocative photographs of the shore in so many of its flighty moods, we thank Mittie Hellmich.

Finally, a big nod of appreciation to Bianca Lenček Bosker, beach bookworm par excellence, for her feedback and forbearance.

Lena Lenček
Gideon Bosker

p e r m i s s i o n s

we gratefully acknowledge all those who gave
permission for written material to appear in this book. We have made
every effort to trace and contact copyright holders. If an error or omis-
sion is brought to our notice we will be pleased to remedy the situation in future editions of this book. For further information, please
contact the publisher.

"The Marginal World" from *The Edge of the Sea* by Rachel Carson reprinted with per-
mission of Houghton Mifflin. Copyright © 1955 by Rachel Carson; copyright ©
renewed 1983 by Roger Christie. • "The Largest Theme Park in the World" from *War
Fever* by J.G. Ballard reprinted with permission of Farrar, Straus and Giroux, LLC.
Copyright © 1991 by J.G. Ballard. • "Mexico" from *T.C. Boyle Stories* by T.
Coraghessan Boyle (New York: Viking, 1998). Copyright 1998 by T. Coraghessan
Boyle. First appeared in *The New Yorker* in 1998. • "Lifeguard" from *Pigeon Feathers and
Other Stories* by John Updike reprinted with permission of Alfred A. Knopf, a Division
of Random House Inc. Copyright © 1962 by John Updike. • Excerpt from *American
Beach* by Russ Rymer reprinted with permission of HarperCollins Publishers.
Copyright © 1998 by Russ Rymer. • "A Change of Scene" excerpt from *Antipodes* by
David Malouf. Reprinted in the United States by permission of Rogers, Coleridge,
and White, London. Reprinted in Canada by Chatto & Windus, a division of Random
House UK. • "A Midnight Love Feast" by Michel Tournier, translated by Barbara
Wright. Reprinted by permission of HarperCollins Publishers UK. Copyright © 1989
by Michel Tournier and Barbara Wright. • Excerpt from *The Autobiography of My
Mother* by Jamaica Kincaid reprinted with permission of Farrar, Straus and Giroux,
LLC. Copyright © 1996 by Jamaica Kincaid. • "Through the Tunnel" from *Stories* by
Doris Lessing reprinted with permission of Alfred A. Knopf, a Division of Random
House, Inc. Copyright © 1978 by Doris Lessing. • "Black Boy" from *Fifty Stories* by
Kay Boyle reprinted with permission of New Directions Publishing Corp. Copyright
© 1980 by Kay Boyle. • "The Beach Umbrella" from *The Beach Umbrella and Other
Stories* by Cyrus Colter reprinted with permission of University of Iowa Press.
Copyright © 1970 by Cyrus Colter. • "I Read My Nephew Stories" from *Everybody*